W9-AHA-950

WALLINGFORD PUBLIC LIBRARY
WALLINGFORD, CONNECTICUT 06492

So
Good

So Good

Venise Berry

WALLINGFORD PUBLIC LIBRARY
WALLINGFORD, CONNECTICUT 06492

A DUTTON BOOK

DUTTON
Published by the Penguin Group
Penguin Books USA Inc., 375 Hudson Street,
New York, New York 10014, U.S.A.
Penguin Books Ltd, 27 Wrights Lane,
London W8 5TZ, England
Penguin Books Australia Ltd, Ringwood,
Victoria, Australia
Penguin Books Canada Ltd, 10 Alcorn Avenue,
Toronto, Ontario, Canada M4V 3B2
Penguin Books (N.Z.) Ltd, 182–190 Wairau Road,
Auckland 10, New Zealand

Penguin Books Ltd, Registered Offices:
Harmondsworth, Middlesex, England

First published by Dutton, an imprint of Dutton Signet,
a division of Penguin Books USA Inc.
Distributed in Canada by McClelland & Stewart Inc.

First Printing, August, 1996
10 9 8 7 6 5 4 3 2 1

Copyright © Venise Berry, 1996
All rights reserved

 REGISTERED TRADEMARK—MARCA REGISTRADA

LIBRARY OF CONGRESS CATALOGING-IN-PUBLICATION DATA
Berry, Venise T.
    So good / Venise Berry.
        p.   cm.
    ISBN 0–525–93885–0   BT 21.95/11.94   3/9L
    1. Afro-American women—Psychology—Fiction. 2. Man-woman
relationships—United States—Fiction. 3. Friendship—United
States—Fiction. 4. Women—United States—Fiction.   I. Title.
PS3552.E7496S6   1996
813'.54—dc20   95–53068
                                                CIP

Printed in the United States of America
Set in Simoncini Garamond
Designed by Leonard Telesca

PUBLISHER'S NOTE
This is a work of fiction. Names, characters, places, and incidents either are the products of the author's imagination or are used fictitiously, and any resemblance to actual persons, living or dead, events, or locales is entirely coincidental.

Without limiting the rights under copyright reserved above, no part of this publication may be reproduced, stored in or introduced into a retrieval system, or transmitted, in any form, or by any means (electronic, mechanical, photocopying, recording, or otherwise), without the prior written permission of both the copyright owner and the above publisher of this book.

This book is printed on acid-free paper. ∞

Acknowledgments

A special thanks goes out to many people who have helped
in the completion of this book:

To God and my special angel, Toni, for guidance from above
To my parents, Jean and Virgil Berry, for constant inspiration
To my brothers, S. Torriano Berry and William James, for
spiritual motivation
To my sisters, ayo, Denise, Joyce, Tyna, Sharon, Stephana,
Vanessa, Bonnie, Poppy, and Valerie, for crucial support
To Everett, Earl, Mac, and Leonard for essential love
To Poppy McLeod and Robert Stein for divine intervention
To my agent, Denise Stinson, for unyielding assistance and
belief
To my editor, Michaela Hamilton, for tremendous enthusi-
asm and enlightened direction

Love is usually demanding, motivating, or frustrating.
Love is often irrational, painful, and unpredictable.
Love is sometimes impulsive, oppressive, or destructive.
But when it's right, love is . . .

SO GOOD!

When Lisa Allen arrived at Brightroad African Methodist Episcopal Church, it was one o'clock and very few cars were in the parking lot. She parked her raggedy buggy in the front row next to a Mercedes. This, she knew, would piss off the owner because no matter how careful she was, her puke yellow Tercel always left dings in other people's car doors.

It was unusually warm and humid in the Chocolate City, despite a faint breeze that blew fuchsia-colored blossoms from Japanese cherry trees. Early April meant the Cherry Blossom Festival was about to begin in Washington, D.C. It was this time of year that the city was most beautiful to Lisa. She often contemplated the contradictions. Not fresh air or graffiti-clean walls—that wasn't what life was all about. The city was life—the good, the bad, the rich, the poor, the ugly, and the gorgeous, all jumbled up together.

Sundiata was getting married today. Although Lisa was happy for her best friend, she had to admit she was jealous too. Now Lisa was the only one of the girls who was not married, and she should have been next. Lisa and Kirby Spencer were supposed to have announced their wedding plans last Christmas. They had been engaged for almost a year. But Kirby out of nowhere accepted a job as an editor at the *Kansas City Star* and told Lisa he needed some space. He said he wanted to leave his options open. "Ain't that a bitch!" Lisa mumbled out loud while checking her lipstick in the rearview mirror. After spending four years with the same man, she just naturally assumed he was the one.

They were a great couple; everybody said so. Kirby stood about six feet one, with short, curly brown hair and one of those scandalous smiles you can't help but love. Lisa at five feet eleven had a real complex about short men. It probably stemmed from Harding Junior High, where she grew three inches without warning in her sophomore year and suffered daily teasing from the other kids. Sylvester Cowan, the shortest boy in her English class, had once whispered in her ear that he liked to climb trees!

Lisa slammed the car door and turned to walk toward the church. A couple of steps away she heard her dress tear. "Shit!" she hissed, turning to see the hem of her dress stuck in the door. She snatched it open and pulled the dress loose, then checked the damage. Thank God it was mendable. She walked up to the front double doors of the church, a huge Gothic-style building with a soaring nave. Lisa admired the large intersecting stained-glass windows and the narrative sculptures below. Those who were into new, slick, modern styles would probably think it was an ugly building, but Lisa thought it was one of the prettiest churches in the city.

The front door was locked, so she tiptoed around to the side, looking for a way in. She tried the side door, but it was also locked. She heard noise inside and beat on the door as hard as she could several times, then waited for a moment. She couldn't help but notice her image in the long plate glass window. At thirty-four years old, Lisa could easily pass for twenty-four. Her olive brown eyes seemed to display a calm, soothing nature. Her nose was about the right size and in the right place. Some days her mid-length black hair was too curly and other days it was too straight. Her biggest problem was an extra twenty-five pounds that loved her and didn't want to leave. There was not a time in her life that Lisa didn't remember fighting and hiding midriff bulge. Maybe it wouldn't be so bad if the weight were spread out more, she thought, twirling around to examine her backside, or maybe more of it should be in her behind; men seemed to love big butts.

Lisa heard a loud screeching sound inside and pounded again on the wooden door. At last she heard footsteps, and an older lady with blondish red hair and large, wrinkled hands finally opened the door. Lisa immediately recognized her as Sundi's aunt Jessie. She looked huge in the long, oversized Nigerian blue adire print gown she wore.

"Lisa . . . baby . . . how you doing?" Aunt Jessie said with a smile and held her arms out wide.

"I'm okay, Aunt Jessie. How's life been treating you?" Lisa answered and leaned in to hug her.

"No complaints, child. I'm thankful for every day that God lets me hang around this old earth. Come on inside. I know Mira wants to see you." Aunt Jessie motioned for Lisa to follow her into the chapel, where Sundi's aunt Mira was also dressed in a colorful African batik caftan. Aunt Mira was busy giving orders to Jessie's teenage boys, Jarod and Keith. At twelve years old, Keith was already demonstrating a mature fashion sense with his faded box haircut, pleated black slacks, and mudcloth print vest. Jarod was Mamma's baby, and he'd allowed her to talk him into wearing a miniature kente cloth tunic with matching pants topped by a small, round kente kuffi hat.

Aunt Mira stopped in the middle of her sentence when she saw Lisa. "And don't run off until— There she is! I was just asking about you, Lisa. Wasn't I, Jessie?" Aunt Mira yelled across the room and rushed over to grab her.

Aunt Jessie nodded and hurried off to make sure Jarod and Keith stretched the white ribbon across each pew correctly.

"Hi, Aunt Mira," Lisa said, trying to muster up a smile. She dreaded the conversation that she knew would follow.

"You look good, honey. Picking up a few pounds, but don't worry, 'cause men like healthy women," Aunt Mira said, squeezing her hand as she spoke. "Where's that cute guy you had on your arm last year when I saw you? It wasn't hard to see he was crazy 'bout you. You two will be walking down this aisle next."

Lisa felt tired already and the wedding was still a couple of hours away. In her mind she fumbled with the truth, but a lie came out instead.

"He died," she answered flatly. Lisa fought the immediate joy that she felt when she watched Aunt Mira's mouth drop. Then she couldn't help but laugh. "I'm sorry," she said. "That's not true. We broke up. He moved out of town."

Aunt Mira eyed her for a moment, then offered a crooked smile. "That's too bad, honey. You know I worried about you when Sundi told me you went back to school for another degree. What is it that you're getting again?"

"A Ph.D.," she responded, and sighed deeply. Lisa didn't know why people felt she needed their opinion of her life decisions, but she steadied herself for the blow.

"You know all that education probably scared him, honey. Men like to be the breadwinners. They need to believe they're in control."

Lisa didn't want to hear that, but at the same time she knew it was true to some extent. She took a deep breath and responded sharply, "Well, that's their problem, Aunt Mira, not mine."

"Hey, you two, we could use some help over here," Aunt Jessie yelled as she and the boys tried to move a large heart-shaped archway toward the center of the floor.

Lisa set her purse on the back pew and followed Aunt Mira over. They pushed and pulled at the arch, but minutes later sweat was pouring from Lisa's forehead and the archway had moved only about an inch. They tried again, and this time the edge got caught on a crack, and the seven-foot arch fell crashing across the back pew. Everybody ran in a different direction as flowers and bells scattered everywhere. For a moment they just looked at one another and then back at the heart.

The church was such a dark, majestic place, and that seven-foot heart had brought a necessary brightness to the gloom. Maybe it was an omen, Lisa thought. She sometimes had a sixth sense about such things. As a child she had often played with a Ouija board for hours at a time. But after seeing *The Exorcist*, she never touched it again. It still made her nervous just to think about it.

"I guess we should get this mess cleaned up," the taskmaster, Aunt Mira, said. "Jarod and Keith, pick up the bells and flowers. And let's see if we can stand this arch upright," she said, turning to Jessie and Lisa.

Keith conned Jarod into doing most of the work by telling him that they would play a game and whoever collected the most ornaments would win. Ten-year-old Jarod ran through the sanctuary, picking up two and three at a time, while Keith mainly hid behind the pulpit. The women tried to lift the arch with no success.

When Jarod didn't see Keith, he realized he'd been tricked and began a search that easily located his brother's hiding place.

"You better help or I'm gonna tell Mom," Jarod told him loudly.

Keith ignored the threat. He shoved his hands in his pockets and peeked around the walnut stand at his mother, who was busy talking to Lisa and his aunt Mira. "Go away, boy, and mind your business," he warned.

"Keith, Jarod, what are you two doing?" Jessie called as her radar kicked in. "Come on over here and give us a hand with this arch."

"You make me sick sometimes," Keith said as he reluctantly headed toward his mother and the arch.

"I don't care 'cause I won anyway," Jarod teased, and followed his brother.

Everyone struggled to get the arch into an upright position. Then, after putting as many of the ornaments back on as they could, they all stood in silence. Most of the bells were broken and the flowers smashed. The once-radiant arch looked kind of pitiful. It reminded Lisa of a snaggle-toothed old man who still believes he's sexy.

"I guess I should go see Sundi. I'm sure she's wondering where I am," Lisa said, breaking the silence.

"Her dressing room is down the left corridor . . . one, two, three, fourth door on the right," Aunt Jessie explained.

"I'll see you guys later," Lisa said as she began walking slowly toward Sundi's dressing room. The closer she got to the door, the more Lisa found herself dreading the situation. Weddings were so confusing right now. She wanted Sundi to be happy, and she was sincerely happy for her, but she couldn't help that it hurt. Sundi had never even wanted to be married, Lisa thought. She hadn't been seriously looking for anyone. But here she is experiencing her big day, and I'm alone again.

Lisa hesitated, then knocked softly.

"Come in," Sundi called from inside.

Lisa forced a smile as she opened the door and stepped in. Then she smiled for real because Sundi was truly a beautiful bride. Her mother, Mrs. Fransis, was crying and fiddling with the veil that was attached to Sundi's African crown hat. When Sundi had called Lisa earlier that morning, Mrs. Fransis was crying then too. Lisa never understood why people cried at weddings. Crying when you're happy seemed like such a waste of emotion.

Sundiata Karif was not her given name. Sundi had changed it about ten years ago, when she got involved in the Pan-Africanist movement. But even a name change and her work with lots of black causes hadn't made Sundi give up capitalism or material luxuries long enough to be true to a real grass-roots movement. Her business of selling handmade baskets was doing better than she had ever imagined, and she was thinking about expanding it into a national distribution line.

"Anybody else here?" Sundi asked as Lisa entered the dressing room.

"Just your aunts and the boys," she answered. "Is there a needle and thread somewhere?"

Mrs. Fransis pointed toward a chipped oak cabinet under the window. "On top of that cabinet."

"Where's Danielle?" Sundi asked without missing a stroke on her nails with the clear acrylic polish.

"I haven't talked to her today, but you know my big sis almost as well as I do. She'll be here, drama and all, don't worry," Lisa assured her.

"God, I'm nervous," Sundi said.

Her mother bent over and hugged her tightly from behind. "There's nothin' to be 'fraid of, baby. Marriage is a wonderful part of life," Mrs. Fransis said, smiling with pride.

Sundi's mother and father celebrated their fortieth anniversary last month. They had a big party with more than two hundred guests back in Greeneville, Tennessee, at the Sheraton. Lisa couldn't imagine spending forty years with the same man. It was like a pair of old worn-out shoes: They feel good but look like shit. Besides, Lisa thought, in most of those "lifetime" marriages the woman has had to put up with a lot of shit to make it last. She often heard them say things like "He was wild at first, but he finally settled down." In today's marriages, wild at first usually ends up in divorce.

Mrs. Fransis was upset when Sundi told her she didn't want to get married in Greeneville. But Mr. Fransis laughed and said, "Let the girl live her life." He always said that when Sundi tried different things. He was very proud of his only child. Every time she accomplished something, Mr. Fransis felt as if he had accomplished it. Whenever she told him about a new experience, he tucked it away in his memory for future recall.

It was an hour's drive to the Knoxville airport from Greeneville. Mr. Fransis had driven Mrs. Fransis to the airport a week ago, along with her two sisters, Mira and Jessie, and Jessie's two sons. The rest of the family had arrived yesterday in a rented van. After the services they planned to load everyone up and head back down to Greeneville.

"What are you afraid of, Sundi? You love him, don't you?" Lisa asked, carefully stitching the small tear in her hem.

"It's got to be love," Sundi said, showing a confident smile. "I don't want to be without him."

Sundi's confidence would soon be put to the test because her future husband, Chris, had been born in a small farming village on the Lekki Peninsula but had grown up in Lagos, the capital of Nigeria. It was that fact that worried Lisa more than anything else. Whenever she thought about Sundi's husband-to-be, she remembered a frightening story she'd heard from a friend at work. This girl had married a Nigerian man, and he moved her and the kids over to Africa. When she told him she was unhappy and wanted to go back home, she quickly discovered that legally the children would stay with their father. She was forced to make a difficult decision. Stay there and live an unhappy life or leave her babies. She chose to stay.

Lisa knew that Chris was very Americanized, but she also knew that African men were used to a different kind of woman. Their macho mentality often clashed with the ideas of successful, independent black women. And then again, when she thought about it, that stereotype couldn't really be limited to African men. A lot of black men in the United States seemed to think the same way.

It was hot and musty in the dressing room, and even worse, Lisa couldn't ignore the sinking feeling in the pit of her stomach as she found herself staring at Sundi. Her smooth, dark skin seemed to glow in the dim light. Sundi was five feet six and weighed about 120 pounds, all of it in the right places. Sundi's dreadlocks were the only problem Lisa could see. Lisa never liked dreadlocks on anybody and definitely wouldn't wear them herself. She felt she had too many things going against her naturally to screw up something on purpose.

It was obvious that Chris loved Sundi's dreadlocks. He seemed to love everything about her. But that wasn't enough for Lisa. She was afraid that Sundi was jumping into this marriage too quickly, and her recent birthday probably had a lot to do with it. Sundi and Chris had dated for more than a year. She admitted that Chris was a special guy, but she also said it wasn't a big deal. Then, right after she turned thirty-six, she was suddenly in love. Her decision, Lisa thought, was connected with the fear that many black women their age had: a fear that they might never get the chance to love and be loved by a good black man.

Danielle suddenly burst into the room. She was Sundi's maid of honor. "Hallelujah!" she yelled in her imperious manner. Her long, silky hair was tangled, and her dress was slung over her arm.

"The place is getting packed, y'all," Danielle said as she hurried out of her clothes and into her African caftan. She sat down and straightened her black stockings, then wiped the mud off her black leather pumps with a tissue.

"You look happy," Sundi said sarcastically.

"I'm excel-laan-tay!" Danielle replied, sucking each of the fingers on her right hand as if she'd just finished eating greasy fried chicken.

Danielle had recently dyed her black hair an auburn color that matched her hazel contact lenses. She reminded Lisa of that light brown Shani doll advertised just before Christmas in several magazines. Lisa couldn't help but smile. She admired her big sis. She was a resourceful career woman, yet she was also a down-to-earth sistergirl with few pretenses. As an executive in Saurus Advertising, she proved she could hang with the big boys, yet around the girls she was always just Dannie.

There was a knock at the door, and a girl entered who looked a lot like Sundi: same size, same skin tone, same hairstyle, even the same dress. Danielle and Lisa couldn't take their eyes off her. Apparently there would be more than one bride, and Chris would have to pick Sundi out of the group. Sundi had mentioned this African tradition, but Lisa didn't think she would actually go through with it. Most women would have a fit if someone else was wearing the same outfit, but somebody else in your wedding dress was truly deep.

"Karen, this is Danielle Mead and Lisa Allen," Sundi said. Karen nodded but didn't speak to them. She simply borrowed Sundi's redbrick lipstick and left.

"This is going to be interesting," Danielle said, eyeing Sundi from across the room.

"It was Chris's idea. He seemed to think it was important," Sundi explained.

"As long as you're happy, who cares? Right?" Lisa added, setting Sundi's veiled crown hat on her head.

"Turn around. Let me see," Danielle told her, admiring the unique African embroidered wedding dress and crown. Sundi twirled in place to display the handmade gown of a royal gold print. It draped loosely to the floor under laced dolman sleeves and a dipping peasant collar.

Around her neck Sundi wore a beaded *ilorin* necklace from Chris's family. When his father, Orun, arrived three days ago he gave Sundi a traditional *idigba*. The wooden container was carved from a colorful calabash shell, and inside it held the *ilorin* necklace, which he said had been a gift to his grandmother from an oni, or priest-king, and represented the gift of life. The *idigba* also included other symbolic items: two kola nut seeds reflecting the union between the two families, a small jar of honey to assure the sweetness of married life, five alligator pepper pods for the birth of five children, and an African orogbo nut, symbolizing how Sundi and Chris would grow old together.

The trio stopped primping as the music started. It was show time.

The wedding began with Reverend Fields and a Yoruba priest taking their places side by side in front of the altar. A Yoruba wedding song was played on an African tension drum by Chris's uncle Cothi. He beat a vibrant rhythm with a curved drumstick, varying the pitch an octave or more by squeezing certain strings along the side with his knees. While he played, Lisa walked into the chapel with Chris's college friend Sobati. She was annoyed that Sobati stood only five feet six, and she towered over him. They were followed by Danielle and Chris's cousin Sylla. Danielle threw her head high in the air and glided down the aisle on Sylla's arm.

Cothi's performance was followed by Aunt Mira, who played the traditional American wedding march on the piano. As Lisa stood and looked at the spectacle, she couldn't help but notice that the stupid archway looked lopsided. Little things like that bugged the shit out of her.

Chris stood with a broad smile across his face in the front of the room. He looked regal in a long, flowing agbada tunic over loose matching pants. A gold-dust pattern called sika futura hugged the trim of the garment as a sign of ancestral status and a signal to Olorun, the god of the sky, to guard the ceremony so that all would go well.

Everyone watched the bride march slowly down the aisle with Sundi's father. But after a moment the groom shook his head no. His friends and family cheered, shouting as if they were on a game show, and the music stopped. This is truly some crazy shit! Lisa thought. The first bride unveiled and moved quickly out of the aisle. The music began again, and another bride took her turn walking slowly toward Chris. When she was about half-way, he again refused, and his guests rejoiced. Lisa got a kick out of watching the faces of those who didn't know what was going on: Noses were wrinkled, eyebrows were raised, and mouths were twisted. One woman actually tapped Mrs. Fransis on her shoulder and began asking questions.

Finally Sundi floated down the aisle, and Chris smiled the biggest smile. He met her halfway, and they walked arm in arm to the altar.

Chris looked at Sundi as if she had single-handedly eliminated apartheid. Lisa smiled as the memory of a double date with them came back to her. It was a Luther Vandross concert. The hound dog she had come with stopped to talk to everyone in the au-ditorium. He even left her for more than an hour, probably chas-ing some other woman. She would never forget how bad she felt with an empty seat next to her, listening to Luther croon live while Chris and Sundi snuggled together like high school sweet-hearts. At this point in my life I'd pay for that kind of attention, Lisa thought.

The crowd settled down as the ceremony began. Reverend Fields stepped forward and spoke: "We gather in this holy place to witness and bless this marriage between Sundiata and Chris-tian before God. We come together to encourage and support these two young people as they move their lives toward the won-derful common goal of sharing true love."

Lisa looked nervously around the church. She knew it was stupid, but she couldn't help but think about Kirby and how this should have been their wedding. She had sensed that some-thing was wrong between them, but she had wanted it to work so badly that she had let the problems slide and ignored all the warning signs. Kirby was a freethinker with little ambition. Lisa was a critical thinker driven to achieve. But every woman has one man in her lifetime who makes her weak in the knees.

The Yoruba priest handed Chris a small glass of brown liquid. Although English was the official language of Nigeria, he spoke in Yoruba through the whole ceremony. The guests didn't know exactly what the priest was saying, but Chris sipped from the glass and spoke in English: "As I drink, I pray for a love that is joyful and understanding."

The groom's full name was Christian Ologbo. Sundi Ologbo, Lisa thought. It wasn't one of those names you'd dream of writing over and over in your notebook as a teenager.

The priest handed the glass to Sundi. She carefully took it and recited her lines: "As I drink, I pray for a love that is strong and secure." She drank from the glass and handed it back to the priest.

According to Sundi, Chris planned to live in the United States. It was a decision Sundi didn't think made his mother very happy. She had refused to come to the wedding with his father and two cousins.

As Lisa shifted her feet, she took advantage of a clear view of the entire gathering. Her eyes searched through the crowd until she spotted a cutie pie in the second row. With his deep sideburns and faint five o'clock shadow, he looked very mature and distinguished. Maybe that's what I need, an older man, she rationalized. Then she flashed him one of her best smiles.

The character behind Mr. Distinguished must have thought she was smiling at him because he grinned and blew her a kiss. Then he made the ultimate mistake of opening his mouth wide enough to show his two front gold teeth. Lisa quickly looked away and frowned. He actually thinks he looks good with that shit in his mouth, she thought. He looks more like an idiot who couldn't resist a "buy one, get one free" sale!

Reverend Fields continued. "Do you, Sundiata, take Christian to be your lawfully wedded husband?" Sundi turned and looked lovingly into Chris's face.

"Yes, I take thee, Christian, in sunshine and in rain, in sickness and in health; for all the days of my life, I'll love you," she responded.

"Do you, Christian, take Sundiata to be your lawfully wedded wife?"

Chris smiled. He had not taken his eyes off Sundi since they walked down the aisle. "I take thee, Sundiata, in good times and in bad, in joy and sorrow; for all the days of my life, I'll love you."

Sundi had told Lisa that the main thing she liked about Chris was his strength. She said that he was different from a lot of black American men she'd dated: He wasn't afraid to take responsibility. Lisa could definitely understand that. It would be nice to find a responsible man who was not into playing games, she thought. She'd even be willing to play the same game, but she didn't want to play solitaire while he jumped all over a checkerboard!

Lisa continued her survey of the room. She stopped at her sister, who was staring at her husband, Roger. He sat three rows back with their four-year-old daughter, Kim, on his lap. Danielle and Roger had been married for fifteen years. Although she hadn't really wanted kids, Danielle had grown to love Kim. Lisa examined Roger's strong, rounded face and his broad chest. He was such a great guy, she thought. Hardworking, understanding, and affectionate. And he truly loved Danielle. When she got pregnant and wanted to have an abortion, he spent days talking her out of it. He needed that baby in his life, and Kim would always be Daddy's girl.

Lisa looked down at her stomach. She was ready to have a couple of kids. She couldn't walk past the baby section in a department store without drooling. She felt a strong, throbbing feeling in her chest as she watched Danielle's smile suddenly change to a distant look of sadness.

To the outside world Danielle had the perfect life. She was one of those girls who went to college to find good husbands. Roger was finishing law school when they met, and she couldn't get much better than that. They'd settled into a great life over the years. They had a big house in the suburbs and all the other material possessions of upper-middle-class status. But Lisa knew Danielle was still not happy.

The African priest handed the couple their rings. Sundi reached first, but the priest gave Chris his ring instead. Sundi looked upset for a second, but her smile returned when Chris slipped the gold band on her finger.

"I offer you this ring as the symbol of a love that is true, a love that will last forever," he said.

Then Sundi took Chris's ring and slid it on his finger, saying, "I offer you this ring as a symbol of an unending love, a love filled with faith, hope, and determination."

"By the power vested in me and with the divine blessings of God, I now pronounce you husband and wife." After the minister said those time-honored words, Sundi and Chris kissed, and the music floated up through the ceiling and on into heaven.

People mingled in the churchyard, while an assortment of African and American music played loudly through two large speakers that sat on the back of Sobati's truck. Chris's cousin Sylla had taped an eclectic mix including the rhythm and blues of Toni Braxton, rap artists like Queen Latifah and a Tribe Called Quest, along with several African high-life songs by such greats as King Sunny Ade and Fela Ransome-Kuti.

The bride, groom, and family members were still inside taking pictures, but the yard was crowded with people who hovered over tables of food and drink: buffalo wings, fruit salad with mangoes, bananas, and pineapples covered with shredded coconut, warm doughnut-shaped sweet balls, fufu, fried plantain, seeded chili, and an African dish called akara, which included black-eyed peas, onions, and shrimp.

Roger sat near one of the tables, stuffing sweet balls in his mouth, while Kim drank fruit punch out of a plastic cup. Danielle strolled over to them. She kissed Roger lightly on the lips and gave Kim a big hug.

"How's Mamma's baby?" she asked, kissing Kim on the forehead and then on both cheeks.

"Hi, Mom," Kim responded. "You look pretty."

"Thank you, sweetie."

"Sorry we were late. I didn't finish the Wallace session in time." Roger apologized without being asked.

Danielle sat down and lifted Kim into her lap. "Did they finally settle?" she asked.

"No," Roger said, gulping sparkling water.

"Now what?" Danielle asked, obviously annoyed.

"As Eddie Murphy says, half."

Danielle rolled her eyes at him. "Maybe she deserves half. You ever thought of that, Roger? She worked just as hard as he did while they were together."

"She was caught with another man, Danielle. What she deserves is a swift kick."

Danielle looked at her husband with a blank stare. Then she stood abruptly and walked away, pulling Kim along behind.

The two of them joined Lisa in the middle of a conversation with Tina and Carol, two women who irritated Lisa immensely.

"That ceremony didn't make sense to me," Tina was saying. Danielle caught her in the middle of talking shit as usual about something she knew nothing about.

"It's an African custom, Tina," Lisa tried to explain. "When Chris chose Sundi, it proved his love. He knew her above all others."

"So what would've happened if he'd have chosen the wrong one?" Carol asked.

Danielle stared at the two of them and shook her head. She had a theory that these two women hung together so they could balance out each other's ignorance.

"He didn't, did he?" Lisa answered with an attitude. She was sure they had worked all that out; after all, it *was* a tradition.

Seeing that Danielle intended to stay, Tina and Carol made excuses and left. They didn't care for her arrogance.

"It was a nice wedding, wasn't it?" Lisa asked Danielle. She bent down and stole a bite of Kim's cookie. Kim frowned, pulled the cookie away, and crammed the rest of it into her mouth.

"Sundi looks happy," Danielle answered dryly.

"Chris is a good guy, Dannie," Lisa added, noting her sister's piss-poor mood. Lately Danielle was always the temple of doom when it came to marriage.

"I just think Sundi jumped in too quick, that's all."

"Don't start," Lisa warned. "Just 'cause you're not happy, don't bring Sundi down."

Kim tapped her aunt on the leg and called her name several times. "Aunt Lisa . . . Aunt Lisa." She held her arms high in the air until Lisa lifted her up. The child settled comfortably on her right hip.

Danielle cut her eyes at Lisa's comment. "Fine," she said caustically, "I'll just bite my tongue."

"Good girl!" Lisa told her sister and patted her on the top of her head as if she were a puppy.

"Go to hell," Danielle mumbled, jerking her head back.

At that moment Sundi, Chris, and their families joined the reception and were surrounded by well-wishers. Danielle, Lisa, and Kim made their way through the crowd. When they reached Sundi and Chris, everybody hugged. Then Chris was pulled away by his family.

"So, Sundi, you've joined the ranks of the obligated. I just hope it's what you want," Danielle joked.

"It's hard to believe, ain't it?" Sundi replied, ignoring the funky comment.

"I believe it," Lisa said reassuringly. "I'm ready to find the love of my life. As a matter of fact, it's time for all of us to settle down and *act right,* isn't it?" Lisa added, speaking directly to Danielle, who turned her head.

Chris walked up behind Sundi and tapped her on the shoulder. "Come greet some of my friends and family."

Sundi smiled, then turned to follow him. Danielle watched as Chris marched ahead of Sundi until she finally caught up and grabbed his arm to slow him down.

"She's going to be following him for the rest of her life," Danielle said.

"Maybe that's okay with her," Lisa suggested. "We all gotta do what we gotta do."

Danielle ran her hand through the back of her hair and smirked. "Yeah. I hear you talking that shit now. We'll see what happens when you find this perfect love you're looking for."

Lisa didn't want to hear the love is pain lecture, so when she noticed the cutie pie from the second row and another man talking with her brother-in-law, she changed the subject.

"Danielle, who's that next to Roger?" she asked.

"I don't know, but we can find out," Danielle answered, taking the hint gracefully. "Come on, Kimi. Let's go see Daddy."

As Lisa followed Danielle across the grass, Kim ran ahead and grabbed Roger's hand. When the two sisters strolled up, Lisa's eyes met the cutie pie's, and they grinned at each other.

"It's really a simple case. You need to look for liability—" Roger said. He stopped talking when he noticed Danielle and Lisa standing beside him.

"Ryan Jackson and Walter Henderson, this is my wife, Danielle, and my sister-in-law, Lisa Allen."

"Hi." Lisa smiled hard, directing it at Walter.

"Hi," Walter said, and smiled back.

Roger noticed that Lisa raised her eyebrows as Walter's name rolled off his tongue. "Ryan is an old client, and Walter is a new one," he added.

"Enjoy the wedding?" Lisa asked as she evaluated the information. Since Roger mainly handled divorces, it was a real possibility that this interesting man in front of her was available, she thought.

"Yeah . . . it was pretty okay," Ryan answered even though Lisa wasn't talking to him.

"It was nice. Different, but nice," Walter added with his big brown eyes glancing around awkwardly.

Lisa noticed he seemed nervous, so she decided to be as friendly as possible. She wanted him to feel comfortable moving ahead if he wanted to. She struggled to organize the many thoughts that raced through her mind.

"We've met before, you know," Walter said, finally breaking the silence.

"You look familiar, but I can't remember," Lisa replied, lying through her pretty teeth. She didn't remember him, but she truly wanted to!

"The Singletons' house in Silver Spring, a couple of months ago," Walter explained, trying to jog her memory.

Lisa had gone to the Singletons' party, but she didn't remember him.

"I was with Anthony," Walter added.

"Oh, yeah," Lisa said, but she still didn't have a clue. Who the hell was Anthony?

There was another awkward pause while she tried to come up with something clever to say.

Then Ryan spoke. "I'm gonna grab some eats. Anybody else want some?"

"No," Walter replied, and Lisa just shook her head as if she were shooing him away.

Then, as if it were planned, Danielle pulled Roger and Kim toward the swing set behind the church. Lisa focused on the gorgeous creature standing in front of her. She liked the fact that she had to tilt her head slightly upward to look at him even in her heels. And his broad shoulders somehow made her feel smaller. He definitely had potential, she thought.

"Do you know the groom?" Lisa asked. Her smile grew a little wider when she noticed that the ring on his finger had been removed.

"We work together," Walter responded, bouncing slightly with the beat of the music.

"At National Computers?"

"Only part-time. I'm an accounting supervisor at Amtrak."

This is definitely my kind of man—two jobs! Lisa thought.

Walter shifted his tall, lanky body and spoke forcefully in his heavy Southern accent. "I don't plan to work forever. So I figure if I work hard now, I can retire by fifty or fifty-five and enjoy the rest of my days. And what do you do, Lisa?"

"I'm back in school at the University of Maryland in College Park."

"An intelligent woman," Walter commented, pouring himself and Lisa a glass of punch. "When will you finish your degree?"

"I should be finished with my course work this semester, but the dissertation will take a year or more," she answered, taking a sip from the glass.

"Oh, you're working on a Ph.D.," Walter said with an even deeper smile. "In what?"

"Communication studies," she answered. He has such a great smile, Lisa thought. Straight, shiny white teeth; he actually reminded her a little of Arsenio Hall without the flash. She noted the long eyelashes and prominent nose. His narrow chin was sexy with the touch of salt-and-pepper hair that covered it. He was truly a doll. Not fine, like most women look for. What Lisa meant by *doll* was that he had subtle good looks, well-groomed fingernails, and good taste in clothes. She liked the way he carried himself with assurance and treated her with respect.

"Let me see something," Lisa said, and took Walter's right hand in hers. She could feel the sparks flying. "I read palms," she explained, then began working out the tension with a hand massage. Next she slowly traced the lines in Walter's palm with her index finger. "You're going to have a long, prosperous life, Walter Henderson. See this *M*?" Lisa asked, tracing it seductively across his palm. "It means money, magic, and me."

Walter laughed. He sensed the connection too and wanted to know more about this woman.

It was bold, Lisa knew it, but it felt good, and what the hell, she thought. It was working!

Lisa and Walter turned to watch the crowd gather around Sundi and Chris as they started an African dance ritual. Chris circled Sundi while rocking back and forth; then Sundi repeated the motion, ending in his arms. It was another African custom that represented their affection and commitment to each other. As other couples were invited to join in, Lisa thought about asking Walter if he wanted to dance, but she decided the time would be better spent eliciting vital statistics.

"You married?" she asked rather bluntly.

"Not anymore. Anybody grabbed you up yet?" Walter shot back, almost responding too easily. Lisa found herself wondering what might be wrong with him.

"No," she answered.

"I'm surprised!" Walter said sincerely.

Bingo! He's interested, she thought. At that moment Lisa decided to go for the gusto. "How about getting some coffee or something after this?"

"I'm supposed to meet a friend," Walter said, hesitating. "But I guess he can wait."

They both stood there grinning at each other for a while. Lisa thought about all of the couples she knew who had met at a wedding. Who was she to question tradition?

Sundi motioned to Danielle and Lisa. "Come on, you two, I want some pictures with the girls," she called, her eyes bright with happiness. Lisa excused herself and reluctantly left Walter. She felt that uneasy feeling rising inside her again. She took a deep breath, fighting to push it back down, and thought: I can't wait till I get my chance to shine. I'm gonna make the guy who's smart enough to marry me very, very happy.

Before they could take the pictures, Danielle ducked into the church, saying she needed to go to the rest room.

Lisa watched as Sundi and Chris thanked the guests that were leaving. Roger tapped her on the shoulder from behind. "You seen Dannie?" he asked.

"She went inside. She should be right back."

"I've got to go. When she comes back, tell her I'm gone home and Kim is with me."

"Okay. Bye, Kimi. Give me a hug," Lisa said, bending down. Kim reached up and threw her arms around Lisa's neck. Then Lisa watched them both disappear behind the church and into the parking lot.

Lisa waited with Sundi until Danielle returned; then the girls had a ball posing in front of the camera. They acted as if they were posing for *Jet* magazine's society page. They took several pictures with Chris; then Sundi had the photographer take a few pictures of "the girls" only.

Lisa waited purposefully to see how long it would take Danielle to remember her child. Poor Dannie, Lisa thought. She tries, but she's not the best mother in the world. Danielle finally asked about Kim thirty minutes later. When Lisa explained that Roger had taken her home, she watched the expression on Danielle's face go from pleasant to angry. Lisa hated the way Danielle and Roger played tug-of-war with their child.

Sundi tried to cheer Danielle up. "Thank you for being my maid of honor, Dannie."

"No problem, Sundi. The wedding was beautiful," Danielle replied.

Lisa couldn't believe Danielle had finally said something positive.

"Everything was perfect, wasn't it?" Sundi smiled, a satisfied smile.

"Beats the courthouse any day," Danielle teased, since she and Roger had gotten married at the courthouse.

"That was your idea, Dannie," Lisa reminded her.

"I know. I spent my money on the honeymoon," Danielle added and winked.

Chris walked back up and interrupted the conversation. "Ready?" he asked Sundi.

"Okay . . . in a minute," she responded.

"Lisa, I'm leaving too," Danielle said. "What are you doing after this?"

"Oh, I didn't tell you guys. I got a date." Lisa smiled, then grew upset as they both looked surprised.

"With who?" Danielle asked, playing mamma.

"In the gray suit . . . Walter," Lisa said, pointing at him proudly.

"Not again, Lisa," Sundi said with a look on her face that sent a pain through Lisa's right temple and eye.

"What?"

"Ball one . . . strike three," Sundi teased.

Lisa hated it when Sundi played these damn games. "Are you gonna tell me or what?" she asked again.

"He's in the middle of a divorce."

"And?"

"His soon-to-be-ex caught him with his male lover!"

They all moaned at the same time, but Lisa's moan was for real. Her luck with men had been the drizzling shits lately.

The memory of last Valentine's Day confirmed those thoughts. She had opened her office door to find a deliveryman on the other side holding a beautiful bouquet of roses. For a second she fantasized. Maybe they were an apology from Kirby or a gift from a secret admirer. Then, as she smiled a big smile, he asked for a woman down the hall!

Chris approached the girls again, this time very irritated.

"It's time to go," he said sternly. "The limo's here."

Sundi nodded and started to follow him.

"Sundi . . . the bouquet!" Danielle yelled.

"Oh, yeah!" Sundi hustled to the top of the church steps and yelled as loud as she could, "Excuse me, everyone . . . excuse me. I need all of the single ladies to gather round, please."

Lisa didn't want to go anywhere near a bouquet, but Danielle dragged her over to the crowd anyway. She stood beside Lisa and held her elbow so she couldn't move. Sundi turned her back to the group and tossed the bouquet over her shoulder, aiming it in Danielle's and Lisa's direction. It bounced off a couple of eager hands, over to Danielle's outstretched arms, and she batted it into Lisa's chest. Lisa's reflexes kicked in, and she pulled the bouquet close. Sundi hurried over to them, beaming. "I'm glad it was you, Lisa," Sundi said.

"Yeah . . . anyone in mind?" Danielle teased.

Personally Lisa didn't think it was funny as she cast a dirty look over at Walter. "Not anymore."

Chris pulled Sundi toward a small bench, where they sat down. Sundi took off her shoes and stockings. Chris removed his shoes and socks. Sundi's aunts knelt in front of the newlyweds with a washtub and began washing their feet while reciting a traditional African verse.

"We wash away the trouble of your past," Aunt Mira said.

"So that your future will begin fresh and new," Aunt Jessie continued.

After they had dried their feet, Sundi and Chris picked up their shoes and tiptoed across a silky white cloth that Keith and

Jarod had laid across the ground between the bench and the rented limo. In the midst of a shower of rice, Sundi and Chris got into the car, waved, and drove away.

The clouds parted, showing a mixed blue-gray sky, and the sun was drifting downward as the guests gathered their things and headed for their cars as well.

"You coming?" Danielle asked.

Lisa nodded. She was ready for this day to be over. "I . . . guess I should make an excuse to Walter," she told Danielle.

"He should be excused, all right—excused from the human race," Danielle said, her witty satire at work.

"Dannie, you're sick. That man has the right to live his life any way he wants to," Lisa said, defending him, even though deep down she agreed with her sister.

"It's such a waste," Danielle added. "It would be different if he were ugly."

"Amen," Lisa mumbled.

"Well, I'm outta here." Danielle winked and started walking toward her car. Lisa turned to follow her. She didn't really feel like saying anything to Walter. What would she say?

"Doing nothing is probably one of the most tiresome things people can do with their lives. It is very monotonous, and there is no reason to stop and rest."

This was one of Danielle's favorite mottoes. She had it hanging in a gold frame on her office wall. Beneath the motto was a bookcase that held a dictionary, a crystal vase with several dead roses, a large picture of Kim and Roger, and a shelf full of books on advertising and marketing designs.

Danielle began working for Saurus Advertising nine years ago. At the time it was an all-black company run by Lawrence Cole. Danielle had met his son, Lawrence Junior, when they took a public relations course together in their sophomore year. Lawrence was considered a nerd in those days. He wore large black-rimmed glasses and carried a briefcase before they were fashionable. He had a crush on Danielle, and although she was never interested in him in a romantic sense, they became friends immediately. Lawrence stimulated her mind. He thought deeply about everything, and Danielle loved the challenging debates they often had. They kept in touch for many years before Danielle interviewed at Saurus. Lawrence had already been married and divorced when she came on board.

When his father died, Lawrence took over Saurus Advertising

with a new vision. He had built it into a multicultural conglomerate, branching out from advertising to include public relations, marketing, and media management.

Danielle playfully sang the jingle from the Specialty Press account and twirled from side to side in her red, high-back leather chair. She had chosen the bright red color over a normal black because she believed red had magic. She always wore red to conference presentations. She loved the way people stared at her in her red convertible Mercedes. And her red leather chair always got her creative juices flowing.

She had not been able to get this jingle out of her mind since the meeting this morning. "When you feel your back is up against the wall, Specialty Press is the one to call. No job's too big, no job's too small. Specialty can do it aaaaaaaaall, Specialty can do it all. . . ."

Danielle threw her head back and allowed a huge smile to cover her face. The tune had come from the creative talent of Derrick Wells, her new executive assistant. Danielle had written the lyrics. When they presented the jingle to the president of Specialty Press, he loved it and put the firm on retainer immediately. Danielle would have a five-thousand-dollar bonus on her next check, and Derrick might get a bonus as well, although not in cash.

Danielle thought about Derrick a lot. Some days she couldn't get him off her mind. If she were younger and not married, she would have checked him out long ago. Derrick had grown up in a well-off part of Hampton, Virginia. His father, Casimer Wells, was a vice-president at Volkers Systems Contractors, which built aircraft carriers and polluted the Chesapeake Bay. His mother, Cinda, had taught music at Hampton University for twenty-six years. They wanted Derrick to go to Hampton, but he chose Howard University to get farther away from home. As a top graduate of the advertising program, he went on nine interviews before he finally decided to accept the executive assistant position at Saurus.

As she hurried to the afternoon wrap-up meeting, Danielle felt the energy inside her grow. She eagerly anticipated seeing her young protégé. She entered the conference room and quickly surveyed the faces. This meeting included only account representatives. They were getting ready for the annual board meeting, and everyone had a part to play. Cynthia and David sat on the right side of the table. David nervously shuffled papers, and Cynthia carefully freshened her lipstick. Janis entered and sat on the left side next to an empty seat where Derrick should have been. Danielle took her seat at the far end, near the window, and stared at Friday afternoon's commuter traffic. Lawrence Cole, Jr., entered and occupied his usual place at the head of the large black lacquer table. He leaned forward, pushing the large square glasses back on his nose, and started a discussion about the quarterly accounts.

"The numbers for this quarter look good so far. We seem to be working more efficiently, which means more profits," Lawrence explained. He noticed during his talk that Danielle was not listening. "Danielle, would you agree?" he asked to bring her into the session.

Danielle jumped slightly after hearing her name. "Yes . . ." she answered, then hesitated. "I will need reports from everybody on the current accounts by next Friday's meeting."

Lawrence nodded in Danielle's direction and continued his discussion.

Derrick rushed in almost an hour later. Danielle smiled as he sat down near her chair. The smell of his cologne was invigorating.

"You're late, Derrick," Lawrence snapped.

"I'm sorry. I was working on the Bennett account," Derrick responded.

Danielle suddenly gave Derrick a dirty look across the table.

"I thought that was David's client," Lawrence said.

"I'm still trying to finish the ad for Goadans," David nervously explained. "They didn't get the material to me until yesterday."

"When's the deadline?" Danielle asked, trying to clean up the situation.

"Friday. Right?" Derrick said, smiling at Danielle, who didn't smile back.

"I can finish it. I've got some time before I meet with Stephens again," Cynthia, another account rep, volunteered.

Danielle eyed Cynthia. She had learned to be cautious after last year's Christmas party, when she overheard Cynthia putting down one of her ideas to Lawrence. Cynthia was a climber, and she didn't mind using other people's backs to get as high as she wanted to go.

"I've already started, and I'd like to continue if it's okay," Derrick said, speaking directly to Lawrence.

"I have no problems with it. How about you, Danielle?" Lawrence asked, looking at her so intensely she found herself looking away.

"It's okay with me," she answered reluctantly.

"Good. Is that it? Okay, let's go home." Lawrence got up quickly and left the room. The others followed in single file.

Danielle walked into her office. She sat down at her desk and lit a cigarette just as David knocked and stuck his head inside.

"Hey, I'm sorry about the Bennett account."

"You should have brought it up, David, not Derrick. It's supposed to be your project, and you've got to stay in control."

"I know . . . I'm sorry."

"Have a good evening, David."

He nodded and shut the door. Danielle looked through a couple of folders, but her mind wasn't focused. She took a long drag from her cigarette. There was another knock on the door, and Derrick opened it before she could respond. He walked in, closing the door behind him.

"What were you trying to prove, Derrick?"

"I just didn't want to lose the account."

"I told you about David in confidence. You were going to help me, not hang me!"

"Hey . . . I'm sorry. I was just trying to do good," Derrick apologized. He moved around behind Danielle and began massaging her shoulders.

"You're so tense," he said, gently rubbing her shoulders, neck, and back.

Danielle closed her eyes for a moment and enjoyed the power in his fingers. She wanted him but needed to resist. She reached for her cigarette, but Derrick took it away and put it out in the ashtray.

"I'm gonna make you a healthy and happy lady," he said, working down to her lower back.

Danielle stood up abruptly and walked away from him. "Derrick, I don't think we should do this," she said in a voice that was less than sincere.

"I know you're unhappy, Danielle, and I'd just like a chance to change that," he explained, and walked toward her. Danielle watched as he stopped at the window and closed the blinds. She moved over to the door and stood in front of it. She knew she should open the door and tell him to leave, but instead she locked it, took his hand, and led him over to the couch. He kissed her neck, twirling her hair to the side and out of his way. She kissed his lips, and he kissed back passionately. Then Derrick slowly unbuttoned her blouse.

"I'm not sure about this, Derrick," she pleaded unconvincingly.

"Everybody's gone. It's okay," he assured her.

Derrick reached inside her beige bra and carefully pulled out each of her breasts as if he were handling raw eggs. He kissed them, first the left, then the right. Then he delicately sucked each nipple like a newborn puppy savoring his first meal. She unzipped his pants and felt her way to the expanding excitement in front. Their lips slid in and out of sync as they dropped to the floor.

Derrick slipped easily inside her. His hips pushed in a rhythmic, circular motion. Danielle closed her eyes. She wanted to scream because it felt so damn good, but she held on to the excitement. Suddenly she grabbed the small of his back and pulled him closer in ecstasy. Derrick felt it too and kissed her full on the mouth. They rocked harder and faster until they both lay still and satisfied.

———

In the 1960s the University of Maryland was separated into three primary campuses: Baltimore County, College Park, and Eastern Shore. Eastern Shore was the traditionally black campus, but with integration more minority students chose the other two, and enrollment declined.

At eighteen years old Danielle Allen chose the College Park campus. She was admitted in the fall of 1977, and her first experience was exciting. Along with hundreds of other students, many black, she was housed in integrated dorm facilities. True integration was the ideal, so most black students were assigned to rooms with white roommates, but as the semester moved forward, partial integration became the reality. Those black students changed assignments, and a number of floors in the dorms remained integrated, while the majority of rooms were segregated.

Gaithersburg, Maryland, represented another kind of life for Danielle. It was one of those D.C. suburbs that offered their residents safe, comfortable lifestyles. It had award-winning parks, a two-million-dollar community recreation center, and a top-notch school district. It was the perfect place for perfect families, a planned community with acres and acres of bland uniformity. Even the weather was as close to perfect as you could get. With the Blue Ridge Mountains on its west side and the Chesapeake Bay on its east, spring and autumn remained sunny and dry, while the summers were warm and the winters were mild.

The Mead residence was a four-bedroom, two-story brick colonial set on a half-acre lot with a stone driveway. It had an elegant master bedroom with a whirlpool sauna tub, a designer kitchen, and two fireplaces, one in a showplace living room that had never been used.

It was dark when Danielle finally made it home. She had called earlier and had Reba, her housekeeper, pick up Kim from day care. As she opened the front door, Reba was gathering her things.

"I'm glad you made it back. I needed to go, so I called Mr. Mead. He's on his way home too," Reba explained as she stuffed several magazines into her tote bag.

"Where's Kim?" Danielle asked, pissed that Reba had called her husband.

"She's in bed, but she may not be asleep yet. I got to go," Reba replied, and hurried out the door.

Danielle slipped into Kim's bedroom. She was asleep, so she pulled the brightly colored animal bedspread over Kim's shoulders. She picked up her colors and coloring book off the bed and laid them on the small white nightstand. Danielle smiled as she watched Kim shift to her side and pull Tweety Bird closer to her chest.

She shut the door and ambled into her own room down the hall. She sifted through the mail and stopped to read a letter concerning Gaithersburg's most successful fund-raiser, Holiday Cheer for Children. Each year the committee sponsored different events like a Winter Wonderland or the Holiday Village of Lights. Admission to the event was a gift for a child, and the gifts were to be donated to worthy causes. As coordinator last year Danielle had made the benefiting charity the Howard University Hospital.

She tossed the letter back on the dresser and moved her head in a circular motion to relieve the tension. She had undressed and crawled into her Victorian king-size bed when she heard Roger at the front door. She pulled the ivory comforter over her, grabbed an *Emerge* magazine, and pretended to read. Then she waited for Roger to come into the bedroom.

As she waited, Danielle remembered how his love had invaded her heart so long ago. She thought about the life they shared and wondered how she could chance throwing it all away. In her senior year Danielle joined the Black Student Union to appease Sundi, but she got involved because of Roger Mead, a third-year law student at Georgetown who gave free legal assistance to the group. The group's main purpose was to protest unfair actions on campus, such as black students being followed around in the bookstore like criminals. But they also established social outlets like parties and cultural events.

When Roger first stepped to the front of the room to speak, Danielle remembered holding her breath. He was fantastic, always well dressed and used proper English. The only outward sign of his involvement in the Black Power movement was the shapely Afro that surrounded his head. Roger was aggressive yet gentle. He was exactly the kind of man Danielle wanted to spend the rest of her life with. She volunteered to serve on the legal committee with him. They spent many evenings looking up cases in the Georgetown law library together. Danielle even told him she was interested in going to law school someday, hoping it would somehow bring them closer.

On their first date Roger picked up Danielle for dinner around seven. He immediately noticed that she was different from his last girlfriend. She was ready when he came to the door, and she even offered to pay for the movie, since he had bought dinner. He was intrigued by her humor and honesty. And he liked the fact that she was strong and confident, but open enough to show him a softer side. It was as if they had loved each other all their lives.

Danielle admired Roger's wisdom. He had a good attitude about life and wanted to accomplish something. He was mature and levelheaded. He looked forward to the responsibility of taking care of a family. After they had shared their hopes and dreams, spending the night, and ultimately their lives together, seemed natural.

Roger walked into the bedroom and reached over to kiss Danielle. She allowed him to kiss her lightly on the lips, then quickly went back to her magazine. Roger sat on the bed, slipped his hand under the covers and beneath her gown. He felt his way up and across her bare stomach.

"Roger!" Danielle whined and shrugged him off. He stopped, staring at her for a moment, then started again.

"Danielle!" he said, imitating her tone as he wrapped his arms around her small body.

Danielle wiggled away and turned her back to him, pretending to concentrate harder on the magazine. Roger shook his head, then took off his suit jacket. He hung it in the closet along with his pants. Next he threw his shirt, socks, and underwear into the hamper and crawled into bed beside her. He tried again to pull her close to him, but she continued to resist.

"What is it, Danielle?" he finally asked.

"I just don't feel like it tonight."

"Or any night," Roger said cynically. He lay back and began to count the speckles on the ceiling out loud.

Danielle tried to ignore him for a while, but finally she couldn't stand it any longer. "I hate that."

"I know," he responded calmly, still counting.

"Roger!" Danielle put her hand over his mouth, and he grabbed her arm. They wrestled across the bed and were soon laughing. It ended with Roger straddled on top of her. He kept the backs of her arms pinned down against the bed so she couldn't move, then leaned down and kissed her. She tried to fight but was too tired.

"I," Roger said, kissing her forehead, "love"—he kissed her nose—"you!" He kissed her on the lips, and to her own surprise Danielle closed her eyes and kissed him back. Before she knew it, she was on top and he was moaning and calling her name.

Sometime later Roger had fallen asleep, but Danielle lay wide-awake. Her fingers played softly in his hair, and he batted her hand away like an annoying fly. Danielle turned, lay flat on her back, and quietly created her own orgasm. She began breathing deeply, in and out, until the climax, when her body tightened and she held it all in. She remembered Derrick's warm hands and lips sliding across her body. Danielle savored the memory for a moment. She should have felt some sort of guilt, but she refused. She wanted badly to be back in Derrick's arms. He had made her feel whole again. She checked to be sure Roger was still sleeping, then turned over on her side, closed her eyes, and quietly cried herself to sleep.

Sundi and Chris spent their honeymoon in Ocho Rios, Jamaica. Once a small, quiet fishing town, it had become a thriving tourist mecca. Sundi loved how the large golden sun made all the colors on the island, from the dark green trees to the clean white sand, seem more vibrant. The ocean was a clear blue, nothing like the brown, muddy water at Colonial Beach on the Potomac River.

It was Sundi's first time in Jamaica, but Chris's third. He'd come twice with his parents as a teenager. Much of the landscape and many of the people reminded him of his own home, Lagos Island. On one side of Lagos was the Apapa Port, which hosted large foreign ships, and a popular tourist area covered most of the other side.

Sundi and Chris had rented a room on the island that included a kitchen because Chris claimed he didn't want to eat just anybody's cooking. Sundi liked to cook, so it didn't bother her most of the time. But tonight, as she opened the curtains and stared at the intensity of the moonlight through the treetops, she hated the frying plantain on the stove. They were supposed to be in bed by now, making mad, passionate love. Instead Chris had been on the phone for almost forty minutes. Sundi dragged herself back over to the kitchen. The plantain had turned a golden brown and looked like overripened bananas, so she took them out of the vegetable oil and laid them on a paper towel to drain.

"We'll be back in a few days. It can't wait until then, Sylla?" Chris asked his cousin. Sundi twisted her nose and mouth at the sound of Sylla's name. He was Chris's cousin and best man, but Sundi couldn't stand him. Actually, it wasn't Sylla she disliked but the fact that he still seemed to come before her where Chris was concerned. Chris had told her over and over again that Sylla was one of the few people in America that he could depend on. But Sundi saw very little evidence of that. Sylla was a leech, always wanting money and favors. He had borrowed part of the money Chris had planned to buy her wedding ring with and couldn't pay it back in time, so Chris's father had had to come to the rescue.

Sundi attacked the plantain with a large spoon, dumping a pile on a paper plate. She walked over to the couch and dropped the plate on the table in front of Chris. He didn't look up from his telephone conversation to see the disgusted look on her face.

Sundi fumbled around in the closet and pulled a pack of birth control pills from the bottom of her suitcase. After slipping one in her robe pocket, she carefully put the pack back at the bottom. She walked over to the couch, trying to force herself into a better mood. She sat next to Chris and twisted her body so she could watch his lips flow easily across his teeth.

As Chris listened to Sylla, he was skimming through an island brochure. Sundi smiled, remembering that it was Chris's passion for reading that had brought them together in the first place. He loved libraries, and so did she. The fact that Chris could read at the age of four was a great accomplishment, since many of his friends could speak two or three languages, but most couldn't read or write. He was Iyoma's only child, and she had taught him all that she knew. Orun was proud of his son's educational achievements, since he himself had attended only six years of school. He agreed with Iyoma that Chris's education should be nurtured and supported.

Chris finished high school and spent a year at Lagos Teacher College before his father agreed to send him to America to study computers. Orun and Iyoma made the decision to send Chris to Howard University in Washington, D.C., because his older cousin Sylla was finishing school there and Chris would have a place to stay and family support. Chris immediately fell in love with the nation's capital. He finished his bachelor's and master's degrees in computer science at Howard and accepted his first job offer at National Computers in Alexandria. Even after graduation, his nightly ritual continued to include spending at least an hour in the library after work.

One Wednesday evening a little more than a year ago, as Chris sat at a table in the reading area of Prince William Public Library, he found himself distracted by the arrival of a pretty young woman. Sundiata Karif carried an armful of books to the table across from his. She did not look up to see the pool of brown eyes that absorbed her. Sundi sat down, spreading the books into three small piles. Then she systematically started skimming through them and marking specific pages with neatly torn strips of white paper.

Chris watched as her fingers turned each page meticulously. He noticed the spark of light that flashed from the small ring on her left hand. His heart was saddened by the thought that she might be married.

When Sundi got up and went to the rest room, Chris sat for a moment staring at the door. He fought an overwhelming urge to find out what she was reading. He finally gave up and strolled over toward her table, pretending to search through the books on the shelf behind it. Then he turned his attention to his real purpose.

The open book on top was called *The Black Women's Health Book*. He skimmed the title of the open chapter, "Sick and Tired of Being Sick and Tired: The Politics of Black Women's Health" by Angela Davis. At first Chris looked quickly back and forth between the rest room and the table, but soon he became wrapped up in the article, which discussed a National Black Women's Health Project. He was very surprised that he had never really thought about black women with health problems and that such problems were important enough for the development of an independent forum. Suddenly he realized how limited his knowledge really was. The idea of black women with separate political issues from black men seemed to him to be an oxymoron.

"Excuse me," Sundi said, standing behind him.

Chris was startled by the soft voice. "Oh . . . I'm sorry . . . I'm sorry," he told her, and hurried away.

Sundi watched Chris walk nervously back to his table. She looked around to see if anything was missing, then went back to her task.

Chris tried hard not to let her catch him looking, but their eyes met several times. He was so embarrassed that for the first time in his life he didn't know what to say. It was as if he had been caught peeping in her bedroom window and they were waiting for the police to arrive.

Sundi finished marking her sections, gathered up the books, and carried them around the corner and into the copy room.

Chris panicked as he watched her stand up and go. He wanted to know her name. He wanted to see her again. When she disappeared behind the reference shelves, he decided to follow. At the edge of a bookcase he spotted her across the room at the Xerox machine. He thought for a moment about what he would say if he approached her. He would apologize for what had happened earlier and maybe ask her name. By that point he would be able to tell whether or not she was interested and he could decide what to do from there.

Chris ventured over toward Sundi. He was about to stop when she turned and smiled at him. He broke into a nervous sweat, nodded, and rushed into the restroom. Inside, Chris tried again to build up his courage. He would be honest. He would tell her he wanted to get to know her. American women liked honesty, so she would probably be flattered by his attention. He pushed the door open and looked toward the Xerox machine, but Sundi was not there. He looked around the room and still didn't see her. He hurried over to the front doors and checked outside, then walked up and down every aisle on the second floor. Sundi was gone.

Finally Chris returned to his table and sadly sat down. But he found a grin when he saw the health book from Sundi's table sitting in front of his chair. He picked up the book and turned to the page that was marked by the white strip of paper. It was the chapter he had started to read. Then he saw the note: "This is a very good chapter in a very good book. I hope you find time to read it. It also makes for some very good discussions. Sundiata Karif 360-8760."

Sundi smiled lovingly at Chris. They were now on their honeymoon, and she hadn't even realized that day that he was the man who would win her heart. As the Caribbean moonlight cast a bright glow across the room, it gave Sundi a chill, and she grew tired of waiting for Chris to get off the phone, so she began to tease him. She held her finger over the cut-off button on the telephone, threatening to push it down. Chris shook his head no, while she nodded yes.

"Okay . . . okay, see you then, Sylla," Chris said, quickly hanging up the phone.

Sundi laughed and eased onto his lap. She held a piece of the plantain to his mouth with her fingers.

Chris opened his mouth and chewed. "Ummmm, good," he moaned.

"Let's stay two weeks instead of one, Chris," Sundi suggested.

"Got to get back to work," Chris replied in his no-nonsense voice.

"Your job wouldn't disappear if we stayed one more week."

Chris didn't respond. He hated it when Sundi questioned his authority, and she knew it.

"What did Sylla want?" she asked, changing the subject.

"Nothing. He's having some problems."

Sundi hated that Sylla was trying to live the good life with their money. He made a decent living working as a city assessor but lived in an expensive downtown Washington apartment and drove a used black Saab that he couldn't afford. Chris, of course, didn't care to think about that. Where Chris was concerned, Sylla embodied all the characteristics of the sainted monkeys. He saw no evil, heard no evil, and spoke no evil.

Sundi smiled a phony smile, jumped off Chris's lap, and hurried into the bathroom. She shut the door and stood in front of the mirror. She removed the pill from her pocket and popped it in her mouth. She turned on the cold water, caught a little in her palm, and swallowed.

The honeymooners spent their first three days going back and forth between the hotel room and the beach. On the fourth day they rented bicycles and rode across the countryside. The Jamaican people were warm and friendly. When they stopped to ask directions from an elderly man sitting on the front porch of his wooden one-room shack, he invited them to enjoy bread and wine. Sundi noticed as he spoke how the lines around his eyes and mouth gave him a unique depth of character. He was obviously someone who had experienced a full life. A crooked cane leaned against the broken chair, but when the man walked slowly inside to get the bread, he didn't use it. He poured the wine into tiny cups and broke off uneven pieces of bread with his hands. Then he told them stories about how the local bay area was once a pirate's cove and that there were still remnants of an old cannon and guns there that were used by the volunteer militia.

Of all the places they went, Sundi and Chris both agreed that Dunn's River Falls was the most beautiful spot on the island. It was a waterfall that flowed down a limestone rock formation. Sundi forced Chris to make at least six different trips up the handmade trail to the top. Each time they stopped to play in the small pools of ice-cold water at various levels. Sundi committed the word *chorrera* to memory after the old man told them the name Ocho Rios was adapted from *chorrera*, which meant "waterfall" in Spanish.

On the morning of their fifth day, Sundi closed her eyes and lay on the beach, enjoying the heat of the sun on her face and the cool of the sand on her back. Chris cautiously tiptoed out of the water and up to her. Without warning, he shook his hair so that the water fell all over her body.

She leaped up, yelling, "Ahhhhhhh, Chris!"

He turned and hustled back into the waves. She followed but

only got her feet wet. She trudged back to her towel and sat down pouting. Sundi pouted a lot. She was a very spoiled child despite her parents' modest income. And once they had stopped spoiling her, she continued to spoil herself. It was nothing for Sundi to spend two or three hundred dollars on an outfit. She didn't have a closet full of clothes, but what she had was quality.

Sundi squinted toward the water as Chris dived beneath it. He sometimes reminded her of a child who had been forbidden to laugh. It seemed that his life had always been one of seriousness and purpose. Sundi noticed that he was different in Jamaica. She thought maybe it was the ocean that somehow made his spirit brighter. Whatever it was, she loved how that liquid energy seemed to move him closer to her.

Chris approached Sundi again slowly. He extended a seashell he had picked up in the water.

"Friends again?" he teased.

Sundi took the shell and indifferently tossed it behind her. "No," she said, poking out her lips babylike.

"Please," Chris begged. He secretly loved that look. "I'm waiting for you to kiss me," he said, smiling.

"So?" Sundi wanted him to suffer, a little. She got up and walked away. She studied the ground in search of unique twigs, tiny pieces of bark, and dried tree roots from the edge of the beach, and she picked up several with interesting shapes and odd colors. These she would incorporate into the handmade baskets she sold. She would interlock the dried tree roots to the plastic base of a basket and cover it with a twisted weave of willow, bamboo, or cane. Or she might decide to pair the unique treasures she'd collected into a decorative zigzag pattern.

Sundi had started weaving baskets as a hobby to earn extra money when she was a student at the University of Maryland, but it was Danielle who talked her into approaching several shops around the school to see if her baskets would sell. They sold very well, and Sundi started a business that grew so quickly she'd never had to put up with a nine-to-five.

Sundi's independence made Chris both jealous and proud.

He was proud because she reminded him of his mother, who, despite tradition, had always found her own way. Yet he was also jealous because her business was a threat and it took away his edge. He wanted to provide for her, take care of her, and be responsible for her. It was what he had been taught to do.

Sundi returned to her spot on the beach and sat inside the same sand imprint. She opened her denim tote and dropped her newfound treasures into an empty plastic bag. She lay back, covering her eyes with her arm.

Chris came up to her and dropped to his knees by her side. He pressed his lips onto her stomach and blew. Sundi giggled like a six-year-old.

"I love this place . . . I love you," Chris said as he kissed Sundi's stomach several times, making loud, smacking noises. Then he turned to lie on his back, using her stomach as his pillow. Sundi watched Chris's chest rise and fall. As she rubbed her hand up and down his muscular arm, she thought about how different their backgrounds really were, how much they didn't know about each other. But she believed in the power of love, and she planned to hold on to that belief.

"I wish we could stay like this forever, Chris," Sundi said, stroking his closely cut head of hair.

"We will," Chris assured her. "And life is gonna be even better when our love is bonded by a child."

Sundi looked upset for a moment. She hesitated, then spoke: "Chris, don't you think maybe we should spend some time together before we have a baby? We need to get more comfortable with each other and our marriage."

Chris wasn't listening. "Hey," he said, stroking her foot with his thumb, "wouldn't it be great if we made him right here?"

Sundi found that their last couple of days on the island went by too quickly, and the last evening was the worst. She spent the whole day dreading their return. She didn't want to get on that plane the next morning. They finished dinner and left the Coral Restaurant, heading back to their hotel. Sundi stopped to give Chris a big hug, then planted a sloppy, wet kiss on his parted lips. "Happy one-week anniversary, babe," she whispered in his ear.

Chris was annoyed. He didn't care for public displays of affection, unless they were initiated by him, and she knew it. They walked in silence for a while. Sundi's white two-piece cotton dress swayed in the evening breeze as they walked past brightly lit signs from tourist shops, restaurants, and clubs and into their hotel.

"Let's go to Kelly's for a drink," Sundi suggested, pointing at the hotel's bar and putting on her best sad puppy dog face.

"No . . . not tonight," Chris said.

"Come on, Chris, please," Sundi pleaded, rubbing her knuckles down the middle of his back as they stood in front of the elevator.

"I don't feel like it," Chris told her, and pushed the up button several times.

"Well, I'm going to have a drink before I come up to the room," Sundi told him, and turned to walk away.

"You can order a drink in the room, Sundi," Chris suggested.

"I don't want to drink in the room, Chris. I want to be around people and music. We've only got one more night. Come on, let's enjoy it."

"I said no!" Chris said, his tone telling her that it was final.

Sundi stared at him for a moment and then decided she would test the waters. "You know we're not in Nigeria, Chris."

"You're my wife now, Sundi, and things aren't the same," Chris said, frowning at her.

"I hope this also means that you plan to stop going out with Sylla and your friends anytime you want to."

Chris didn't respond, so Sundi shrugged her shoulders, rolled her eyes, and walked toward the bar.

Chris looked around the lobby, which seemed almost deserted, and gathered the courage to speak. "You expect to be my wife and run the streets acting like a whore?"

"A whore!" Sundi said, turning back toward him. She put

her hands on her hips, and her neck swayed back in a typical black woman stance.

"I didn't say you were one. I said you were *acting* like one." Chris tried to explain, lowering his voice as another couple entered the lobby and moved toward the elevators.

"Big difference," Sundi said, and stormed away. Then, suddenly, she did an about-face and marched right up to one of the hotel bellhops. "Do I look like a whore to you?" she asked bluntly.

The bellhop's brown face blushed to a burgundy shade, and he gave her a puzzled look. He didn't have time to answer before Chris snatched her arm and pulled her into the elevator. Sundi saw the look of indignation on Chris's face and decided she would back down for the moment. But within that stern silence on the elevator she was laughing inside because *she* had taken control, for a minute or two anyway.

When Sundi and Chris arrived at National Airport, Sylla was on time. Despite his average size and shape, his dark skin and bald head made him easy to spot in the crowd. He waved when he saw them enter the terminal.

"Hey! How are the lovebirds?" Sylla asked.

Chris shifted his eyes over toward Sundi briefly and faked a smile. "Fine, man. How are you?"

Sundi didn't respond, so Sylla made sure to direct his next question to her.

"You have a good trip, pretty lady?" Sylla took the larger bag out of her hand as he asked.

Before she could answer, Chris and Sylla began talking in Yoruba. They were walking faster than Sundi, so they quickly pulled away from her. She trailed along, not really caring what the problem was this time.

Sundi stopped at a magazine stand and looked for something that she might want to read. She selected an *Ebony* in which Robin Givens, post Mike Tyson, loomed across the cover with a sexy and determined intensity. The issue included stories on ways to love yourself, ethnicity, and the full-figured women in control. This would keep her occupied for a while.

Up ahead, Chris and Sylla had stopped walking. Chris pulled out his checkbook, made out a check, and handed it to Sylla just as Sundi caught up to them.

"Thanks, man," Sylla said. He folded the check three times and stuffed it in his pants pocket.

"Don't worry about it. And I'll see you later tonight," Chris replied, putting his arm stiffly around Sundi.

Sylla grinned and hurried off. "I'll get the car, you guys get your other bags, and we'll meet out front."

Sundi and Chris walked toward the baggage claim area.

"We don't have that much left in our savings, Chris," Sundi said quietly.

"It doesn't matter," Chris replied.

Sundi stopped short. "It does matter, Chris! How are we gonna afford a baby if you keep giving our money away?"

Chris turned to address her. "He helped me many times when I was in school, Sundi."

"So now you gotta take care of him for the rest of your life?"

"Our family helps each other. That's what we do."

Sundi dropped the blue duffel bag she was carrying on the floor and walked past Chris.

"Try helping me for a change," she said.

It was a Wednesday, and Lisa hated Wednesdays. It seemed bad things always happened to her on Wednesdays. She had agreed to meet Danielle for lunch at a new place on Fifth Street and Avenue E, Senor Pablos. And although she didn't feel like being bothered, she drove up to the block and parallel parked in the first space she found. Danielle waved when she saw her coming down the street.

"You're late," Danielle said as Lisa stopped beside her to catch her breath.

"You're trifling," Lisa shot back, just to let her know she was not in the mood.

Danielle raised her eyebrows and cocked back her head. "Excuse me!" she replied as she followed Lisa inside.

The walls were painted a bright gold with maroon trim. It was the perfect atmosphere to soothe Lisa's battered soul. They followed the hostess over a small wooden bridge with large goldfish swimming beneath a trickling waterfall.

"I'm so silly sometimes," Lisa admitted to her sister as they sat down across from each other at the table.

"You dug out Kirby's letters and read them again, didn't you?" Danielle guessed.

"Even worse, I called him and really got my feelings hurt," Lisa said, cradling her head in her arms on top of the table.

"No, you didn't! What happened?"

"He was busy . . . he had company. I hung up, had a good cry, and finally fell asleep."

"Poor baby," Danielle said, patting her left breast. "Want some?"

"Ha-ha—very funny!" Lisa responded in between chuckles. "I'm so damn tired of being unhappy!"

"Lisa, you could be married and still be unhappy. Look at me," Danielle told her.

Lisa picked up her menu. "And why are you unhappy, Dannie? Roger is as close to perfect as a man can get."

"That's the problem. Roger is too perfect. There's no excitement, no passion. Just Roger and his perfection."

"Well, if Roger's not a good one, then I'm truly in trouble."

"Buy a lifeboat because we're all sinking," Danielle told her as she scanned the lunch entrées.

"Maybe I should just give up now and save myself some pain," Lisa joked and took a sip of water from the glass in front of her.

Danielle closed her menu. "I'm sorry to inform you, but pain is what life is all about."

"So what's the point?" Lisa asked.

Danielle never answered.

After they had ordered, Danielle discussed her most recent episode of consumer decadence. She showed off the extravagant diamond tennis bracelet she'd bought at Wishbone jewelers. Lisa admired the bracelet, then sat engulfed in her own thoughts. She thought about how much simpler life had been when she was a child. She thought about the many hours she'd spent perfectly happy by herself reading and daydreaming. She thought about her youthful dreams. She had wanted to see Egypt and Africa someday, to buy a horse and name it Sango, which meant "crash of thunder" in Yoruba. At one time she even thought she might become a world-renowned poet like Nikki Giovanni.

Her dreams had been fed by her high school English teacher,

Mrs. Winters, in her senior year at Duncan. She won an award from the Poetry Society for one of her favorite pieces, "If I Were the Clothing Worn by Your Precious Body." Lisa tried to remember the poem but only parts of it filtered in.

If I were the clothing worn by your precious body,
I would constantly caress your warm satin skin with love.
I would shape your brilliant muscles like the mellow impact of
strength and hug the innermost crevices of your torso in
an ultimate embrace.
You would know no other beauty to match the hot, vibrant,
massaging cloth I would be.

Lisa hesitated, searching her mind for the next verse. She stopped for a second to nod and smile at a self-absorbed Danielle, then continued.

If I were the clothing worn by your precious body,
I wouldn't bind your handsome qualities as others have tried.
Instead I would enhance and accent them to the extent of
ecstasy.
I wouldn't hinder your sensuous movements, but support their
every imaginable impulse.
You would know the glamorous, soothing rhythm of my
presence.
If I were the clothing worn by your precious body, you would
experience a unique depth within the realm of my soul.
You would believe in the graceful creation of an everlasting
love and you would be satisfied to remain inside my in-
timate delights . . . forever.

Lisa had to laugh at herself thinking about how naive she had been about love then. That poem was a tribute to the first man in her life. It was dedicated to their love and its innocent perfection. It started out as one of those loves she'd seen in the movies—wonderful and exciting, the kind of love that fairy tales are made of. It was the best kind of love—until she caught him necking with Belinda Johnson in the backseat of his father's station wagon.

"Lisa, I asked how's school coming?" Danielle said in an annoyed tone. "You know I hate it when you tune me out like that!"

"Sorry," she mumbled.

The waiter brought nachos and a chili con queso dip.

"So, you going to school anymore or what?" Danielle asked, grabbing a chip, dunking it into the cheese, and popping it into her mouth.

"Yeah, I'm still in school, but it may not make any difference," Lisa answered, picking up a chip and covering it with the red sauce.

Danielle's brow wrinkled, and her lips curled downward. "What the hell does that mean?"

"Just what I said," Lisa responded sharply. "I'm supposed to complete my course work this semester, but if I don't get my ass in gear, that might not happen. My comps are scheduled for this summer, but who knows if I'll be ready? And the dissertation—who knows if I'll ever figure out what I want to do with that? It's still just a pipe dream for next year."

"You're pathetic, you know," Danielle told her as she opened her napkin and set it on her lap, then picked another chip from the basket.

"I know," Lisa agreed, wiping her hands on her napkin. Not only was her love life the pits, but she was screwing up her education, and that had always been one place where she was on top.

When Lisa first decided to go back to school for her Ph.D. in communication, everyone thought she was nuts. She had been out of school for eight years writing speeches for a local politician, when she started teaching part-time at Delaware Technical and Community College in the District.

It was a voice and diction class, and Lisa was very nervous, hoping that she wouldn't sound totally inexperienced. Her first lecture was about the importance of proper breathing. The students participated in a number of simple exercises. They inhaled and exhaled for a couple of minutes. Then she had them stand and form their mouths into perfect Os. She coaxed them to say "O" softly, pushing very little air from their lungs, then loudly pushing more air out and building the intensity. By the end of the class a crowd had gathered outside the door. And when Lisa dismissed them, she overheard one student tell another, "This will be a cool class if all I have to do is breathe. I do that automatically!" By the end of that semester Lisa knew she wanted to make teaching her career.

The waiter brought their food. He set the burrito plate with refried beans and guacamole in front of Danielle. Lisa had ordered chicken fajitas. Of course, Danielle, who *never* ate much, didn't finish her food, while Lisa, who had *no* willpower, sucked down everything in sight. Danielle ended up leaving half a burrito on her plate. Lisa eyed it for a while, and when Danielle offered, she ate it, then felt guilty.

As Lisa drove out of the District, heading back to the school, she noticed, as she always did, the distinct difference in neighborhoods. In Maryland the streets were much cleaner. The buildings were newer. The people even seemed happier. Somehow her life was better when she was here. School had always been the one place she felt safe and comfortable.

When Lisa first received the graduate fellowship from the University of Maryland, she was ecstatic. Walking next to the redbrick Georgian buildings on her first day back brought memories flooding in of when she, Danielle, and Sundi were a very unlikely trio on campus in the eighties. Lisa was a freshman, Sundi was a junior, and Danielle was a senior. Lisa chuckled as she realized that Danielle and Sundi were actually buddies, while she was more of a pest who was always up under them.

She had gone to college to follow Danielle. It was ironic, Lisa thought. She always felt Danielle was much smarter than she was. In high school and college Danielle was always the honor student and Lisa brought home average grades. Yet Danielle had barely finished her B.A., and here Lisa was working on a Ph.D. Lisa had come to understand that success was more about learning the system than learning the knowledge.

A story she'd heard years ago in day camp came to mind. She couldn't remember it exactly, but it was something about a group of animals getting together to start a school. They established a curriculum that included things like running, climbing, swimming, and flying. The rabbit was first in her running class but had a nervous breakdown when her teacher made her swim. The bird was the best in the flying class but couldn't climb a tree. He hurt his wing when he tried and dropped to sixth in his flying class. The beaver was an excellent swimmer, better than the instructor, but couldn't pass the flying class. And the fish flunked her running class because she refused to get out of the water. In the end an abnormal snake who could swim well, climb, run, and fly a little was chosen valedictorian.

Lisa had come back for her Ph.D. with a different attitude. She was focused and more motivated, at least in the beginning. The first year she ran on adrenaline alone. She got As in all her classes, and her student evaluations as a teaching assistant were great. In the second year her drive continued, but the third year had become boring. She just coasted along because many of her classes seemed to be rehashing information she already knew.

It was this fourth year when Lisa's heart truly sank. She finally had to admit that the three-year program she had planned would probably take six or seven instead. When the department admitted a second black Ph.D. candidate in the fall semester, Lisa was excited. She thought she would finally have someone to relate to. She had begun to feel so isolated in the process as the only African-American. When Eunice Decker arrived, she quickly found out that her presence would not make a difference. Although they had acknowledged each other in the halls, they had never actually become friends. And every now and then they ate lunch or dinner together, but the conversation was always distant.

The problem was that Eunice followed the warning. It said that black folks should not hang together too much and should not write a dissertation on a black subject and should not be too active in black causes. In this way they could avoid the negative stigmas that were automatically attached to blackness. This warning was based on a myth that was omnipresent. It was an unwritten rule that everyone knew was wrong but followed anyway. The basic premise of the myth was that the farther black people moved away from their blackness, the better they could fit into the system, and the better they could fit into the system, the more successful they could be. Lisa had always fought the myth. She didn't believe things could get better if black folks ran away from who they were. This was the area she was interested in, and she chose to pursue it. She knew her path was more difficult, but she liked who she was, and she was proud of what she had accomplished, so she refused to acknowledge the myth.

Lisa parked her car in lot 14 and hustled into her office four minutes late for her one o'clock speech class. Taped to her door were three pink message slips from someone named Walter. Lisa snatched the messages down, unlocked her door, and tried to remember who Walter was. Nothing came, so she stepped into the office and reached inside her class folder to get the work sheets for the day. She panicked when she saw that she hadn't even typed them yet. Lisa took a minute to think about what she could do instead.

"This is a good day for impromptu speeches," she said out loud. Then she rushed downstairs and into the sweltering classroom, where unfortunately maintenance wouldn't get the air-conditioning working until winter. The students sat in the room, very unconcerned about her tardiness. Several were reading, some were talking, and a couple stared out the window in a daze. She began a short lecture on impromptu speeches to get their attention.

"How many of you feel you are good at speaking without preparation?"

Only six of the thirty students raised their hands, and Lisa could have picked those six out herself.

"Jill, why do you feel you are a good impromptu speaker?" she asked.

"I'm just comfortable in front of people, and I have confidence," Jill answered, ignoring the dirty looks she received from other students, who didn't appreciate her aplomb.

"What about someone who doesn't feel that they're good at speaking spontaneously . . . Jerry, you didn't raise your hand."

Jerry scooted around in his seat before speaking. His eyes darted back and forth between Lisa and the open window behind her. "I just can't think of the right words to say, like in an emergency."

"Okay, let me ask another question. How important do you guys think it is for your chosen career to be able to express yourself at the spur of the moment?"

Lisa searched the room for a face that might have an answer. Finally the only sophomore in the class, Dan, uncrossed his legs, leaned forward, and spoke up. "I want to be an actor, so I know I need to be able to think on my feet."

"Good! What about you, Marcus?" Lisa asked because Marcus was probably the shyest student in the class.

"I'm going into computers, so I don't have to worry about speaking to people. I'm just taking this class to fill a requirement," he answered and scooted down in his seat.

"But why do you think it's a requirement, Marcus?" Lisa asked, keeping the spotlight on him.

"I think they're just trying to get as much money as they can out of us!" Marcus said, rolling his eyes up into his head.

Jill, the designated talker in the class, spoke up again. "You still need to know how to talk to people about the computer, Marcus," Jill said, looking at Lisa for support.

"That's right." Lisa quickly chimed in. "You will need to be able to talk to your boss or colleagues about a variety of topics —often spontaneously. Understanding impromptu speaking can help all of you to be more successful in your careers. The more you speak in public, the better you become at it. When there's no preparation time, you are forced to use previous knowledge. In an impromptu speech you can also use your opinions, but they should be supported by specific examples. Today we're going to practice impromptu speeches. For this exercise you can choose any topic you're familiar with."

Now Lisa was on a roll. She sat on top of the desk and hooked her left leg under her right. "The most important part of impromptu speaking is to organize the information quickly. You should try not to ramble. First, you need to choose your topic based on a subject you know something about. And second, you should think of the major points you want to make about that topic. In this exercise you will need at least three major points. Then identify examples you can use to support each of your major points. And finally, conclude with a summary and maybe even a projection for the future. I want you to talk for about three minutes. Now, who wants to try it first?"

Lisa surveyed the room, watching as the students wrinkled their foreheads, shifted their eyes, and scratched the back of their necks. Things were going very well so far, she thought.

Amy, Lisa's second most vocal student in the class, beat Jill in raising her hand, so Lisa acknowledged her first. Amy stood up and moved to the front of the class. Lisa hopped off the desk and sat in a chair in the front row.

"Okay, my speech is going to be about the Supreme Court because when presidents nominate people to the Supreme Court, it is often tied to certain issues, ideas, and favors rather than based on how good that person might be. Sometimes this is a good thing, and sometimes it's not. For example, Thurgood Marshall was the first black person to be nominated and appointed to the Supreme Court by President Johnson, and his appointment was largely based on the civil rights movement. President Reagan nominated and appointed the first female, Sandra Day O'Connor, during a push for women's rights. Recently President Bush nominated and appointed Clarence Thomas to the Supreme Court not because of his qualifications but because of his color and party affiliation. Thomas replaced the outgoing Supreme Court justice Thurgood Marshall, but he is a conservative mind and thinks nothing like Marshall. So even though he is black, he will probably not help us to continue the push for true equality. Unfortunately, as Americans we have come to accept this political game playing. We allow the government to do whatever they want without repercussions. It's ridiculous and needs to be stopped!"

"Very good, Amy," Lisa said, clapping, so the class would join in. "Where did you pull that information from?"

"It's a paper I'm working on in my political science class."

"Very good. See how easy it is? Who's next?"

No hands went up. "Should I choose somebody?" Lisa asked. She waited a moment, but there were still no brave souls. "Why don't you go next, Cassel?" she suggested, pointing at the chubby boy in the corner.

"I knew you was gonna choose me," Cassel said, reluctantly taking his place in the front of the room. Lisa flashed him a wide smile. Cassel stood up and took a deep breath but allowed his shoulders to slump. Lisa motioned for him to stand up straight. He did and began, "Rap is an important form of black music today. . . ."

This is going great! Lisa thought as she sat and listened. Suddenly she looked at the pink message slips and remembered who Walter was. He was the guy at Sundi's wedding, divorced, gay, bisexual, whatever, she thought. How did he find me?

The last student finished his speech five minutes before the end of class, so Lisa made several additional comments about confidence, presentational style, and inner knowledge, then dismissed them. As they shuffled out into the hallway, she waited to talk to Cassel.

When he walked past the desk, she stopped him. "Cassel, you got a minute?"

"Yeah, Ms. Allen?"

Lisa hesitated, trying to organize the words correctly in her mind. "Cassel, when I called on you today, you said, and I quote, 'I knew you was gonna choose me.' How would you need to say that same sentence if you were working at IBM or if you were in a class with a teacher who's not as understanding as I am about black dialect?"

"What?"

"Do you know how to say, 'I knew you was gonna choose me,' in the way that would be acceptable to people in other environments?"

"I knew you were going to choose me," Cassel said, exaggerating the words and twisting his mouth as if it hurt.

"Good! I just wanted to make sure you knew. See you tomorrow." Lisa smiled and pushed him into the hallway.

She gathered her papers and hurried out the door, stopping only to throw the three pink message slips into the trash.

The sign outside read LUCKY'S. It was a nice place in Takoma Park, Maryland, packed full of buppies glad to see another Friday night happy hour. Lisa walked around slowly, looking for Danielle or Sundi. An interesting man brushed past her. She noticed right away his very inviting butt and thought: You can get a much better ride when there's something to hold on to. She blamed it on reflexes when she reached out and touched it. He turned around and looked dead in her face, so Lisa flashed him her famous smile. He couldn't help but smile back; then he turned and continued pushing his way through the crowd.

Lisa had a love-hate relationship with nightclubs. Once she got inside, she always managed to have a good time, but the thought of going in nauseated her. It all stemmed from a high school experience in her senior year. One night as she sat talking with her friends in a local club, Nelson walked in. Lisa could still see that night vividly in her mind. She was crazy about Nelson Hays, but he didn't know it. In those days it wasn't ladylike to be aggressive, so Lisa sat straight up in her seat and stared in Nelson's direction, trying to catch his attention. Eventually he felt the intensity of her look, glanced over, and smiled. Lisa just knew he was about to come to her table when Anna Miller sashayed her fast ass over to him, whispered something in his ear, and they danced for the rest of the night. Two weeks later they were going together. Lisa was so hurt that she decided that would never happen to her again. If she lost another man, it would be because he was not interested, not because he didn't know she was!

Lisa finally saw Danielle on the dance floor, looking as good as any twenty-year-old out there. She caught her sister's eye, and Danielle pointed to a table in the corner. Lisa walked over and sat down in a seat next to the one Danielle's jacket was slung over. She glanced around, looking for her friend with the soft, round behind. Instead her eyes were forced to linger on a sweet lump of brown sugar standing under an exit sign. His silver-framed glasses complemented the wide, tempting lips that sat on top of a salt-and-pepper beard. Lisa subtly moved her purse and Danielle's jacket from the chair next to her, caught his eye, and motioned for him to come over. They smiled at each other and exchanged several glances as he sat down.

"You having a good time?" Lisa asked.

"Sure. I've never been here before," he responded, looking around the room intently.

"Are you here with someone?" Lisa asked, crossing her fingers.

"I'm meeting a friend. Oh, here she comes now."

Of course she had to be this little skinny thing, with light skin and long hair, Lisa thought. He jumped up, kissed her, and gave her the seat.

"Honey, this is—" He stopped, waiting for Lisa to finish the sentence.

"Lisa," she said, smiling coldly.

"I'm Jackson, and this is Shelly."

Lisa nodded and sat there pissed. She looked around the room to avoid looking in their direction and luckily spotted Sundi. She motioned for her to join them. Sundi sat down on the other side of Lisa, moving Danielle's jacket to the ledge behind her. The waitress appeared carrying a round tray.

"You guys want anything from the bar?" the waitress asked.

"Rum and OJ," Lisa said. "Quickly," she added. "As a matter of fact, bring two."

"What's that?" Sundi asked and pointed at the drink Danielle had left on the table.

"A piña colada," the waitress answered.

Sundi took a sip. "Give me one of those, a virgin," she said. Good old Sundi, Lisa thought. Always the designated driver.

She ordered Danielle another drink, since her glass was half empty, and the waitress left. Someone stopped by the table to speak to Jackson, and when he started to write down his number, Lisa noticed that he was left-handed. This made her feel much better because there was a myth in the Muslim faith that during Creation God decided the people behind his right hand would be sincere and happy while the people behind his left hand would be the opposite. Lisa nodded to Shelly. She could have him.

A short cocoa-colored guy came up behind Sundi, tapped her on the shoulder, and asked her to dance, but she turned him down. This pissed Lisa off. She had told Sundi a zillion times not to say no the first couple of dances. From an informal study that she had conducted Lisa was convinced that there was the silent code among men at these places. She hypothesized that if women didn't dance with the first couple of guys who asked, they might never get asked again. She believed this because every other guy in the place who wanted to ask was watching the brave soul, who took that long walk across the room and got turned down. That of course would scare them, and the fear could mark the entire table for the rest of the night.

"Who picked this place?" Sundi asked, obviously in her prudish mood.

"Danielle called me," Lisa replied, and frowned at her.

The record ended, and Danielle came up behind them. She pulled an empty chair from the table behind her and dropped into it. "Isn't this great?" she said, out of breath.

"I don't think Sundi likes it here," Lisa told Danielle, playing instigator.

Danielle patted her forehead with a napkin. "Is there a problem, Sundi?"

"I thought we were going to be at your house. Chris would have a fit if he knew I was here."

"It's good to know men are the same all over the world," Danielle said with a smirk.

Danielle's in rare form tonight! Lisa thought.

Sundi frowned. "This place ain't nothing but a meat market."

"Actually, it's a deli and these are *choice cuts*." Danielle corrected her. Then she and Lisa hissed as they watched a pair of long, muscular arms and rounded cheeks sway past the table. They moaned in unison: "Umm, umm, umm." Of course he was Lisa's first choice. She watched that tempting ass walk away for the second time and wanted to follow it. Next time maybe I will, she thought.

"Sometimes you act like you're not even married, Dannie. How does Roger feel about all this?" Sundi asked. She was really tripping. Lisa wondered what was wrong but decided not to ask right then.

"You take care of your husband and let me handle mine," Danielle told her scornfully.

The waitress brought the drinks just as another record started, and the same guy asked Sundi to dance again. Lisa liked his style. Determination is the key to success, she thought. Sundi turned him down again, but this time they didn't let her get away with it.

"Go on, Sundi, have some fun!" Danielle urged.

"Yeah . . . go ahead," Lisa added.

Sundi hesitated but finally got up. Once she was out on the dance floor, Danielle and Lisa watched as she started to loosen up. She moved her hips to the beat and allowed her shoulders to bend with the rhythm.

"What's up with her?" Danielle asked just to keep the conversation going.

"I have no idea," Lisa responded, and took a big gulp from the glass in front of her. Danielle started to bounce in her seat to the music, and Lisa wiggled her hips a little.

"Why are we just sitting around? We're here to have fun, aren't we?" Danielle asked as her eyes stopped on her next victim at the bar. "You know Travis?"

"No," Lisa answered, and shook her head. Lisa knew Danielle had had a couple of drinks, but she didn't know how many until she motioned to the guy at the bar. Surprisingly he got up and came over to the table smiling.

"Lisa, this is Travis."

"Louis." He corrected her. It was embarrassing, but Danielle was feeling no pain.

"Oh, yeah . . . right. Come on, let's dance," she said, and pulled him through the crowd and onto the dance floor.

Lisa caught a glimpse of Jackson on the dance floor with Shelly. God is good to me, she thought. He couldn't dance worth shit either.

Lisa inspected the rest of the crowd on the dance floor as the music built to a heightened frenzy. Folks were dressed to the hilt in satin skirts, crepe jackets, lace blouses, palazzo pants, chemise dresses, double-breasted Venetian suits, cotton poplin shirts. They wore Italian leather shoes and platform pumps, pillbox hats and embroidered head wraps, dangling gold-toned earrings, mesh chokers, class rings, pendants, woven disk bracelets, and even sunglasses.

Lisa turned her attention toward the doorway, where she spotted a definite showstopper entering the club. He was younger, maybe twenty or twenty-five years old, but had a smile that could rival hers, which was hard for Lisa to imagine. His deep widow's peak forced you to focus on that perfectly sculpted face. He was too perfect, except for that widow's peak, which meant that he'd lose his first wife. Lisa frowned as some bimbo came up behind him, threw her hands over his eyes, and played peekaboo. When he turned around to hug the girl, his sexy braided ponytail dangled four inches down his back. Lisa knew immediately that a relationship with this man would be like a firecracker. There would be a flash and a bang; then it would fizzle out!

The other women in the room caught his scent and rushed

at him like hungry catfish toward a dangling rubber worm. He knew he had this power, and he casually took control.

The record ended, and Danielle and Sundi returned to the table. Danielle drained the rest of her first drink in a couple of quick gulps.

"So what's the latest, ladies?" she asked, surveying the room with eagle eyes.

"I think I'm finally getting Kirby out of my system," Lisa answered proudly. "I burned every one of his letters last night, one at a time." Danielle and Sundi clapped and cheered her on.

"A toast to Lisa!" Danielle said, raising her other glass. Lisa and Sundi lifted their glasses, and they all clinked them together.

"Did you ever get your five hundred dollars and cassette player back?" Sundi asked Lisa. She would have to mention that, Lisa thought. She hadn't told Danielle because she didn't want to hear her mouth.

"You gave that man five hundred dollars?" Danielle screamed.

"I didn't give it to him. It was a bond. I'll get it back."

"He was a jailbird too, Lisa!" Danielle yelled, loud enough for everyone in the club to hear. Lisa shrank down in her seat.

"Twenty-three warrants for parking tickets," Sundi whooped.

"I don't know where you find 'em, Lisa," Danielle told her jokingly.

"The Goodwill bargain basement," Sundi answered, and she and Danielle shrieked with laughter.

Lisa struggled to hold back a smile. "Ha! Ha! Ha!" she said in an exaggerated manner. "I got news for ya. I met a new guy with real potential last week. He's a security guard at First National Bank." She was lying, but she needed to get them off her case.

"Hold that thought. I gotta go potty," Danielle said, jumping up and hurrying toward the rest room. Lisa watched the heads turn as Danielle swished by. Even the showstopper followed her hips across the room with his eyes.

Suddenly Lisa perked up. They were playing one of her favorite songs, "So Good," an oldie by Al Jarreau. There was something about that song that made her lose all self-control. She frantically looked around the room, hoping to connect with someone for a dance. When that failed, she closed her eyes and squirmed rhythmically in her seat.

When she felt a tap on her shoulder, Lisa turned around to find the showstopper standing there and almost pissed on herself. She couldn't believe he wanted to dance with her. She followed him mechanically to the dance floor and leaned into his arms. She took a deep breath. He smelled great, like mountains and beaches all mixed together. As they rocked back and forth, Lisa turned her head so that her breath would blow hot on his neck. She stroked the base of his head gently with her hand in sync to the beat. He pulled her tighter in response. Lisa opened her eyes to check for the ponytail and make sure this was real.

The song ended much too quickly. As they pulled apart, Lisa planted the experience in her memory for a private late-night smile. He led her back to her seat and thanked her. No introduction, no small talk, just that phenomenal smile. His eyes turned to Danielle. Lisa sensed an automatic connection between them.

"Lots of beautiful women at this table," he said, and winked at Danielle. Then he nonchalantly turned and strolled away. Danielle watched until he disappeared into the crowd.

"That's Derrick," she whispered excitedly to them. "I've gotta tell you something, but it's between us, the girls." Danielle scooted closer to them.

Sundi and Lisa exchanged glances. So that was the famed Derrick, they thought. They had heard a lot about this Nubian warrior since he started working at Saurus. They nodded, giving their allegiance to Danielle.

"We made love for the first time last week, and he's unbelievable! The man had me crawling up the walls of my office!"

Lisa's first reflex was to scream. She hadn't seen her sister this happy in a long time. But at the same time she didn't believe what she had just heard. Danielle was actually having an affair on Roger.

"You're out of control, Dannie. You have a husband and daughter to consider here," Lisa finally told her.

"I need my life back," Danielle explained. "I need to discover who I am again. I'm more than a mother and a wife. I want to be happy."

"That kind of happiness doesn't usually last," Sundi warned.

Danielle looked over toward Derrick and sighed. "Right now I don't really care."

After seeing Derrick, Lisa could almost understand her sister's lunacy. She remembered a time, not so long ago, when she had dated a man more than ten years younger than she was. Ross was her fantasy, an excellent lover. Lisa had always heard people talk about size being important, but Ross taught her that size didn't mean a *thang* 'cause he definitely had that *swang*. It was the first time she came with a man inside her. And it was the first orgasm she'd ever had worth remembering.

As Lisa sipped on her second drink, she thought about how she used to sneak out of her office during lunch to meet Ross for what they called their "afternoon delights." Or he would call her in the middle of the night for a special "midnight rendezvous." While she waited for him to arrive, she'd almost drive herself crazy in anticipation. By the time Ross hit the door, he probably thought she was some kind of sex maniac because she couldn't wait to jump on his bones. They rarely made it into the bedroom.

Ross was always ready too. Sometimes she wondered how he walked through the hall to her apartment with his dick erect like that. She licked her lips and smiled at the memory of those wonderful times. Once when she opened the door, Ross had already unzipped his pants and that smooth, chocolate Fudgsicle was sticking straight out of the wrapper. Delicious!

"So, Lisa, have you had time to check this new guy out?" Sundi asked, waking her out of her reverie.

"Everything works perfectly!" she said triumphantly. Once Lisa started lying, it was easy to continue. She figured if she had a lover right now, he would be perfect or she wouldn't have him. So it really wasn't a lie; it was more like a vision.

"It always does on the rebound," Danielle teased.

Rebound, my ass, Lisa thought. I ain't had a man in six months. If he existed, he definitely wouldn't be on the rebound.

Derrick could go nowhere that night without Danielle's constant surveillance. And except for that compliment, one dance, and another wink or two, he didn't pay much attention to her. She watched as he flirted with the peekaboo cutie at the end of the bar. Lisa could see Danielle's green-eyed monster waking up.

"One of my vendors says she has to be celibate every other month to cleanse her body. I was thinking I might try that," Sundi told them, and waited for a reaction.

"She married?" Danielle asked, ignoring the basic premise of Sundi's statement.

"No," Sundi answered.

"Got a boyfriend?" Danielle continued.

"A real nice guy . . . I met him once," Sundi answered.

Danielle was ready for the punch line, and of course Lisa was in it: "Next time it's a celibate month, call Lisa. Maybe she could hang on to a hard-up man!"

Danielle and Sundi both laughed, and so did Lisa. But Lisa wasn't laughing at her joke. She was laughing at Danielle's jealous ass foaming at the mouth when Derrick slipped out the door behind that cute young thing. Lisa laughed some more when she saw Danielle take the small oriental umbrella from her drink and break it into several tiny pieces.

Danielle was ready to leave not long after that, and somehow Lisa found herself sitting outside Derrick's apartment with her. Danielle was too drunk to drive, so she had talked Lisa into driving her over to his place. Lisa's attempt to change her mind on the way had failed miserably.

"You sure I can't talk you out of this, Dannie?"

"Lisa, you promised," Danielle pleaded.

"Come on, let me take you home instead," Lisa said.

Danielle twisted her mouth. "Girl, give me the keys." She fumbled in her purse, found a twenty-dollar bill, and handed it to Lisa. "This should cover your cab ride back."

"Okay, it's your life. Go see if he's home. I'll wait."

Lisa sat in the car while Danielle got out and stumbled to the door.

Derrick took a long time to answer. Lisa shook her head and watched as Danielle impatiently rang the bell again and again. He finally opened the door in his beige terry-cloth robe. He stood tall and confident with his bare chest exposed. His lips curled slightly as Danielle burst past him to comb the one-bedroom apartment for the other woman. She searched the bathroom and hall closet, then moved on to the bedroom, but found no one. Derrick stood in the doorway, waiting for her to finish. She soon returned, looking apologetic, and almost as if he had planned the whole scene, he held out his arms. Danielle fell pathetically into them.

She waved from the doorway. Lisa watched the door shut, waited around for a minute to be sure, then got out of the car and walked toward the hotel on the corner to catch a cab.

The next morning Danielle drove around for hours, thinking about her situation. She had loved Roger Mead immensely when she married him, and she still loved him, but she was not in love with him. She thought about how people said he was arrogant, foolish, and bullheaded when he went into a partnership with Victor Wilson and John Craig. They started their law firm in the District right out of Georgetown's law school with most of the start-up money coming from Victor's trust fund. A neighbor's dog had bitten him when he was six years old, and Victor still walked with a slight limp in his left leg.

They were three of the sixteen minorities admitted to Georgetown in 1977. Roger didn't apply to any other school but Georgetown because that was the only place he wanted to go. He loved the District and wanted to be in the middle of it all: the Supreme Court, the House, the Senate, and, of course, the White House.

He had grown up not far away in Mayfair Mansions, a public housing project in Northeast Washington. It was built as part of a policy plan for the year 2000. A series of urban growth corridors had been designed around the railway transit system when thousands of black families migrated to D.C. from the South, hoping to get good government jobs.

His mother, Julia Mead, moved to D.C. looking for a better life for her and her two kids. She was tired of the Southern redneck intolerance in Mississippi and needed to live in a place where freedom was real. The nation's capital was supposed to be such a place. Julia's brother Samuel lived in D.C., and he had invited her and the kids up many times. When Julia finally arrived, she was disappointed. Her naive hope and excitement gave way to a harsh reality.

As the older child, with one sister, Chloe, Roger did all he could to help out. His mother received welfare assistance, some food stamps, and health care coverage, but she also worked part-time in the laundry at the Westerbeck nursing home.

Roger's father was only a memory in the back of his mind. His grandmother had once told him that right after his third birthday, Roger Senior moved somewhere in California because he swore he was going to be a movie star. Nobody had heard from him since. Without a father figure, Roger was left to create his own existence in a family of women.

When Julia didn't find work after the second month, Samuel took her down to the welfare office. It took another two months to get the first check; then they moved to Mayfair Mansions. Julia resented welfare each time the check came, but she knew she couldn't live without it.

Despite temptation, Roger stayed away from the street hustlers, pimps, and drug dealers. He did the best he could to protect and care for his mother and sister. He became a man, using Mr. Shaw, his tenth-grade political science teacher, as a model. It was Mr. Shaw who inspired Roger to go to law school. He would listen intently as Mr. Shaw went off on one of his many tirades about the unfairness of the system. He came to understand why Mr. Shaw complained about how discrimination deprived black folks of opportunities for decent education and employment. And he knew he wanted to do something about it.

As Danielle drove into her driveway, she didn't know how to tell Roger that she needed to get away. He wouldn't understand because he had never run away from anything in his life. She turned off the engine and sat looking straight ahead. She thought seriously about lying to her husband. But what kind of lie would it be?

She checked her makeup in the rearview mirror, got out of the car, straightened her pink linen skirt, and walked up to the door. She put her key into the lock, but before she could turn it, Roger yanked the door open. Danielle stumbled inside. She caught her balance and tried to walk past him, but he grabbed her arm.

"You gonna tell me what the hell's going on, Dannie?" he yelled.

Danielle tried to pull away but couldn't.

"Where have you been?"

"Nowhere."

"Don't tell me nowhere and you've been out all goddamn night!" Roger said, squeezing her arm tighter.

Danielle yanked her arm away and looked up at him. She finally had the nerve to say what she'd been thinking for months. "What do you want from me, Roger? I can't do it anymore. Okay? I can't pretend we're happy and everything's okay, because it's not." She stepped away and caught her breath.

Roger's brow wrinkled, and he loosened his grip on her arm. "And what does that mean? Every relationship goes through these periods."

"I'm not happy, Roger, that's what it means!" Danielle yelled. "I cry all the time, for no reason. I don't know how to explain it. I don't know what's wrong, I just gotta get away from here."

"So take a vacation. I can look after Kim for a while," Roger said thoughtfully, despite his anger.

Danielle half smiled. "Why do you have to be so damn nice, Roger?" she asked. "I'm talking about a separation, not a vacation! I don't know what else to do!"

"How about working through this like a responsible wife and parent, Dannie!" Roger said, and stepped toward her. He wanted to grab her shoulders and shake some sense into her but instead he pulled her to his chest, trying to hold her close.

Danielle wriggled out of his arms. "That's the problem, Roger. I don't want to be responsible anymore. I'm sick of being responsible! Can't you understand that?"

He shook his head because, just as she thought, he couldn't understand. He had been responsible all of his life. He didn't know any other way.

Kim walked into the hallway, rubbing her eyes. "Mamma."

Danielle picked Kim up. "Hi, babe. You getting ready for school?"

"We're talking here, Danielle!" Roger said.

"I gotta get Kim ready for school," she responded coldly.

Roger sensed that he was losing something precious, and he was willing to fight to keep it. "She doesn't have to go to school today. Would you put her down and talk to me?"

But for Danielle this battle didn't matter because the war was already lost. "I'm tired of talking, Roger. I'm tired, period," she said, and carried Kim into her bedroom and shut the door.

Roger hesitated, staring at the closed door. Finally he grabbed his briefcase and left for work.

Danielle drove Lisa to Union Station. They were running late. The pollution seemed thick that morning, and Danielle found it hard to breathe, so she rolled up her window and turned on the air conditioner.

"I know you don't want to talk about it, but I'm really worried about you, Dannie. This thing with Derrick has gone too far."

"It's exactly where I want it to be," Danielle responded, adjusting the air vent so that the cool air blew directly on her.

Lisa rolled up her window too. "You must be going through the change or something. That might explain this craziness," she said. "Are you sure you're gonna be all right?"

"Me all right?" Danielle answered, forcing a smile. "Who used to save you from the Crawford boys all the time?"

"That was many years ago," Lisa reminded her. "And we were kids then."

Danielle shot her a dirty look. "If I could handle the Crawford boys at seven, I know I can handle these two men at thirty-seven."

"When you called Cletus your boyfriend you broke his brother Mason's heart. I don't think you handled it very well."

"At least now I understand how men can do this kind of shit," Danielle continued.

"What do you mean, you understand?"

"You really don't plan to fall in love with somebody else. It just happens. I mean, you're not necessarily innocent or guilty."

"Bullshit!" Lisa threw back at her big sister.

"Who shit?" Danielle responded playfully.

"You're full of shit!" Lisa told her. "You know you still love Roger."

"I love them both, but in different ways," Danielle admitted as she stopped at a red light and turned to look at her sister.

"So you would accept this situation if it were Roger who was playing?"

"Hell, no!" Danielle shouted. "I wouldn't accept it, but I would understand it, and that's the difference. I'm not ready to give Derrick up. I've got to see where it goes."

Lisa shook her head in disbelief. "You would be crazy to leave Roger for that kid, Dannie!"

"I didn't say I was going to leave Roger. We're just going to take a break for a while. But when I do decide, you'll be the first to know," Danielle assured her.

They found a parking spot in lot C. Danielle took Lisa's garment bag and tote out of the trunk. Then they stopped briefly to watch the aftermath of a fender bender nearby. An older Chevy Impala had hit a cab while it was pulling out of its parking space.

A tall brown-skinned man, wearing a blue jacket with the Amtrak emblem on it, happened to be walking by, and he immediately took control. He ordered the man with him to go inside and call security. Then he stepped between the two drivers.

"Just take it easy," he told them, using his presence to keep them apart.

"Stupid bitch . . . she should've watched where she was going," the cabdriver spit out, pointing his finger in the lady's face.

"I said I'm sorry. What more do you want, asshole?" the lady shot back, unafraid.

Up went the man's middle finger.

Lisa stepped closer to get a better look, then suddenly ducked behind Danielle's red Mercedes. Danielle looked down at her sister and back over at the tall ebony brown man looking toward them.

"What's wrong with you?" Danielle asked.

Lisa didn't respond right away; she was slowly inching her way to the other side of the car. "Shhhh!" she finally hissed. "I'm going to get my ticket."

Danielle watched Lisa crab-walk between cars and over to the entrance. She rubbed the back of her calves, just thinking about the pain. She watched two additional security guards arrive, then picked up the suitcase. As Danielle entered the terminal, Lisa was standing behind a wall, beckoning to her.

"What in the world are you doing, girl?"

"That was that guy from the wedding. Remember Walter? He's been calling me at work, and I just didn't want to deal with him today. I forgot he worked here."

"That's the one Sundi said was gay?"

"Right. Come on, I've got to get on the train before he comes back inside," Lisa said, grabbing her bag from Danielle and rushing toward the train.

"So if he's gay, why is he calling you?" Danielle asked, following close behind.

"Hell, I don't know. He's divorced. Maybe he's bisexual."

"You bought your ticket already?" Danielle asked.

"Yeah, come on," Lisa urged while concentrating on the entrance. As Walter entered the terminal, she stopped behind a large post.

"You look really silly," Danielle said.

"Just stand right there. Don't move," Lisa replied while peeking over Danielle's shoulder.

"I'll be here Monday evening at ten to pick you up," Danielle said, hugging Lisa.

"Okay," Lisa said, returning her hug. "I'm going to make a run for it." She stepped out from behind Danielle and heard a man's voice call her name.

"Lisa . . . Lisa Allen," the voice called.

"Oh, well, Lisa, I've got to go," Danielle teased.

"Don't leave yet," Lisa begged as she turned around and smiled at Walter.

"I thought that was you. How are you?" Walter said as he reached her.

"Uh. Fine . . . good . . . How are you?" Lisa said, and tried to fake another smile. "Walter, this is my sister, Danielle."

"Hi," Walter said, and extended his hand.

"Hello," Danielle responded with a grin that spread from ear to ear.

"Did you get my messages?" Walter asked Lisa.

"No . . . ah, yes. But I've been in and out of town," Lisa answered nervously, shifting her bag to her opposite hand.

"Here, let me take that for you," Walter told her, grabbing the garment bag.

"Well, I really do have to go. I'm already late," Danielle slipped in, winked at her sister, and walked away.

Walter continued. "I called eight different departments at the University of Maryland before I found a Lisa Allen in communication studies. I've been leaving messages for weeks."

"I only got a couple of messages," Lisa lied again, and ran her tongue across her teeth.

"So what happened at the wedding? I thought we had something pretty special; then you disappeared."

"Oh, I'm sorry. My sister wasn't feeling well, and she rode with me. I looked around for you, but I didn't have much time."

"All aboard," the conductor yelled.

Walter glanced at the claim check as they walked closer to the train. "Chicago, huh?" he said, and waited for her response.

"A communication conference," Lisa answered, glad for an excuse to move toward the train.

"Staying long?" Walter asked, walking beside her.

"Just the weekend."

"Chicago's a long way for the weekend. You're gonna spend most of your time on the train," Walter teased.

There was something about him that Lisa really liked. She

got that same knotted feeling in the bottom of her stomach—a combination of pain and pleasure—as she watched his forehead wrinkle and the sides of his mouth curl when he smiled. Lisa could tell intuitively that he was the kind of person who enjoyed feeling good and being happy. He seemed so much like the kind of man she was looking for. She didn't need a rich man, or a brilliant man, or even a fine man, just a man who knew how to enjoy life. Someone who knew the difference between love and sex, living and surviving.

"It gives me time to relax and work through some things," Lisa finally answered. "I can't relax on a plane."

"Taking a break from a husband or boyfriend, I bet," Walter said.

Now that was definitely a loaded question, Lisa thought as she shook her head and smiled broadly.

As they reached the train, the conductor called again, right in Lisa's ear: "All aboard!"

Walter handed her the bag. "Have a good time, Lisa Allen," he said, grinning.

Lisa was grinning too. She couldn't stop. There was something special about this man. She couldn't deny that. But she also couldn't ignore the fact that he was gay or at least bisexual. She couldn't deal with that. After sitting on the first available seat by the window, she watched Walter from a distance.

She opened up the *Washington Post* and skimmed through the entertainment section. Her eyes stopped at the daily horoscopes. She looked up her sign, Libra, and read out loud: "Uranus is in charge of your destiny, which means it's a great day for taking care of self. Avoid promises of love and happiness, as they could be insincere."

She folded the newspaper back up and laid it on the seat beside her. Walter could have been a promise of love and happiness, she thought as she disappointedly watched him discuss something with a security guard. The man has too much baggage, she thought. Why is he putting me through this torture if he's gay? Maybe he's not gay? Why would he have an ex-wife if he's gay? The questions raced through her mind like the tortoise past the hare until Walter turned toward the train and looked her way. Lisa was surprised when he saw her and waved. He shot her a big smile, but she smiled back only halfheartedly as the train pulled away.

Seventeen hours later Lisa got off the train near downtown at Union Station in Chicago. She caught a cab over to the Hyatt Regency, where the conference was being held, glad to check in and stretch out in a real bed.

It felt strange to be back in Chicago—to be home. Lisa and Danielle had grown up on the South Side in Avalon Park, off Seventy-ninth and Cottage Grove. She had always been fascinated by the fact that Avalon Park was once swampland. Her high school history teacher had explained how the swamp was drained in the early 1900s, when the city built the Seventy-ninth Street sewer system.

Her parents, James and Laura, owned a small home in the middle of the block. It was an average two-bedroom house, so she and Danielle had to share a room. She remembered clearly how her mom collected owls because she had once read that an owl was the constant companion of Athena, the Greek goddess of wisdom. Everywhere you looked in the house there were glass, wood, metal, plastic, paper, brass, copper, gold, and silver owls staring at you. Lisa used to have nightmares about those eyes, but her mom wouldn't get rid of them. She just told Lisa she'd get over it as she got older, and eventually she did.

Danielle, Lisa, and their mother had moved to D.C. after the divorce. Danielle was seventeen, and Lisa was fifteen. By that time more than ninety-five percent of Avalon Park was black. Chicago had begun to lose its steel mills, and that had caused a lot of people to be out of work. Their father was one of those people. When James lost his job, he and Laura started to argue all the time. Laura yelled at James about not trying hard enough to find another job, and pretty soon James started yelling back. He left the house every morning to look for work, but each time he came back with no luck.

For a long time Lisa thought that that was the reason they

had gotten divorced. But Danielle later told her the real reason was Mrs. Rollings, who lived down on the corner. Mrs. Rollings was a very pretty honey-brown woman. She always wore a lot of makeup on her perfectly designed face. You couldn't help but notice that she had lots of blush on her tan cheeks, ruddy red lipstick painted on full lips, and dark eyes set off by blue eye shadow. She didn't work, but Lisa and Danielle saw her many times at the bus stop on their way to school, her clothes always molded to a perfectly shaped body.

After a couple of months of trying to get a job, James had noticed Mrs. Rollings too. Somehow he ended up leaving their house each morning and spending the day with Mrs. Rollings. Her husband found out about the affair on the coldest day in January. The rumor was that he knocked Mrs. Rollings around and put her out. She stayed with her sister for a while, and James continued to see her. When Laura found out, Lisa and Danielle expected the same kind of explosion, but Laura simply locked herself in her room for a week. One month later later they moved to D.C. with their grandmother.

Laura's friends in the neighborhood kept her up on everything that happened after they moved. They told Laura about Mrs. Rollings's moving into the house with James for over a year. They told her about how Mr. Rollings would sit out in front of the house in his car and cry or honk the horn for hours. They also told her when Mrs. Rollings left James and moved back in with Mr. Rollings.

Lisa stopped in to see her father, but he wasn't in. She left a note stuck in the screen door. The house looked the same, she thought as she got back into the car. The grass was neatly cut, and the pale green paint still looked good despite several years of wear. There were a number of such houses sprinkled throughout the decay. Families like theirs who had been in the neighborhood for many years. Families with little money but lots of pride who were hoping to help restore the area someday.

As Lisa drove the rental car through the area, she realized that Avalon Park had become another testimony to life in urban America in the nineties. It was full of run-down and abandoned buildings, gang symbols spelled out across worn walls, vacant lots that served as a dumping ground for garbage bags full of trash, old televisions, chairs, piles of wood, and empty crack vials.

It made Lisa hurt inside to think about how unfair America was to black folks. They seemed to be the last group accepted as true Americans. Only a few superstar athletes and entertainers were allowed to truly realize the American dream. It was ironic that many of the soldiers fighting and dying for America in the Gulf War were black yet President Bush had the nerve to veto the civil rights bill one year later. Lisa was concerned that black folks were asleep and there was no Prince Charming around to wake up their sleeping bodies!

On Saturday afternoon Lisa conducted her workshop on effective multicultural communication. It was always fascinating for her to see how many people get through their lives not listening to or thinking about anyone but themselves. She started the session by explaining that the only way for people to achieve more effective multicultural communication was to better understand and accept other people and their cultures.

A major segment of the workshop was a discussion about stereotypes. Lisa passed out a worksheet, and the participants wrote down all the stereotypes they could think of concerning specific cultures.

"Okay, now, which of the stereotypes do you honestly believe?" Lisa asked the group to get the discussion started.

A white lady in the back of the room raised her hand, and Lisa pointed at her.

"Latinos are rude and insensitive," she said without hesitation.

"Okay, why do you believe that?" Lisa asked, ignoring the rumbling around her.

"I had lunch with two Latina colleagues, and they talked to each other in Spanish for at least five minutes, knowing I couldn't understand them."

"How often did that happen?" Lisa asked, stepping to the chalkboard.

"Only once. I haven't been out with them since."

"So on the basis of this one incident with two Latinas, you have confirmed this as a norm for all Latinos?" Lisa asked, allowing her to clarify her response.

Seeing Lisa's point but not wanting to back down, the lady nodded her head and shrugged her shoulders.

Lisa drew a circle on the board and placed an X inside. "We all have a comfort zone," she told the group. "We spend our lives creating this comfort zone. Our homes are set up so that they are comfortable. Our desks are arranged in a comfortable order." Lisa turned to the lady who had spoken. "You have your comfort zone, and those two Latina women you went to lunch with have one as well. How is your comfort zone different from theirs?"

The lady hesitated. She looked down at the top of her table, then over at the clock.

"It's okay," Lisa assured her. "There is no right or wrong here. We are simply trying to help people understand how the cultural experience works."

"I guess Spanish would be a part of their comfort zone," the woman finally responded.

"Yes, it would. What type of company do you work at?" Lisa asked.

"A bank," she answered.

"Would it be safe to say that they are allowed to speak very little Spanish on the job?" Lisa asked, and the lady nodded her head. "So, if you think about it, they are out of their comfort zone all day at work," Lisa continued.

Several hands rose around the room. Lisa pointed at a tall Latina lady near the front to get her perspective.

"Did you tell these women how their actions made you feel?" the Latina lady asked.

"No. I didn't know how to tell them," she replied nervously.

"You should have just told them how you felt. I don't understand why people feel they can't talk to us," the Latina lady continued, very agitated.

"How long had you worked with these women before you asked them out?" a white man near the door blurted out.

"A couple of years. We would speak in the hall or elevator, but that was the first time we went to lunch together."

Lisa continued to probe her situation. "And after waiting two years, why did you finally go to lunch with these ladies?"

"I got the idea from my kids," the lady explained. "My son and daughter were participating in a school program where they each have pen pals in Mexico. They seemed so excited I decided to try to get to know these women. They weren't from Mexico, but they were from that same culture."

Lisa stepped away from the board and over to the front table: "It was a great idea, but for the wrong reason." Lisa stopped the discussion to illustrate. "What you did is called the guinea-pig syndrome by people of color. Let's invite a minority to lunch today. It is seen as a very patronizing action."

Lisa went on to clarify. She explained to the group that minorities wanted to be respected within their cultural aesthetic, but accepted as human beings. She expanded her idea to include all people: gays and lesbians, women and men, kids and adults.

The discussion made Lisa stop and think about her own comfort zone. She was allowing it to keep her from getting to know Walter. She couldn't deny the spark between them, but she also couldn't handle the inner conflict she felt because something inside told her to let it go.

On her way back to D.C. Sunday night, Lisa planned to enjoy some quiet time. She wanted to catch up on her reading and get some sleep. She had finished eating a hamburger and settled comfortably at a booth in the dining car reading a new horoscope book on sex and marriage when she felt someone hovering over her. She thought it was a porter, so she finished reading the sentence before looking up. When she finally lifted her head, no words would come, only an uncontrolled smile.

"I'm glad you're smiling," Walter said, balancing himself as the train took a slight turn.

"What are you doing here?" Lisa asked, excited that he could be so romantic.

"Looking for you," he answered.

That's the right response, Lisa thought. But it's from the wrong man! "Why?" she had to ask.

"Would you believe love at first sight?"

Lisa shook her head from side to side but allowed the edges of her mouth to bend upward a little.

"Destiny?"

"No."

"How 'bout déjà vu?" Walter continued.

"Definitely not," she answered with a big smile.

"That's too bad, because they're all true," he told her, and motioned to the seat across from her. "You mind?"

Lisa shook her head no and actually wiped sweat from her forehead as the porter appeared.

Walter picked up the menu, studied it for a minute, and then marked his selections on the entrée card. The waiter took it and disappeared.

"When is your birthday?" Lisa asked. She crossed her fingers under the table and silently prayed: Please Lord, not a Virgo. Kirby was a wishy-washy-ass Virgo, and I can't take another one.

"The big bad lion, that's me!" Walter answered, smiling a dangerous smile.

Bold and aggressive on the outside, but warm and tender, a pussycat, inside. Lisa liked Leos.

"And you're a Libra," Walter said confidently.

"How did you know?"

He pointed at one of the horoscope books on the table. Lisa shifted her books around on the table nervously. But she had to admit, she liked a man who paid attention to detail.

"Are we compatible?" Walter asked.

Lisa didn't answer right away. "Some say yes, some say no."

"What do *you* think?" Walter continued, not letting her off the hook.

"I don't know yet. I don't know you," Lisa answered honestly. She was feeling very confused.

Walter cupped her hand inside his two warm, strong palms. "I was hoping we could change that."

Lisa pulled her hand away and formed the crucial question in her mind. "I need to be honest, Walter."

Walter leaned forward and looked into her face. "I want you to be honest," he said, crossing his arms and maintaining his serious look.

"You're supposed to be gay." Lisa had looked down as she spoke, but her head snapped up to catch his reaction.

The comment didn't surprise or upset Walter; Lisa found that very strange. Instead he hesitated for a moment. Then his smile returned, and he let out a loud laugh. "That's why you disappeared at the wedding and didn't return my calls."

Lisa raised her eyebrows and nodded.

"Boy, the gossip in this town is mighty powerful, but in this case it's wrong. I assure you, I'm not gay!" Walter told her adamantly.

"Maybe gay is not the right word, since I also know you recently got a divorce. Would that make you bisexual?" Lisa asked, and waited nervously for his response.

"I'm neither, Lisa. But I have a very good friend who is a transvestite, and my ex-wife hated him. I understand she's told several of her friends that that's why I divorced her."

Lisa watched Walter cautiously. She knew the man could be lying, but she found herself wanting to believe him. "Can I ask your version of why you got divorced?"

Walter's beer arrived, and he took a drink. "I finally woke up and realized that I didn't have a life of my own. My whole existence revolved around her. I needed a life, and I decided to get one. Unfortunately she didn't appreciate that."

Lisa's stomach churned as she tried to clear her head.

"Are there any other questions burning in your mind, Lisa Allen? I have nothing to hide."

"Just one," she said. "You said you were at the Singletons' party with Anthony. Who is Anthony?"

Walter laughed, and Lisa had to laugh with him, remembering she'd lied that day and acted as if she'd understood. "Anthony's my roommate," Walter finally told her. "He's divorced too, and he had a spare bedroom in his house. It's a shame black men can't be roommates nowadays without folks thinking they're gay."

Lisa sat back and smiled warily. She was happy and wanted to scream as loud as she could, but she held it inside.

"You believe me?" Walter asked in a gentle yet forceful tone. He stroked the back of her hand, then sandwiched it between his palms again. "At least let me prove it to you." Walter lifted her hand to his soft lips and pressed hard.

Lisa still wasn't completely convinced, but she smiled and allowed him to keep her hand this time. She felt a strong, suggestive energy well up inside her. "We'll see" was the only response she could come up with.

Sundi and Chris closed on their four-bedroom condo a few weeks after they returned from their honeymoon. Their living room looked like a forest. There were fifteen or twenty plants, large and small, all grouped together in front of the sliding glass doors. A colorful map of Africa hung on the wall, and African drums and sculptures were scattered throughout the room.

Although Sundi had set up a room downstairs as the workroom and office for her business, her baskets were everywhere. Many sat around the living room; others were in the den and kitchen. The bathroom as well as the bedroom hosted several. Some were made using a pairing weave, with two similar color and texture strips woven together, and others had a Japanese weave, in which contrasting colors and textures were combined for variation. Some of the baskets were ribbed, some were matted, and others had sharp spiral lines. Sundi could make a basket out of almost anything: rope, strips of material, shoelaces, tree roots, willow coils, bamboo, reeds—anything. She made her baskets versatile because people used them for everything: floral arrangements, cosmetic storage, and toiletries. Fruit baskets were popular at Christmas, and baskets also sold very well during Easter.

Sundi had contracts with about twenty-five stores in the

greater metropolitan area. After returning from a long day of restocking client stores in Baltimore, Sundi slid her key in the lock and pushed the front door open. She stepped into the house and stopped when she saw the television was on.

"Chris?" she called, knowing it was too early for him to be home from work. She quickly scanned the area for a sign.

Sylla lifted his head over the back of the couch and smiled. "Hi, pretty lady."

Sundi dropped her briefcase and several baskets on the kitchen table. "What are you doing here, Sylla?" she asked peevishly. "Where's Chris?"

"He's still at work. I just needed a place to cool out till Chris got home," Sylla told her. He grabbed a handful of greasy potato chips and shoved them greedily into his mouth.

Sundi couldn't believe she had come home to find Sylla in her house, sprawled across her couch. She walked over and stood in front of him. "How did you get in here?" she snapped.

"I used the key Chris gave me," Sylla said, patting his pants pocket.

"He gave you a key? When did he give you a key and why?" Sundi asked. Her eyes surveyed the room, moving from Sylla's jacket thrown across a chair to his tennis shoes by the door, a messy pile of newspapers laid on the floor in front of the couch, and a dirty plate, bowl, and glass set on the coffee table.

"Sundi, I've never understood why you don't like me. What have I done to cause this feeling?" Sylla asked, sitting up straight.

"Because you're a leech and we're not going to take care of you!"

"I only take what my cousin is willing to give. How does this make me a leech?" Sylla asked. "You guys have lots of money. You have your own business, and Chris makes a good salary."

"It's our money, Sylla, not yours. We want to have a kid sometime in the future," Sundi screamed. She knew she was going too far, and Chris would have a fit, but she let it all out anyway. "We can't afford to take care of your sorry ass!"

"I'm sorry you feel that way. Because I know my cousin feels differently," Sylla told her.

"Give me the key, Sylla," Sundi asked, holding out her hand.

Sylla's eyes narrowed, and his body stiffened. "I will give the key to Chris if he asks, but I will not give it to you!"

"This is my goddamn house too, and I want that key!" Sundi said defiantly.

Sylla ignored her. He turned toward the television.

Sundi was enraged. She grabbed his jacket and threw it at him. "Get the hell out of here!" she screamed.

"I will leave when Chris comes home, if he wants me to leave," Sylla said angrily.

Sundi took a deep breath and lowered her voice. "I'm not going to argue with you, Sylla. I'm going to call the police." She immediately picked up the phone and dialed 911.

Sylla's eyes grew wide as he watched her. "I see Chris and I need to have a long talk," he said. Then he grabbed his shoes and jacket and hurried out the door.

Sundi knew that Chris would be furious when he found out what she'd done. But she didn't have the energy to worry about it. She locked the door and turned off the television. She moved almost mechanically through the bedroom, taking off her clothes. She stepped into the shower and let the water run through her hair and down her back.

Sundi wanted to cry, but she held it in. She wondered if she and Chris would ever make it through this awkward period. She cringed because it was not only Sylla that bothered her. Many things about Chris seemed to irritate her more than before. Now that the newness had worn off, Chris was a space invader. He was no longer the person she loved and adored from afar, but a permanent fixture in her life. The two-bedroom apartment that had been just right for her was now a four-bedroom condo that was still too small. The perfect life she had created for herself had changed, and everywhere she looked, her space was being gobbled up by her significant other—by love. Chris was her husband, and she was willing to try to deal with his habits, but she'd be damned if she was going to put up with Sylla coming and going in their home as he pleased.

Sundi suddenly felt a cold rush of wind. She turned the water off and wrapped the towel around her. She stepped out into the bedroom and heard the television on again.

"Chris," she called to no response.

Sundi tossed on a large batik caftan and entered the living room to find Sylla sitting on the couch again.

"What the hell are you doing back here?"

"I was just thinking, pretty lady. This is my cousin's house, and since he gave me the key, I have as much right to be here as you do."

"If you don't get the hell out of here!" Sundi screamed in disbelief. She picked the telephone book off the cabinet and threw it at him. It landed on his foot, and he let out a loud cry of pain.

At that moment Chris put his key in the door, and it swung open. He walked into the room as bitter tears streamed down from Sundi's eyes and Sylla bent over moaning.

"What's going on?" Chris asked as he set down his newspaper.

"Cousin, I need to talk to you," Sylla said, and jumped up.

"Why are you crying, Sundi?" Chris asked, walking over to her.

"Why does he have a key to our house, Chris?"

Chris paused. He was surprised by her question. "We've always exchanged keys. I have one to his apartment too."

"I want him to leave now, Chris, and he can't keep that key!"

"You can't put Sylla out of my home, Sundi. He's my family!" Chris responded harshly.

"This is our home," Sundi replied, in a calm voice. "I want that key, and I want him gone. If not, I'm leaving."

Chris looked at Sylla, then back at Sundi. His face was tense, yet confused. "Sundi—"

"Look, man, it's okay. I'll go," Sylla volunteered. "Here's your key. Sorry about causing problems," he added, and hurried out the door.

Chris took a last glance at Sundi and hurried out the door after him. "Sylla, wait!" he called.

Sylla stood next to his car, rubbing his sore foot. "I can't believe how your wife treats me, man," he said in a sad voice. "I don't know why she doesn't like me."

Chris's face turned a maroon color to reflect his embarrassment. "You didn't do anything to her, man?" he asked. His eyes darted several times between the house and Sylla.

"I was just lying on the couch, waiting for you to come home, and she tripped."

"We will work this out. I promise," Chris told him.

"I don't know what you're going to do, cousin. But you know I support you, right?" Sylla asked, and put his arm across Chris's shoulder.

"I know. Thanks, man," Chris said apologetically.

Meanwhile Sundi watched Sylla and Chris through the window. She knew Sylla was telling him how he was mistreated. She expected Chris to swallow the story whole.

When Sylla drove away, Sundi went back into the bedroom to dress. Chris came back inside. He headed for the bedroom, where he exploded. "Dammit, Sundi, do you know what you did! You made me look like a fool! Like I have no control in my own home!"

Sundi stood rigidly flexing her fingers down by her side. "I don't care how it looked, Chris. You gave him a key to our house without even discussing it with me. I'm paying part of the mortgage on this place. I have something to say about who gets a key!"

"Sylla is my family, just like Danielle is yours. Didn't you give Danielle a key in case of emergency?" Chris asked.

"I asked you about giving Danielle a key, and you said fine," she replied. "Plus, Sylla was not in here on an emergency."

In his anger Chris's chest seemed to expand with each breath. "This is unacceptable, Sundi!"

Despite Sundi's best effort to control them, the tears came again. "And it is acceptable for Sylla to use our home like his own personal flophouse? When I asked him to leave, he refused." She frantically wiped her face with the back of her hand. "He finally left, and when I went to take a shower, he came back."

"He came into the shower?" Chris asked, looking concerned for a moment.

"No. He stayed in the living room."

"So how was he hurting you, Sundi?"

It felt as if the air had become thick and dense. Sundi was sick of explaining herself over and over again. "I don't think it's too much to ask to come home—to our home—without your cousin here sprawled across the couch. Chris, I have to try and work through our differences, but Sylla's not my husband, and I don't have to put up with his bullshit!"

Chris stared at Sundi with a pained look on his face. He knew things were difficult lately, but he was trying to adjust just as she was. He tried to remember to put the toilet seat down when he finished. He kept his clothes out of the living room, and he had even washed dishes two or three times. He was doing the best he could, but now she had gone too far. Chris stormed into the bedroom, lips tight, eyes forward, and Sundi followed.

"I don't know what you want from me, Sundi," Chris said. He grabbed his cologne, two pairs of pants, and three shirts out of the bedroom closet and headed toward the den. "I have made an effort to satisfy you, but you don't seem to care about me at all."

Sundi blocked his path. "Dammit, Chris! We need to talk this through."

Chris pushed past Sundi. "I've tried to explain to you how I feel, but you don't want to hear it," he said. He tucked the newspaper under his arm, went into the den and slammed the door behind him.

"I'm not your child, Chris. I'm your wife!" Sundi screamed at the door.

Chris dropped onto the couch and scooped up his newspaper. One of the headlines reported that unemployment in Alexandria had dropped to three percent. Chris put the paper down and looked at the light flicker beneath the door. Unemployment was not what he was concerned about right now.

His mind was suddenly pervaded with distant images of the mainland in Lagos where deteriorating shantytowns were filled with ex-farmers who wanted to explore opportunity in the big city. His family had lived in North shantytown until his father raised enough money to start a fabric and clothing shop for tourists down on South Beach. He later expanded to three shops with the help of his wives: Ekiti, Azane, and Iyoma, Chris's mother.

Chris remembered at five years old stocking the lower shelves of his mother's shop, which also carried food. Although he loved the sweet corn, rice, and yams that his mother received weekly from her family in the rural country, he never liked the rural country. The only evidence of Western civilization he saw in his mother's village was a set of pink foam rollers that Iyoma had given to her cousin Senta as a gift. Since kinfolk shared, that gift made its way around the village. Every day Chris would chuckle as those curlers would be proudly displayed on the head of a different woman. One relative wore them as she snacked on a breadlike substance called chapatis. Another had them on as she pounded yams into fufu for the evening's meal. Eventually, when the novelty wore off, the tropical climate won and their hair was allowed to return to its natural form.

It was not until this moment that Chris realized why he didn't like the rural country. His visits there had always pointed out the narrowness of life's opportunities. His male relatives worked in the fields that surrounded the village most of the day, and the females cleaned and prepared and cooked food, while caring for the children. Chris had grown up in a family where specific roles were accepted and learned. Because he was a male child, he was allowed to help his mother only until the age of twelve; then a new regime began. Manhood made such behavior inappropriate. This was a tradition that he had watched his mother fight.

His mother came from a line of strong Yoruba women, yet she was lost in a world of antiquated tradition. Over the past twenty years she had watched women in Nigeria take on a number of forbidden positions. They were farming alongside and without husbands; they took part in the production of salt and palm oil; they made pottery and became proficient weavers; they were excellent healers, musicians, dancers, and overall creators.

Although Iyoma had many cousins who remained subordinate to male authority, her mother and grandmother had planted stories in her mind that would not go away. Iyoma had cultivated those stories into a rich garden of ideas about real womanhood.

There were precedents for this newfound power in ancient Yoruba tradition. His mother often told him stories of how the oba (king) chose a number of women in the palace to hold high positions. First, Iya Oba, the king's mother, was highly respected for her wisdom, and Iya Kere, the king's treasurer, was one of the most trusted people in his court. Special worship services were organized by Iya Nasa for the king to enhance his spiritual well-being, while Iya Lagbon, the mother of the crown prince and the king's wife, was well loved and respected. Finally, his favorite story involved the Iya Monari, a female executioner who had the strength and fortitude of any man.

Once colonialism had taken over, Nigerian women were removed from their prominent positions. Colonial bias pushed Nigerian women back into a more domestic lifestyle, a status that lingered on. Chris's mother had been among those women who refused to go backward. Despite the appearance of her husband's authoritative control, Chris knew Iyoma basically did what she wanted. He had always admired the independence of his mother, and that was part of his attraction to Sundi. Yet he also felt the need to be in control. It was an important part of what made him a man. It was tradition.

Sundi sat in the lounge of the Hyatt around five o'clock in the evening, sipping on an iced tea. It had been three days since she and Chris had spoken anything other than basic directives. Sundi had tried a number of times to apologize. She was not sorry for what she had said to Sylla, but she was sorry for her comment about putting up with Chris's customs. Although that was how she truly felt inside, she had known better than to say it out loud. And even worse, she hadn't meant it the way Chris had taken it.

After three days of trying to restore peace, she was startled by Chris's call this morning. In a brief conversation he asked her to meet him at five-thirty in the lobby of the Alexandria Hyatt. She was hoping this was his way of making up. She wore one of his favorite outfits: a thin black scalloped jacket with gold buttons that accented her small but shapely breasts. The matching skirt ended six inches above her knee, and she highlighted her long legs under sheer black panty hose.

Sundi sat and watched groups of busy people shuffle in and out of the two glass elevators. As they floated up and down, the waiter brought her another iced tea.

"I didn't order this," Sundi told him.

"It's from the gentleman at the bar."

Sundi turned to see Chris sitting on a stool. He nodded and raised his glass to her.

As Chris walked over to the table, Sundi watched him closely. She liked the way his legs moved in slow, rhythmic strides. She loved the fact that he was so sure of himself and so masterful in his ability to love her.

"Excuse me," Chris said as he reached Sundi's table. "I've been watching you for a while, and I was wondering if I could get you to tell me your name."

Sundi just stared at Chris for a second, then decided to play along. She smiled quickly and answered, "Sundiata," with just a slight hint of enthusiasm.

"You're very beautiful, Sundiata. Are you meeting someone here?"

"Yes, I'm meeting my husband," Sundi told him. She crossed her legs and watched Chris's eyes focus on them, then move back up to her face.

"Well, I should be going then," Chris said, turning away.

"No, stay awhile," Sundi told him, and pointed to the seat across from her. "He's not coming right away."

"Thank you, pretty lady." Chris acknowledged her gesture and sat down. "My name is Christian Ologbo, and I'd like to know as much as I can about you, Sundiata."

"Why?" Sundi asked, not wanting to seem too easy.

"It will help me to understand your beauty."

Sundi watched Chris for a moment, trying to see if he was for real. He didn't change his expression, so she responded: "My beauty fades every day. Is that all you're interested in?"

The ends of Chris's mouth wrinkled. "Bravo. You see right through me," he told her. "What I'm really after is your soul."

Sundi returned a seductive glance and took another swallow of her iced tea. "What do you want to know?" she asked.

"Whatever you want to tell me," Chris answered, finishing his glass of rum and Coke.

"Well, Sundiata is a very loving and generous person. She's also a smart and independent businesswoman. But she gets lonely sometimes, and there are periods when she feels sad."

"Lonely and sad!" Chris spit out with emotion. "That's impossible. Who is this husband you're waiting for? He must be an idiot."

"It's not really his fault," Sundi replied. She had to smile when she realized that she was defending him. "We haven't known each other very long, and we're still trying to work things out."

"What kind of man do you love, Sundiata?" Chris asked as he moved his leg forward to rub up against hers. Sundi felt a sensation that ignited a heat wave from that spot and flowed through her entire body.

"I think he's probably a lot like you," Sundi answered. "Kind, compassionate, exciting, and very confident."

Chris touched her smooth brown face with his fingertips. "Run away with me, Sundiata. This husband could never make you as happy as I could."

Sundi thought carefully about her next answer. She leaned forward on the table, allowing her breast to press against his arm. "I couldn't do that to him. Despite his faults, he's very special to me."

A bellhop entered the room and looked around for a moment. Then he walked over to their table. "Here you go, Mr. Ologbo," he said, handing him a room key.

Chris jumped up, pulling his eyes away from Sundi for only

a moment. He reached in his pocket and gave the bellhop five dollars.

"Thank you. Let me know if you need anything else," the bellhop said before hurrying away.

Chris turned to Sundi and fell right back into his role. "If you can't leave this husband for good, then give me one night—one night with the woman of my dreams."

"The woman of your dreams, huh?" Sundi repeated the line, wanting to believe it.

"Yes, you are the woman of my dreams, Sundiata," Chris assured her. "I want to start all over again," he continued, and took her hand. He pulled her out of the seat, and they headed for the elevator.

Sundi felt the magic growing inside her again as she followed him inside.

Lisa circled the area nine times before finding a parking space three blocks from her apartment. With the air-conditioning in her car broken, that extra ten or fifteen minutes felt like an hour. Something is always wrong with this damn car! Lisa thought as she parallel parked.

She dragged herself up to the front door of the renovated row house on New Hampshire Avenue. The large bay windows and brick front were accented by the oak doors. The downstairs apartment was a two-bedroom occupied by the owner, Rita Belmont. Rita's husband had left her the same year she retired, so she had taken a portion of her pension and renovated the upstairs into a one-bedroom apartment. Lisa was her first tenant.

The houses on either side had also been renovated. The Willises lived on the left. They were a yuppie white couple with two children and a cat. On the right side were Ruth Moller and her son, Arthur. Lisa knew them very well since she had tutored Arthur last year in English. He was an honor student, quiet and meticulous. He had been courted by all of the top colleges and universities until he did poorly on his SAT test.

The house directly across the street was a major eyesore on the block. The yard was full of trash that had gathered from everywhere, and the grass was allowed to grow every summer, all summer without fail. The worn yellow paint was peeling, and one of the shutters was barely hanging on. Every time Lisa passed the house, she felt like walking across the street and snatching the damn shutter down. Usually she tried to avoid looking in that direction.

Lisa walked slowly up the two flights of stairs to her apartment. She unlocked the door and went straight back to her bedroom. She pushed the play button on her answering machine, then kicked off her shoes and threw pieces of clothing in the rocking chair as she listened.

"Hey, Lisa, this is Vanessa. Girl, I got some great gossip. . . . Mrs. Allen, this is First Bank Visa and your payment is past due. If you have already sent the payment, thank you, if not please contact Mary at 1-800-555-9789. . . . Lisa, I can't wait to see you again this weekend. I'd like to get together before then. Call me, and I'll come running."

Lisa shivered when she heard Walter's voice. She flung herself across the queen-size bed, closed her eyes, and thought about him. He seemed so perfect—too perfect. They had enjoyed several lunches together and one movie, and he was slowly easing his way into her heart. In the movie when they held hands she wanted to let go and couldn't. She often found herself daydreaming about the potential of the love he offered. Lisa's serenity was disturbed by the loud thumping of the bass from a car stereo. She got up and went into the living room. She turned on her stereo, then sat on the couch. She noticed how the gray, blue, and beige abstract design perfectly matched the two steel blue butterfly chairs that sat off to the left. She glanced over at her computer but didn't feel like working.

She moved into the kitchen, got down her small glass teapot, and filled it with water. She placed it inside the microwave and set the timer for one minute. She pulled a box of tea bags and the sugar bowl out of the cabinet just before the bell to the microwave rang. When she reached for the steaming water inside, the doorbell startled her, and Lisa burned her finger on the hot glass. "Shit," she hissed.

The doorbell rang again. Lisa plunged her finger in a tub of butter on the counter and went to the door. She looked out the peephole and saw Danielle dancing next to Kim. She quickly opened the door, and Danielle rushed into the bathroom. All Lisa saw was a purple streak from the silk blouse she had bought Danielle for her birthday last year.

"Hi, Kimi," she said, holding out her arms for a big hug. But Kim ignored her and went straight toward the hall closet. Lisa grabbed her from behind and kissed her on her face several times. Kim pulled away and wiped the kisses off with her sleeve. She continued her trek to the hall closet and opened the door. When she saw she couldn't reach the box she wanted, she turned to Lisa and pointed. Kim knew it was her box, and it contained her toys: building blocks, crayons and coloring books, a plastic tea set, an Etch-A-Sketch, two black Barbies, six or seven black children's books, including Lisa's favorite, *The Black Snowman*, by Phil Mendez, and three Dr. Seuss classics. Lisa didn't move. She stood and stared at Kim, smiling, so Kim put her hand on her hip and said, "Hurry up, Aunt Lisa!"

"No! Why should I get that box for you and you just finished wiping off my kisses?" Lisa teased as she walked over to the closet and pulled the box down from the shelf. She held it over Kim's head so that she still couldn't reach it.

"Only for a kiss," she told her. Then she leaned down, and Kim gave her a quick peck on her cheek. Before Lisa could get the box on the floor, Kim started pulling toys out of it.

"Don't bribe my kid for kisses. She'll grow up to be a prostitute," Danielle said, emerging from the bathroom.

"You truly *are* ill," Lisa responded, shaking her head.

Danielle dropped down on the floor beside Kim and grabbed a set of building blocks, stacking one on top of another in a tall pile.

"Where you coming from?" Lisa asked.

"Nowhere. I just had to get out of the house for a while."

Danielle purposefully knocked over the stack of blocks she had built. They flew all over the floor, and Kim squealed in delight.

"You straighten things out yet?" Lisa asked.

"Nope. He won't talk about it. He's still acting like everything is fine. Roger hates to deal with conflict."

Lisa remembered her tea and returned to the kitchen. Danielle got up and stood in the doorway.

"I know what I'm *supposed* to do, but it's not what I want to do," Danielle told her, and started to flick the light switch on and off like a bored child.

Lisa pulled a tea bag out of the box and dropped it in the pot. "Stop that!" Lisa scolded. "You're going to do what you want to do anyway, so I don't know why you're tripping."

"I just wanted your advice, sister dear," Danielle said, faking sincerity.

Lisa threw her hands in the air. "Oh, no! You'll never get to blame me for this mess!"

"Blame you?" Danielle asked, and stepped into the kitchen. She opened the refrigerator, picked several red grapes off the stem, popped them in her mouth, and closed the door.

Lisa poured the tea in a cup. "Want some tea? Because that's all I've got to offer . . . no advice."

"Blame you?" Danielle repeated with her mouth still full of grapes.

"Nothing is ever *your* fault, Dannie," Lisa explained.

"That's not true."

Lisa dumped three spoonfuls of sugar in her cup and stirred it. "The Que party in 1979? You knew Tim would be there with Teresa. You broke them up on purpose."

Danielle sat down on the barstool. "And if I knew then what I know now, I would've let her have his sorry ass. But that wasn't my fault. If it was true love, my presence wouldn't have mattered."

"How about the accident with Roger's car in 1981?" Lisa asked as she blew on the tea, then took a sip.

"Now how was that my fault?"

"You had your turn signal on. The man thought you were going to turn. That's why he pulled out in front of you."

"I did not have my turn signal on!"

"I was there, remember?"

Danielle sat quietly for a moment, then spoke in a serious tone. "Yesterday I decided to leave Roger, and the day before that I planned to break it off with Derrick. Today I don't want to see either of 'em, and tomorrow I'll want 'em both."

The phone rang, and Lisa picked it up, glad for the distraction. She recognized her father's voice immediately. "Hi, Pop," she said in a cheerful tone. Danielle jumped in front of her, waving her arms and shaking her head.

"Yeah, I'm sorry I missed you too when I was in Chicago. . . . Sure, it was a good conference."

Danielle mouthed the words "Don't tell him I'm here." Lisa smiled and nodded that she understood.

"You'll be here next week, Saturday is June third? Of course, you can stay with me, the couch lets out into a bed, but Dannie and Roger have that huge house over there. Wouldn't you and your friend be more comfortable with your own room?"

Danielle began shaking her head and waving her arms wildly again.

Lisa held in her laughter and ignored Danielle's theatrics. "Oh, Pop, you know Dannie doesn't hold that against you. It was an accident. As a matter of fact, she's here right now. Why don't you ask her yourself? Just a minute."

Lisa handed Danielle the phone and held her hand over her mouth to stop the laughter.

Danielle shot Lisa a death threat with her eyes. She put on a fake smile and took the receiver.

"Hi, Pop. I heard you're coming next weekend. . . . Yes, you know you can stay with us. What's her name? Dorthea. No problem. Here, Kim wants to talk to you. Kim, come say hi to Pawpaw."

Kim ran into the kitchen and took the phone in her tiny hands. Danielle pointed a threatening finger at Lisa, then poured herself a cup of tea.

They listened as Kim answered each one of her grandfather's questions with care: "Uh-huh . . . Yes . . . No . . . I go to school . . . preschool . . . Yes . . . I miss you too . . . Okay . . . here's Mom."

Danielle took the receiver back and smiled more sincerely this time.

"Okay, Pop. We'll see you this weekend. Bye-bye."

"Bye, Pop," Lisa yelled from a distance. The moment Danielle hung up the phone, she lunged for her little sister. Lisa darted into the living room, slipped, and fell across the couch. She let the laughter out. Danielle picked a small blue pillow and hit Lisa several times. Kim decided to join the fun. She picked up a pillow and hit her mom across the leg. Danielle grabbed her daughter and began tickling her stomach. Kim finally got away by rolling across the floor.

"You know, this one could be nice," Lisa reminded Danielle.

"I'm sick of meeting every woman he sleeps with. How many is this, nine or ten?" Danielle asked, turning back toward the kitchen.

"She's only number five, I think," Lisa said, smiling.

"Well, dammit, she's five too many," she added, picking up Lisa's cup of tea and gulping it down.

Lisa scowled at her and snatched the cup from her hand. "Dannie, how can you of all people deny anybody happiness, no matter where it comes from?"

"Aunt Lisa, could I have some juice?" Kim asked, standing behind her.

"Sure, babe," Lisa told her. She grabbed Kim's Daffy Duck cup from the cabinet and opened the refrigerator.

"What did you forget to say?" Danielle asked Kim as she stood in the middle of the floor, anxious to get back to her toys.

"Please," Kim offered immediately.

Danielle returned to the previous conversation. "I don't think this is about his happiness. It's like he's trying to find us a new mom or something."

"Those women are not trying to be our mother, Dannie. You've always got to overdramatize things. Besides, they never last long. Six months, a year at the most, and he'll be off on a new tangent."

Kim took the cup from Lisa's hand and instantly turned toward the living room.

"Wait a minute, miss," Danielle called to her. "What else do you need to say?" .

"Thank you," Kim yelled on her way out the door.

"At least he ain't bringing that last cow back. What the hell was her name . . . Geraldine?"

"Pearline." Lisa corrected her and laughed.

"I shouldn't ever forget that one. She stayed drunk all the time and threw up all over the bed in the guest room, remember? I had to have the comforter dry-cleaned, and I threw the damned sheets away when they left."

"Oh, girl, you should be a star in one of those B movies," Lisa told her, placing the back of her hand on her forehead and leaning back just a little to speak with an exaggerated tone. "Life is so terrible! Why me? Oh . . . woe is me."

Danielle and Lisa suddenly heard a loud crash in the living room. They both jumped up to see what had happened. Kim had stacked up another pile of blocks, only to kick them over, imitating her mom.

Although she would never admit it, Danielle and her father were very much alike. Lisa could see it clearly. They were both selfish and felt that their perspective was the only perspective. Danielle had had a hard time accepting her father when he first called several years ago, but Lisa had wanted to get to know him. She was excited because she hadn't seen him in ten years. When he came to their mother's funeral, he said he wanted to be a part of their lives again. Danielle and Lisa fought about it, but finally Lisa won. She had come to like her father, and she didn't hold a grudge about the divorce. She was glad to have him back in her life.

In all the stories that Danielle remembered about her father, the main point that seemed to ring true was that James Eugene Allen was a hustler. His life could have gone either way—toward excellence or mediocrity. He chose mediocrity. James was the only kid in his family to go to college in the fifties. At seventeen years old he attended Lincoln University, a historic black college in Jefferson City, Missouri. By the end of his second year, with a full social calendar and a grade point average of 1.1, James was forced to drop out. He moved to Chicago, where he worked during the day at U.S. Steel South and hustled on the pool table at night.

Danielle loved the story about how her parents met. Almost every day after work James would stop at Corine's Cafe for dinner. Some days he would order pork chops smothered in gravy, mashed potatoes, and sweet potato pie. Other days he'd get fried chicken, macaroni and cheese, greens, and sweet potato pie. Then he'd take off for Willie's Tavern to shoot pool, gamble, or just talk shit with the fellas for the rest of the night. About midnight James would drag himself home, sleep until six in the morning, and start all over again.

Laura Belland changed his routine. James had had dinner many times at Corine's before he noticed Laura. Her beauty was natural. She didn't have time for makeup and long red fingernails. She knew what she wanted out of life, and she was determined to get it. Laura was a part-time student at the University of Chicago and a waitress at Corine's. The restaurant was located about seven blocks from where James worked on Ninety-fifth Street. Laura noticed James right away, and she knew he wasn't the type of man she wanted in her life. He was a gambler with no roots. She hated the way he and his coworkers sat in the cafe talking loud and ignorant. She hated waiting on their table because they were rude and obnoxious and tipped poorly.

James's chance encounter with Laura came one day as he clowned around with his friends about his success on a recent date.

"She was fine, man, wanted me right there in her father's livin' room," James told eager ears.

"And what did you do?" Ben asked.

James stuck out his chest. "I got the pun-tang, what chu think?"

"Man, you got it with her parents in the next room?" Chase asked sarcastically.

"I ain't got no reason to lie to you! Just 'cause you ain't gettin' none," James responded crassly.

"I gets my willie off when I need to, and I don't have to *lie* about getting it" Chase threw back at him.

Laura frowned at their conversation. She dropped the check on the table and quickly turned away.

James and his buddies bantered for a few more minutes. As they paid the check and rose to leave, James stood up and turned around. Not looking, he bumped into Laura with a tray of food in her hands. The tray spilled onto her chest and across the floor.

"Ahhh, shit!" Laura hissed at him as she wiped mashed potatoes from her uniform and stooped down to clean up the floor.

"I'm sorry," James said, bending down to help her. A second waitress brought a broom and started sweeping up the broken plates and glasses.

"That's okay, I'll get it," Laura told James, but he ignored her and kept wiping at a pile of peach cobbler. "I said that's okay."

"You sure?" James asked, anxious to get out of the center of attention anyway.

"Yeah, I'm sure," Laura told him, while wiping up collard greens.

James did not stand up right away. He noticed for the first time Laura's full cherry lips that needed no color to stand out. He saw the delicate ears that held two silver hooped earrings. His manhood was roused at the sight of her full cleavage.

That night when Laura got off work, she walked past James's red 1955 Crown Victoria parked in front of the café.

"Hey! Wait a minute," James yelled, jumping out of the car and running toward her. "Hi," he said, struggling to catch his breath.

"Hi," Laura responded, cool, no smile.

"I'd like to really apologize for this afternoon by driving you home," James told her.

"No, thank you. My bus stop is just on the corner," Laura said, and began to walk away from him.

James followed her to the bus stop. "But it's not a problem, honestly."

"It's not necessary."

James stood and watched that stubborn young woman sit at the bus stop. He couldn't think of anything to say. Danielle could just imagine her father waiting in nervous anticipation. And when the Ninety-fifth Street bus came to a stop, Laura smiled softly at him and got on.

James sat outside Corine's three nights that week, and every time Laura chose the bus. The second week he waited five nights. The third week, every night. Laura even changed her schedule to avoid him. But four months later, as she finished mopping the floor, she looked outside and saw his car. She put the mop and bucket away in the closet and went into the rest room to wash her hands. Laura brushed her hair back into place and got her purse out of her locker. She walked out of the front door of the café, over to his car and got in.

James Allen arrived from Chicago with his friend Dorthea on Saturday evening. As Danielle opened the door, she noticed that James was aging well. It was hard to believe that more than twenty years had passed since his divorce from her mother. Women described James as ruggedly good-looking. His round head balanced his short, stocky body. He had bushy eyebrows and a large, flat nose that somehow accented the mustache above his thick brown lips.

Danielle hadn't bothered to clean up, but the house didn't really need it anyway. She had a maid who came in once a week to do the big things like dust, mop floors, and clean windows. In fact, she had spent most of the day flipping through photo albums.

Danielle immediately noticed that Dorthea was more reserved than James's last girlfriend. She wore a wide-brimmed woven hat that matched her lavender two-piece flowered dress. Her ensemble was accented with pearllike buttons and matching pearl earrings. She was definitely not one of James's regular floozies. Danielle showed them to the guest room and left them to unpack. She went into the kitchen to finish her tuna casserole. As she turned to put the milk back into the refrigerator she almost bumped into Roger standing behind her.

He put his arms around her and kissed her passionately. Then his hands worked their way into her pants from behind, and he caressed her bottom.

"Roger, we have company," Danielle said softly, surprised yet excited by his attention.

Roger seductively slid his lips down her neck. "Come with me for a minute."

"Maybe later. I need to get this casserole in the oven."

Roger pushed her gently up against the refrigerator and began to grind against her: "Now, Danielle. I need you now," he whispered.

Danielle felt a spark with Roger that she hadn't felt in a long time. She set the milk on the cabinet and followed him into their bedroom.

Ten minutes later it was over. Roger was in the shower, and Danielle lay across the bed swallowed by her dreams. She allowed her legs to fall open and played with the soft brown hair inside. She closed her eyes and imagined Derrick's face. She stroked his thick, muscular shoulders, kissed his hairy chest and stomach, then tasted his ample thighs. Danielle imagined the potency of Derrick's lips as they slid inside her thighs and his tongue stroked her in just the right place. She felt the explosion and screamed his name.

"Derrick! Is that his fucking name, Derrick?" Roger hollered as he stormed out of the bathroom and past the bed.

Danielle's eyes jerked open at the sound of Roger's voice. She tried to speak but couldn't. She watched as he grabbed his blue suit jacket and starched beige shirt out of the closet, then stormed out of the room. Danielle lay there for a moment. She felt like crying, but the tears didn't come. She lay still and wondered what to do, until she heard a knock at the door.

"Yes," Danielle answered, voice raised slightly in an effort to sound okay.

"I just wanted to see if I could help with anything in the kitchen," Dorthea said timidly.

"Sure," Danielle said. "You can make the salad. Just grab what you need out of the refrigerator. I'll be out in a minute."

Danielle showered and dressed from habit. Then she joined Dorthea in the kitchen. Dorthea had rolled up her sleeves and was washing lettuce, tomatoes, and onions. Danielle finished mixing the ingredients for the casserole. She listened to Dorthea, but her mind was still fixed on Roger.

Dorthea talked about how she and her husband, Samuel, had helped to create the Woodlawn Organization in Chicago in the 1950s. The group wanted to clean up the neighborhood, and they also organized a boycott of Southside Grocery on Sixty-third Street because the primarily black customers felt they were being cheated with extremely high prices.

Danielle put the casserole in the oven and watched Dorthea chop the salad ingredients: celery, onion, tomatoes. As she described her son, Quenton, who had joined the Air Force at nineteen and made it his career, Danielle couldn't help liking her. Her husband had died three years ago, so he hadn't got to see Quenton make second lieutenant. Dorthea was all alone in Chicago since her son was currently stationed in Japan, and James had answered her prayers.

"Where are the bowls?" Dorthea asked, finally ready to toss the salad.

Danielle reached over and pulled a glass bowl out of the cabinet. "Right here.

"How did you and Pop meet?" Danielle asked, truly interested by now. This was the first woman he had brought to her home who seemed to have some sense.

Dorthea leaned back against the wall and smiled. "Your father joined the choir at Woodlawn Baptist Church six months ago. He says he did it to meet me. We were introduced by a mutual friend, and we've been inseparable ever since."

"Speaking of Pop, I wonder what he's doing," Danielle asked.

"He's probably still asleep. I don't drive, so he had to drive all the way by himself."

"You don't drive? How can you stand it?" Danielle asked.

"I've never needed to drive, so I just didn't learn."

Danielle glanced over at her keys on the counter. "I'd go crazy without my car. Even if I'm not going to use it, I want it sitting in the driveway waiting for me."

"I know a lot of people who feel that way."

Lisa rang the doorbell, but she and Kim didn't wait for anyone to answer. She used her key to open the door. They had just returned from a matinee movie and a trip to the mall, so Kim was excited.

"Look, Mom, at my earrings!" Kim said, handing her the bag.

Danielle opened it and smiled. "Those are so pretty. Kim, this is a friend of Pawpaw's, Miss Dorthea."

Dorthea held out her hand, and Kim took it. "Hi," they both said.

"Where's Daddy?" Kim asked, and grabbed the bag from her.

"He's gone to work for a little while. Go put your earrings in your room, so you don't lose them," Danielle said.

"You must be Lisa," Dorthea said, holding out her hand again.

Lisa shook hands with her, then grabbed a slice of carrot off the cabinet. "Yes, I am. How was the trip?"

"Good, it was fine. I want to thank both of you girls for inviting me here. It seemed very important to your father that we meet."

"I'm glad you could come," Lisa said, then winked at Danielle.

They sat at the dining room table and talked for a long while. They laughed easily together. Lisa sensed she was good people. Danielle was surprised that she found herself hoping her father could hold on to this one.

Since Dorthea had never been to the city, the next morning was designated for sight-seeing. They drove past Capitol Hill, toured Frederick Douglass's home, and took pictures in front of the Howard University sign. Inside the Smithsonian, Danielle watched as James held Dorthea's hand. They stopped in front of Archie Bunker's chair, and had a good laugh remembering the episode where Sammy Davis, Jr., kissed Archie Bunker.

Around midnight Danielle lay on the couch in the living room, switching through the channels on the television with the remote control. She was avoiding the bedroom. She didn't want to face Roger. She heard a noise in the kitchen and lifted up to see who it was. James smiled at her as he got himself a bowl of casserole and stuck it in the microwave. He got a can of beer out of the refrigerator and joined her in the living room.

"What are you doing up?" he asked.

"I can never get to sleep before midnight."

James sat next to Danielle on the couch. "That nap I took messed up my sleepin' pattern. How ya doing, Dannie?"

"I'm fine, Pop. I've finally realized that life is gonna move forward with or without me."

The bell on the microwave rang, and James got up to get his bowl. "I know what cha mean. I made a mess of things in my life, and now it's too late to change most of 'em."

As Danielle watched her father, she tried to remember when he became a bad guy in her life. She had loved him while she was growing up. She still loved him even through the divorce.

James reappeared in the door, blowing the steam from the bowl. "You and Roger having problems?" he asked.

"What makes you think that?"

"Because I know where he is right now, Dannie. Distant, moody, feeling unloved and unappreciated," James explained, then took a bite of the casserole.

"You don't have to worry about Roger and me. We'll be fine."

James felt the urge to put his arms around his daughter, but he suppressed it. He knew she was hurting inside, just as he had been many years ago. "Just be careful, Dannie. Before you and Roger make any serious changes in your lives, think them through carefully while there's time."

Danielle disregarded her father's comment. She couldn't believe he was trying to give her advice. "That's what you and Mom didn't do, right?" she snapped.

He spoke with his mouth full. "I'm sorry it was Laura who died, Dannie, instead of me. I know you hate me for that."

"I don't hate you. Or blame her death on you," Danielle replied.

James set the bowl down on the coffee table and chose his words carefully. "I don't know how to change things. I'm doing the best I can."

Danielle had to tell him how she felt, but she didn't think it would do any good. She just couldn't love him again, not the way she used to. "Well, maybe your best ain't good enough, Dad. Maybe it's too late."

"Is there anything I can do?" James asked. He cringed, afraid of the answer he might receive.

Instead Danielle kept talking. "If you could have anything in the world right now, Pop, what would you ask for?"

"Of course it would be your forgiveness, Lisa's forgiveness, and Laura's too. I'd want my family back," James told her, then stood up and paced the floor. "I missed Laura and you girls so much. I should've been there when you were growin' up . . . becomin' ladies."

Danielle had started something she didn't want to finish. She flicked quickly through the channels: Lifetime, Family Channel, TNT, USA, CSpan, ESPN, and BET. She didn't want to listen. She tried not to listen, but she knew she had to.

"Dannie, I was just too stupid to understand how important the years were as they passed. I was stubborn and thought I could make myself happy in other ways. But it didn't work."

Danielle turned the television off and threw the remote on the coffee table. It slid across the table and hit the floor. She now knew what had made him the bad guy. "You didn't call or come see us, Dad. Why?" she asked.

James hung his head. He thought about all the times he had picked up the phone but put it back down or had got on the freeway and turned around. He knew he couldn't explain, but he tried. "Because it hurt too much, Dannie. I thought if I could forget, I could stop the hurt. I didn't know what else to do."

"What about our hurt, Pop?" Danielle threw back at him. "Did you ever think about anybody other than yourself? Lisa and I didn't know if you hated us or what. You didn't even remember our birthdays."

"I remembered 'em, Dannie. I'd drink myself into a coma, and still I never forgot your birthdays," James explained, scratching the top of his head. "I didn't know what to say to you guys. I didn't know what to do."

"Well, it doesn't mean much now," Danielle said, standing up and walking toward the fireplace mantel. She fingered a picture of her, her mother, and Lisa. It was one of the happier times they shared after the divorce.

James walked toward his daughter with his arms outstretched. "I know I can't change what happened, but I'm tryin' to make things different now, Dannie. I'm gonna ask Dorthea to marry me."

Danielle stepped back. His announcement made her upset yet peaceful at the same time. "If she makes you happy, that's great for you, Dad."

James continued to move toward her. "For the first time in a long time, this is not only about me, Dannie. That's what I've been trying to say. This is the first woman I've loved since your mother, and I want us all to be close." James put his arms around Danielle. "I wanna feel like I have a family again."

Danielle stood rigid against his touch. "We'll never be a family like that again. Dorthea can't replace Mom," she told him, pulling away.

"I'm not trying to make her your mom," James said, his forehead wrinkled as if he were in pain.

"So why do we have to accept her? What difference does that make? We're not living with her; you are," Danielle replied, and stepped farther away.

"You know what I mean, Dannie. I've tried to figure out what went wrong."

"And do you know?"

James rubbed his fingers together nervously. "I know I was

never honest with myself or your mother," he said. "I blamed everything on her. I told myself if she had believed in me and motivated me when I lost my job instead of complainin' and fightin' all the time, I'd have never ended up down the street."

"That's bullshit! You chose to jump in bed with that woman," Danielle yelled. "Mom had nothing to do with it!"

"I know that now. But the choice I made then was between Laura all the time fussin' 'bout money and being responsible and Miriam telling me how wonderful I was and how she couldn't get enough of me." James cautiously looked up at Danielle. He felt the distance and knew she needed more time. "I know you can't understand this, but I made the only choice I could make at the time."

Danielle examined her father's face. His eyes were red and glassy, and he tried desperately to smile. She knew his love was real, but she'd always known that. She just wanted him to suffer because her mother had suffered. She also knew he was telling the truth when he said he didn't know what to do. Danielle knew it was true because she now found herself in the same situation. This truth was dangerous for her because she had to admit, at least to herself, that she was not being honest. She was at the point in her marriage where there was only one choice to be made.

At Grambling State University in Grambling, Louisiana, Walter Henderson's name was well known between 1977 and 1982, when he was a starting forward on the basketball team. Walter studied just enough to pass his classes with Cs and occasional As and Bs. Most of his As and Bs came in math. Formulas and tables seemed to be second nature. But his family wasn't interested in his math ability; instead they wanted him to be a professional basketball player. When that didn't happen, they quickly lost interest in his education. Despite an average GPA, Walter had graduated in the top ten percent of the math department. He got a job offer from an alumnus and a fan in D.C. to work with Amtrak in accounting. He took it and moved to the big city three days after graduation.

The month of June was heating up, but the weather didn't have much to do with it. Lisa had finally decided that this weekend she was ready to take her relationship with Walter to the next level. She wanted to love him, and she believed that he felt the same way. As she sat in her living room waiting for Walter to arrive that Friday night, Lisa also realized that waiting had become her latest pastime. They had spent the last three weekends together, and so far this was her major complaint. Walter was always an hour or more late, and Lisa hated waiting. She watched the door, looked at her watch, then got up to check her hair in the mirror. Why do men never think to call? Lisa thought.

When Walter finally rang the doorbell, he pushed it six or seven times. She took her time and checked her appearance once more in the mirror. Lisa couldn't believe he had the nerve to rush her. She walked slowly to the door, practicing her best pissed look on the way. But it was no use. When she opened it, Walter hurried inside and kissed all the piss away.

"Hi. Been waiting long?" he asked with boyish excitement.

Lisa hesitated, then lied. She didn't know why. "No . . . not very long."

"I have a great evening planned."

"What?" Lisa asked, and lifted her overnight bag onto her shoulder.

"It's a surprise," Walter teased. He took the overnight bag from her and headed for the door.

"Tell me, Walter," Lisa said as she followed him out the door.

Walter stopped and grinned. "I'll tell you this. I have to go to New Orleans on business, and I want you to come with me."

He continued to smile, and so did Lisa as he took her hand and pulled her toward the car.

"When?" Lisa asked between steps.

"In a few weeks . . . at the end of August."

Walter opened the car door and threw her bag in the backseat on top of his.

"It sounds great. I'll try to get time off," Lisa said as she slipped into the passenger's seat. She had to smile when she realized that he had gotten away with being more than an hour late. I guess that's why they do it, she thought. Because they can.

"You gonna tell me where we're going?" Lisa asked a second time, and scooted next to him.

"I can't. It's a surprise," he teased.

"I hate surprises, Walter."

"Not this one. You'll love this one," he told her, and started the car.

"Colonial Beach?"

"Nope," he said, and slowly pulled out of the parking space.

"But you told me to bring my swimsuit."

Walter shook his head as he stopped at a stop sign. He pulled Lisa close to him, and they kissed. At that moment there was no traffic, no passersby, and no sun or moon. The only thing Lisa noticed was the peaceful way he made her feel.

When Walter parked the car in front of a large Spanish-style villa, Lisa had to admit she was impressed. It was a beautiful trilevel house with a partial brick front. The inside was a bit cluttered for her taste, but she saw potential. She imagined what she would change if it were their house. The brown and orange shag carpet, a relic from the seventies, would be the first thing to go. The drapes also were a cheap brown cotton weave. Lisa gave it a five on a scale of ten. The rating jumped to eight when she saw the indoor pool and hot tub.

"Whose place is this?" Lisa asked.

"A friend. He's out of town, so it's all ours for the night," Walter answered, and winked.

"Where's your swimsuit?" Lisa asked.

"Right here," Walter said, pulling on the elastic under his pants. "Go get your suit on so we can jump in that hot tub."

Lisa pulled the swimsuit out of her bag and dangled it in front of him. She had surprised herself and brought her two-piece. It had been awhile, years in fact, since she had worn it. Lisa smiled; somehow the extra weight didn't matter with Walter. He made her feel like Olive Oyl in a Popeye cartoon.

"You can change in there," Walter said, pointing at the bathroom door along the left wall.

After Lisa hurried inside, Walter opened a wooden box on the coffee table and took out a small bag of white powder. He carefully arranged two thick, long lines and two short, thin lines on a square piece of glass.

Washington, D.C., had been a strange experience for a Southern boy out of Louisiana. Walter quickly got involved with a life he'd only heard about. The first time he tried cocaine, it was awful. He snorted up the two lines of white powder and immediately began to blow it back out. He felt as if his nose were on fire, and water ran from his eyes down his cheeks. He rushed into the bathroom and held his head under the cold water. That seemed to help briefly. But as the burning feeling subsided, it was replaced by an incredible feeling of serenity. It was a feeling Walter wanted, even needed, over and over again. Getting high had become a habit, but only on the weekends. Walter convinced himself that it wasn't a problem because he got up and went to work every day. He was positive he could stop anytime.

Lisa stepped in front of the bathroom mirror, pulled her peach blouse over her head, and unsnapped her lace bra. She absentmindedly ran her tongue across her teeth as she wiggled into the bikini top and bottom. She held in her stomach while she loosely braided her hair. She opened the drawer to search for a rubber band and found instead toothpaste, aftershave, cocoa butter lotion, and a three-pack of condoms. Overcome by curiosity, she looked down in the bottom of the cabinet. She found a box of bobby pins and also noticed several magazines underneath a bag of cotton balls and extra rolls of toilet paper. She pulled out one of the magazines and stared at the cover. It was a man dressed as a woman. Inside were other pictures in a variety of poses. Lisa fought the doubt she suddenly felt. They had spent so much time together she refused to believe that he had been lying to her. She replaced the magazine in about the same position she found it and hurried into the living room.

She trembled as she stood for a moment watching him snort up the two thick lines of coke.

"Whose place did you say this is?" she asked.

"A friend I hang out with sometime. Why?"

"How close is this friend?" Lisa continued, and cautiously sat in the chair across from him.

"What's with all the questions?" he asked, patting a spot next to him on the couch.

"I was just wondering."

Walter stood up, kicked off his shoes and socks, and pulled his pants down, showing purple baggy swimming trunks that camouflaged his small, bulging stomach.

He motioned to Lisa. "Here," he said. "Try this."

"No. That's okay."

Walter walked over to her. "You ever been high and made love before?" he asked. He brushed his hand across her cheek and seductively began rubbing his fingers around her ears.

"I've smoked marijuana and made love afterward."

"Well, magnify that feeling a thousand times and tell me you wouldn't love it." He leaned over and kissed a spot on her chest. "Come on, babe . . . would I let anything happen to my girl?" he coaxed.

Lisa stood up and walked away. "Walter, I want to trust you so badly," she said.

"What's wrong?" he asked, and joined her in the middle of the floor.

"I just don't know what to believe, Walter. I think I love you, but I'm still not sure who you are," she said. Lisa looked down at the floor and shifted nervously from one foot to the other.

"Just tell me what the problem is, Lisa, and I know we can work through it," he pleaded.

Lisa led the way to the bathroom and pulled out one of the magazines. She handed it to Walter.

"I'm sorry," he said immediately. "I should have told you. This is the friend's place that we talked about on the train. He's a transvestite."

The memory of that conversation flooded back into Lisa's mind, but she was not convinced. "Where is he again?" she asked.

"He's out of town for the weekend, but if you don't feel comfortable here and want to go, Lisa, it's okay. We can go."

Lisa watched his eyes dart back and forth as he spoke. She sensed that he was nervous, but she didn't think he was lying to her. "Why haven't I met him, Walter?"

"I didn't think you were ready. But I've never lied to you. I don't judge my friends by their choice of lifestyles."

Lisa tried to satisfy her doubts. His explanation made sense. People did have the right to make their own choices. Walter had

become an important part of her life in the brief time they had
spent together. She felt so safe with him she just wanted to wrap
herself in his arms and never go back into the outside world.

"You gotta trust me, Lisa," he said, and put his arms around
her. "If you want to meet him, you can."

Lisa took one look into his warm, soft brown eyes and released an uncontrolled smile. He handed her the glass, and she
hesitated, then sniffed up each of the short lines. She felt her
nose burn and itch slightly. Then her head started to feel light
and spacy.

"I'm so crazy about you, lady," Walter whispered from behind her. "I wouldn't let anything happen to you." Then as if
he had read her mind, he wrapped his long, muscular arms
around her waist and held on to her tightly.

"Could you repeat that?" she asked. She couldn't hear it
enough.

He spun her around to face him. "I'm crazy about you, Lisa
Allen, and I hope you believe that I would never let anything
bad happen to you."

That was all she needed to hear. They could have sent the
loony wagon because Lisa was gone. He picked her up and carried her to the hot tub. In the midst of her euphoria, Walter's
touch was magical, his laugh was perfect, and his love was a
masterpiece.

Two days later, as Lisa whirled around and around in a giant
teacup with Kim, she could feel the jerk chicken she had for
lunch slowly rising. When the ride ended, they headed back to
Sundi's booth at the fair. Kim stopped to pick dandelions along
the way. When one pocket was full, she started on the other.

The Multicultural Festival in Columbia, Maryland, had a temporary amusement park with several rides, including a merry-go-
round, a Ferris wheel, and the giant teacups, and the festival
itself offered ethnic foods, arts, and crafts. Sundi had rented a
booth to sell her baskets. Last year she had made more than a
thousand dollars in one day.

"It's not applicable to black women," Danielle told Sundi as Lisa and Kim approached Sundi's booth and caught the end of their hot debate.

"How can you say that? I know there are some differences, but there are also similarities," Sundi argued as she wove a reddish brown shredded root through a coiled oval basket.

Danielle was helping Sundi by dipping strings of the thin shredded root into a shiny waxed substance and laying it across the table next to the others. "Black women have been liberated all their lives," she continued. "Our great-great-grandmothers didn't have the luxury of deciding they were tired of staying home."

"All I'm saying is we still have to work together to accomplish anything," Sundi replied, and picked up a strand of the dried, waxed root.

Lisa jumped into the conversation. "But we can't separate our struggle from black men; it's all the same."

"You guys aren't listening to me," Sundi told them, trying to clarify her point. "It's not that I want to split from black men and the black struggle. I could never do that." Sundi's hands skillfully molded a curving root into place as she continued. "It's just that I believe there's strength in numbers. We need to work with white women, not against them."

"The last three positions in my department have been filled by white women," Lisa said, slightly agitated. "The trick now is to hire white women under the category of minorities to avoid bringing in ethnic minorities."

Kim's hair was blowing too freely, so Danielle pulled it into a ponytail. "That's why the attack on affirmative action is so ridiculous. Even though the numbers for white women have risen significantly in every field, minorities, especially blacks, are still being filtered through one and two at a time."

After getting away from her mother, Kim dumped a handful of dandelions in Lisa's lap. Then she ran off to pick more. Not thinking, Lisa picked up a dandelion and began pulling the petals off one by one.

"The problem is that we're all fighting over the same pie," Sundi observed.

"And as long as we're fighting each other, we don't have time to deal with the real problem," Danielle added.

Lisa tossed a handful of dandelion petals into the air and watched them float slowly to the ground. "Haven't you read the latest *Newsweek*?" she finally asked. "White males are worried. Life is not as easy as it used to be. There aren't as many jobs. Getting into school is more difficult."

"So now they know how we've felt all our lives! How our parents and grandparents felt!" Sundi snapped.

"It's even deeper than that. White women are their sisters, daughters, mothers, cousins, wives, and girlfriends. If two applicants are equally qualified, one black, one white, who gets hired? Somebody who's like you or a stranger believed to be inferior?" Danielle asked.

The conversation stopped as Sundi put down the basket she was working on and waited on an elderly black customer who bought a set of three baskets, each fitting inside the other. Sundi had been set up only a couple of hours, and she had already made more than three hundred dollars.

Lisa slid down to the end of the picnic table and continued to destroy dandelions. She thought about Walter and his invitation. "I should go with him, I shouldn't. I should go with him, I shouldn't. I should go with him."

"You shouldn't," Danielle commented.

"Don't start, Dannie," Lisa said.

"What do you really know about this guy, Lisa? Have you disproved the rumor that he's gay?"

"Yes. He's definitely not gay."

"You know sex don't prove nothing. I've heard bisexuals are excellent lovers," Danielle warned.

Sundi glued the ends of two roots together. "You know, a friend of his ex told me she doesn't believe it, and she's known Walter and Brenda a long time."

Danielle put a strand of wet root down long enough to point

her finger at Lisa. "Well, I hope you're practicing safe sex with him anyway."

"Look, I'm taking care of my business, and you need to do the same!" Lisa said, and rolled her eyes. She couldn't stand it when Danielle harassed her.

"It's only because I love you, Sis," Danielle teased. "And AIDS ain't nothing to play with no matter how sweet and wonderful you think he is."

Lisa had become irritated by the conversation. She didn't understand why she was always the one who had to be chastised like a child. "Okay, okay, Dannie, give it a rest."

"Has he at least been tested?" Danielle asked, concerned about her sister.

"As a matter of fact, he has. What about Derrick, has he been tested?" Lisa said, throwing it back in Danielle's face.

"He says he's fine, but I haven't had sex with Derrick without a condom."

"Have either of you guys been tested?" Sundi asked tentatively. "I haven't."

"Well, honestly, I don't want to know." Lisa's stomach churned inside. She had lied. She didn't know if Walter had been tested or not. They had discussed it several times, but then they both pushed the issue to the side.

"I know I'm fine, and since my sister doesn't want my advice about her trip, I'm gonna go ride the bumper cars," Danielle told them. "I feel like hitting something. Come on, Kim, let's go ride the car-cars."

Kim dumped another handful of dandelions out of her yellow-stained hands and into Lisa's lap. "Don't tear these up, Aunt Lisa," she instructed as she grabbed her mother's hand. They hurried toward the amusement park.

Lisa and Sundi sat in silence for a minute. Lisa watched a couple in love walk hand and hand past the booth. Sundi reorganized her display table, moving three of the more colorful baskets toward the front.

"So, how's the newlywed game, Sundi?" Lisa finally asked.

"We're losing, miserably" was her immediate response. "We're back in the same bedroom, but we haven't really worked things out. And truthfully I'm sick of bending over backwards to make him comfortable."

Lisa returned to tearing dandelions to pieces. She felt sorry for her best friend. "Why can't you be yourself? You're a nice person, Sundi."

"I'm too damn nice. That's the problem. Girl, this old lady at the store yesterday dropped a jar of pickles, and while I cleaned up the mess, she stole my coupons. I hate pickles!"

Lisa had to laugh. She could see Sundi cleaning up the mess as if it were *her* job. Danielle and Kim returned.

"The line was too long," Danielle explained, flopping down at the picnic table next to Lisa.

"Look what you did!" Kim yelled, pointing at the torn-up dandelions scattered on the ground.

"I'm sorry, I forgot," Lisa told her.

Kim wrinkled up her face, not caring about Lisa's purpose. She hit her on the leg and ran off to pick more.

"Since I've got Chris back in the bedroom, I'm playing model wife and step stool to keep him there," Sundi admitted.

"Is it working?" Lisa asked.

"He's happy," Sundi answered, twisting her mouth.

"It's usually women who hold out on sex to get what they want," Danielle said, teasing Sundi.

"I don't really give a shit anymore," Sundi told them, shaking her head.

"Show me a woman who says she can do without sex, and I'll show you a woman who has never had an orgasm." This was familiar territory for Danielle. She acted as if no other woman had ever had an orgasm. Lisa and Sundi had once described their moments of climax to her because she swore that they were missing out. They tried to explain that everybody's experience was different. Lisa even gave her a book one Christmas called *The Moment of Climax*, but Danielle never bothered to read it.

Out of the three of them, Sundi was the one who needed sex

the least. So Lisa had to laugh when she thought about Chris's threatening her with the loss of it. Once Sundi had gone for a whole year without sex. Lisa knew that was an impossibility for her. She'd be like one of those dogs that attacked people's legs.

"I think I've made my decision, you guys," Lisa finally announced. "I'm going to New Orleans with Walter next week."

"New Orleans is nice," Sundi said supportively.

"I don't know why you're tripping. You already had your mind made up," Danielle told her with a wry face, and shrugged her shoulders.

Danielle reminded Lisa so much of their mom when she did that. Whenever their mother didn't agree with something, she would twist the right corner of her mouth around as if it somehow soothed her disdain and shrug her shoulders. It got to the point where she didn't even have to say anything. She'd just twist her mouth and shrug her shoulders, and they knew exactly what she meant.

"Honestly, Lisa, I'm worried. This man seems to be filling up your life. You haven't talked much about school and finishing your Ph.D. lately."

She was right, Lisa admitted to herself. She had definitely slacked off. "I don't need a Ph.D.," she joked, and let out a loud sigh. "I've got love."

"Paleeese," Danielle and Sundi both screamed at Lisa at the same time.

"I'm gonna finish the damn thing," Lisa said sternly. "All I need to do is pass the comps this summer, write the proposal and dissertation. I've worked too hard not to finish."

"All I can say is he must have a golden dick, because you have truly let your guard down," Danielle said.

"Why do all of our conversations end up on the subject of sex?" Sundi asked antagonistically.

"What else is there? It's a man's world. I'm just a squirrel trying to get a nut," Danielle answered, and they all burst out laughing.

"I got one for you guys. Why do you think Eve coaxed Adam to eat the forbidden apple?" Lisa asked.

" 'Cause a man wrote the book!" Danielle yelled out, and since her answer was better, Lisa let it ride.

Lisa finished reading the last paper for her introductory speech class. She took a moment to skim through her notes, then wrote a "B–" at the top near the center and circled it. She entered the grade in her notebook and filed the paper in her class folder.

She took a deep breath; it felt good to be finished. Probably the worst part of teaching was grading papers, she thought. But at least she was doing something she believed in now. Lisa's previous job of writing speeches for Congressman Theodore Page had been a farce. She quickly discovered that he was a true male chauvinist asshole, and her job was to help him sound good. It was sad, Lisa thought, that he didn't learn anything from her speeches. He would simply read them with his extensive oratory skill, sprinkling in emotion and conviction where necessary; then he'd go back to his good old boy network and talk the same trash. The job paid well, and he liked Lisa, so she hung in. Every time she talked about quitting, he gave her a raise. She knew he needed to keep her around because her chocolate skin was good for his liberal front.

The day Lisa quit was the day she knew the congressman had gone crazy. As they sat in his office one evening discussing an upcoming speech at his alma mater, he casually reached over and felt her breasts with both hands. Then nonchalantly he said, "I've always wanted to do that." Lisa sat there for a moment. She was shocked and confused. But Page went right back into the discussion as if nothing had happened. Finally Lisa said, "Excuse me." She hurried out of the room, got her purse out of her desk drawer, and walked out the door.

She mailed her resignation and didn't even go back to get her personal things. She had a friend bring them to her. Lisa had thought about suing, but she didn't believe in burning bridges unless she had to, so she just walked away. The last thing she heard was that the congressman had lost his reelection bid and was running an insurance company somewhere in Connecticut.

Lisa thought about Walter, and on impulse she picked up the phone to call. It rang once, twice; then his answering machine kicked on.

"I'm sure your call is the one I've been waiting for. Don't hang up or I'll never know . . ." Walter's voice said on the other end.

"Hi, Walter," Lisa said. "Just calling to see what time you're coming by. Call me as soon as you get home."

She set the phone down in its cradle. Walter had somehow become a very special part of her life, yet she knew so little about him. Everything was wonderful when they were together, but when they were apart, she couldn't help the panic that emerged inside. Lisa wanted so badly to trust him, to love him.

Just then the phone rang.

"Hello," she said into the receiver.

"Hey, baby," Walter's voice sang in a capricious tone.

"Hi, where are you?" Lisa asked.

"I just got home, and I heard the voice of this beautiful woman on my machine."

"So you figured it was me?"

"I have to admit, I tried this other honey first," Walter teased.

"That's not funny!" she told him. "How long is it going to take you to get over here?"

"Well, Brenda dropped by and said she needs to talk to me, so I'm not sure. Maybe I could go another time," he said apologetically.

"But I really wanted to show you off at the graduate social tonight, Walter. I told everybody you were coming," she pleaded.

"I'm sorry. Maybe I can meet you there later. Where is it again?" he asked in a deep, smooth voice that eased some of the tension away.

"Beckley Hall, fifth floor, room five-oh-six," she told him.

"I'll try to get away, I promise."

"Walter—" Lisa started to speak.

"Just a minute, babe," he said, stopping her in midstream. Lisa struggled to hear the conversation as he turned his attention to someone in the background, but she couldn't understand. "I got to go, sugar. I'll try to get there."

Lisa slammed down the phone. She found her hands were shaking as she pulled her burgundy houndstooth pantsuit and matching pumps out of the closet. She wasn't used to dealing with extra baggage, and she wanted his ex-wife to go away. There were no kids to connect them, so the woman needed to get a life!

Lisa went into the bathroom to wash her face and brush her teeth. Everybody was expecting Walter, and now she had to make excuses. She thought briefly about not going herself but rejected the idea. She would only feel worse at home alone.

At the social Lisa didn't begin to mingle until she finished her second glass of wine. She was hoping that Walter would show, so she glanced at the door every time somebody walked in. She and her office mate Vanessa spent most of the time together. Vanessa was probably the person in the department Lisa felt most comfortable with. She knew she could split a verb or drop an "ing" without being judged. She later joined her adviser, Dr. Carol Javier, the newest faculty member in the department, at the far end of the room. As it grew later, she realized Walter wasn't going to make it.

On the drive home she found it hard to control the anger building inside her. She didn't appreciate being dumped tonight for his ex-wife, and she was sick of trying to justify his actions. Hell, for all she knew he and the woman could be in bed somewhere right now.

Lisa reached her apartment and hurried upstairs. She listened to her messages, hoping Walter had left one, but he hadn't. She picked up the phone and called his number.

"Hello," Walter said in a sluggish tone.

"Hi. What are you doing?" she asked as she kicked off her shoes.

"I must have nodded off. Is the reception over? How was it?" Walter asked, then yawned.

"Okay . . . I told everybody you couldn't make it because you preferred to spend the evening with your ex-wife."

Walter abruptly sat up in the bed. "You know that's not true."

"No . . . I don't know," Lisa continued, unbuttoning her blouse.

"You have to forgive me, baby, or I can't go back to sleep," he begged.

Lisa frowned. She'd heard that shit before. "So am I supposed to care or what?"

Walter used his sexiest voice. "What can I do to get you to forgive me?" he asked.

"Come over here right now because I want to see you," she whispered, and unfastened her bra.

Walter stood up from the bed. "Now?" he asked.

"If I have to wait more than thirty minutes, Walter, I am not going to let you in," she added, removing her pants and stockings.

"I'll be there in twenty." He hung up the phone, pulled on his sweatpants from the weight bench, grabbed his shirt and his shoes, and rushed out the door.

11

The sun pouring through the large stained-glass window created shifting patterns across the altar. Pew by pew, the congregation stood up and marched toward the front to give their offerings to God. Chris hated this public display. He felt giving was a personal act, and he refused to buy into the capitalistic lure that rattled the other souls into following suit.

Sundi and the rest of the row stood according to the directions of the usher. They walked past Chris, who crossed his arms and stared straight ahead with no remorse. They headed quickly down the right aisle toward the two altar boys in front, dressed in black pants and starched white shirts, who held large gold plates out to accept the blessed green paper and change.

In front of Sundi an elderly man removed a wad of bills from his pocket, peeled off ten dollars, and dropped it into the plate. Sundi dropped in her white envelope, which contained twenty dollars—ten for her and ten for Chris. She was followed by a heavyset woman dressed in a green knit oversized top and pleated skirt who carefully separated three one-dollar bills and let them go.

They marched past the choir singing "How Sweet His Name," took a quick turn, and moved back up the center aisle toward their seats. Sundi entered the pew and sat down next to

Chris. The deacon blessed the offering, and as the last of the congregation made their way back to their seats, the choir sped up the tempo of the song. They easily moved into the faster beat, hands clapping, feet stomping. They sent a message to the Holy Ghost himself. Sundi forgot Chris's embarrassing action for a moment and let the music pass through her. The powerful pulses flowed through her bloodstream, and the energy bound her to this almighty being.

When the service ended, Chris found himself in the receiving line behind Sundi despite his objections. It wasn't that he didn't believe in church. It was that he chose to worship in his own way, in a more private way. He periodically agreed to go to church with Sundi for appearances only. As they inched their way forward, he wondered who had come up with such a crazy idea. Why should he have to stand in line and shake hands with people he didn't know? He became more annoyed when he saw that three deacons, four ushers, and the preacher had positioned themselves directly in front of the door. The stiff greetings were repeated over and over—some sincere, some not.

Sundi reached for the soft, chubby hand of Reverend Fields. It was hot and moist, just like his face, which glistened with perspiration. Unfortunately the reverend's condition was not from a powerful and moving sermon, but from the heat of the bright lights necessary to videotape his sermons. Sundi smiled and offered her greetings. Chris nodded his head and followed Sundi from palm to palm. They both burst out the door and into the sunshine.

On their way to the car, Sundi heard a voice in the parking lot. She turned around and saw a client she needed to contact. "Hey, Lyle!" she called, and started toward him, then remembered Chris. She turned back around. "I'll be right back."

Chris was disturbed when he got into the car. He watched as Sundi and Lyle leaned against a black Chevy Geo and talked. He saw Sundi grab the hem of her T-neck jumper when the wind blew it upward. He also saw Lyle's eyes move up and down her body in a coupling gesture.

Sundi was excited when she got back to the car. "Lyle wants

to order another thirty baskets between now and Christmas for his two stores. He wants ten of the Japanese weave, and I only have five, so I need to get busy. We're going to have lunch tomorrow to sign the contracts."

Chris didn't respond. He started the car and looked straight ahead as they drove out of the parking lot. She didn't notice his mood in her excitement. On the ride home Sundi was absorbed in planning the order and Chris was filled with jealousy.

When the couple entered the condo, Sundi headed right to the kitchen and got herself a grape soda. Chris stretched out on their beige sleeper sofa and turned on the television. He stopped on a rerun of *The Cosby Show*.

"Chris, you want anything?" Sundi called to him from the refrigerator.

"No," he replied. His voice bristled.

Sundi opened the can, took a couple of swallows, and headed back to the living room. She sat down next to Chris on the sofa.

"On second thought, I think I would like a soda," he said, not looking directly at Sundi.

She took a deep breath and rolled her eyes. She hesitated, then got up to get the soda.

"So you're having lunch with Lyle again?" Chris called to her in the kitchen.

"Yeah, that's what I told you in the car. He wants thirty more baskets," Sundi answered as she walked back into the living room and handed him the soda.

"So why do you have to have lunch with him? Why can't you just go to his store and drop the baskets off?"

Sundi brushed her hair back with her hands and closed her eyes. She was so tired of this jealousy shit. "Chris, what's the big deal about having lunch with Lyle? You know he's just a client."

"But he don't seem to know it!" Chris shouted at her.

She dropped onto the couch next to him and took his hand. "I've been working with Lyle for almost ten years. I think it's safe to say if we wanted to get together, it would have happened before now."

"It's not just about lunch, Sundi. Sometimes people don't

want something until they see somebody else with it. Like this soda."

Sundi opened her mouth to reply but stopped. She knew jealousy was like gas: It usually built up inside and came out funky.

She decided to deal with it from a different approach. "I like to see jealousy in my man," she whispered in his ear playfully. "But this time there's no need. Lyle doesn't want me, and I definitely don't want Lyle, except as a client."

Chris gave Sundi an awkward glance, with his nose turned upward, but he smiled, then turned off the television.

"Why'd you turn off the TV?" Sundi asked in a raised voice.

"I don't feel like watching it now," he said sullenly.

"But I want to watch it, Chris," she told him.

"Turn on the one in the bedroom. I think I'm going to read," he said as he picked up the latest issue of *Emerge*.

"I don't want to watch the one in the bedroom! I want to watch this one!" Sundi told him. She reached for the remote control, but Chris quickly snatched it away from her. Sundi reached around him and couldn't get to it.

"Dammit, Chris, sometimes you really get on my nerves," she said as she went into the bedroom and shut the door.

Chris sat and watched the bedroom door for a minute, then turned the television back on. He simply wanted her to know how it felt to be teased.

Sundi threw herself on the bed, buried her head in the nearest pillow, and screamed.

Lisa knew something was wrong when Sundi stopped by her office without calling first. Her face was flushed, and her eyes were glassy. Lisa's office mate, Vanessa, had left to get coffee, so she shut the door to allow her best friend to vent in private.

"I've only been married three months, and so far I feel like the bad outweighs the good," Sundi told her, squeezing the well-used tissues in her left hand harder.

Lisa scooted her chair closer and handed Sundi a few clean tissues. "Marriages are hard work. You knew that going in."

"I don't mind hard work, but this is bullshit," she complained, resting her head in her cupped hand on the edge of the desk.

Lisa moved several books out of her way. "Tell me something good about the marriage, Sundi."

Sundi thought deeply for a minute. She couldn't think of anything at that moment. "It's like he sees me differently now. I'm like a slave whose duty is to cook, clean, and fuck him when he pleases."

The phone rang, but Lisa didn't answer it. "You can make it work, Sundi; you've just got to keep trying."

"The strange part is that I don't mind doing those things for him, but I want to know that he appreciates it."

"I don't know what to tell you. You know what my experience is like when it comes to relationships."

Sundi dropped her eyes to the floor and shifted her feet under her chair. "I don't expect you to have the answer. I guess I just wanted to tell somebody how fed up I am. I'm always the one who has to compromise. I give and give while he just takes and takes."

Lisa chuckled. "Sounds like an extreme case of the Big Daddy syndrome."

"Shut up, girl, I'm serious," Sundi said, half smiling.

"I'm serious too. You can't ignore that *man thing* when you're trying to figure them out. They need to be in control. They have to have the power!" she explained, handing Sundi the whole box of Kleenex from the top shelf of the bookcase.

Sundi tossed a handful of tissues in the trash. "That's true," she mumbled.

"The problem is that too many of them don't know how to be a real Big Daddy. A *real* Big Daddy takes care of everything so that his woman can concentrate on being beautiful and taking good care of him. A real Big Daddy is somebody who knows where he's going, so a woman doesn't mind following him. Too many men today are nighttime Big Daddies and daytime Baby Hueys."

Sundi laughed along with Lisa this time. Then she blew her nose into several new tissues and lost her smile again. "I've got to do something, Lisa. I can't get through to him anymore. He used to hold me in his arms at night until I fell asleep. Sometimes he seems so cold and distant now. I can't live like this."

"If he used to do those things, Sundi, they're still there. You can get them back."

"I'm not so sure," she said, shaking her head.

"Maybe I could talk to him?" Lisa said, not because it was something she wanted to do, but because it seemed the right thing to say.

"No. His manhood might be damaged if he listened to a woman, any woman."

"So, get a man to talk to him for you. How about Roger or, even better, his cousin Sylla?"

Vanessa returned from her coffee break, opened the door, and quickly sized up the situation. "I'm sorry," she said, backing out the door. "Come get me in the lounge when you're finished."

"That's okay," Sundi said, jumping to her feet. "I'm on my way out."

Lisa got up too. She walked Sundi to the front door of the building.

"How could I talk to Sylla? He's more of an asshole than Chris."

"Maybe that's why Sylla fights with you, Sundi, because you don't talk to him and he feels left out? He and Chris were very close until you came along."

Sundi took a deep breath and tried to smile. "Maybe you're right. Chris does listen to Sylla like he's the voice of God himself. It's worth a try, I guess."

"Well, Sylla's not going away, so you might as well try to deal with him," Lisa told her.

Lisa remembered something her mother used to say: If you're not getting three hugs a day, that means you're not giving three hugs a day. Lisa liked hugs, and she knew Sundi needed a hug, so she gave her a big one. "Let me know how it turns out, okay?"

Sundi nodded her head. "Thanks, Lisa," she said, bounding down the stairs.

———

Sundi planned the discussion with Sylla from beginning to end. Mustering up all her nerve, she called and asked him to meet her at the condo. Just hearing his voice made her realize how truly desperate she was.

When the doorbell rang, she answered it immediately, and Sylla stepped inside, sporting a wide grin. He stood in the doorway, waiting for her to invite him the rest of the way in. Sundi motioned toward the couch and followed him over.

"So, what's on your mind, pretty lady?" Sylla asked, breaking the ice.

"We need to come to a better understanding, Sylla," Sundi explained. "I know you and Chris are close, and the fact that we're always fighting bothers him."

Sylla leaned back and made himself comfortable. "So what do we need to do?" he asked. "Uh . . . Could I get something to drink please?" he added before she could respond.

Sundi gritted her teeth together, then got up and entered the kitchen. "We've got orange juice, water, and grape soda."

"Orange juice, please," Sylla replied with a broad smirk across his face.

Sundi poured a large glass and took it in. "Let's call a truce, Sylla," she told him. "I love Chris, and I want to make him happy. But I don't know what to do anymore."

Sundi sat in the overstuffed chair across from Sylla. She prayed this anguish would be worth it.

Sylla maintained a serious look on his face. He knew she could not separate their family. He and Chris were blood, and it was good that she had finally realized that. "You have to let him be a man, Sundi. Black women have castrated black men in this country. We don't allow it in Africa."

"So what does that mean? I'm too old to play the diphead role."

"Chris doesn't want a diphead," Sylla told her after taking a swallow of his juice. "He's always been attracted to strong, independent women like his mother, but he also respects his father. It is a state of balance that you have to achieve, Sundi, in order to make Chris happy."

"That's what I've been trying to do," she said skeptically. She couldn't believe she was actually listening to Sylla.

"I could talk to my cousin for you. He will listen to me," Sylla offered as he finished his drink.

Sundi cautiously looked at Sylla's face. She was surprised he had offered to do what she wanted so easily. "And why would you do that for me, Sylla?" she asked.

"Because I want Chris to be happy too, and he does love you, Sundi," he told her through a half smile.

Sylla approached Chris with a rejuvenated spirit that evening. The library was closing when he caught up with him at the elevator. Chris pushed the button for the first floor, and the door slammed shut.

"I had a long talk with Sundi today, man," Sylla told Chris.

"About what?" Chris asked with a look of disbelief.

"She's hurting, Chris. That's why she lashed out at me, and you need to talk to her," Sylla replied.

"I can't talk to her, she's crazy," Chris said stubbornly.

The elevator door opened, and they stepped outside. "She's crazy, and you're caught in her madness," Sylla warned. "She wants to apologize, and you should let her. What more can she do but apologize?"

"Why should she apologize, Sylla? She's not sorry. Sundi does whatever Sundi wants, whenever she wants," Chris said as he headed for the front counter.

"Look, Chris, she's not a Yoruba woman, she's American."

"I know she's American. These men have ruined their women. They let them run all over them in this country. They're such wimps!" Chris spoke in such a loud, angry voice that a librarian crinkled her nose and motioned to him to be quiet.

"And you have chosen to marry such a woman, so now what?"

He set the pile of books on the checkout counter and handed the clerk his library card. "I can't be less than who I am, Sylla," Chris stated firmly.

"Is it a wimp who accepts an apology or a wise man?" Sylla asked, slapping his cousin's back in support.

"If she comes to me, I will listen," Chris finally agreed.

Sylla flashed a huge grin at the lady behind him. "I know you love her, man, and Sundi is basically a good woman," he added. "But like most American females, she thinks she is still a beautiful wild mustang who is to be adored from afar. We all like wild mustangs, but there is no need to have such a creature in our home."

Chris put his library card back in his wallet. "Sundi will always be a wild mustang, man. Somehow I just have to learn to live with that." He grabbed up the pile of books and hurried out the door.

The guilt behind failure can swallow you up whole the way a python swallows a rabbit. Questions like who, what, when, and where can no longer be answered in neatly arranged phrases. Danielle's guilt was so much a part of her now that she had come to know it too well. She answered all the questions over and over again but did not like the answers. She hated the guilt yet loved it at the same time because it made her feel alive. She was no longer the Danielle who played by the rules and accepted the system. She was a rebellious, scandalous woman doing what she wanted to do.

The experts call it middle-age crisis, but in black communities it's often called the knocking on forty door blues. It happens as people start to see their life as half empty rather than half full. They tend to get paranoid and lose control. The fear of looking crazy to everybody else is erased by the overwhelming rush of pleasure people get when they free themselves to focus on self: to satisfy their own needs, to achieve their own goals, and to fulfill their own desires. These people buy new sports cars and clothes and even find younger partners to appease their egos. Danielle had been singing the knocking on forty door blues for more than a year. It was as if she didn't know any other tune, and now she was living her song.

Late one Thursday afternoon, as she sat on the floor at Derrick's apartment between his long brown legs, she thought about this guilt. Derrick poured himself another glass of wine. He was wearing only his shorts, and the muscles in his thighs turned hard and strong as he bent over to stand up.

"It's about that time," Danielle said, pulling the blanket tighter.

"I know you don't want to leave me," Derrick teased.

"But you know I have to, Derrick," Danielle told him.

He strolled into the kitchen, his back glistening with beads of sweat. He opened the cabinet door and pulled out a jar of peanut butter.

"I wish we could stop playing games, Danielle, and just be together," he said.

"Be careful what you wish for," she warned.

"I hope I get it and soon," he told her, dipped his finger into the jar, and put it in his mouth.

She joined him in the kitchen and playfully rubbed her nose against his back.

"We still on for dinner?" he asked, turning around.

"Of course," she answered.

Derrick dipped his finger in the peanut butter jar again and this time smeared it across Danielle's lips. He seductively licked and sucked it off. "I don't know if I'm ready to let you go yet," he said.

"You could probably make me stay a little while longer," she said, tempting him with a kiss. As she reached up to hold him, the blanket fell to the floor. She had nothing on beneath the blanket.

"You know we might never leave the apartment at this rate," Derrick told her as his hands caressed the small of her back.

The couple moved awkwardly intertwined in each other's arms toward the couch and made love again under the red and yellow flickering lights of his fake fireplace. It was an hour later when they emerged from the shower and dressed.

"Maybe you could bring Kim tomorrow. I'd like to meet

her," Derrick said. He stretched his lengthy arms inside his blue jean shirt.

"She's not ready to see me with another man yet, Derrick."

"I'm not just another man . . . or am I?" Derrick asked, looking into her eyes with a fire that burned too brightly.

"You know what I mean," Danielle said affectionately, and turned away.

"Sometimes I think you enjoy this attention," he added. "He's at home waiting and I'm here waiting. Two lovesick puppies at your mercy."

Danielle laid her head on his chest and softly caressed the long crease in his back. "You don't believe that," she whispered.

And Derrick smiled beneath his frown. "No, I don't."

When Danielle made the decision to leave Roger a week later, she hurt badly inside, even though she tried to hide it. But somebody had to be unhappy, and Danielle was not willing to continue in that role.

Roger sat in the hallway, listening to the bumps and squeaks of Danielle and Kim moving around upstairs. He massaged the back of his neck with cold, rough hands to ease the pain. It was the same pain he had felt when his sister, Chloe, eloped with a car salesman twelve years ago and moved away to Denver. It was the same pain he had felt when his mother remarried and moved to St. Louis in his senior year of college.

Roger had focused as intensely on his own family as he did on his mother and sister. But it was all falling apart again, and he couldn't stop it. He watched as Danielle and Kim came down the stairs. Danielle set the two suitcases on the floor and stood in front of him.

"I'll let you know as soon as I'm settled," she said.

"Danielle."

"Roger, please don't say it."

"You should stay here with Kim. I'll go somewhere else."

"Thanks, but no. I need to do this, Roger, and I need for you to understand. You always did a better job of taking care of her than I did anyway."

Danielle held her arms out to Kim, who stood looking at her critically.

"You're not going to give Mom a hug good-bye?"

Kim shuffled her feet and looked down at the floor.

"Please. You know I can't leave without a hug from you."

"Good, then you can stay here with us."

"I can't do that either, baby. Remember what we talked about upstairs?"

Kim nodded her head.

"Then come on and give Mom a big hug." Danielle held her arms out again, and this time Kim ran into them. They squeezed each other tightly. "I'm going to call or see you every day, okay?"

"Okay," Kim answered, backing up and navigating her way to her father's legs. Roger put his arms around Kim and watched as Danielle picked up her bags and carried them out the door.

"Bye, Mom," Kim said, hugging her father.

Danielle blinked back the tears and shut the door.

She settled into her room at the Residence Inn as well as anyone could settle into a hotel room. It was one of those home-away-from-home hotels with a small kitchenette, bath, and living/bedroom area. Sundi and Lisa had both asked her to stay with them, but she refused. Danielle could be very stubborn when she'd made up her mind.

Sundi couldn't believe she had really left Roger. She wondered if her best friend had lost her mind, and she needed to find out. Danielle had just finished putting her wet hair in curlers when there was a knock at the door. Danielle wrapped the towel around her head and opened it.

"Hi, Sundi," she said, opening the door and stepping back.

"Hey," Sundi said, walking across the room and over to the window. She looked around the room as if she were a police detective searching for clues. "You finally did it, huh?" she asked sarcastically.

"Yeah, it was about time, wasn't it?" Danielle joked, taking the towel from around her hair.

"I'm really sorry, Dannie. I was hoping you guys would work it out," she continued.

Danielle plugged up the blow dryer. "Don't be sorry . . . I'm not."

Sundi finally sat down at the table. "You know, you really could stay with us."

"Sorry, but I need my freedom. I mean, that's what this is all about, right?" Danielle asked, and turned on the blow dryer.

"I don't know, you tell me," Sundi hollered over the noise.

Danielle raised her voice too and spelled it out for Sundi. "That's it—f-r-e-e-d-o-m."

"You had dinner yet?" Sundi asked as she opened a *Homeland Authentics* catalog and flipped through the pages.

"Derrick is coming by pretty soon to take me out."

Sundi nervously stood up. "Oh . . . I guess I should go."

"Stay. He'll be awhile. How's Chris?" she asked, and aimed the blow dryer at the front of her hair.

"Fine. He's out somewhere with Sylla and his other cronies."

"Sounds like life is not a bowl of cherries in the Ologbo house either," Danielle teased.

Sundi watched quietly as Danielle finished drying her hair. "You know, I will never give you the chance to say I told you so," Sundi finally told her. "We're going to work out our problems over on Trenton Street."

"Good, because I'm working out my problems too. Just not in the way you and Lisa think I should," Danielle replied.

"Danielle, leaving Roger is something, but how could you leave the baby? That's what I don't understand!" Sundi finally said, shaking her head in confusion.

"I never was thrilled about being a mother, Sundi. You know that. Roger took on most of that role. Her school and friends are all over in Gaithersburg, so I left her where she would be comfortable. There was no sense in disrupting her life too."

Sundi looked into her eyes for the truth. "Do you regret having her, Danielle?"

Danielle stared at Sundi and suddenly smiled. "Sometimes I regret marrying so early and wonder what my life would have been like if I had done things differently. But no, I don't regret having Kim. She's the only thing we did right, and she was an accident."

Danielle took her red paisley dress out of the closet while Sundi studied a page of the catalog.

"I don't think we're ready for kids yet, at least I'm not," Sundi eventually told her.

"And I take it Chris is ready."

"He thinks we're working on it now. The same things I love about him I've come to absolutely hate, Dannie. He's strong and aggressive. He takes charge and I love that, but I don't like being stepped on in the process."

"I'm probably the last person who needs to give somebody advice about marriage," Danielle said, taking off her robe and stepping carefully into the dress.

"You were married for a long time."

Danielle moved in front of the mirror. She leaned in and smeared her lips with redbrick lipstick. "Just be honest with yourself, Sundi. Life is too short to be unhappy."

"So are you really happy now, Dannie?" Sundi had to ask.

"Happiness comes and goes. I'm content with my decision for now."

The phone rang, and Danielle answered it. "Hello . . . Yeah. I'm ready . . . okay." She hung up the phone, and Sundi began walking slowly toward the door.

"You can go with us if you'd like, Sundi."

"No . . . That's okay. We'll go some other time."

"Didn't you tell me once that Sundiata meant 'hungry lion'?" Danielle asked.

"Hungering lion." Sundi corrected her. "I think that describes me well, don't you?"

"Yeah . . . that's you or at least it *was* you," Danielle reflected.

"What do you mean, it *was*?"

"Just be careful, Sundi, because marriage changes things. It should be safe and secure and, if you're lucky, satisfying. But you have to stay hungry, you have to eat every bite."

Sundi reached the door, then turned back to Danielle and smiled. "Can you believe my mom named me *Bernetta*?"

Danielle tried to call Lisa several times after she moved, but Lisa kept hanging up on her. When Danielle showed up at Lisa's apartment early Saturday morning, she beat on the door for a long time before Lisa finally let her in. They didn't speak at first. Danielle followed her into the bedroom and sat on top of a pile of clothes in the rocking chair in the corner. She was too lazy to move the blue sweat suit, black jeans, red sweater, and beige nightshirt that wrinkled beneath her. Lisa tried to listen to Danielle's mumblings, pack for her trip to New Orleans, and enhance her positive spirit at the same time.

"*I am a unique and wonderful person,*" Lisa's voice on the cassette tape proclaimed.

"I am a unique and wonderful person." Lisa repeated the affirmation.

"So, are you ever going to speak to me again?" Danielle asked.

"You're silly for leaving him, Dannie," Lisa told her, "and I'm not going to support this craziness." She picked out a pair of flat blue slip-ons with tassels and stuffed them in her shoe bag.

"I didn't ask for your support, did I?" Danielle told her, agitated because Lisa didn't understand.

The tape continued: "*I do not accept the limitations that others try to place on me. My possibilities are limitless.*"

"Mom always said, 'A good relationship is nurtured in time, strengthened with sensitivity, and secured through communication.' I still believe that," Lisa told her sister.

"Sure you believe it. You've done the things you wanted in life. You didn't get married early, have a kid, and stop living."

"I do not accept the limitations that others try to place on me. My possibilities are limitless," Lisa said, echoing the tape. "If you call this living, you can have it, Dannie. I'll take a great kid like Kim and a good man like Roger anytime."

"You've always thought Roger was the perfect man, haven't you, Lisa?"

"I will accept the things I cannot change and change the things that I can."

Lisa pulled a fur puff from a can of black shoe polish and started to buff her black leather pumps. "I think he's as close to perfection as a man can get," she answered, then agreed with the affirmation. "I will accept the things I cannot change and change the things that I can."

"Well, you can have him. He probably should have married you anyway," Danielle said, not looking up at her sister.

"What the hell does that mean?" Lisa asked, obviously annoyed.

"You guys have always loved each other," Danielle continued, this time looking her sister directly in the eye.

"He's been my brother-in-law for ages; of course I love him. You talk so stupid sometimes!"

"That's right. Don't listen to me. I'm a crazy woman right now," Danielle agreed as she lifted herself up and pushed the pile of clothes onto the floor.

"I give myself permission to make positive changes in my life."

"Now, that's one I agree with," Danielle yelled toward Lisa, and repeated it as loudly as she could. "I give myself permission to make positive changes in my life."

Lisa stopped packing to stare at her sister. "I don't believe this is a positive change, Dannie. It's one thing to have a fling with this kid, but you've stepped over the line."

"How do you know what's over the line for me? Why can't I do what makes me happy?" Danielle whined.

"And you honestly think Derrick's going to make you happy?" Lisa asked, then chuckled as she put her tennis shoes into a plastic bag and pushed them into the bottom of her suitcase.

"You think I'm supposed to stay in this marriage with Roger and be miserable?"

"I am confident that I will accomplish my goals in life."

"Obviously not," Lisa replied caustically. "I am confident that I will accomplish my goals in life."

Danielle snatched a fingernail file from the top of the dresser and began to clean under her nails as she spoke. "Well, I don't know if I'd marry Derrick, but I do know . . . his dick is my command," she joked.

"That's your problem, Dannie," Lisa warned, sifting through her panty hose until she found two good pairs. "This is no longer about sex. You've left your husband and your daughter, and it's not funny."

"I am living my life based on my choices and not allowing chance to rule."

Danielle stared silently at her baby sister. She knew Lisa was telling the truth, but the truth was not what she wanted to hear.

Lisa repeated the motivational phrase. "I am living my life based on my choices and not allowing chance to rule."

"So I suppose Walter's sexual ability has nothing to do with your running off to New Orleans," Danielle finally said.

Lisa folded a pair of jeans from the laundry basket and tucked them into her suitcase. "It's a lot more than that with Walter. I think he could be the one."

"It can't be that serious, Lisa. You've only been seeing him a couple of months."

"I have this feeling, Dannie, and don't try to ruin my life just because yours is all fucked up."

"You had that feeling with Kirby, remember?"

"I deserve happiness and fulfillment in my life."

"I deserve happiness and fulfillment in my life," Lisa repeated as if she were speaking directly to Danielle. "Kirby could have been the one. He just couldn't hang."

"Well, I'm still waiting to meet the man that *can* hang with you!" Danielle told her jokingly.

"I think Walter's the maaaaan!" Lisa said, dipping her shoulders and twisting her hands as she spoke to give the word more emphasis.

Danielle hesitated. "Just take some time and get to know him, that's all I ask. You see the problems I'm having with Roger, and Sundi's complaining about Chris. If he's the one, it'll work out."

"I am the best I can be, and I'm getting better every day."

"I am the best I can be, and I'm getting better every day," Lisa echoed, then continued her conversation. "It feels so good to be with him, Dannie. It's like he's the answer to all of my prayers."

"Well, continue to pray on it because you know Mom's favorite line: 'Just because it feels good to you doesn't mean it's good for you.' "

"I like who I am, and I enjoy being me."

Danielle and Lisa repeated together, "I like who I am, and I enjoy being me."

"Real love takes time, Lisa," Danielle added. "Roger and I have tried to get it right for fifteen years."

"I don't want to wait any longer. I want to have a baby while I'm young enough to enjoy it."

"Believe me, no matter how young you are, childbirth is *not* something you will enjoy."

"I prevent harmful stress from occurring in my life at all times."

"I prevent harmful stress from occurring in my life at all times," Lisa said, while pulling two dresses and a couple pairs of pants out of the closet and laying them on top of her garment bag. "How can you *not* see bringing Kim into the world as special, Dannie?"

"You know what I mean," Danielle replied. The tape clicked off, and Danielle flipped it over. "Contrary to popular belief, all women aren't mothers, Lisa. Kim is great, but she's her father's child, and she is right where she should be."

"I will not allow the attitudes of others to impact me in a negative way."

"I will not allow the attitudes of others to impact me in a negative way," Lisa mumbled. "Isn't that strange? You have everything I need to be happy, and you don't want it." Lisa tossed a pair of black jeans onto a pile on the floor headed for the laundry.

"Nothing can *make* you happy except yourself, Lisa. Get a

grip, girl. Walter's wonderful now because you guys just met, but give it time."

"When I set a goal, I reach it. Nothing can stop me from accomplishing my goals."

Lisa sorted through the underclothes in her top drawer. "When I set a goal, I reach it. Nothing can stop me from accomplishing my goals."

"Don't ignore me, Lisa. I'm very serious."

"I just want to have a good time, Dannie. I want to be happy. The same thing you want, right?"

"I'm not saying don't have a good time." Danielle continued lecturing. "Just be careful. Can you do that for me?"

"I never overcommit, and I get things done on time."

Danielle and Lisa repeated the affirmation in unison: "I never overcommit, and I get things done on time."

Lisa pulled out a black sexy teddy and tossed it into a side compartment.

"You're going to take that with you?" Danielle asked with her mouth hanging open.

Lisa smiled, nodded her head, and dropped it in her suitcase.

"I am a winner. Determination is the key to success, and I have determination."

"I am a winner. Determination is the key to success, and I have determination," Lisa agreed.

I have determination too, Danielle thought. This was her life and she needed to live it—her way. She couldn't help it that Roger and Kim didn't understand. She couldn't help it that Lisa and Sundi didn't approve. She only knew that she had to make a change. She had to move on with her life, despite how much it hurt.

"I'm going to get out of here," Danielle said as she stood up and walked toward the bedroom door. "No need to see me out. You finish your packing and have a good time."

"You take care of yourself, Sis," Lisa whispered as she disappeared through the door.

"You do the same," Danielle replied softly.

Lisa had never been to New Orleans before, so her enthusiasm brought a new excitement to Walter's visit home. First they went on a walking tour of the French Quarter. Although the houses were gorgeous, they were packed too close together for Lisa's taste. Many had been restored, commanding royal attention with large French doors, wrought-iron balconies, and beautiful private gardens. Lisa felt the spirit of mixed cultures and evolutionary change erupt inside her as they passed a small outdoor park named after Louis Armstrong, who had grown up in New Orleans, and listened to an impromptu concert by local jazz artists. The ragtime sounds flowed through the cobblestone streets, past Pirate's Alley, where William Faulkner once lived. Sounds of zydeco floated down St. Ann Street, alongside the historical architecture of the Mahalia Jackson Theater of the Performing Arts.

Lisa and Walter strolled down Basin, Canal, and the famed Bourbon Street. Then they ate gumbo and beignets in the French Market. Lisa found out quickly that beignets were very messy. She laughed at Walter, who had powdered sugar on his nose, so he blew hard across the table, and it scattered all over her black and burgundy patchwork vest. He laughed.

Lisa tried to wipe the powdered sugar off. "That's not funny, Walter."

He stopped laughing. "I'm sorry. Here," he said, and wet his napkin in his water glass. "Try this."

Lisa wiped off the rest of it and smirked at him. "Thanks."

"You tired yet?" he asked.

"Not yet," she replied. Despite walking all day, Lisa felt energized.

"Good, because we still have a lot to do today." Walter took her hand and led her back to the car. They drove by a fascinating area once called Black Storyville. He explained that it used to be a red-light district with famous clubs and restaurants, prostitution, and gambling. Great musicians like Jelly Roll Morton, Leadbelly, and Louis Armstrong had made their fame there. Lisa cringed as she looked at the deteriorating housing project that now stood as a monument to the historical legacy.

Down by the Gulf, they walked hand in hand under a bright August moon, arms swinging like young sweethearts. Lisa concentrated on his warm fingers between hers and prayed that she'd never have to let go. The last time she had felt this good was during a trip to the Bahamas as an undergrad.

She had been surprised at how romantic the men were. They had treated her as if she were a precious gem to be protected and adored. That's how Walter made her feel all over again.

Lisa kept that memory stored in a special place. She hadn't thought about that Bahamian cabdriver Bennie in a long time. He took her to a club out of the tourist area. There were wrought-iron tables and chairs. The ceiling was covered with wicker fans, baskets, and handwoven rugs. As Lisa thought back, she could almost taste the cool planter's punch and see the hot limbo dancers testing their agility, bending lower and lower under bamboo poles.

Dwane, the lead singer at the club, was a *fine* honey. She had noticed him right away. He had hazel-colored eyes and a smile that made her feel good all over. As she and her date enjoyed the show, some guy came over to the table and quietly spoke to Bennie. He nodded his head and five minutes later excused himself. It caught her off guard when Dwane came over to her table, sat down, and started to rap. He told Lisa how good she looked and how he'd been watching her from the stage. They talked briefly about her vacation and his career. Then he invited her back to the show the next night as his guest and left.

Lisa was flattered and pissed at the same time. It looked like a setup to her, and she definitely wasn't no pass-around pack. When Bennie returned, she asked him to explain, and he said it was their custom. If she wanted to go out with Dwane, she had every right, so out of respect he had given Dwane the chance to ask. Of course Lisa went back to the club the next night as Dwane's guest and had another great evening of being pampered and adored.

She also remembered the one asshole she met that week on her way home. When she changed planes in Atlanta, her transfer gate was at the opposite end of the airport. As she lugged her large blue tweed suitcase and matching satchel across the floor, trying to make the connection, she heard an irritating noise, "Pssst . . . pssst."

Lisa looked around. The only person near her was a tall, slender guy dressed in faded jeans and a white jacket, leaning against the wall. Lisa ignored him at first. She was feeling too good to deal with his bullshit. Then she heard it again, and when she turned around to give him a dirty look, he said: "Hey, baby, why don't you put those bags down and come talk to me a minute?"

Lisa was sure that that man told stories about her today because she cussed him up and down that airport. She couldn't believe it. He didn't say, "Let me help you with those bags," then rap along the way. Mr. God's gift wanted *her* to put *her* bags down and miss *her* plane to talk to him! Welcome back to America.

Before heading back to the hotel, Lisa and Walter stopped outside a quaint little house in the middle of a residential block. It had been a long day, and Lisa didn't really feel like visiting anybody.

"Where are we, Walter?" she asked, slightly irritated.

"I just need to stop for a minute . . . come on," he said, walking up to the door and knocking softly.

A tall, elderly, big-boned lady opened the door wide and smiled when she saw him. "Wally!" she blurted out as they hugged.

"Hi, Mamma!"

Walter turned and gave Lisa what she thought was his biggest grin ever before he followed his mother into the house.

Lisa was dumbfounded. She felt her heart beating frantically and tried to calm herself down. She stepped inside behind them and shut the door.

Mrs. Henderson went to the back door and called for her husband. "Walter . . . Come inside. Junior's home."

Mr. Henderson dropped his cigarette on the ground and hurried up the back steps. He was met halfway by Walter. They hugged for a long time and patted each other on the back. Lisa stood nervously in the hallway, waiting to be remembered. Mrs. Henderson suddenly turned and smiled at Lisa and pointed to a chair.

Mr. Henderson and Walter entered the house, and Walter walked over and stood behind Lisa's chair.

"Mom, Dad, this is Lisa."

"Hi," his mother said in a sweet, sugary tone.

"Hello," his father echoed.

"Hi," Lisa responded back to both of them, awkwardly.

"Wally, I have your favorite, bread pudding," his mother said, speaking to him as if he were twelve years old again.

Mrs. Henderson rattled around in the old wooden cupboards, tiptoeing to reach the three bowls she brought down. A well-worn enamel countertop flanked the entire wall under the window where she cut hunks of bread pudding.

Walter sat down at the table between his father and Lisa. It was a pine dining table in the corner of the room lit by an old brass chandelier. Mrs. Henderson brought the dishes over and served large helpings to her husband and son. Lisa noticed how beautiful she was. Her brown, slightly graying hair was pulled back into a bun, and she had very few wrinkles in her face.

"How about you, Lisa?" Mrs. Henderson asked.

"Yes, please," Lisa replied. She hadn't had bread pudding since her grandmother had made it years ago.

Mrs. Henderson set a bowl and spoon in front of Lisa, then got everyone the drink of his or her choice: milk, water, or sweetened tea. Walter straddled the chair and tore into the pudding as if he hadn't eaten all day.

"How long you here for, Junior?" his father asked. Walter's father couldn't deny him if he wanted to, Lisa thought. They looked just alike. Why is it, she wondered, that men seemed to get better-looking as they grew older without even trying and women had to struggle to maintain just a little sense of dignity?

"Just tonight, I gotta get back tomorrow."

Lisa looked carefully at Walter. He had just lied to his parents. They would be in New Orleans for the weekend.

"You look good, son," Mr. Henderson said, nodding toward Lisa as if she had something to do with it. Lisa blushed and took another bite of the delicious pudding.

Walter sensed that Lisa was nervous and put his arm around her. He swallowed the pudding in his mouth, then spoke. "Mom, Dad, I wanted both of you to meet Lisa because I'm going to marry her."

Lisa stared hard at Walter. He had just said the *M* word. Men never say the *M* word, especially men who are just getting over a divorce. An old boyfriend of hers once compared it to getting kicked in the nuts, twice.

"How's Brenda, Walter?" his mother asked, smiling at Lisa at the same time.

"Brenda is as okay as Brenda can get, Mom. She's my ex-wife, remember?"

Walter got up to get a second helping of pudding. He grinned at Lisa, and she absorbed all of that wonderful grin.

"Lisa . . . how you like New Orleans?" his father asked, and winked at her.

Lisa smiled. She knew she was going to like him. "It's great, Mr. Henderson."

"Maybe you guys can come again and stay longer next time," Mr. Henderson continued.

"I hope so," she replied, still smiling.

"What do you do, Lisa?" Mrs. Henderson asked as she dished a second helping of pudding for her husband before he could finish the first.

"I'm in school and I teach."

"You need to be careful nowadays. Kids are crazy. Killing teachers and each other," Mr. Henderson said and shook his head. "I bet you're a good teacher and your students love you."

Lisa's nervous jitters returned. "I try," she said, then got up to put her bowl and spoon in the sink. She sat back down at the end of the table in a trance as Walter told his parents all about them: how they met, how he felt about her, and why he planned to marry her. She knew at that moment that he was the one.

They didn't speak much during the drive back to the hotel. Walter kept watching Lisa. He wondered what she thought of his folks and how she felt about his announcement. Lisa was busy wondering too. She formulated thoughts about New Orleans, Walter's parents, and the surprising *M* discussion.

Inside the hotel room Lisa quickly peeled off her clothes and scooted under the covers in her birthday suit. She struggled to think of a good way to bring up the *M* word. After all, if Walter was thinking about it, she thought they should think about it together. Suddenly everything was going right in her life, and Lisa was almost scared to breathe because any minute things might change back to normal.

She listened to Walter hum "Mighty Love" by the Spinners while he shaved at the bathroom sink. She decided the best approach would be to handle it jokingly.

"Hey, Junior!" she called. Walter didn't respond at first. "Junior!" she yelled again.

"What?" Walter said, appearing in the doorway with his face half covered with white cream. The water on his bare chest sparkled in the amber light. Lisa was mesmerized for a moment. Wouldn't it be wonderful if he were the one? she thought.

"Why did you tell your parents that?"

"What?"

"That we were gonna get married."

Walter stepped out of the bathroom and walked toward the bed. His shorts hugged that wonderful round behind. He kissed her lightly, leaving traces of shaving cream across her lips, then went back into the bathroom.

While Walter finished shaving, Lisa brushed her hair and thought about her next move. She had brought it up, and he hadn't responded, at least not the way she wanted him to. What did that mean? She didn't want to seem anxious, but she had to get the issue out in the open.

Walter came out of the bathroom, patting his wet face dry with a thin white towel. He went inside his suitcase, got out a little bottle with several joints in it. He still hadn't said a word. He lit a joint, lay on the bed beside Lisa, and played in her hair.

"You didn't answer my question!" she reminded him when she couldn't stand it any longer.

"We are gonna get married!" Walter insisted with his usual confidence.

Lisa almost believed him, but she refused to get her hopes up. "You don't *know* that," she teased, taking a drag off the joint and handing it back.

"You're right, I don't know," he said. He suddenly hopped out of bed, and Lisa panicked because she thought her remark had upset him somehow. She was ready to apologize because she didn't want anything to come between them tonight. She watched as Walter put the blunt in the ashtray and knelt at the side of the bed. He looked as if he were about to pray, but instead he took her hand and held it in his.

"Lisa Elaine Allen . . . will you marry me?"

"Are you for real?" Lisa asked, grinning as hard as she ever could.

"I'm on my knees, woman. What more do you want?"

Lisa smiled. She wanted and needed him more than she would admit. "Nothing, that's all I want!" she finally answered.

Walter and Lisa kissed as they had never kissed before. Lisa was giving this man all of her: her heart, her soul, her life. She took another drag of the joint, then put it out. She pulled Walter back onto the bed and slid her tongue across his chest and down to his belly button. She dived down even farther, tickling every crack and crevice she could find. She nibbled and licked and sucked until he cried out for mercy. Then something different happened. He returned her ardent emotion. His tongue was magical, creating a series of brightly colored rainbows in her heart.

That next morning Walter woke up early. He gently shook Lisa until she was awake. She opened her eyes and saw that silly grin on his face. She imagined for a second how great it was going to be to wake up to that grin every day.

"Let's do it this weekend," Walter said.

"Do what?"

"Marry me right now!"

She lifted herself up. "What? . . . Walter, you're nuts!"

"I'll call in. We can stay over the Labor Day weekend for our honeymoon." That was what she loved most about him: his spontaneity. It was so exciting to be with Walter. He enjoyed each moment. He got all he could out of every day. He was helping her to enjoy life again too. And she truly loved him for that.

"This is happening so fast, Walter," she said, letting her voice of reason take control.

He held his hand out to her just beyond reach and said: "You only live life once, baby, come on . . . grab hold."

Lisa hesitated, then grabbed that beautiful black hand. "Okay," she said. "Let's do it. I love you, Walter Henderson." What else could she say? She wanted to feel this way forever.

Walter picked up the phone and dialed happily.

Lisa's wedding was much different from her sister's and best friend's. Walter's mother told her about a small country chapel at the edge of town. They shopped all day for a dress. Since it wasn't the large formal wedding she'd dreamed of, Lisa settled on a pleated white silk dress with an off-the-shoulder neckline and a hem that fell just below the knee. For her headpiece she wore only a headband covered with baby's breath, and her bouquet was made of white cymbidium orchids.

In the backyard of the chapel was a beautiful wooden Victorian gazebo with three handcrafted wooden archways leading to it. The gazebo was surrounded on three sides by unique gardens. A breathtaking tulip garden was on the left, with more than five hundred brightly colored bulbs. There was a perennial garden on the right with basket-of-gold, geraniums, and daisies all intermixed within a dark green Mexican sage bush. Behind the gazebo was a wonderfully wild field of golden mustard that followed a long, winding creek.

As Lisa stood side by side with Walter in front of the preacher and next to his parents, she contemplated her happiness. There were only two things missing from her wedding: Danielle and Sundi. She glanced over at Walter's grin. He was everything she wanted in a man, and he was going to be hers.

"Today we celebrate the joining of Walter Michael Henderson and Lisa Elaine Allen in holy matrimony. This union is not to be entered into lightly, but carefully as a sacred bond." The preacher read the words from a book in front of him. "Do you, Walter Michael Henderson, take Lisa Elaine Allen as your wife? To love, comfort, and support her throughout your years together?"

Walter's grin grew wider as he said, "I do."

"Do you, Lisa Elaine Allen, take Walter Michael Henderson as your husband? To love, comfort, and support him throughout your years together?"

"I do." Lisa heard herself saying the magical words.

"Would you exchange rings now?"

Walter reached in his pocket and pulled out the bridal set that he and Lisa had chosen a few hours before. He slipped the engagement ring and wedding band on her finger one at a time. Lisa then took his wedding band from a small pearl purse she carried and slipped it on his left-hand ring finger.

The preacher handed the couple white candles. "May this

flame burn forever in your hearts," he said, and lit each one. "I present these candles as symbols of the passion and love you share. By the power vested in me, in the presence of God's holy fire, I now pronounce you husband and wife." The preacher finished and closed his book as Walter's and Lisa's lips touched gently.

It stormed every day during Chris's mother's visit to the United States. That week in August was a perfect tribute to Iyoma's tornado mentality. She was set on destroying anything between her and her son, and Sundi stood directly in her path.

Sundi tried everything to get on the woman's good side, without success. She cooked, cleaned, and even washed her dirty clothes. After two days Sundi needed a break, so she tried to slip away to the mall. Iyoma followed. How could she tell her husband's mother to get lost and still maintain peace in the valley?

For Sundi, malls were wonderful places to go when things were heavy on her mind. The brightly lit shops at Iverson Mall seemed content to absorb the worry and sorrow that she brought inside that evening. Trying to lose Iyoma, she hurried past a half-off shoe sale, something Sundi rarely did. As she rushed through the deserted department store, she found herself in the baby section, the last place she wanted to be with her mother-in-law. The conversation in the past two days had been consistently peppered with sarcastic comments about babies.

Iyoma held up a tiny red and white dress with lace around the cuffs and hem. "Isn't this cute?" she asked Sundi.

Sundi nodded and tried to keep moving, but Iyoma called

her back. "Sundi, wait," Iyoma said. "We need to talk because I'm worried."

Sundi stopped. Her parents had taught her to respect her elders. "There's nothing to worry about, Mamma Yoma," she assured her. She knew what was coming but thought it really wasn't anybody else's business when she and Chris decided to have kids.

"So you will have a child for my son soon?" Iyoma asked.

Sundi looked nervously down at the floor. "We're waiting until we can afford it," she answered.

"Afford it? Sundi, children *are* wealth. They are your future," Iyoma told her with a smile.

"First, Chris and I need time to work things out together," Sundi tried to explain.

She turned and headed over to the junior department and quickly picked up a purple flowered skirt off the sales rack. Iyoma continued to stalk her, but like her son, she was not ready to listen.

"You can have children?" Iyoma asked.

"I can if I choose to," Sundi responded, shooting a dirty look her way.

"A woman needs children to be complete, Sundi."

"I don't believe that," she snapped, holding on to the anger that was growing inside her. She wanted so badly to tell this woman to mind her own business. She wanted to tell her that Chris was a grown man and they didn't need her meddling. She wanted to end his family's interference and simply love her man.

"But Chris does!" Iyoma continued.

Sundi tried to block her out as she stood in front of a full-length mirror and held a short blue skirt with a matching blue and yellow striped top against her to assess its fit.

"Sundi, Chris is a Nigerian man. He needs more than you can give him," Iyoma said in a stern voice.

"Did he say that?" Sundi asked, challenging her statement.

Iyoma positioned herself between Sundi and the mirror. "No."

"Then how can you?"

"Chris is to marry a Nigerian girl at home, Sundi. It's been planned since they were small. He *loves* Kiara."

Sundi dropped the skirt and top on the floor and stared at Iyoma in disbelief. Another woman, no way, she thought. She had refused to let Iyoma rattle her until now. This was too much for her to deal with calmly. She didn't believe it, but what if it was true? Maybe he used to love this other woman, but he didn't love her now. He couldn't love her now.

All the way home Sundi thought about how she would approach Chris concerning this revelation from Iyoma. She needed to hear from him what it all meant. She decided the best way to handle it was not to confront him in front of his mother. She wouldn't give her the satisfaction of seeing them argue.

As they entered the apartment, Sundi set her packages in a hall chair. Chris wrapped his arms around her waist and kissed her on the neck in a superficial display of affection.

"What did you buy to make yourself beautiful for me?" he asked.

Sundi fashioned a phony smile at Iyoma. The satisfied smirk on her face drove Sundi wild. She suddenly couldn't hold it in. She stepped out of his arms.

"Chris, can we talk in the bedroom?"

"About what?"

"I just need to talk to you, *please*?" Sundi said in a scratchy voice.

Chris stole a quick look at his mother, who sat down in the living room. She started skimming through a magazine, pretending not to listen.

"Why can't we talk out here?" Chris asked, asserting his control.

"I said *please*," Sundi repeated, only to please his ego.

Chris didn't move. "Whatever it is, we can talk out here."

Sundi hesitated, but as she watched Chris walk arrogantly into the living room, the words just burst forth. "Okay, tell me about Kiara," she yelled.

Chris instantly looked at his mother, and then he did something that sent chills through Sundi's small body. He lost his confidence for a moment. Sundi had spent a lot of time studying his reactions to things, and he always stood his ground when he thought he was right.

"Mamma . . . I told you to let me handle it," he said, cutting his eyes at Iyoma.

"I'm sorry, son," she said insincerely; then Iyoma left quickly, slipping into the den.

"What the hell is this about, Chris?"

"My father wants me to come home and help him run the tourist shops."

"So you're going home?" Sundi asked.

"I don't know, Sundi. I don't know what I'm going to do right now," he continued, his face furrowed with confusion.

"And this Kiara, who is she?"

Chris didn't look at her as he spoke. "She's just a girl back home. We were going to marry until I met you."

"When were you going to tell me all this?" Sundi asked. She sank down in the overstuffed chair and waited for a response.

"Look, we can talk about it later when Mom leaves."

Fury surged up inside Sundi. She was sick of putting her heart on hold for his manhood. She was tired and wanted this thing to be settled. She didn't want to wait for anything. "I want to talk about it now, Chris!" she screamed.

Chris glanced at the door of the den and took a deep breath. "Leave it alone, Sundi," he warned, and walked away. It was the one thing that Sundi hated, and she knew exactly what it meant. He was finished with the conversation, and she would not get anything else out of him until *he* was ready.

"Fine, Chris! I'm sick of this bullshit anyway. I'm going to bed!" she yelled, rolled her eyes, and stomped into the bedroom.

When Iyoma heard the door to the bedroom slam, she cautiously entered the living room. "Where's Sundi?" she asked. "I need a clean washcloth."

"She's gone to bed, Mom," Chris told her.

"She goes to bed before you?" Iyoma asked with concern.

"It's okay, Mom. If I want something, I can get it," Chris explained.

"So why did you marry?"

Chris didn't respond at first. He saw what his mother was trying to do, and he chose not to let her agitate him more. "I asked you to let me talk to Sundi about returning home."

"I know, but we were having such a good time. I'm sorry," Iyoma apologized.

Chris opened the linen closet to get the washcloth. "You know I haven't decided to come back yet, Mom."

"I just want you to give it serious thought, son. Your father could use your help, and Kiara is still waiting," Iyoma reminded him.

"Kiara is not a part of my life anymore."

Iyoma raised her eyebrows. "Are you sure?" she asked.

Chris handed her the cloth. "Good night, Mom," he said, and watched her go back into the den.

Chris struggled to keep his thoughts in order. He was sick of his mother and his wife. He knew he couldn't continue to live like this. He was tired of fighting about everything. He needed a break. He entered the bedroom, shut the door, and sat on the edge of the bed. Sundi didn't move. Sleeping together was all a facade for Iyoma's benefit anyway. They hadn't made love in weeks.

Sundi waited silently while he took off his shirt and pants and climbed under the comforter. "Chris, I'm really struggling to understand things, but you just seem to be piling more shit on," she finally told him. "Could we please talk about this?" She knew he wouldn't budge if she didn't take a more compliant role. She hated playing these games, but the goal, she told herself, was to get what *she* wanted in the end.

"Don't ever do that again!" Chris vented in her direction.

But Sundi continued to push. "Just tell me if you love this Kiara?" she asked, needing to hear him say what she thought she already knew.

Chris took a deep breath. "No," he said.

Sundi repressed a smile and moved closer to him. "Do you love me?"

"I don't know, Sundi. I don't know if this is love or not!" Chris muttered.

She was hurt by his response, so she shoved him hard from behind. "What do you mean you don't know?"

Chris lost his balance on the edge of the bed and fell onto the floor. "Damn, Sundi, that hurt!" he said, rubbing a sore knee, which had hit the floor first.

Sundi laughed when she saw his face scrunched up in pain. "I didn't know you were that close to the edge. I'm sorry, Chris." She reached out her hand to help him up, but he didn't take it.

"What you need to do is grow up. This whole argument is ridiculous!" he said, lifting himself up and crawling back into bed.

"It's not ridiculous if you are planning to go back home and marry some other woman," she explained. "I've got too much invested to let you go that easily."

He leaned over and kissed her shoulder. "I may not have a choice. My father is not well, Sundi."

"Chris, we talked about this. I don't want to leave America; it's my home. You said you wanted to stay here too," Sundi pleaded.

"So what does that mean? Fuck me and what happens to my family across the water?"

"You know that's not what I'm saying." Sundi sat up in the bed. She wanted to make him understand that she needed him here as well.

"That's what it sounds like to me," Chris continued angrily.

"Why do you always have to act like you're so perfect?" Sundi asked. "I have needs and feelings, Chris, just like you."

Chris shot a disgusted look her way. "It's not like my needs and feelings are being satisfied, Sundi. This is not a marriage—it's a joke! And honestly I'm sick of it too."

The tension in his voice was so dense that Sundi couldn't respond. Chris turned off the lamp and turned his back to her. Sundi searched through the darkness but could barely see the curve of his back through the liquid that collected in her eyes. She was afraid she could lose him because Iyoma was not like

Sylla. Iyoma didn't want to compromise. She was determined to have it her way.

Keeping something from Iyoma was like trying to keep daylight from a rooster. On her last day in America, while Sundi was out on a delivery, she slipped into her son's bedroom. Each time she was left alone in the house, she had systematically searched a room. She tiptoed around, looking inside drawers, through closets, and even under the bed.

She found a couple of photo albums and some old letters in the closet because Sundi kept everything. She dug into shoe boxes, old purses, and sacks but found nothing of interest. When she reached to move a small suitcase from the top shelf, the back of her hand touched the lightbulb, and she jerked away from the heat. Her elbow hit a suitcase above her; it tumbled down and spilled open. Iyoma knew she had struck gold. She tucked a small plastic case into her jacket pocket, then made sure everything was back in its place and left.

Chris came home from work early and loaded the blue BMW with Iyoma's suitcase and two boxes of gifts, souvenirs, and necessities hard to find in Africa. On the way to the airport he stopped at the bank, went inside, and handed the teller a check.

"Just a minute," the teller said, then went to her computer and began to type.

"You sure this is all right with Sundi?" Iyoma asked.

"Sure, Mom . . . don't worry."

The teller returned. "One hundred, two, three, four, five . . ." She counted out a thousand dollars, and Chris slipped it into a small envelope.

From there they headed to Dulles International. Iyoma knew there was not a lot of time before she would be on a plane back home, so she had to talk fast.

"She should be pregnant by now, Chris. There must be something wrong."

"It takes time, Mom," Chris answered, and took a deep breath. He was almost as sick of this conversation as Sundi was.

"Six months is plenty of time."

"It's only been four months, Mother."

Iyoma continued to press him. "Soon it will be six, then what?"

Chris sped up to make it through a yellow light. "Can we not talk about this now?" he asked.

"What if she can't have kids?" Iyoma asked relentlessly.

"I don't think that's the case," Chris assured her.

"Then what if she doesn't want kids?" Iyoma continued, squeezing her hands together in anticipation of what she already knew.

"I know that's not true," Chris answered confidently.

"Okay . . . okay . . . but all I'm asking, Christian, is that you consider Kiara at home if something *is* wrong."

Chris stopped the car at a red light, then turned to face his mother. "I love Sundi, Mom. We're having some problems right now, but I don't want to leave her."

"So make Kiara your second wife," Iyoma offered.

Chris was very surprised to hear his mother say this. She was his father's third wife and had always complained. She hated the fact that Orun had been her father's friend, and she was only fifteen when her hand was given in marriage. She rebelled and went to Europe to study instead. She spent a year away before she decided to honor the tradition and accept her place by his father's side. Chris thought about how, in some ways, this tradition scared him, and it was part of the reason why he married Sundi. He wanted to make his own choices.

Chris parked in the short-term lot and carried the bags inside the terminal. Once the luggage was checked, they walked past the gift shop, toward Gate 21.

"Well?" Iyoma said, still determined.

"This is America, Mom. You can't have two wives," Chris reminded her.

"You could come home. Remember, we need you at home."

Chris didn't hide his irritation. "I'll think about it," he said, just to get her off his back.

"Your father needs your help, Chris. You are his only son."

Iyoma was very proud of that. It gave her status in the family. Orun's other two wives had given him only daughters.

"Here's your gate," Chris said, pointing toward a couple of empty seats.

There was an awkward silence as they sat down in the waiting area. Finally Iyoma spoke again: "I'm only trying to help, Chris. Kiara loves you, and she's willing to wait."

"It's just not the same now," Chris tried to explain. "I don't love her, Mom."

"First call for Flight Seven-five to New York. We'd like to board those with small children, our first class and mileage-plus passengers, and those needing additional time to get settled first," the flight attendant called over the PA system.

Iyoma stood up. "Please think about it," she requested once more.

Chris handed her the envelope from the bank. "I will . . . I promise," he said, standing as well. Chris kissed his mother on the cheek. He didn't want to admit it, but it was a relief to see her go.

"I love you, Chris," Iyoma told him, then slipped the package of birth control pills out of her jacket pocket and into his hand. Without saying another word, she turned and walked quickly down the ramp.

Sundi finished washing the dishes while listening to a jazz station on the radio. Her mood was lighter because she knew Iyoma's plane was in the air by now.

Chris came into the apartment slowly. He clicked off the radio and walked into the kitchen. "You finished yet?" he asked, though he already knew the answer.

"No, here, make yourself useful," Sundi responded, handing him a dish towel.

Chris took it hesitantly. He dried a couple of bowls, then put the towel down.

"If I went home, would you go with me?" he asked.

"I've always wanted to visit Africa, but I don't want to live there, Chris. You know that," Sundi said.

Chris walked into the living room, knowing she would follow.

Sundi picked up the towel and dried her hands. "Have you decided something?" she asked, right behind him.

"I don't know. Maybe, maybe not," he told her and shrugged his shoulders.

The fear returned. "Dammit, Chris, we talked about this before the marriage. You said you wanted to live here!" Sundi yelled.

Chris let out a deep sigh. He closed his eyes and wished away the throbbing pain inside his head. "I've been thinking about my family, my father's sickness. Maybe I should go back and help. Things have changed, Sundi. My family needs me," he explained.

"And I guess I don't need you?" Sundi asked. She felt the pressure too. She knew she was losing him.

"I don't know what you need anymore."

"Well, I guess you'll do what you have to do then, and so will I," she told him. She walked back into the kitchen to finish the dishes and waited for him to follow this time.

A minute or two went by, but it seemed like forever to Sundi. She wanted to go back into the living room. She needed to see what he was doing, to know what he was feeling, but she knew she couldn't. She had to wait.

"What's that supposed to mean?" Chris finally asked, coming to the doorway.

Sundi finished drying the dishes as she spoke. "I'm not going to move to Africa, Chris. My friends, family, and business are here."

"Can't you stop being selfish and think about me for once?"

"I am selfish, Chris. I've always been selfish. You knew that when you married me," Sundi responded dryly.

"And I guess I'm not the progressive man I thought I was," Chris replied. "I can't help it, Sundi. I want the kind of wife I dreamed about as a boy."

Sundi put the dish towel down. "Somebody like that girl Kiara?" she asked curtly.

"This has nothing to do with Kiara! Why don't you see that?

It has everything to do with us!" he shouted, and threw his arms up in the air. "Nothing we planned has happened, Sundi. Our life together is still uncertain. Like the baby we should be anticipating by now!"

"So what, Chris? I'm not pregnant! What is it with you guys and babies?" she yelled with her hand on her hip.

"Children are a reflection of our life together, Sundi. Can't you understand that?"

"And what happens if I get pregnant? Will things change, or do you plan to bring a baby into this mess we call a marriage?"

Chris's look of sincerity suddenly changed. "If I decide to go home, you're welcome to come. I do love you, Sundi," he said. Then he tossed the pack of birth control pills on the counter and walked straight out the front door.

Sundi picked up the pills and swallowed hard. She knew she couldn't explain them away. She tried to think, but it was impossible. Her mind was clouded, and it was hard to separate her thoughts. No matter how she looked at it, her marriage was eroding. It almost seemed an impossible fate to avoid.

Danielle hung up the car phone after saying good-bye to Kim. She missed her daughter much more than she thought she would. She was headed over to Columbia Avenue to meet Lisa and Sundi. It was Adams Morgan Day. Lisa had gotten back from her trip to New Orleans that morning. She called to say she would meet them at Sundi's booth around one. She didn't give Danielle much information about the trip, and that made her suspicious. But it didn't matter, her big sister could never have guessed the news she was about to hear.

The area was crowded with a variety of vendors. There were tables of ceramics, displays of original artwork, and makeshift tents filled with painted glass, handmade pottery, and sculptures. As usual, Sundi's baskets were selling briskly.

"Hey, how's it going?" Danielle asked as she approached the booth.

"Pretty good," Sundi replied, and finished wrapping a basket for a customer.

Danielle sat down in the empty chair behind the table. "Lisa hasn't made it yet?"

"Nope. It's just me and my baskets."

"How's the home front?"

"I think the war is over and my side lost," Sundi replied, then sat down in the chair beside her.

"Don't give up unless it's what you want, Sundi. You know the man loves you," Danielle told her. "And when a man loves you, you can make it work if you pay attention."

Before Danielle could finish her prophetic advice, Sundi got up to help a customer who couldn't decide between a heart-shaped coiled or round woven basket for his girlfriend. Sundi talked him into buying both and returned his change just as Lisa bounced over and held out her half-carat diamond engagement ring and wedding band.

"I got married in New Orleans!" Lisa blurted out, grinning from ear to ear. She watched as their eyes widened and they stared in shock.

Danielle and Sundi gave each other quick glances and forced phony smiles toward Lisa.

Then Danielle asked what Lisa thought was a really stupid question: "To Walter?"

Lisa scowled. Her sister was so ridiculous sometimes. "Who else but Walter?" she responded.

Danielle started to pace around like a tiger fed up with the bars on the cage. She was frightened, upset, and excited at the same time. She opened her mouth to speak, but she didn't know what to say.

"You guys could be happy for me!" Lisa told them. "You both make me sick sometimes. You act like I'm not supposed to have any happiness!"

Sundi stepped in cautiously for Danielle. "That's not true, Lisa, and you know it. We're happy for you. We're just surprised. Right, Dannie?"

Lisa dramatically threw her hand up in the air and took another look at her rings. "It really doesn't matter what you guys think because I'm Mrs. Walter Michael Henderson now!"

"Are you nuts, Lisa? Are you on drugs or something? Who the hell is this guy?" Danielle hollered past her. "I don't know him. You don't even know him!"

Danielle waved her arms in the air frantically, but Lisa didn't care. She twisted her mouth and ran her tongue across her teeth. "Cut the theatrics, Dannie. I'm grown," she said coldly. "I don't need your permission or approval!"

"Obviously you don't know what the hell you need! And what about school?" Danielle continued. "You've had a hard time focusing as it is!"

Sundi motioned for them to lower their voices as she stepped back behind her table to sell two of her Japanese woven baskets to a young couple.

"Lots of people get degrees while they're married," Lisa said in a softer but just as determined tone. "Get off my back about that bullshit!"

"This is crazy, Lisa. How could you rush into something like this?" she asked.

Sundi joined them again, and Lisa noticed that Danielle's voice became strangely calm.

"I just don't understand what's going on with you. I don't know what I'm supposed to do anymore," Danielle said and lowered her head.

Lisa tried to explain, hoping that her sister would try to understand. "I'm finally happy, Dannie. And you don't have to do anything except be happy for me because everything was perfect. Even my horoscope said go for it. So I did."

"You're not serious, Lisa? This has to be *Totally Hidden Videos*, right?" Danielle asked, looking around for a camera.

Sundi had to laugh at her comment, but Lisa stared blankly at them both and waited. She didn't crack a smile. She couldn't believe they would do this to her. This was her time to be happy, and, dammit, they weren't going to deny her this!

"Where is Walter?" Danielle finally asked as if it hurt. "Too chickenshit to be here when you told us?"

"I didn't want him to be here. I knew you would act an ass, just like you're doing!"

"Oh, my ass is not the problem here, little girl," Danielle said, grabbing Lisa's hand and looking at the rings again.

Lisa snatched it back. "I'm not a little girl, even though you

wardrobe was impeccable. He stood about five feet eight, with a round, muscular bald head, complemented by an off-black mustache that filtered down into a short goatee. Roland was the kind of man who had a number of women waiting by the phone for his call.

When Danielle stepped inside the small two-bedroom apartment, only three people had arrived: three women, one white and two black. She didn't know any of the women, but she noticed immediately that they were very young. She figured they must be new contestants in Roland's game of human Jenga. He would build their pile of hopes higher and higher until that moment when everything would come crashing down. Derrick led Danielle into the living room and found a spot on the black leather couch. Then he excused himself and went into the kitchen to get them something to drink.

The football game was in the second quarter. The Houston Oilers led the Minnesota Vikings, 7 to 0. Critics were projecting that both teams had the potential to make it to the Super Bowl.

"All right!" Danielle yelled as she watched Warren Moon avoid a sack and scramble four yards for the first down. On the very next play he threw a forty-five-yard pass to Ernest Givens for a touchdown.

Danielle looked around to see where Derrick was with her drink. She fought a pang of jealousy when she saw that he was talking to one of the women. Her mind processed the situation quickly. The first thing she noticed was that this woman wasn't built like the average white woman. She was well endowed in all the right places. She wore skintight black pants and a black tube top that struggled to hold everything inside. She also observed that Derrick was much too attentive.

The doorbell rang, and Ben, another of Derrick's friends, came in with his girlfriend, who was also white. Danielle had met them several months ago at a party in honor of Ben's promotion.

Danielle got up and walked over toward Derrick and his conversation companion. She smiled at both of them, took her drink from his left hand, and quickly turned to go back to her seat.

"Wait, Danielle, this is Monica," Derrick said quickly.

Danielle turned back around with a blatant air of confidence. "Hi," she said, forcing a smile.

"Monica and I have known each other for years. She's a nurse over at Mercy." Derrick put his arm around Danielle's shoulder and squeezed it. "Monica, this is Danielle."

"It's nice to meet you," Monica said, holding out her hand.

Danielle nodded at Monica, gave Derrick a "sure you right" look, and went back to her seat.

By the time everybody settled in front of the television, it was halftime, so Roland turned down the sound and turned up the stereo. Rap music blared, starting with Salt-n-Pepa, moving on to Digital Underground, and ending with Ice-T. Danielle was fascinated that they didn't seem to mind screaming to hear one another talk.

She got up to refill her drink after watching Roland and the girl he had favored for most of the evening dance frantically in the middle of the living room floor. The girl's short yellow skirt rose higher and higher as she rocked her body to the beat. Roland moved in closer, placing his hand strategically on her behind and thrusting himself into her thigh.

Danielle returned to her seat somehow embarrassed by the whole scene. She motioned for Derrick to move over, but instead he pulled her down on his lap and started gyrating beneath her. Danielle turned various shades of red as she struggled to free herself.

"Let go, Derrick," she pleaded. That seemed to make Derrick's attention get even worse. He rubbed his hand up and down her leg, then up her thigh. As he reached up between her legs, Danielle leaped about two feet in the air. Derrick jumped up behind her, pumping his pelvis to the beat. He tried to pull Danielle out to the middle of the floor, but she fought like a nice-sized trout on a fishing line. He finally gave up, grabbed a pair of sunglasses off the coffee table, and began a wild and erotic dance by himself.

In what proved to be one of those precious Kodak moments, the group started chanting: "Go, Derrick, go, Derrick, go, Derrick, go, Derrick!" And Monica soon took her cue, hopping up to dance with him. The sexual connotations between them pissed Danielle off. She tried not to watch the disgusting public display as they suggestively felt and pushed against each other in the middle of the floor, but she couldn't help it. She felt a headache coming on; she was suddenly uncomfortable and irritated.

She realized that she couldn't compete with the women in the room. She was definitely not twenty-one anymore. Her hips, chest, and stomach had spread. And although she still looked very good, she no longer wore that perfect size eight. She watched as everyone laughed and enjoyed the sensual performance. The louder the audience got, the nastier Derrick seemed to get. Before Danielle realized it, he was standing in front of her again. He threw his left leg in the air and started to hump toward her face. She stood up, turned away, and stumbled outside to get some air.

She sat out on the stairs and listened to the pulsating beat from inside. For the first time Danielle realized she was happy with what she saw in the mirror every morning. She didn't want to be twenty-one again. That was not what this was about.

After what seemed like an eternity, Derrick finally opened the door. "Come on back inside, Dannie. The game is starting," he said in his cool, controlling manner.

"I think I'm ready to go home," she told him without looking up.

"What about the game?"

Danielle stood up and held out her hand. "Derrick, either take me home or give me the keys. You can get a ride with Ben or Roland."

"What's wrong with you tonight, Dannie? I thought we were going to have some fun."

"And this is what you consider fun?"

"I just danced with the girl. We didn't go in the bedroom and fuck!"

"It depends on how you define the word!"

"Well, I'm not ready to go yet. But here," Derrick said, pulling the keys from his pants pocket and handing them to Danielle.

"You're not coming with me?"

"I'm not a puppy, Danielle. I don't want or need a leash!"

She stood up and walked down the stairs and over to the parking lot. She wanted to turn around to see if he was still watching, but her pride wouldn't allow it.

The next morning Danielle's nightmare weekend continued. She anxiously answered the knock on her hotel room door. She felt this way every Saturday morning when Roger brought Kim over or she picked her up. She stood nervously in front of her estranged husband while Kim rushed inside.

"Hi," Danielle said.

"Hi," Roger replied. "Can we talk out here for a minute, Dannie?" He stepped away from the door to let her pass.

Danielle walked outside and shut the door. "What's wrong?" she asked.

Roger looked exhausted. His face was stolid and worn. "I went to Kim's teacher conference yesterday, and her teacher says she's become very mean and cold to other children lately. Apparently last week she hit a little boy in the head with her book, and yesterday she pushed a girl down for no reason. I talked to her, and I thought maybe you could try too."

Danielle sensed the pain in Roger's tender heart. She wanted to reach out to him, but she fought it. She still loved him, but she didn't know what kind of love it was anymore. She needed this time to find herself. "I'll see what I can do," she told him.

They both hesitated, as if they needed to say something more, but Roger finally turned around and walked away. Danielle went into the room and joined Kim.

When she searched her daughter's face, she always saw her mother. Laura was in those small brown eyes, the tiny, curved lips, and the soft, caramel-colored hands. She and Lisa had been in college when their stepfather, Charles, called to tell them that their mother had had a massive heart attack and died instantly. From the day Kim was born, Danielle felt she was somehow a reincarnation of Laura. She looked just like her in all her pictures. And Kim was also what elderly people called an old soul.

She seemed to know and understand things she really shouldn't at her age.

"Mamma, get my colors, please," Kim hollered as she sprawled across the bed. The little girl opened her coloring book and flipped through the pages, looking for just the right picture. Danielle reached in the top dresser drawer and tossed the crayons onto the bed. Then she gathered her courage and sat on the bed beside Kim. Danielle opened another coloring book and picked up a gold crayon.

"Not that page," Kim told her, and took the crayon out of her hand.

"I'm sorry, which one can I do?" she asked.

Kim turned several pages in the book and pointed. "This one."

"Thank you," Danielle said, and started to color the designated page.

She colored the sun a bright gold and the leaves on the tree forest green. Then she chose a reddish brown for the turtle's face and legs. "Kim, can we talk?" Danielle finally asked as she colored the turtle's shell turquoise.

"Uh-huh," Kim replied nonchalantly.

"Your teacher says you've been real mean to the other kids lately, and I just wanted to know why." Danielle lifted her eyes slightly to look at Kim's face.

The child continued to color as she spoke and never changed her expression. "Those kids just made me mad."

Danielle put down the crayon and leaned closer to Kim. "What did they do to make you mad, baby?" she asked.

"They bothered me. Said stupid things," Kim replied.

"Like what, Kim? What did the little boy say to make you hit him with your book?"

Kim set down her crayon and looked directly at her mother. "He wanted to be my friend, Mom, and I told him I didn't want him as a friend. I didn't need any friends. But he kept bothering me." She pulled a purple crayon out of the box and colored the candy circle on the lollipop.

"I still don't understand, Kim. Why didn't you want him as

your friend? We all need as many friends as we can get," Danielle explained and put her hand on Kim's arm. Kim jerked away.

"You don't need friends," she told her. "You don't need me and Daddy," she said, focusing on her picture with added determination.

"Oh . . . that's not true, baby. You know how much I need you. I'm so sorry about all of this," Danielle apologized, hesitant to reach out and touch her again.

Kim continued to color, but she slowly started to go out of the lines. Then she began to mark through the picture with long, broad strokes of blue, pressing harder and harder until the crayon finally broke in half.

"Kim, stop that and look at me."

Kim pulled away again, then kicked the colors and coloring books onto the floor. She scooted out of her mother's reach, up into the center of the bed. "Leave me alone!" she screamed.

"It's me you want to hit, isn't it, baby?" Danielle asked. She crawled onto the bed and knelt in front of her. "Go ahead and hit me, Kim. Come on. Hit me as hard as you can."

Kim sat watching her mother for a long time. She wanted to hit her. But she also wanted to hug her.

"You don't want to hit your friends at school, Kim. You want to hit me. So come on and do it. Get it out of your system," Danielle coaxed her.

Kim didn't need to be told a third time. She bent her tiny body over and bolted straight toward Danielle. She rammed her head into Danielle's shoulder, swinging her arms as hard as she could. Danielle didn't try to protect herself. She embraced the pain. When her daughter finally got tired, she reached out and pulled her into her chest. They held on to each other tightly, eyes closed, hearts pounding.

"I'm so sorry, Kim. I know this is hard on you," Danielle said.

"You're not sorry or you wouldn't be gone," Kim cried.

Danielle felt nauseated. She didn't know what to say to make it right. "We've spent every weekend together since I left, Kim. You know you're the most important person in my life."

"But you're not coming back, are you?"

Danielle took a deep breath. She wanted to feel her blood flow again. "I don't know. I can't promise you that," she told her.

"Then I hate you," Kim said. She looked up into her mother's face when she said it but did not move from her lap. "You and Daddy hate each other, and I hate you both!"

"I love you, Kim, and I know your daddy loves you too. This is not about our love for you. We were having a hard time living together. Your daddy and I needed some time apart to think things through," Danielle explained. "I'll make this up to you, I promise."

She continued to hold Kim close to her. She thought seriously for the first time about her decision, about the choice she'd made. She was confused about love now. Sometimes it was fear, sometimes it was joy, sometimes it was loneliness, sometimes it was happiness, and now it was hate. It all seemed too complicated.

Greeneville, located in the Great Valley of East Tennessee, is surrounded by mountains with scattered thick forests. It was the home of the seventeenth president of the United States, Andrew Johnson, and his house, tailor shop, and the national monument are the most popular tourist attractions. It's a town that's moving slowly into the twenty-first century. Greeneville has had the same mayor for more than twenty years, and his monthly salary recently reached two hundred dollars.

Sundi and Chris arrived in Greeneville on Sunday afternoon. Her cousin Jarod's funeral was to be held on Monday. Sundi had gotten the call late Friday evening that Jarod had been hit by a car and killed. The drunken driver missed a turn and crashed into Ashman's Drugstore, where Jarod had gone to play video games.

Even though the situation had not improved much between them, Chris felt it was his obligation to be with Sundi at a time like this. As they drove past Benson's grocery store and the Greeneville Community Center, where Sundi had played Dorothy in the local version of *The Wiz*, she focused on his face. It was a gentle face, a handsome face, she thought. It was a face that once brought visions of sunny days and chocolate kisses.

They parked in front of the two-bedroom house Sundi had grown up in and got out.

"Come here for a minute," she said, grabbing Chris's hand and pulling him over to the back of the garage. "There's something I have to do first."

Chris instinctively pulled his hand away but followed her.

As they rounded the corner, Sundi smiled to see her playhouse still standing tall. On top of a small hill, it was made of wooden boards and pieces of tin. To Sundi it was a precious memory of her childhood: her castle. To Chris it looked like the shoddy living area in the shantytown where he had grown up: his nightmare. Sundi crawled into the old leaning structure and motioned for him to follow her inside. He hesitated, then continued.

Sundi sat on a wooden crate and cleaned off one for Chris.

"This is my ritual," she told him. "I always come in here for a few minutes first. It's a way to center myself when I get home."

"You played here as a child?"

Sundi dug an old tennis ball out of the dirt. "I loved it in here. Mom and Dad weren't allowed inside, so it was a place for privacy. The only other person who came in here was my best friend, Mitsi. We used to play and dream. We even planned our futures here."

"Where is Mitsi now?" Chris asked.

"She fell in love with Tanner, who lived down the street. They're married with four kids and live about ten blocks from here. We'll have to get over and see them before we leave."

Sundi touched the side of Chris's face with the palm of her hand. "I do hope someday to have a happy home with kids just like Mitsi."

Chris felt numb inside. Sundi seemed to be trying, but he wasn't convinced.

"Sundi!" Mrs. Fransis called from outside the playhouse.

"I'm coming," she answered, and crawled out the front opening.

"Hi, sunshine," Mrs. Fransis said, holding her arms out.

"Hi, Mom," Sundi replied, and hugged her mother back.

Chris emerged from the playhouse.

"Chris, how are you?" Mrs. Fransis asked. She let go of Sundi and collected a hug from him.

"I'm fine, Mrs. Fransis."

"You call me Mom too, and you bet' not call Lester by anything but Dad. You're the son I didn't give him."

Chris and Sundi got their bags out of the car and walked into the house. Mr. Fransis sat in his favorite chair in front of the television, snoring loudly. Sundi stood for a moment and looked around the living room. It never changed. The red and green calico print couch included beige ruffled overhangs and pillows to match. It clashed with Mr. Fransis's favorite chair, which was green and brown striped.

Sundi led Chris to her old room, which now served as a sewing room. The double bed was still covered with her old brightly colored bedspread splattered with shades of pale yellow, lilac, and hot pink.

"Lester, wake up, Sundi and Chris are here!" Mrs. Fransis said, shaking her husband.

"Leave me alone, I'm concentrating," Mr. Fransis told her, and settled back into his nap.

"Let me do it," Sundi said as she entered the room with Chris. She sat on the arm of the chair beside her father and started to sing, "Just a closer walk with the-e. Grant it, Je-sus, if you ple-ase. Daily walking clo-se to the-e. Let it be, dear Lord, let it be."

"That's got to be my baby's beautiful voice!" Mr. Fransis said, opening his eyes.

Sundi gave him a big kiss on the cheek. "Hi, Daddy."

"How long you been here? Florian, why didn't you wake me, woman?" he asked, curling the edges of his mouth down.

"I ain't studdin' you, old man. Chris, you hungry?" Mrs. Fransis asked, turning her attention to her son-in-law.

"Yes, ma'am," Chris answered.

She hurried into the kitchen. "I got some smothered pork

chops and sweet corn on the stove. Come on and get you some. You too, Sundi."

"I'm not really hungry, Mom," Sundi called, and sat on the floor in front of her father.

Chris got up and followed Mrs. Fransis to the kitchen.

"When are you and that boy gonna have my grandson?" Mr. Fransis asked before she could get situated.

"Don't you start too," Sundi warned him. "That seems to be all Chris thinks about."

"There's nothing wrong with him wanting a child, Sundi. All men want to see their future," her dad told her, and slid his hand over her dreadlocks.

"Sometimes the future isn't so bright. Look at poor Aunt Jessie and Uncle Nathan. We're here to bury a child, and he was only ten years old," Sundi said, picking up Jarod's picture.

"And if you ask your Aunt Jessie and Uncle Nathan, I bet they'd tell you they wouldn't change nothing. Except maybe the boy would have been home three days ago instead of at the store."

"So is the driver still alive?"

Mr. Fransis picked up his glass of lukewarm water and took several gulps. "He's in the hospital. Doctors say he's in a coma. They don't know when he's going to wake up."

"I don't see how this could have happened."

"Happens a lot, baby. He was drunk and fell asleep at the wheel. When he missed the turn, his car jumped the curb and hit Jarod as he was coming out of the store."

"Poor Jarod."

"Poor us. We got to stay here on this earth and put up with that kind of craziness. Jarod is gone on to the good life."

"You have a special way of seeing things, Dad," Sundi said, wrapping her arms around him.

"Just remember, I need a grandson to take fishing with me before I leave this earth."

"What if I have a girl?"

"Well, she can come fishing if she learns how to put her own worms on the hook," Mr. Fransis said, grinning.

"Oh, Lester, stop that nonsense," Mrs. Fransis told him as she came out of the kitchen, wiping her hands on a dish towel. "You know you'll put the worm on the hook for that baby just like you did for Sundi."

The next morning Sundi sat at the kitchen table, skimming through the *Greeneville Sun*, waiting for her parents to get ready. She was reading an editorial about absentee ownership in Greeneville. It talked about how locally owned mom-and-pop stores were being run out of business by larger chains.

She smiled as she looked up and saw her mother straighten her father's tie. They had been together so long they just naturally seemed to fit together. She realized that to some extent the marriage she wanted was a lot like theirs. They had both grown up in Greeneville and lived next door to each other for fourteen years. They were childhood buddies, became junior high sweethearts, and they were married two days after their graduation from Greeneville High.

Chris sat across from Sundi, eating homemade biscuits and grits. He raised his head every now and then to glance at the sports page. Mr. Fransis came into the kitchen, grabbed a biscuit, and sat next to his daughter.

"Remind your mother to give you your grandma's recipe for these biscuits before you leave this time."

"I will, Dad. Is Mom ready yet?"

"No, she's trying to decide on shoes, I think."

"Come on, Florian!" Mr. Fransis yelled with a mouth full of biscuit.

"How's everything, Chris?"

"We're doing fine, Mr.—Dad. Just working hard."

"You know a lot about computers, don't you?" Mr. Fransis asked, opening up the front page of the paper.

"I program them. Mainly I set them up so that you can use the information," Chris explained.

"I don't like computers myself. On some TV show they said they gonna put newspapers on computers. I hope it's long after I'm gone."

"Don't talk like that, Dad," Sundi said.

"Why? I'm an old man. I've lived my life. Now, Jarod, that's a tragedy, but me, I'm ready to go whenever the Lord calls."

"He's off on that kick again," Mrs. Fransis said, entering the kitchen. "I should have warned you and Chris before you got here. He's been talking to the Lord quite often lately. Let me call Nathan and tell him we're on our way."

The ride to Franklin's Funeral Home was a short one. It was just down the street past about fifteen houses, a large open field, and a corner shopping mall. Mr. Fransis parked in the lot across the street, and they got out just as Nathan, Jessie, Mira, and Keith drove up. Everyone walked inside together.

As they entered the room, Sundi looked around at the pool of blackness. More than sixty bodies were covered with black silk tunics, black tapered skirts, black embroidered dresses, black single- and double-breasted suits, black buttons, earrings, belts, stockings, purses, gloves, and shoes.

A small wooden casket sat in front of the room with white roses and silver bows around it. The organist played "His Eye Is on the Sparrow" as people took their seats.

Minister Langel entered and stood beside the casket. "This is a sad day in Greeneville," he began. "It's a day when we have to wonder, What kind of God do we trust? It's a day when we have to ask, What's the purpose of this life? And it's a day when we have to feel that the world is a very unfair place to be."

Aunt Jessie cried out in long, painful sobs. Nathan and Keith held each of her shoulders to offer comfort, but it didn't help.

"But it's also a day when we must recognize the power of our Lord God. We must strive to understand each other better and help our family, friends, and neighbors as they struggle through this loss. And we must accept the temporary nature of our lives here on earth."

Aunt Jessie rushed toward the casket, calling Jarod's name.

She leaned over the small brown body, tears tumbling down. Nathan held on to her, and Mr. Fransis jumped up to give him a hand.

When things settled down, Minister Langel continued. "We will all mourn with Nathan, Jessie, and Keith. We've lost our precious Jarod. A beautiful ten-year-old has died a senseless death in our community. But we should also rejoice today because Jarod's soul has gone home to our Father, the Lord Jesus. He now knows what true happiness is."

When he finished, the ushers guided the congregation, row by row, past the casket. Sundi stopped to study the spiritless shell and felt her knees buckle beneath her. As she lost her balance, Chris caught her and held on tight. She stared into the casket and surveyed the small nose and mouth that were not finished growing. She reached inside and held the tiny fingers that lay across his chest. The tears came suddenly. Sundi cried for the dead child in front of her, but she also cried for the child inside her, still waiting to be born.

After the funeral everyone stopped by Jessie and Nathan's to pay their respects. They passed around photo albums that documented Jarod's existence on earth. They cuddled and cajoled Keith, who still had not cried for his younger brother. They ate ham, baked beans, potato salad, bread, peach cobbler, and cakes of all kinds. They drank coffee, tea, Kool-Aid, and soda, with a little hard liquor on the side.

Sundi spent most of the afternoon serving people, cleaning up, and helping with the food. She wanted to stay busy to keep herself from thinking. When the last guest had left and only family remained in the house, Nathan spoke. "I wanted to say something to my family because when I lost my mother and sister a few years ago, you guys became my family. Jarod was my baby boy, and now he's gone. But I know Mom and Sis will take care of him for me and I'll see him again someday. So I just want you all to know how much I love you and how much I appreciate your concern and support."

Nathan held Jessie in his arms, and they cried together. Jessie pulled Keith into the circle. Mira hugged Nathan from behind and put her right arm around Keith. Then Mrs. Fransis joined her two sisters in the circle along with Mr. Fransis and other remaining family members. Mr. Fransis pulled Sundi close to him. Sundi reached for Chris, and they held on to each other tightly.

The ride back to Virginia gave Sundi and Chris a chance to talk, and for the first time they also listened.

After a long silence Chris initiated the conversation. He was willing to give it another try if she was. "I think we need to reconsider our marriage and what it means."

"What does it mean to you?" Sundi asked.

Chris pulled up behind a white station wagon and read the bumper sticker: FAMILY IS ALL THAT COUNTS. "That bumper sticker says it all. Marriage and family are the same for me. You are my family, and I want kids to be part of us. We will love and take care of each other as a family."

"Marriage and family are also important to me, Chris, but first you and I need to learn how to love and take care of each other. Then we can bring children into the world and love and take care of them."

Chris gritted his teeth in anguish. He wondered if she would ever understand. "I love you and want to take care of you, Sundi. If you don't feel the same about me, just say so."

She didn't answer right away. She read the bumper sticker over and over as the car pulled off. "It's not that, Chris. I do love you," she finally replied. "But a baby means we have to be secure with each other, and that's what I'm missing: security."

"How could you not be secure? You don't believe I love you? You think I'm going to leave you? Do you trust me at all, Sundi?" Chris asked the questions one after another, not waiting for her answers. He was confused. He had done the things she wanted him to do for her, he had said the things he knew she wanted to hear, yet she still doubted him.

"I think we need time, Chris. Time to work through our differences."

"Sundi, there's no more time. Tomorrow is not promised. Jarod's death has shown us that."

"It's so hard to believe that his life was stolen like that," Sundi said sadly. "Life is so precious, and we take it for granted every day."

Chris turned onto the interstate, then took hold of Sundi's hand. "The life I want us to create is just as precious. I want us to bring a child, just like Jarod, into the world."

Sundi turned her head slightly and smiled at Chris. She did love him, and she wanted to make him happy. A baby would mean so many changes, but maybe it was something she should reconsider.

"Did you hear me, Sundi?" he asked.

"Uh-huh," she answered.

The sun was shining brightly and almost neutralized a cool September wind. The rain had stopped, leaving only dirty traces of mud along the side of the road. Life is a lot like walking in the mud, Lisa thought. You can try to cover it up, but every step you take shows anyway.

Lisa had left her class at four but didn't get home until six because her car died out twice. Two bikers helped her push the car into a gas station close by the second time. The attendant fiddled around for almost an hour before he admitted he didn't know what was wrong. Then he told her that the mechanic wouldn't be back for another hour. Lisa was only fifteen minutes away from the house. She turned the key and the engine revved up, so she decided to take a chance on getting home.

As she drove up to the old cedar house in Silver Spring, she realized she had to get used to calling Walter's place home. It was a small three-bedroom and one-bath ranch. Walter had told her she could change anything she wanted, so the first change was to move his weight room out of the third bedroom and into the garage. Lisa then set up her office in that bedroom. She had neatly arranged her computer desk, a worktable, the couch, and the two butterfly chairs. It was crowded but comfortable. Next they hired a contractor to cut a door from their bedroom into the back of the hall closet so that Lisa could have her own closet space.

The final change she planned was an extension in the kitchen area. It was a tiny room, too cramped to move around in, so she envisioned knocking out a wall and turning the back porch into a breakfast nook.

As she pulled into the small gravel driveway and got out of the car, she heard someone call her name. She turned around to see Roger walking toward her. They smiled and hugged. Lisa was actually glad to see him.

"You look great," Roger said, holding on to her left hand.

"Thanks. You look . . ." Lisa hesitated, not knowing how to lie.

"It's okay. I know I need to get it together," Roger said self-consciously.

"Come on inside," she told him.

As they walked into the living room, she set her briefcase down and headed for the kitchen. "How about something to drink? I have apple juice, water, and tea."

"Just water, please," Roger said as he sat down on the couch.

Lisa brought a glass of water from the kitchen, handed it to him, and sat down on the love seat across from him.

"You remembered I don't like ice," Roger told her after taking a big swallow.

"Of course I remembered," Lisa said. "So how are you, Roger?"

He shook his head from side to side. "I'm okay. My partners think I'm crazy. My child probably thinks I'm crazy, but I'm really okay."

Lisa laughed. "You're not crazy," she said. "Dannie's the crazy one."

"That sister of yours is truly stubborn!" Roger admitted, then set his glass down on the coffee table.

"I know. I grew up with her," Lisa sympathized.

"I miss her, Lisa. I haven't loved anyone else for such a long time," he said, fighting the distress. He leaned forward, hesitated, then spoke again. "I'm sorry I just lied, because I've always loved you, Lisa."

Lisa cringed at his statement. She felt strange. She wanted to hold him in her arms and tell him it would be okay, but she didn't dare. His presence now evoked too many memories.

"You've got to get on with your life, Roger," she eventually said. Then she anxiously picked up *Black Pearls* from the coffee table and flipped through the pages.

"I'm doing that, Lisa, but it doesn't seem to help," he said, and got up. He paced back and forth across the floor a few times, then sat next to her on the love seat.

"You have to change the things around you," she told him, shifting her weight to the opposite side of the couch, and putting the book down between them.

Roger picked up the book and opened it. He read a quote by Barbara Jordan out loud. " 'If you're going to play the game properly you'd better know every rule.' Guess I didn't know the rules when it came to your sister."

"You need to stop worrying about her and do something for yourself. Go to new places, meet new people," she pleaded. "I felt the same way you do when Kirby left. But it'll get easier when you stop fighting and move on."

Suddenly Roger laid his right hand on top of hers. Lisa froze as he squeezed it. She wanted to pull her hand away but couldn't. "Maybe I should have married you," he told her.

Lisa stood up and pulled her hand away. These were feelings she wasn't ready for—not now.

"Do you ever think about that night?" Roger continued.

Lisa didn't respond, but she noticed for the first time that Roger's receding hairline was much wider and the gray in his beard was whiter than before. She had been in love with Roger for so long it was hard to let go. But he had always been her sister's husband, and now she had a husband of her own.

"I'll never forget that night, Lisa," Roger assured her.

"I used to think about it sometimes," she said. "But it doesn't matter, Roger, because you love Danielle and I love Walter."

"I know," he acknowledged. "I honestly didn't expect anything to happen. I just needed to make sure you knew how I felt," he explained.

Lisa's eyes dropped to the floor; then she looked back up at him. "I know," she responded softly.

As Lisa watched Roger pull away, she thought about how special her love for him really was. For a long time he had been her hero, he had been her secret love. He had come to her rescue once when they were in school.

Lisa had gone out on a date one Saturday night. The guy she was with got sloppy drunk, and he and his friends started talking negatively about women. When he groped at Lisa's breasts in front of his friends, she screamed, pushed him away, and ran out of the club.

It was late, about two o'clock in the morning, as Lisa headed toward the bus stop. A car full of guys drove past, whistling and yelling obscenities. When the car stopped about a block ahead of her and two of the guys got out, Lisa turned and ran as fast as she could. She ducked into the Sambo's restaurant on the corner despite the fact that black students on campus were boycotting the restaurant because of its racist name.

Danielle and Sundi were on a trip to Richmond to meet with several shops about Sundi's baskets. Since Lisa had a date Saturday night and a test on Monday, she didn't go. She couldn't think of anybody else to call except Roger. He and Danielle had only been dating a couple of months. Roger heard her frantic voice, got up out of bed, and came right down to get her.

He drove her back to her dorm, and they sat in his car, an old black and white Mercury Monterey, and talked for a while. Roger was so much older and more mature than the men in her life. He became her ideal man. She mainly remembered how good he smelled that night. They kissed; it was soft, passionate, and filling. Then, somehow they ended up at a small hotel off campus. His hands caressed every inch of her body, and they made the most wonderful love. It never happened again. But sometimes when she got lonely, Lisa would remember that night and secretly wish he were hers.

She knew that was why she fell so hard and fast for Walter. The feeling he awoke inside her was the same feeling that she had felt for Roger that night. Walter was the second man in her life who could create rainbows in her heart.

Later that evening Lisa waited in the living room for Walter to finish dressing. She carefully examined his ugly blue and gold striped couch and love seat and decided they had to go. She had been dressed for fifteen minutes, while Walter was still busy deciding on the appropriate sports jacket. They say women are particular about how they dress, she thought, and called to him, "Hurry up, Walter!" But she didn't dare go into the bedroom to help because her choices would only confuse him and he would take even longer.

Lisa flicked the television channels, trying to avoid watching the news. It was so depressing. Nothing but murder, death, and more murder. She didn't see how it was that different from soap operas. You could go away for a month, come back, and the same thing would be happening; only the names and places might change.

She finally got tired of waiting and went into the bedroom. She walked in just as Walter was taking a long drag from a joint. She came up behind him and tickled his sides. He choked and coughed from the weed and fell over onto the bed. Lisa giggled and turned to run, but he grabbed her leg and pulled her over on top of him. Walter flipped over and held Lisa down against the bed. With his legs bent around her like a grasshopper, he secured his hold.

"Get up, Walter," she pleaded, still laughing. "You're wrinkling my blouse."

Walter didn't move. He took the joint and placed the fire delicately inside his mouth.

"Walter, I don't want any of that."

"Sure you do," he said as he cupped his hands over her face and blew as hard as he could. Lisa inhaled most of the smoke and started to cough. Her eyes watered, and it was difficult to get air for a minute. Walter laughed as he rolled off her and patted her on the back. She frowned at him, got up, and went into the bathroom. She ran cold water and drank swallows of it from her cupped hands.

"You all right?" he asked, standing in the doorway.

"I told you to stop!" she spit out, patting her face with a wet towel.

"You know you love it," he said, reaching to hug her. Lisa pushed him away and began repairing her damaged makeup.

Walter shrugged and went back into the bedroom.

For a moment Lisa thought about how natural this routine was becoming in their lives. They didn't get high every day, but on many weekends and for lots of events it was included in their habitual activities just like combing their hair. It wasn't that they were junkies out on the street shooting up or anything, she rationalized. They were both educated, intelligent people with good jobs.

She took her taupe silk blouse off as she walked back into the bedroom. While she ironed out the creases, she raised her head several times to watch Walter finally decide on his blue suit jacket. He winked at her, and she rolled her eyes but couldn't stop the smile that followed. Lisa loved Walter more than any other man in her life. Nobody had ever put her happiness first like he did. She put her blouse back on and buttoned it over her black lace teddy. She couldn't believe how satisfied she felt as she took Walter's hand and pulled him out the door. They were late, and they were the guests of honor.

Danielle and Sundi threw a great party. As Lisa and Walter drove up, they could hear music blasting from inside the large recreation room. The place was obviously packed because they couldn't find a parking space. Walter drove around back and down to the end of the winding drive. All the regular spaces were taken, so he drove up over the curb and made a space on the grass.

They walked up to the front door arm in arm, knocked, and stood waiting for someone to open it. As Lisa tried to straighten Walter's tie, he pulled her to him and messed it back up. Danielle finally opened the door.

"Hi, Dannie," Lisa said, smiling as if she had just won the lottery.

"Hi, Lisa," Danielle responded, then looked at Walter, sizing him up quickly. "Hello, Walter."

"Wally, please," he said, and held out his hand. "It's nice to finally meet you officially." Danielle took his hand briefly and twisted her lips to the side.

"Walter, you remember my big sis, Danielle," Lisa said smugly, stepping past her and pulling Walter along. When Lisa and Walter entered the room, everybody greeted and congratulated them. Lisa grabbed Walter's arm and continued to cheese. She wanted everyone to know this wonderful, good-looking man was all hers.

"Not bad, huh?" she whispered to Sundi.

"He's great. You guys hungry?" Sundi asked, and looked him over.

"No. Not right now," Lisa answered as she waved hello to Andre, Raquel, Jackie, and Tony at the bid whist table.

Lisa was surprised to see Andre and Raquel together. The last time she heard, they'd broken up. She and Raquel had worked together in the congressman's office. Lisa also noticed that Jackie had lost a few pounds. She hadn't seen her and Tony since they moved from Gaithersburg to Baltimore a couple of years ago.

Red, yellow, and blue streamers hung from the ceiling, with balloons everywhere. A computer banner that hung on the back wall read: HAPPINESS USUALLY SNEAKS THROUGH A DOOR YOU DIDN'T EVEN KNOW YOU LEFT OPEN. That was probably Danielle's contribution, Lisa thought.

"Congratulations!" James yelled as he and Dorthea made their way toward the couple.

"Daddy, you made it!" Lisa said, hugging him sincerely. "Hi, Dorthea," she added, giving her a hug too.

"Your sister told me the good news. This must be the guy," James said, holding his hand out to Walter.

As Walter shook his hand, Lisa made introductions. "This is Walter, Dad. Walter, this is my father, James, and his friend Dorthea from Chicago."

Lisa heard her name called in a tiny voice, and the crowd parted so that Kim could get through to hug her.

"Hi, Kimi. You having fun?" Lisa asked, picking her up and giving her a big kiss.

"Stop, Aunt Lisa," Kim said, smearing lipstick across her cheek.

"What did I tell you about wiping off my kisses?" Lisa asked, putting her down to tickle her. Kim giggled and ran off to find her mother.

Once Walter met everybody, he headed over to the bid whist table. Lisa didn't even know he played the game.

"I think I'd like to send you guys on a trip to *Boston*," Andre told his opponents. He loved to talk shit at the table when he was winning.

"We'll visit you in Baltimore, sucka, . . . but this one's mine," Tony replied, slamming down the big joker and taking Andre's small one.

"I thought— You need to learn how to play!" Andre yelled at his partner, Raquel, trying to blame the mistake on her.

"If she don't have the cards, she can't play the cards," Jackie teased, throwing out the king of hearts and taking Andre's queen.

"Watch the board," Andre screamed at Raquel again.

"It's just a game, Andre. Get a grip!" Raquel yelled back.

"Now for the set book," Tony said, slapping the table with his ace of spades.

"Not today," Raquel told him, cutting it with a trump and taking the book.

"Saints be praised!" Andre hollered. He jumped up and gave Raquel a high five with both hands. "What a partner!" he added.

Lisa turned her attention to her other guests. She hadn't seen a lot of these people in a long time. It made her realize how secluded her life had truly become since she met Walter. Some of the folks who came Lisa didn't consider friends. She knew they only showed up to meddle. To see the man Lisa Allen had married after only a few months. To see if they could confirm the rumors: Was she desperate? Was it on the rebound from Kirby? Was she crazy and out of control? But Lisa didn't care what they thought. For the first time in a long time she was happy. And happiness was such a small part of life that when she found it, she knew she had to grab it with both hands and hold on as long as she could.

When a popular old dance tune came on by James Brown, the middle of the floor suddenly became crowded with folks doing the funky chicken, the four corners, and the bump. Lisa got a glass of white wine and sat on the couch, away from the activity.

Sundi joined her. "I've been waiting for the crowd to scatter so we could talk. How you doing?" she asked.

"Okay. Just a little tired, but I can't complain," Lisa said, glancing over at Walter.

"You guys settled in yet?"

"Yeah, it's a nice house. But I still have to do some serious interior decorating. It definitely needs my touch."

"Good taste is a rare commodity around here. Look at those shoes Muriell got on."

"Girl, quit!" Lisa said, nudging Sundi with her elbow between laughs.

"How's school coming?"

"You know I postponed my comps till the end of the month?" Lisa replied.

Sundi nodded her head.

"Well, I'm just trying to prepare now as best I can. Walter says I should stop teaching next year and spend some concentrated time finishing everything."

"What do *you* want to do?"

Lisa had to think about the question for a minute because it surprised her. She didn't really know what she wanted anymore. She had started the degree because something was missing in her life, but now that she had Walter, she honestly didn't know. Her life felt complete.

"It seemed like I was lost until he came along," Lisa finally said, taking a sip of wine.

Sundi observed her carefree manner for a moment. "But that doesn't answer my question."

"I can't answer the question, Sundi. But I can tell you what I don't want. I don't want to lose him. I like who I am when I'm with him, and I can't think of anything better than that right now. It's just not okay to be alone anymore. Do I sound crazy?"

"No, it's not crazy. But, Lisa, don't forget that you're a wonderful person with or without him. That's a battle we all have to fight on a daily basis."

Lisa hesitated. "Remember in *Mahogany* when Billy Dee went to see Diana Ross in Europe?"

"Sure. That was a good movie."

"When he left, he told her that success is *nothing* unless you have someone you love to share it with. I know what he meant by that now. That's how I feel."

Ruth and her son, Arthur, came over and stood in front of them.

"I sure miss you living next door," Ruth told Lisa as she stood up and they hugged. "Congratulations!"

"Thanks. I miss you guys too. How's the old neighborhood?"

"About the same. The guy living in your old place seems nice."

"What about college, Arthur? Did you decide?"

Arthur lifted his head but continued bouncing with the beat. "I'm going to Morgan State. I thought about what you said, and I'd like to try a black college first. I'll get my master's at one of the mainstream colleges."

"Great! Stay near home and close to Mom," Lisa said, and gave him a big hug too.

Jackie and Tony lost the bid whist game. They got up as Andre held his fists together high in the air and cheered for himself. "Winner and still champion," he announced to the room.

"I need a partner so I can whoop up on these chumps . . . I mean, champs," Walter said, looking around the room as he spoke.

Derrick volunteered: "I'm in, man!"

Andre added his ritual prayer: "Thank you, Lord, for two new fools."

"Just deal the cards," Derrick replied, handing the deck to Raquel.

"Having fun, ladies?" Danielle asked as she joined Sundi and Lisa on the couch.

"It's great!" Lisa told her. "I really do appreciate the effort. Thanks." She knew Danielle was trying hard to deal with her newfound independence, and she loved her for it.

Sundi looked up to see Chris motion to her from across the room. She gave Lisa and Danielle a disgusted look and dragged herself over to him. As she reached him, he turned and spoke to Sylla in Yoruba and they both laughed.

"Don't do that," Sundi threatened.

"Could you get us a couple of beers?" Chris asked.

Sundi wrinkled her brow and glared at him. "Why can't you get them, Chris?"

"Sundi, these are your friends." He spoke in his native language again to Sylla, and that made Sundi angrier.

"I asked you not to do that."

"He just told me how much he loves you," Sylla teased.

"Shut up, Sylla!" Sundi said aggressively.

"Don't talk to him like that!" Chris ordered. "I was just playing. What's wrong with you?"

"I don't want to be played with tonight, okay?" Sundi answered, rolling her eyes.

"Could you just get the beers, please?"

Sundi stomped out of the room and into the kitchen.

Derrick and Walter were no match for Andre and Raquel. They were up quickly when Raquel made a five no-trump on the first hand.

Andre continued to brag. "Come sit and play, but don't plan to stay, 'cause I'm the king of bid whist, *your majesty Andre*."

Derrick and Walter talked quietly for a minute and then disappeared into the back storage room. Walter pulled out a small container of cocaine, and they each snorted a couple of lines.

Danielle got up and headed for the kitchen. She walked in on Sundi as she stopped short of the door, grinning.

"Shhhhh," Sundi said quietly. She shook the two beers up vigorously, and Danielle laughed.

Sundi tried not to smile as she walked calmly into the living room and handed a beer to each of them. Danielle stood in the doorway and watched.

"Here you go, fellas, enjoy," she said, stepping back as they opened the cans. Beer sprayed everywhere, all over Sylla's brown suit and Chris's blue sweater. Simultaneously they both jumped up and yelled obscenities, while Sundi burst into laughter.

"Just playing, honey," she said coyly as Chris and Sylla rushed into the kitchen to clean up.

Danielle headed back to the storage room to get a mop to clean up the mess. She tried to open the door but found it was locked. She heard movement inside and knocked. She was shocked when the door opened and Walter and Derrick stepped out. Derrick kissed her on the cheek as they hurried past. When Danielle stepped into the room and looked around for the mop, she noticed specks of white powder on the table. She picked up a few of the specks with her fingertip and tasted them.

She suddenly appeared in the living room, moving like a subway train. She grabbed Lisa's right arm and jerked her outside.

Sundi noticed and followed.

Danielle screamed at Lisa as the door slammed shut, "He's a goddamn drug addict!"

"No, he's not. He just does it sometimes. So do I. So what!"

"What's going on?" Sundi asked, joining them outside.

"Walter's a fucking drug addict," Danielle told her, totally ignoring Lisa's explanation.

"Why do you say that?" Sundi asked.

"Because I just caught him in the storage room snorting cocaine with Derrick."

Lisa continued to defend him. "That doesn't make him a drug addict." But Danielle didn't listen.

"And you do it too? What the fuck's wrong with you, Lisa?"

"Derrick was with him! Is he a drug addict?" Lisa snapped back.

"I didn't marry Derrick," Danielle responded with much attitude.

"You're tripping, Dannie," Lisa told her. She wasn't going to argue. This was her night, and Danielle was not going to ruin it.

"Would you tell her something?" Danielle asked Sundi, as if there were something different she could say.

"Yeah. You guys tell me something!" Lisa dared them. She stepped back and moved her neck in a circular motion. "Tell me how it feels to rob the cradle, Dannie. And, Sundi, when are you going back to Africa to share your man? I'm sick of you guys treating me like I'm stupid just because I'm the youngest. I'm living *my* life, and both of you need to get that shit straight! If you can't be happy for me, then that's too goddamn bad! Come on! I'm waiting! *Somebody tell me something!*"

All Lisa remembered as she turned around and stormed back inside was the stunned look on their faces. She'd finally had the chance to tell them what she thought, and it felt good. Who do they think they are? she thought. Shit, I'm grown. She was tired of playing bullshit roles with people, especially her sister.

An old proverb popped into her mind: He who talks too much of happiness summons grief. So Lisa walked over to a wooden coffee table and knocked on it quietly three times. She wasn't going to let evil spirits become jealous of her happiness and take it all away.

"Is everything okay?" James came up behind her and asked.

"Everything is great," Lisa answered, forcing a smile. "I'm hungry. Come on, let's get something to eat."

Outside, Danielle continued to rant and rave to Sundi about her discovery.

"Well done, Mamma Danielle," Sundi finally told her.

"That explains her weight loss and how she doesn't seem to care about school anymore!" Danielle said, not giving up.

"So would a diet and the fact that school is no longer the most important thing in her life," Sundi rebutted.

"I knew something was wrong with him. I just knew it," Danielle said.

"Look, I don't get a real good feeling either, but what can you do?" Sundi asked. "She's in love. You remember what that's like, Dannie?"

"If it makes you this stupid, I don't think I want to remember."

"Well, you should remember. You recently left your husband because of it."

Danielle gave her a crooked look. "I didn't leave Roger for Derrick. My marriage was in trouble long before Derrick came along."

"Whatever you say," Sundi said, and motioned toward the door. "We should probably get back inside."

"Yeah, let's open the gifts so this night can be over soon."

Lisa watched Danielle and Sundi come back inside. As they walked over to the table of gifts, she spotted Walter sitting on the gray love seat in the corner, set her plate down, went over to him, and wiggled onto his lap in true defiance.

"We're ready to open the gifts, everybody," Sundi announced to the crowd, grabbing a couple of boxes and handing several others to Danielle.

"Gather around. Gifts for the newlyweds," Danielle said.

Danielle and Lisa exchanged quick, awkward looks as Danielle handed her baby sister a small silver box. Sundi gave Walter a larger box wrapped in white paper. Lisa tore into her box to find a small framed picture of herself and Danielle as kids. It was during Easter, Lisa remembered. She was about eight or nine years old, and they were standing next to each other. Her hair was short because the day before, Danielle had cut a big hunk out of the top playing hairdresser. Their mother had taken Lisa to the beauty shop to have it trimmed. Lisa smiled when she noticed the matching blue cotton brocade dresses they'd chosen that Easter together.

She looked up at Danielle and had to smile.

"Thanks," she said under her breath, knowing Danielle could hear her.

"Hey, Lisa, look," Walter hollered, and pulled out a hand-woven African mudcloth blanket.

"That's great. Who's it from?"

Walter read the card: "Chris and Sundi."

"Thanks," Lisa said, smiling at Sundi too.

As Lisa tore into another box, the door opened, and everyone was surprised to see Roger walk in. His beard was neatly trimmed, and his jacket was sharply pressed. Danielle hesitated for a moment, then moved toward him.

Kim raced over and grabbed his leg. "Daddy," she said.

Roger bent down and kissed her on the forehead. "Hi, baby."

"Roger, you should leave," Danielle said, trying to steer him back toward the door.

"Come on, Kim, let's go get some ice cream," Sundi said as she took Kim's hand and led her into the kitchen.

Roger hesitated. "Leave? This is Lisa's party. Why should I leave, Dannie? Lisa is just as special to me as she is to you."

"Roger, please don't do this!" Danielle pleaded.

"Do what? I brought Lisa a gift. Where is she?" Roger asked, ignoring her. He worked his way through the group and over to Lisa and Walter. He handed Lisa a small, beautifully wrapped gold gift box. "Here, Lisa. I wish you much happiness."

Roger held out his hand to Walter. "Good luck, man."

Lisa opened the box. Inside was a gold heart-shaped clock.

"Thank you, Roger. It's beautiful."

"It's for the good times," Roger said, giving her a big hug. She hugged him back. She felt so sorry for him. Here in front of her stood a genuinely great guy, and her sister was too stupid to see how rare and wonderful he was.

Danielle tried to pull Roger toward the door again but had little luck. Derrick jumped up to assist, but Roger pushed him back down onto the love seat.

"Get off me, boy!" Roger told him.

"I can handle it, Derrick," Danielle added.

Roger stopped fighting Danielle for a moment and looked hard at Derrick, then back at her. "I take it that's your new man," he said sarcastically.

"He's a friend," Danielle responded automatically.

They both stood on display in the center of the floor. Danielle seemed nervous, an unusual posture for her. She looked at the ground, then fumbled with her watch.

Roger looked around the room at all the faces. He stopped to smile at Lisa again, then walked out the door.

Danielle followed Roger into the hallway and watched him drive off. Derrick walked up behind her as she shut the door.

"Why didn't you tell him?" he asked.

"Tell him what?" she replied, annoyed.

"Were you ashamed to say I'm your man?" Derrick shouted at her. "I want to know, Dannie."

"Derrick, please," she said, waving him away, but Derrick stepped in front of her. Danielle let out a loud sigh. "It wasn't any of his business, okay?"

"What about the people inside? Who do they think I am, Dannie?" Derrick asked, standing his ground.

"A friend, Derrick, okay?" Danielle answered, and tried to move past him, again without success.

"Just a friend? Why don't you tell them the truth?"

"Look, I don't feel like dealing with this shit tonight." She tried to step around him, but he pulled her back.

"I hate it when you put me off like that, Danielle."

"Oh, we gonna talk about what we hate. When did you start doing drugs?"

"Why? Do I need my *mamma's* permission?"

Danielle glared at him intensely. "I don't like it, Derrick!"

"Well, I don't really give a damn what you like. I can't do nothing to please you anyway."

Just then Lisa opened the door and interrupted their argument. "Oh . . . sorry . . . Just checking to make sure everything is okay," she said.

"It's fine, thanks," Danielle answered, pushing past Derrick.

"Hey, Mom, look what Sundi found," Kim said, rushing toward Danielle with a tiny troll doll in her hand.

"Hey! That's an ugly doll, isn't it?" Danielle told her, taking the doll and pulling its hair back to examine the exaggerated face.

"He's not ugly. That's the way trolls are supposed to look," Kim said, snatching the doll away. "Where's Daddy? He knows all about trolls," Kim continued, looking around the room for Roger.

"Your dad had to go home. You can show him tomorrow. Go show Grandpa the troll."

Kim rushed off calling her grandpa's name.

"You gonna be okay?" Lisa asked her sister sincerely.

"I'm gonna be just fine," Danielle replied.

The last week in September Lisa wrote her comprehensive exams. She answered six questions from communication theory to cultural history over a one-week period. While she waited to get her results back, she tried to work on her dissertation proposal, but it just wouldn't come together.

Lisa knew it was going to be one of those days when she woke up that Wednesday morning. She saw too many signs of trouble. Walter had left a hat on the bed, and for superstitious souls that meant a fight in the house. Then she found a dead bee in the bathroom and spilled a glass of milk in the kitchen. Both meant more bad luck. After she repeated her morning affirmations, she settled in to work on the proposal. She was rigorously typing when the computer screen went blank.

"Oh, God, no, not today!" Lisa yelled, looking at the wall where the plug had pulled loose from the worn socket, again. This was the third time this month, and Walter had promised to fix it weeks ago. "Dammit, Walter," she mumbled.

She plugged the computer back in and tried to start over, but her mind went on vacation. She was beginning to hate school. She was sick of her program. She wanted it to be over! She wanted to get on with her life. She needed to enjoy an evening in front of the television, cuddled up under Walter without feeling guilty. She hoped to have babies and be able to spend time loving them.

"Forget it!" she finally decided, throwing her arms in the air. She took a deep, calming breath and glanced at the clock. It was two-thirty, and Walter wasn't due home until six.

She ambled into the kitchen because she hadn't eaten yet and realized she was hungry. She stood for a long time in front of the refrigerator with the door open. She had to laugh because that was the one vivid picture she had of her father before they left Chicago. He hated it when they stood in front of the refrigerator, holding the door open, trying to decide what they wanted. He would pull a dime out of his pocket and say: "You see this dime? That's how much the man takes out of my pocket every minute you stand there with that door open!"

Nothing really looked good, but Lisa finally threw a bag of light buttered popcorn into the microwave. She turned on the television and listened to the *Rolonda* show while ironing her jeans in the bedroom. These are some stupid-ass people, Lisa thought. But she couldn't stop herself from watching as Rolonda explained how the five men on the show were competing for the dog of the year award. Each man took a turn bragging about how badly he had treated the woman in his life while the audience both cheered and booed. Then several of the women came on to verify these stories, some admitting that they were still seeing the men. Lisa couldn't believe these people were on national television telling everybody that crazy shit! They needed to get a clue—buy one or something! She was about to force herself to change the channel, when she heard Walter's keys in the door. She hurried into the living room to meet him.

"What are you doing home so early?" she asked. He'd been drinking or smoking or both . . . she couldn't tell anymore.

"Those assholes suspended me," he said, throwing his jacket across the hall chair and kicking off his shoes.

"For what?" Lisa already knew, but she had to ask anyway.

"Nothing . . . don't worry about it," he answered, storming into the bedroom.

Lisa followed him. "Suspended for what, Walter?" She stood

in the doorway, waiting for an explanation. Finally she had to
repeat her question a third time: "What's going on, Walter?"

"They did a surprise drug test this morning. Don't worry, I
called my lawyer. I'm gonna sue those muthafuckas."

"You went to work high?"

"No. I guess it's from a couple of days ago."

"How long?"

"Just don't worry about it, baby," Walter said as he lay on
the bed and reached for the television remote control.

Lisa snatched it away from him. "How long are you suspended for, Walter?"

He walked into the bathroom but didn't shut the door. "A
week, a month, I don't know. I just gotta clean out my system
and go back and test negative."

Lisa stood in the bathroom doorway. "That's not gonna
work! What if they do another surprise test?" she said in a raised
voice.

"Can't a man pee in peace?" he yelled at her.

Lisa stepped back into the bedroom and slammed the door
shut. She waited impatiently for him to come out.

The toilet flushed, and the door swung open. "You talk like
I'm an addict or something!" he shouted at her.

"Walter, maybe this is an omen. I've been thinking that
maybe we should stop the drug thing anyway," she told him
calmly.

"Well, it's good to know you can do the thinking for both of
us. Thank you!" he responded caustically. Then he hopped onto
the bed and propped his head up on several pillows.

"I didn't mean it like that," Lisa explained, backing off. She
sat on the edge of the bed next to him.

"I know you never mean anything like that," Walter pushed.

"This ain't about me, Walter. What are you going to do?"

"Look, just because you're working on a Ph.D. don't mean
you've got to know everything. Let me take care of me, okay?"
Walter stiffly took one of the pillows from behind his head and
put it over his face.

Lisa wanted to ignore him, but she couldn't. She had to

know. After all this was her life too. "So what do you think about quitting the drug thing, both of us?" she asked again.

"I ain't thinking about nothing right now except getting some rest," he said in a muffled voice from under the pillow.

Lisa pulled at the pillow. "Walter, don't do this. We need to talk!"

He let go after a brief tug-of-war. "I know what I'm gonna do. I'm gonna sing," he told her. "I feel like singing. Is that okay with you, Lisa?" Walter started to sing "I've Been Working on the Railroad" at the top of his voice, making up words as he went along.

"I been workin' on the railroad, all the goddamn day. I been working on the railroad, just wasting my life away. Can't you hear the whistle blowin', blowin' smoke up my ass. Hum hum hum hum hum hum hum hum hum, hum hum hum hum hum."

Lisa never got an answer to her question about quitting the drug thing. But his suspension lasted only two weeks. Walter tested negative and started back to work on the same day. She knew he wasn't doing it as often now, so at least that was something. They moved back into their life together, accepting each other, faults and all.

A four-day project took Walter to Baltimore, where he needed to update several of the accounting files. Lisa scheduled the contractors for the kitchen project while he was gone, so she could surprise him when he returned.

This was the first time she had been left in the house alone. Her excitement had very little to do with the fact that she was renovating the kitchen. As a matter of fact, a new kitchen, cooking, and cleaning didn't thrill her at all. Lisa had never been interested in a traditional domestic life. The way she looked at it, if a man wanted someone to cook and clean, he needed to hire somebody. If he wanted someone to enhance the quality of his life, she just might be able to help and she knew she could make up in the bedroom what she lacked in the kitchen!

D and R Contractors was a small company. When they arrived, she discovered that Dennis and his brother, Ross, were partners, and they did all the work themselves. She hung around and watched most of the time. She wanted to see the transformation for herself.

First they moved the stove, refrigerator, and dishwasher out into the hallway. Then they took the old tile off the kitchen and back porch floors. Later that afternoon they were ready to tear out the wall. Dennis found the foundation beams and marked the area to be removed. He picked up a sledgehammer and turned to Lisa.

"You wanna take the first shot?" he asked.

Lisa paused. "Sure," she replied. "What do I do?"

"Just grip the sledgehammer with both hands and hit the wall inside these markers."

Lisa stepped up to the wall, grabbed the handle, and lifted the sledgehammer. It was heavier than she thought, so when she pulled it back to take a big swing, she found herself struggling to keep it on target. She threw her whole body into it, and the sledgehammer hit the center of the wall, but Lisa tumbled into the wall right behind it. Dennis and Ross both rushed in to help.

"You okay?" Dennis asked, taking the sledgehammer from her clinging hands.

"Yeah. That thing is heavy," Lisa said, smiling.

"I guess we should have warned you," Ross added.

"Well, move back, little lady. Let me try," Dennis told her, stepping sideways toward the wall. He eyed the spot where the plaster was cracked. He took a long hard swing, and this time most of the plaster caved into the other side, leaving a large, uneven hole.

Lisa got out of the way, while Dennis and Ross took turns with the sledgehammer until only the frame remained. They quit for the day about four o'clock but were back at seven the next morning. When they returned, Lisa had already cleaned up the mess on the floor. Ross gave it a final cleaning, then started laying the new tile floor in the breakfast nook. Lisa had picked out a lilac and tan abstract pattern that matched the almond appliances nicely.

Dennis evened up and covered the edges of the wall frame

with plasterboard. Then he replaced the screens on the back porch with combination storm windows. On the third day they primed the walls in both rooms in the morning and started putting on the first coat of paint that afternoon. On the final day they put on a second coat of paint, moved the stove, refrigerator, and dishwasher to their new spots, and cleaned up the last of their mess.

Bachman's Furniture delivered the new oak veneer dinette set that evening just before Walter came in from Baltimore. When he opened the door, Lisa was sitting quietly in the breakfast nook, drinking tea.

"Hey, baby," she said, jumping up to give him a kiss. "Look, it's done! What do you think?"

"What the fuck!" Walter said in an irritated voice.

"What's wrong?" Lisa asked, confused by his response.

"How the hell am I going to pay for this, Lisa?" Walter asked, and dropped his suitcase.

"We had talked about this, Walter. You said the money was in the bank."

"Well, it's not in there anymore," he shouted on his way to the living room.

Lisa was dumbfounded. It seemed every time she tried to do something good lately, it was shoved back in her face. "What happened to the money?" she asked as she leaned against the wall and crossed her arms, bracing herself for the argument that she knew was coming.

"Management said I needed to check into a treatment center by next Monday if I want to keep my job." Walter didn't look at Lisa while he spoke. He sat on the edge of the sofa with his head in his hands.

Lisa walked over to the couch and sat down. She didn't respond to his announcement right away. She stared past Walter and out of the window.

"Don't you have something to say?" he asked, raising his head.

"Like what, Walter? What should I say?"

He stood up and walked over to the patio doors. "Nothing . . .

While I was in Baltimore, I went to a center and talked to the doctors." His eyes were red, and his lips trembled. "I tried, baby, I really did."

"Don't lie, Walter. You didn't try," she said, correcting him.

"How could you say that?" he asked as if he were offended.

"Hiding it from me is not trying, Walter. I knew you hadn't stopped, but I pretended just like you did," she told him. She got up and walked over to him. "You're high right now, aren't you?"

"I just finished off a blunt in the car. It's no big deal."

"It is a big deal, Walter! Don't you get it? They're sending you to a treatment center. You're an addict!"

Walter raised his hand and smacked Lisa across the mouth without thinking about it. "Don't say that. Don't ever say that to me!" he yelled.

It caught her totally off guard, and she backed away, holding her hand over the hot sting of her face. Walter walked toward her, tears filling his eyes. He held out his trembling arms. "I'm sorry, Lisa. I didn't mean it," he said. "I'm so scared right now. I don't know what's going to happen."

Lisa gingerly swallowed her pride and stepped into his arms. "It's okay, Walter," she said, stroking his head. "You'll be fine, and I'll be right here with you."

The two of them drove to Baltimore that Saturday. They spent the night at Kings Inn and made love four times; that hadn't happened since their honeymoon in New Orleans. They said very little to each other as they dressed the next morning.

Walter had chosen Woodbridge Rehabilitation Center. He would stay inside for six weeks, and if all went well, he would be back home by Thanksgiving. He'd continue to work with the program for another six months as an outpatient, attending group sessions twice a week.

Lisa noticed as she started the car that Walter's hands were shaking badly. She reached over and squeezed his leg to reassure him. She followed the map, going north on 695, took the Security Boulevard exit, and turned left down Oak Park to the facility. It was a large fenced-in complex that resembled a minimum-security prison. From the corner of her eye Lisa could see Walter fidgeting in the passenger's seat as the gates opened and they drove inside.

Walter and Lisa said their good-byes in the front lobby, and an orderly showed him to his room. She stood and watched as he disappeared behind two large steel double doors.

Lisa drove back down the driveway, this time noticing the picnic tables, canopies, and lawn chairs scattered around the grounds. One patient in a wool jacket sat on a park bench, puffing frantically on a cigarette stub.

Instead of going directly back home, she decided to drive into downtown Baltimore and have lunch. Somehow it made her feel closer to Walter. She ended up spending all afternoon at the Inner Harbor. She had lunch at the International Cafe within the glass-walled pavilions at Harborplace. Lisa couldn't shake the feeling of impending loss and needed something to hold on to. She missed Walter but for the first time she was forced to admit to herself that maybe her marriage was a mistake. She allowed the devastating thought to seep into her mind for a brief moment only. Then she walked up and down the brick promenade, browsing in every shop on the block until she was exhausted.

Danielle sat in her usual seat by the window in the Saurus conference room. The discussion was a variation of something she'd heard a thousand times, so she turned her focus outside. She envied the serenity of a pigeon resting comfortably on the ledge, while a man on the street tried desperately to flag down a cab. Derrick rushed into the room, late as usual. Danielle could smell his cologne from any distance. She shut her eyes for a moment and let her memories get lost in the scent.

"The final order of business is the Mr. Louis's Bakery account. It seems he's upset because of a lack of organization on our part. Who wants to explain first?" Lawrence leaned back in his chair, eyeing Derrick and waiting for someone to speak.

"I'm now working with Mr. Louis, and I will straighten it out," Danielle volunteered, pulling her jacket together and sitting up straight.

"So what happened?" Lawrence asked, not letting her off the hook as he usually would.

"There was a miscommunication. He was approached with material that wasn't ready," she answered, and glanced at Derrick, who shifted in his seat uncomfortably.

"Derrick, do you have something to say?" Lawrence asked, noticing the tension.

"I have to be honest, Mr. Cole. I did what I was told to do," he responded, not looking at Danielle.

"And who told you to do what?" Danielle asked sternly.

"I'm sorry, Mrs. Mead, but you wanted an early indication of what Mr. Louis thought, and you asked me to speak to him."

Danielle's hands were sweating, and she was ready to explode. "You must be mistaken, Derrick. I did say it would be nice to know if we were moving in the right direction, but I have never asked you to contact Mr. Louis for any reason."

Derrick didn't reply. He simply shrugged his shoulders and raised his eyebrows.

"Well, whatever happened, it's got to be taken care of immediately," Lawrence said.

Danielle contemplated her relationship with Derrick. It was out of control, but she hadn't been able to end it. Somehow she'd gotten in too deep. "Are we finished?" she asked.

"Yes, I think that's it," Lawrence answered.

Danielle hurried down the hall to her office. Once inside she closed the blinds and sat down heavily in her fire red chair. She took several deep breaths, set her elbows on top of the desk, and massaged the back of her neck. "Shit, shit, shit!" she hissed, slamming her fist down on the edge of the desk with each word.

She hadn't seen Derrick in four days, and she felt sick inside. He had been an oasis in the middle of the desert satisfying her thirst. But now she found herself wondering if his water was worth the price.

Danielle stood up to stretch. She raised her arms high in the air and moved her shoulders forward and back. She walked over to the window and opened her blinds to see the outer office. She jumped back quickly when she saw Derrick saunter up to her secretary's desk. He leaned over and profiled for a moment. He was talking and laughing just loud enough to get her attention. Her hazel eyes followed him as he started toward her office door and disappeared behind the wall.

Danielle prepared herself for his entrance. She took out a small mirror from her top right-hand drawer and freshened her lipstick, then shuffled some papers to make it look as if she was busy. She waited for his knock, watching the door like a small, hardheaded kitten that keeps tearing at the drapes. She waited a few more minutes, but there was still no knock. She finally got up, went to the door, opened it, and stuck her head out. Derrick was nowhere in sight.

When she couldn't stand it any longer, she headed for his office, but she had just missed him. So she hurried out to the lobby and down the elevator. She saw him headed for his car and called out, "Derrick, wait!"

He turned and saw her but kept walking. He had unlocked the door and gotten in when she reached the passenger side. He started the engine, and she began beating on the window. He took his time, then finally unlocked the passenger door, and she got in.

"What the hell are you trying to do to me?" she yelled at him.

"Keep your voice down," he told her as he started the car and drove out of the lot.

"So what's this shit you're pulling, Derrick?" she asked, twisting her body to face him.

He stopped for a red light. "You should know all about shit, Mrs. Danielle," he replied.

Danielle frowned at him. "What?"

"You didn't tell me you got a bonus for the Specialty Press account," he said, turning to look directly at her.

"Who told you that?"

"Dammit, Danielle, I trusted you, and you haven't been fucking me, you've been fucking over me all along," he told her as the light changed.

"Derrick, that bonus was not based on the Specialty account. It came from a number of projects I've worked on this year."

He drove forward slowly. "Stop lying, Dannie!" he screamed, and whipped quickly into a parking lot. "The jingle was mine!" Derrick yelled at her as he pulled up to the empty brick building, put the car in park, and turned off the engine.

"Correction. The jingle belongs to Saurus Advertising, Derrick. You're an employee working under their contract. I haven't lied to you about anything!" she yelled back.

Danielle couldn't stand for that gorgeous face to look so pained. She reached out and touched the back of his neck. "I haven't lied to you, Derrick. I swear. I'm crazy about you, and that's a scary statement for me to make."

Derrick examined her face closely. "That's the first time you've said how you really feel."

Danielle smiled weakly. Her candor with Derrick was not planned. It caught her off guard, and she felt strangely vulnerable.

He leaned over to kiss her. "You know I'm crazy about you too, don't you?" he said enticingly.

She shook her head as he slid his tongue between her lips and set her mouth on fire. Danielle pressed her mouth firmly against his, and they kissed passionately. This man was in her blood, and she wasn't ready to let him go. Derrick drove her back to her car.

"How about letting me show you how I feel tonight?" Danielle asked as she got out of the car.

Derrick smiled smugly. "I'm not sure about tonight. Call me," he said, and drove off.

That night Danielle wanted to apologize in her own special way. She called several times, but he wasn't in. Finally she decided to surprise him. Before she went to his apartment, she stopped by the store and picked up two bottles of champagne, a single red rose, and a three-pack of Trojan Plus rubbers. Derrick wasn't home, so she parked across the street and waited.

Danielle sat in her car and smoked a cigarette from her stash under the seat. She popped a greatest hits tape by Natalie Cole into the cassette deck and moaned along with the tune "I'm Catching Hell." She had to admit it was no longer the wild and passionate love affair they'd once had, but sex—great sex, plain and simple.

Ten minutes later, when Derrick's car finally drove up to his apartment, Danielle instinctively scooted down in the seat and watched as Monica, his friend from the NFL party, stepped out of the car. Her short black skirt and high heels said they were going to do more than dance this time. Danielle watched them walk up the stairs together. Then, as he pulled his keys from his pocket and found the right one, Monica reached over and kissed him on the ear. Derrick turned to her and seductively pulled her close. He bent over and allowed her breast to fill his mouth. She turned the key, the door opened, and they disappeared inside.

Danielle's heart pounded; her head throbbed. She had allowed this man to infest her life like a virus. She needed him to block the misery that came from leaving her husband and child. She had hurt a really good man, who had done nothing but love her for as long as she could remember.

She started the car and drove around the block several times before going home. The first time around she noticed the light in the kitchen was on. The second time the light in the kitchen had been replaced by the light in the bedroom. The third time there was no light at all.

She walked wearily inside her hotel room and looked around at the dismal sight that had become her home. It seemed as if aeons had passed since she had felt truly comfortable and secure. The purple flowered drapes didn't match the orange-and-purple checked bedspread. The room was cluttered with suitcases and boxes that couldn't fit into the small closet.

Danielle kicked off her shoes and walked into the bathroom. While her bath water ran, she undressed. She stood erect for a moment, beside the tub, with her hands pressed against her lower back. She closed her eyes and rolled her head in a circular motion, then stepped into the water and lowered herself until she was submerged from the waist down.

She poured bubble bath into the tub, then turned off the cold water, letting only the hot run. It moved slowly over her legs and thighs until the heat covered all of her body. She played for a moment with the bubbles like a child. Her hand waved back and forth, causing rainbow-colored spheres to form and push their way across the surface. They would burst with the wrong touch, then build magically again with very little movement. She finally rested her head on the back wall and closed her eyes.

The phone rang, but Danielle didn't move. After four rings her answering machine came on.

"Hi, you've reached 718-7762. Please leave a name and number, so I'll know it was you. Thanks."

The machine beeped.

"Dannie, this is Roger. Call me, please."

Danielle slammed her fist into the water. She missed him. She had missed him for some time but wouldn't let herself feel it. She used Derrick as her shield, but now that her shield was down, the truth seemed unbearable. She needed her husband and daughter, but how could she go back? It had been so long since she thought of Roger, and good things came to mind. Now she smiled at the sound of his voice on the machine, and she felt special at the thought of his love. She cried as an overwhelming emotion entangled her soul.

The next morning Danielle called Lisa's house five different times with no answer. So an hour later, when Lisa opened the front door, Danielle stepped inside.

"What's up?" she asked in a cautious but cheerful voice.

"You should have called," Lisa told her with an attitude.

"I tried. You didn't answer the phone, and your machine was off," Danielle explained to her little sister in a matter-of-fact tone.

"So next time take a hint," she spit out.

"What the hell's wrong with you?" Danielle asked as she stepped past her.

"I just wanted some time to myself now that my comps are finished," Lisa answered, and headed for the bathroom to brush her teeth.

Danielle followed her. "How'd they go?"

"I'll know next week," Lisa replied.

"How do you think you did?"

"I don't know."

Lisa brushed her teeth and rinsed her face. She couldn't tell Danielle that her comps were not important right now, but Walter was. She couldn't explain how strange it felt being in the house without him or how empty she was inside without the security of his love. She didn't talk to her big sister that morning because she knew she wouldn't understand.

Since Walter's absence, Lisa had spent most of her time cleaning and studying. She had completed a thorough search of the house and found every one of his stashes. Several joints hidden in a box in the hall closet, a small bag of cocaine in the desk drawer in the den, and more joints in the bottom drawer of his dresser. She got rid of it all.

Lisa headed toward the kitchen. "So, what are you doing here, Dannie?"

"I came to hang out with my sis. And I wanted to see the renovation," she replied. Danielle stopped in the middle of the floor in admiration. "Nice . . . very nice."

"Thanks," Lisa said, brushing her hair.

"And how's Walter?" Danielle asked, then helped herself to a banana.

"I don't know. We're not allowed to contact each other until the end of the third week," Lisa told her and poured herself a cup of tea from the pot.

"You can't make fresh tea?"

Lisa rolled her eyes. "Why should I?" she replied, and proceeded to heat up the cup in the microwave.

They both settled comfortably into the plush chairs in the breakfast nook.

"He'll be back in time for the holidays, right?" Danielle asked.

"Yeah . . . the Tuesday before Thanksgiving."

"That's good, because it's a bitch not having a man during the holidays," Danielle added under her breath.

The bell to the microwave rang, so Lisa got up and removed the steaming cup. She pushed a pile of papers across the table and set the cup in front of her. "I see you're still feeling sorry for yourself," she told her big sister.

"It looks like you ain't doing too bad in that category yourself," Danielle said, eyeing her.

"So when are you going to tell me what the real problem is?" Lisa asked.

"It's really not a problem. I just wanted to tell you that Roger and I are going to have dinner tonight, and I guess I'm scared. I know I fucked up really bad this time."

She blew on the hot tea and leaned back. "Yes, you did," Lisa agreed. "But then, when you do something, Dannie, you always do it in grand fashion. So is this dinner about getting back together?"

"Kind of . . . I really want to see where his head is at right now. Maybe he won't want me back. Or maybe he'll take me back just to dog me," Danielle explained, and took another bite of the banana.

"Oh, I see, Dannie. You can give it, but you can't take it."

"Exactly," she admitted.

"Wow, we're even being honest today," Lisa teased, and clapped her hands together.

"How about going out with me for some breakfast or something?" Danielle asked.

"No, thanks. I think I'm going to just eat some leftover spaghetti and keep working on my proposal. I'm almost finished, you know."

"You need any help?"

Lisa stared at her sister for a moment. "Danielle, what's going on? You didn't come here to help me with my proposal."

"That's not true," she objected.

"Look, tell me or get out!" Lisa said bluntly, and pointed toward the door.

"Damn, you're tripping today."

"I just can't deal with any bullshit right now, Dannie. There are too many other things going on."

"Okay . . . okay." Danielle stood up and walked over to the center cabinets. She hesitated, thinking about what she was going to say. "I'm ready to go home, Lisa." She had finally found the truth that was lost somewhere inside her. "Roger, Kim, and even Gaithersburg were a crucial part of my happiness, and I've been

an idiot. I never should have let them go." Danielle closed her
eyes, wishing the fear away.

"Ahhhhhhhhh! I can't believe it!" Lisa screamed at the top
of her lungs. She jumped up, ran across the floor, and threw her
arms around her big sister's neck. "Of course he'll take you back,
girl! The man loves you."

Danielle started squeezing her hands into fists. "I wish I were
as sure as you are, Lisa."

"Dannie, you guys belong together. Roger knows it, and
thank God you finally see it too. Do what you do best and work
this shit out!" Lisa said, ignoring her doubt.

"I remember Mom used to say, 'You know you're getting old
when after flying high for one night, you find yourself grounded
for days.' Boy, do I feel old!" Danielle said and hugged her sister
back.

It was about seven o'clock that night when Danielle arrived
in front of the house she used to call home. For a minute she
sat in the car absorbed in memories. She saw Roger standing in
front of her at those black caucus meetings. She pictured the
way his eyes always shifted upward when he tried to think of
something. She watched his lips move in a persuasive rhythm.
She stirred inside with familiar emotions.

Danielle got out of the car. She walked up to the door, said
a quick prayer, and rang the doorbell. The porch light came on,
and Roger opened the door.

"Hi," she said anxiously.

"Dannie, how are you? Come on in," Roger said.

Danielle followed him to the kitchen and stopped to get herself
a glass of water. Roger stood in the doorway, eyeing her cautiously.

"I needed something to drink. You don't mind, do you?" she
asked, pulling the cold water from the refrigerator.

He handed her a glass from the cabinet. "No."

Danielle surveyed the piles of papers spread across the dining
room table as she poured water into the glass. "Things must be
hectic at the office for you to bring work home," she said, nodding toward the mess.

"Things are chugging along. Victor's wife had the baby. A seven-pound boy. So things are rough while he's gone."

"How did the Wallace case turn out?" she asked, nervously sipping the water.

"She got the kids, the house, the BMW. He got screwed on several levels."

"Sorry."

"Don't be. He was having an affair too."

Danielle tried to smile, but she couldn't. How ironic, she thought. She negotiated million-dollar advertising accounts every day but now stood in front of this man overwhelmed in silence.

"You look good, Roger," she finally told him.

He leaned against the counter next to her but didn't speak. But when Danielle looked into his face, his eyes told her most of what she needed to know. They gave her the courage to continue. "I guess there's no easy way to say this."

"I've missed you, Dannie," Roger said, pulling her into his arms.

Danielle held him tightly. "Roger, I'm so sorry. I don't know what happened," she blurted out. She knew an apology wasn't necessary but needed to apologize anyway.

"It's okay," Roger whispered. "You're home, and that's all I need."

Danielle opened herself up to Roger's love again. Now that she knew how powerful real love was, she vowed never to let it go. She wanted to be a better wife this time and a better mother. Danielle had so much to say to Roger, but she struggled, forming sentences in her mind that never made it to her lips. She laid her head on his shoulder and thanked God for Roger's unchanging love.

Danielle, Sundi, and Lisa chose to go jogging out at East Potomac Park on Saturday afternoon to start their day. Lately the
time they spent together seemed so limited. Each was engulfed
in her own realm of self-pity. Their goal was to run up to the
tip of the peninsula and back. They ran up the hill at a slow but
comfortable pace and made it to the top with no problems.

They stopped to take deep breaths in and out, and waited in
front of a statue called *The Awakening*, which depicted a half-
buried man who was painfully pulling himself up out of the
earth. As they looked at the statue, each of them thought about
how it related to a part of her life. Danielle saw it as her awakening, now that she was back with her husband and daughter
and her affair with Derrick was over. Lisa felt the statue had to
be a sign that Walter was waking up through his program and
would return home well. Sundi thought it represented her real-
ization of how precious life is and the fact that she had finally
decided to throw the birth control pills away.

Danielle had worn her bright yellow and raspberry warm-up
suit, Sundi was dressed in an oversized Dallas Cowboys sweat-
shirt and blue stretch pants, and Lisa had borrowed Walter's
zip-neck fleece pullover and forest green sweats.

"Come on, ladies, we've got a full day ahead. Let's get on down the hill," Sundi finally said, starting to jog in place.

"Slow your happy ass down," Danielle told her. "Whose silly idea was this anyway, jogging in the middle of winter?"

"It's only October, so stop making excuses and get it in gear. Move it! Move it! Move it!" Sundi yelled like a drill sergeant in the army.

They followed orders and took off running and laughing at the same time. They had passed the halfway mark when Lisa's knee gave out. She grabbed it and stopped, waving the others on, then walked the rest of the way. Danielle and Sundi started to race to see who could reach the car first. Sundi easily beat Danielle. She stood gloating, until Danielle fell across the hood and moaned loudly, gasping the thin air.

Lisa reached the car several minutes later. She got out the keys and opened the door. "So where to?" she asked as she got in and started the car.

"I'm starving. Let's go to Georgetown for a late breakfast?" Danielle answered.

"Actually I'd prefer an early lunch. How about you, Sundi?" Lisa asked.

Sundi was sprawled out across the backseat, huffing and puffing. "What about this funk? We did just finish running," she replied, without opening her eyes.

"Speak for yourself!" Danielle joked, sniffing up under her arms. "I smell fine, and I was the only one who worked hard enough to sweat."

As Lisa backed the car out of the parking space and headed for Georgetown, she couldn't help but notice that they all looked a mess. It was one of those rough and rugged days. Danielle's long, silky hair was tossed all over her head. Strands in the front stuck straight up, and the back lay flat down. Sundi's dreadlocks looked even worse, if that was possible, and she had large bags under her eyes, as if she hadn't slept in days. Lisa looked at her nubby fingers. She had chewed on her fingernails so much that she didn't have any left.

"Ohhh, I like that black leather coat and those boots," Danielle said, pointing to a lady crossing New York Avenue.

Lisa shielded the sun from her eyes with her right arm and looked. "It looks like you."

"Yeah, I got good taste. It's my good sense that I have to worry about," Danielle said, feeling sorry for herself.

"You're back with Roger. Stop whining," Lisa told her.

"Why don't you use that thing up there to block the sun? That's what it's made for," Sundi observed from the backseat, pointing to the visor.

"Because I don't need to," Lisa told her, turning the corner and lowering her arm as the sun ducked behind several clouds.

"Excuse me, Miss Thang!" Sundi added, lying back down.

"It's Mrs. Thang to you!"

They drove ten blocks down Wisconsin Avenue past historic town houses that had been converted into clothing boutiques, restaurants, and specialty stores. Danielle nudged Lisa when she noticed that Sundi had fallen asleep. They both shook their heads and listened for what sounded like the beginning of a snore. Finally Lisa broke the silence.

"You know, Roger *is* a good man, Dannie. You should be happy."

"I know, and I'm such a bitch because I don't appreciate him like I should," she admitted. "But I do love him, and I'm going to try to do better."

Lisa gave her a questioning look.

"You know it's not like I want to be a bitch. I'd like to be a better person than I am," Danielle explained. "But what can I do? We both know I'm just not cut out for the typical wife and mother thing." Lisa pulled up behind a double-parked car and waited for the left lane to clear.

"As long as it's over with Mr. Young and Wonderful," Lisa told her supportively. "That's what matters."

Danielle winked at her baby sister. "He was *too* young and *too* wonderful."

Lisa pulled around the parked car. "I think Roger knows you

well enough after all these years, Dannie. I doubt if he's expecting a typical wife and mother."

"Mom once told me that 'Men are a lot like thumbtacks. They're only useful if they have two good heads, and both are pointed in the right direction.'" Danielle and Lisa both burst into laughter.

Then Lisa's voice turned serious. "I sure hope Walter's head is pointed in the right direction when he gets out."

"He's trying, Lisa. That's all you can ask," Danielle said reassuringly.

"Well, I know one thing. If he's not pointed in the right direction, I'm through with fairy tales."

"Bullshit!" Danielle said, shaking her head and lightly hitting her sister across the shoulder.

"Who shit?" Lisa asked, following along.

"You're both full of shit!" Sundi joined in as Lisa made a left turn down M Street.

"Look who decided to wake their tired ass up," Danielle teased.

"I been awake, listening to you two and your sob stories," Sundi told them, then sat up and patted down her dreadlocks.

"Like you don't have sob stories too," Lisa replied, and pulled into a vacant parking space.

Sundi got out of the car and pulled two quarters from her purse. "Of course I have sob stories, everybody does, but I'm determined not to complain anymore. I married the man. I'm still living with him, so I need to just deal with it."

"Have you heard from his mother since she left?" Danielle asked, shutting the car door.

Sundi put the quarters in the meter. "Please don't mention that woman. I know she found those pills and gave them to him. Chris is not the kind of man to snoop around in my closet."

"Mothers love their sons and raise their daughters," Lisa joked, locking the car doors.

They walked four blocks to Wisconsin Avenue, then another

two blocks to Nino's. Lisa was in the mood for a grilled chicken salad.

Sundi unwrapped a stick of spearmint gum and popped it in her mouth. "I know one thing: I'm through feeling bad," she announced as they sat down at a booth in the corner. "He made me so mad last week I shocked the shit out of him. I moved into the den!"

"You didn't!" Danielle and Lisa cried together.

"Can you believe he gave his mamma a thousand dollars out of our savings account? Hell, no wonder she thinks children are wealth!"

They shrieked with laughter as the waiter brought water to the table, but the laughter stopped when a mixed couple walked in. The guy, a dark-skinned, good-looking Wall Street type, was with a pale, average-looking white girl. They were seated at the table across from them.

"Why do they do that?" Danielle asked, narrowing her eyes. "If they're going to dump us for white women, they could at least get somebody that looks good."

"I thought you said Monica looked good for a white girl?" Sundi asked, hiding behind her menu.

"She wasn't looking that damn good," Danielle answered, and made a clicking sound with her teeth.

They sat in silence and watched as he pulled out her chair and took her coat, playing a game called gentleman. Danielle put her finger in her mouth, as if she were trying to make herself throw up.

"I bet he wouldn't act like that if he was with one of us," Lisa said, turning away as the waiter arrived.

Once the waiter took their orders, the conversation continued.

"Maybe we should cross over like they do. Maybe they know something we don't," Sundi said.

"I'd cross over if I could have Tom Selleck," Danielle fantasized.

Lisa scrunched up her face. "Not me, Laurence Fishburne is the man."

"He's not white," Danielle corrected her.

"I don't care what color he is, he's *fine!*"

Danielle shook her head, and smiled at her sister's antics. Then she changed the subject. "Sundi, did Lisa tell you she passed her comps?"

"No, she didn't tell me," Sundi said, surprised. "When did you find out?"

Lisa shrugged her shoulders. "A few days ago. I'm just glad they're over."

"And what's next?" Sundi asked.

"I gave my adviser a brief outline of my dissertation proposal, and I'm just waiting now for her feedback," Lisa replied, shifting in her seat to get comfortable. "I'm using your idea, Sundi, about studying communication between African-American and African couples."

"I've talked to several couples who said they would participate," Sundi said.

"Maybe you'll document my theory that men are the same all over the world," Danielle joked.

"They're not the same, Dannie. There are good ones, bad ones, and in-between ones. The problem is that there aren't enough good ones to go around," Sundi explained.

"We might have to face the fact, ladies, and share one," Lisa added.

Danielle immediately copped an attitude. "Bullshit! I ain't sharing nothing."

"Are we being a hypocrite?" Lisa asked her sister.

"I don't care! I'm not going to share and *know* I'm sharing. It took me a long time to share with you. And I only did it because Mom forced me to."

"Remember back home in high school when some of those girls acted so desperate? They would do battle over the *sorriest* men," Lisa said.

"I remember when Tina and Merriam shared that *Negro* like idiots," Danielle explained.

"You're kidding," Sundi responded in disbelief.

Lisa continued the story. "One had a baby by him, and they

would take turns watching the kid while the other spent time with him."

Sundi twisted her face. "Those women are on the talk shows every day."

"Yeah, but I don't know those women," Lisa replied. She watched as two white women came into the restaurant and stared at the interracial couple. She saw them settle into a table not far away, then noticed that they were scanning the room. Searching, she thought, for other unprepared, curious black men disgusted with the problems of life, hoping in some way to lose their worries within an opposite world.

Why was it so painful to see a black man and a white woman together? It happened all the time now, but it still made Lisa sad. She had dated a white man once, but there was something missing, something was wrong. Maybe it was the innate sense of belonging or a shared historical experience; whatever the reason, it didn't feel right. She knew a relationship for her had enough problems without adding race to it.

"Black men today are spoiled rotten. Half of them want you to take care of them," Danielle said, reflecting on Derrick.

Then Lisa finished the sentence. "And the other half are taking care of white women."

"That's not true," Sundi argued. "Sometimes it's really love."

"Sometimes . . . Did you guys see Oprah's show last week on interracial marriage?" Lisa asked.

"Yeah, it was deep," Sundi said.

"This lady had the nerve to say she didn't see a black man when she looked at her husband," Lisa continued.

"Was she blind or what?" Danielle asked cynically.

"No, she was stupid," Lisa blurted out.

Sundi objected. "How do you guys know what that woman sees?"

"I know she couldn't miss the fact that he was black as my shoe," Lisa answered, and they burst into laughter.

Lisa examined the brown external color on her left hand. She knew the importance of her black culture and understood the powerful tapestry of her color. But she wondered if any of it mattered anymore.

"Why do we let black men drive us so crazy?" Sundi asked.

"Because we can't do without 'em," Danielle answered immediately.

"Haven't you guys heard?" Lisa added. "There's no black or white; we're all universal."

"Yep. Let's face it, girls. There's only one important color in the world nowadays, and it's green." Danielle waved a twenty-dollar bill in the air.

"Green for money or envy?" Sundi asked.

"A little of both," Danielle replied. She thought about the life she was returning to, and it made her both happy and sad. She could be the good wife and mother. She could be the successful career woman. She could focus on her family and be a responsible adult. But could she be happy? Danielle took a bite of her spinach pasta and resolved to love Roger for who he was, rather than who she wanted him to be. He was a special man, and she knew she was lucky to have him back.

The first snow had fallen, but it was melting fast. It covered all the trees, the ground, and the bottom of the Potomac Mills sign that Sundi and Lisa passed as they walked inside. Sundi stopped to stare into the display window at T J Maxx, admiring the red and green dresses positioned between sparkling colored Christmas tinsel. Her mind was not on business today, but she did need to finalize an upcoming Christmas order for one of her clients.

As they entered Baskets Galore, Sundi went straight over to her display.

"Hello, Wilma," she called, passing a rack of wind chimes and brushing them slightly to hear the whimsical sounds.

"Hi, Sundi," Wilma said, stacking a row of candles on a shelf. "The oval willow baskets are all gone, and I only have two of the twined bamboos left."

"How many more do you want?" Sundi asked as she carefully checked each of her baskets for possible defects.

"Ten more of the oval willows—people seem to love them— and five additional bamboo. I'd also like five of the interlaced dish style baskets we talked about last time."

As Lisa waited for Sundi, she flipped through several of the cards. She picked up one and read the outside. "Have you noticed as time goes by, men tend to get more loving and easier to understand?" Then she opened it to read. "Me neither!" Lisa had to laugh because it was definitely true.

Sundi noticed a small piece on the base of one basket that was working its way loose, so she pulled a small stick of glue out of her purse and repaired it. "I've only got three of the new interlaced baskets left, but I should be able to make a couple more by next week. Does color matter?"

"No. I'll leave that up to you," Wilma told her, finishing the last row of candles.

Sundi completed her business quickly, and she and Lisa headed for the nearest shoe store. Lisa wanted to pick up a new pair of black boots.

"So, what's the big secret you wanted to tell me?" Lisa asked as they pushed through the preholiday crowd.

"You have to promise not to tell Dannie because I don't want to hear her mouth yet," Sundi said.

"Please. Who cares what she says?" Lisa replied from behind her.

Sundi slowed down to let Lisa catch up. "I'm going to have a baby!"

Lisa stopped short. "You're pregnant?"

"Yep!" Sundi said, stepping out of the way as anxious shoppers rushed by.

"Does Chris know?"

"Not yet."

Lisa saw the food court to the left of them and changed direction. "Let's sit down for a minute," she told Sundi. "Do you think Chris is going to stay?"

"I don't know what he's going to do, and it doesn't matter."

"Don't tell me you think a baby is going to *make* him stay, Sundi!" Lisa warned her as they reached an empty table.

"Of course not," she replied. "I know that doesn't work these days. I want to do this, Lisa. I'm ready. When I saw Jarod lying in that casket, I knew this was the right thing to do."

For the first time in a long time Lisa was speechless. But there was one burning question that needed to be addressed. "What if Chris does decide to go back home? Would you and the baby go with him?"

"I'll have to deal with that problem if it comes up," Sundi replied, half smiling.

Lisa filtered the information through her mind. "So, if necessary, you're ready to raise this baby by yourself."

Lisa decided she was not going to sound like Danielle, drilling Sundi with negatives. So they both sat quietly for a moment.

Sundi looked around the room contemplating her decision. Then two children suddenly ran past screaming.

"My child is not going to act like a heathen in public," she said angrily.

"We'll see," Lisa teased.

Lisa's eyes followed an older woman who walked slowly and deliberately toward the table across from theirs. She sat down and searched through a small blue tote bag she carried. She took out a cup and a small bottle of something. She poured just a little into the cup and took several sips periodically. She looked as if she had traveled miles and slept very little. It was obvious that she was by herself, and that made Lisa sad. Danielle was right, she thought, the holiday season was a lousy time to be alone.

Sundi broke the silence first. "So how's Walter?"

"We had a good visit. He's lost a little weight. And it was a little awkward, but he seems to be doing well."

"He'll be home in a few weeks, and you guys can start all over."

"I'm kind of scared, Sundi," Lisa said. "Somehow it felt different when he held me."

Sundi shifted her purse to the other side. "What's wrong?"

"I don't know if we can start over," Lisa said, and leaned forward on the table.

"Do you still love him?" Sundi asked.

Lisa smiled as she thought about the question. "Yeah, I do."

Sundi squeezed her hand. "Then you can start over. You two deserve a second chance, Lisa."

"I know you're right. Sometimes Walter acts like the biggest asshole in the world, and other times he's Mr. Perfection."

"The question is, Can you live with that, based on your delicate sense of balance?" Sundi asked, pushing two dangling dreadlocks out of her face.

"I'm going to try. He's everything I prayed for, Sundi. Although I should have been just a little more specific with my description to God," she said jokingly.

Sundi set her hand on her stomach. "Things will work out. For both of us."

As they smiled at each other, Lisa couldn't help but feel jealous of Sundi all over again. She had somehow found a way to compromise and maintain her love. Lisa wanted to do the same. She remembered that her horoscope for the day said: "Listen with your heart and not your mind." So she did. And instead of feeling sorry for herself and embracing the jealousy, she focused on the happiness she felt for Sundi, who was trying to turn her marriage around.

Chris was late getting home from work that evening. But when he entered the house, he knew something was up. The table was set, lit by a flickering candle, and the smell of his favorite dish, curried chicken, filled the air. Sundi smiled and motioned for him to sit down. He smiled back, washed his hands, and sat with reserved enthusiasm.

After the meal Chris strutted to the couch and clicked on the television. He knew what this kind of treatment meant. He flicked the remote and stopped on a basketball game, waiting for Sundi to make her move.

She put the food away but left the dishes until later. She hated this routine, but she knew it would ultimately get her what she wanted. She joined Chris in the living room, sitting close beside him.

"So, you need anything?" she asked, turning slightly to the left to make sure that their thighs touched.

"I'm good," Chris responded stiffly, and turned his attention back to the television.

Sundi watched as B. J. Armstrong leaped into the air to sink a layup. There were two minutes left in the half. The Celtics called a twenty-second time-out, and a commercial came on.

"Chris," Sundi said, "we need to talk. I really need to know if you think you're going home."

"I haven't decided, Sundi," Chris told her. He thought he knew where the conversation was headed.

Sundi readjusted her body, slipping her left leg under her right to see his response better. "I realize things haven't been great lately, but you've got to let me know how you feel."

Chris knew she was waiting, but he took his time. The game came back on, so he watched it instead. "Yes!" he yelled as Scottie Pippen stole the ball and dribbled it back down the court for an easy two points.

"Chris . . . did you hear me?"

"I heard, Sundi. I just don't think now is the time to discuss it," he said sharply.

Sundi sat in silence staring at Chris. She wondered if she had done the right thing. Somewhere in the back of her mind there were pictures of what her married life was supposed to be like. She couldn't find them. She hated that she questioned his sincerity; she hated that she wasn't sure of his love. And she couldn't help but be afraid that this baby would only add to their problems.

Chris tried to ignore her, but after a while he couldn't take it anymore, so he clicked off the TV. "Okay, okay, you want to talk about it. Fine! Let's talk!" he said, very irritated.

Sundi ignored his attitude and said, "I need to know where I fit into your life, Chris."

"Where do you want to fit in, Sundi? You tell me," Chris replied, turning the question back to her.

"What's the future gonna be like for us, Chris?" Sundi rephrased her question and lifted her eyes to see his face.

Chris fell back against the couch with his arms crossed. "If something happens to my father, I may have to go back home. Maybe not forever, but for a while."

Sundi noticed immediately that he said "not forever." Maybe

he was coming around, she thought. "What would happen if I went with you for a little while but didn't stay?" she asked.

"I guess we'd have to work that all out somehow. I don't know, Sundi. I don't have all the answers."

"All I'm asking, Chris, is not to be treated like property," she continued.

"You know, Sundi, I don't complain about all the money you waste on clothes, and shoes, and other junk because you make your own money and you have the right to spend it any way you like, but there are some things I can't accept, I won't accept."

"But do you hear how you talk?" she asked him. "You act like you're God himself and I have to follow your ten commandments."

"I don't think respect for me as your husband is too much to ask."

"And what about respect for me as your wife?"

Chris jumped up, knocking one of her baskets off the coffee table. Out of sheer habit alone, Sundi retrieved it.

"That's the problem, Sundi! You always have to challenge me! What do I have to do to get you to understand what marriage means in my culture?"

"Why does it always have to be about you, Chris? What about me? What about us?" she asked as she stood to face him.

" 'Us' is nonexistent, Sundi. You do whatever you want anyway. So what's the point?"

Sundi put her hands on her hips and steadied herself. "You don't talk to me, Chris. You bark orders at me. And you didn't do that before we were married. That's the point," she yelled.

"And you never ignored me before or treated me like I was incompetent or stupid or something!" he yelled back.

"I don't want to do this anymore, Chris, so if we're going to stay together, we have to find some middle ground here."

He looked her directly in the eyes. "I married you because I thought you were the kind of woman who would be willing at least to consider my needs in marriage."

"What about my needs, Chris?" Sundi said, still not backing down.

He suddenly realized that changing her was a hopeless cause, and this revelation forced him to smile. "You can't help it, can you?"

"I'm just trying to get you to see both sides. We both have to give things up."

"I've already given up my dignity, Sundi, by staying in a marriage where I've been lied to and my judgment is constantly questioned."

"I'm sorry I lied, Chris, but I didn't know what else to do. I wasn't ready to deal with a baby on top of everything else."

"So just answer one question for me?" he asked, then hesitated. "You say you love me, Sundi, but what does that mean?"

"It means I would do almost anything for you, Chris, except allow myself to be stepped on," she replied angrily.

"I don't want to go back home, Sundi. I want to stay here with you. But I honestly don't know if that's possible. I want a family. I want to build a life together," Chris told her, and waited for a response that didn't come.

Sundi smiled at him.

His eyes traced the shapely figure in front of him. He wanted so much to love her the way she wanted to be loved. But this was an impossible relationship, and he knew he couldn't take much more.

Sundi stepped toward him. "Remember how we used to talk for hours about everything?" she asked. "I miss that."

Chris reached for her hand. "I want to trust you, Sundi."

She brushed her hand across his chest, then watched the look in his eyes soften. They were glassy, as if he were about to cry, but of course he wouldn't. He was too old, and watching a few Montel shows hadn't convinced him otherwise.

"Chris, I'm pregnant," she finally told him, in the babylike tone of voice that she knew turned him on.

He eyed her carefully and listened to the echo of the words she'd just said. "You're going to have a baby?"

Sundi nodded her head. "We are."

He pulled his arms around her. "What I'm gonna do with you, Sundi?" he whispered through a runaway smile.

"Just don't stop loving me. That's all I ask," Sundi answered, and kissed him softly on his ear. "Please don't stop loving me," she repeated, and pressed her lips against his.

Sundi started to unbutton Chris's shirt. She knew this would trigger his instincts, and it did. He stopped her because he liked to undress himself. She watched and waited. When Chris finished unbuttoning his shirt, he took it off and flung it onto the floor. He then pulled Sundi's blouse over her head and dropped it as well. She followed his lead until they were both undressed. Chris sat down on the couch and guided Sundi onto his lap. He moved inside her, slowly and deliberately, while she moaned from the good feeling.

Chris was soon into his routine. He took his rightful place on top, giving her everything he thought she wanted. He centered his attention on making her body and mind feel good. Sundi rubbed her hands down his back and worked her body under his. She knew what he liked, and she wanted him to have it all.

In the afterglow they lay in each other's arms and watched Michael Jordan sink the last basket for the Chicago Bulls to give them a 99 to 96 win over the Boston Celtics.

Sundi snuggled closer into his chest. Chris squeezed her tightly. Both contemplated their victories.

In honor of Walter's return, Lisa decided to host her first Thanksgiving dinner. She had watched a local chef on television cook a turkey a couple of weeks before and scribbled notes down on a paper towel. He used a brown paper bag to cook it in. First he soaked the bag in butter and oil. Then he sprinkled paprika, pepper, seasoning salt, and onions all over the bird. He popped the turkey into the bag and slid it in the oven for six hours. It looked pretty simple to Lisa, so around midnight she took two paper sacks from the grocery store and did everything she'd seen the chef do. She checked the oven to make sure it was hot enough and slid the turkey inside.

They usually ate at Danielle's for Thanksgiving, but this year Lisa had a lot to be thankful for. Walter had been home for two days, and things seemed to be better. He was distant and moody sometimes, but it didn't last long. And he was still the charmer she married, loving and responsive most of the time. With the turkey in the oven, she went into the bedroom to lie down. When she looked at the empty bed, she remembered that he had been gone most of the evening. He hadn't said where, just grabbed his coat and told her he'd be back. Lisa tried not to listen to the annoying questions that crowded her mind. What was so important out there? Were drugs involved? Was it his ex-wife? How could she help? She had fallen asleep for what seemed like only moments when her nose filled with a harsh, burning smell. She opened her eyes to see black smoke channeling its way into the room and across the ceiling.

Lisa leaped off the bed, ran into the kitchen, and opened the oven to find a ball of fire in place of her turkey. She screamed and grabbed potholders, trying to pull out the rack. She hit at the fire several times with the potholders, the rack fell out of the oven, and everything hit the floor. Lisa glanced around the room and grabbed the flour canister. She dumped the flour on top of the fire, and the flames disappeared.

She stood and looked at the mess. Her turkey and her new floor were ruined. She slid down the cabinet and sat on the floor, cursing Walter for no real reason, except that she hadn't seen him all night. Tears rushed down her face without warning. It was as if she couldn't do anything right. She couldn't cook; she couldn't get a good man; she probably wouldn't even finish her damn Ph.D. program.

Lisa didn't hear Walter come in behind her. He looked at the mess and at Lisa's tears. He dropped to his knees to comfort her, chuckling at the same time. "It's okay," he mumbled.

His humor incensed Lisa. She cried even harder and pushed him away from her.

"It's okay, baby. . . . It's just a turkey," he said in a more sincere effort to console her, still fighting the urge to smile.

Lisa kicked the turkey across the floor, then grabbed her foot in pain. She cut her eyes at Walter as he laughed out loud again. "I'm not even crying about the turkey," she finally told him. "I don't care about the damn turkey! Where the hell have you been all night?" Lisa hit Walter as hard as she could on his arm. He just continued to laugh and dodged her next blow.

"I had to take care of some business. What does that have to do with this mess?"

"This mess represents our marriage, Walter!" she spit out.

"Whoa! Where did that come from? I thought we were getting our marriage back on track," Walter said, turning serious.

"What track are we on and where is it going?" she asked.

"You take everything to the extreme, Lisa," he said, disgusted. He got up and walked into the living room to skim through the pile of mail.

She was close behind him, waiting to hear the words she needed to hear. "Walter, I'm serious!" she screamed, snatching the mail from his hands. "Can't you hold a decent conversation with me anymore?"

"I'm doing the best I can, Lisa, and I'm sorry if it's not good enough!" he yelled back, and walked away from her over to the patio doors.

"Don't do that," Lisa said, throwing the letters on the buffet. "Don't act like it's my fault because I want too much."

Walter turned around. "Did I say you wanted too much?"

"Can you at least tell me what's out in the street that's so important, Walter?" she continued, staring at him intensely.

"Nothing, Lisa. It's Thanksgiving. Can't we get into this another time?" he pleaded, then headed back into the kitchen, grabbed the roll of paper towels, and started to clean up the mess.

"When, Walter? You've been home for two days, and it's starting already," she said, not letting up. "At least help me understand why this isn't working."

Walter didn't answer her right away. He picked up the turkey and set it in the sink, then threw the charred paper bags in the trash can. "You really want me to tell you what's wrong?" he finally asked.

"Yes. That's exactly what I need to hear from you. What is the problem?"

He turned to face her, wiping the grease from his hands on a paper towel. "You're the problem, Lisa. You're what's wrong," he said. "You want to live in a fantasy world. You're stuck in *The Cosby Show*, in the good life, where everybody's always happy, and if there's a problem, it's solved in thirty minutes. Real life doesn't work like that, baby. It's more complicated, and most of the time for poor folks it's downright unfair."

Lisa was stunned for a moment. Of course it's my fault, she

thought irritably. He's never responsible for anything. She sat down at the white oak dinette and formed her thoughts into sentences. "What's wrong with wanting a nice life, Walter? Why can't I want to be happy?"

"You can want happiness, Lisa, but I can't make you happy. And the funny thing is . . . I knew this was going to happen," he added as he sat down across from her.

"What do you mean, you knew?"

Walter surveyed the breakfast nook she had created. He loved it, and he loved her too. He wanted to get lost in those deep brown eyes. "I'm as close to Prince Charming and the fairy tale as you'll probably get, Lisa, but I'm still not good enough."

Lisa watched Walter walk out of the kitchen and thought about his words. Maybe it was her fault, she thought. Maybe she did want too much. She believed in fairy tales, and she had hoped to create one of her own. She loved that line from Kathleen Turner in *Romancing the Stone* when she told her agent she was a hopeful romantic.

Lisa picked up the phone to call Danielle and tell her about the turkey. Her big sister had a good laugh. She was cooking a ham just in case, so she said she'd bring it over.

Lisa sat in the front room window, watching the willow tree sway back and forth with the breeze. Walter was gone again when she got up Thanksgiving morning. As Danielle, Roger, and Kim drove up to the house, she thought about how great it was to see them back together. Thank goodness somebody's marriage was moving in the right direction. A poster in her office of an old African proverb came to mind: "Every morning in Africa a gazelle wakes up. It knows that it must run faster than the fastest lion or it will be killed. And every morning a lion wakes up. It knows that it must outrun the slowest gazelle or it will starve to death. So it doesn't matter whether you are a lion or a gazelle: When the sun comes up, you had better be running!" That was how she had felt every day since she met Walter, as if she were constantly running to or from something.

Walter returned just before Sundi and Chris arrived. Lisa was relieved. She had only haphazardly explained his absence. Everybody had a good laugh about her turkey disaster; then they settled down to a dinner of ham, green beans, macaroni and cheese, mashed potatoes, pumpkin pie, and green Jell-O, which was Kim's contribution.

After dinner they talked, as many middle-class black folk do, about the needs of urban black Americans. All the same old issues came up: education, institutional racism, the Reagan-Bush legacy, welfare, black movies, and rap music. No solutions, no changes; they just sat around and reassured themselves that they were doing all they could by getting inside the system and pulling one or two of "the unfortunates" along with them.

As the conversation ended, Sundi, Chris, and Roger turned on a bloody vampire movie, while Walter ran to the store to get more beer. Lisa wasn't in the mood for bloodsuckers—she felt drained already—so she went into the kitchen to start on the dishes.

Kim, worn out from the excitement of the day, had fallen asleep, so Danielle took her into Lisa's office and laid her on the couch.

Walter returned and brought the beer into the kitchen.

"I'm sorry about earlier," he told Lisa.

Lisa couldn't help but smile. She dried her hands and hugged him tightly. He returned her hug.

"I'm sorry too," Lisa said.

Walter grinned, grabbed three beers, and headed into the living room.

"Wasn't that sweet!" Danielle teased her baby sister as she entered the kitchen from the side door.

"You know, in some states folks get shot for meddling," Lisa said lightly, and continued to rinse an already clean plate.

"Well, actually it makes me think I owe you an apology," Danielle said, wringing out the dishrag and wiping off the stove.

"For what?" Lisa asked, confused.

"You did good, Lisa. He really is a nice guy, and I am glad to see you happy."

Lisa smiled while arranging several plates on the bottom rack of the dishwasher. That was something she never thought she'd hear her sister say. "Thanks" was the only response she could come up with.

"You guys should come to Vegas with Roger and me for New Year's Eve."

Lisa didn't look at Danielle as she spoke. She put the last of the glasses in the dishwasher and shut the door. "I'll ask Walter about it.

"Dannie, how do you know when love is going to be strong enough to survive all the crazy things life throws at you? I mean, how did you know you and Roger could get through something like the thing with Derrick?"

Danielle stopped cleaning the dinette table for a moment. "I honestly don't think you can know until it's all over. When the wall isn't smooth anymore and you can see the cracks and holes from all the battles, but it's still standing."

Lisa leaned against the cabinet. "I've always been jealous of your relationship with Roger. You know that, don't you?"

"No, you weren't. You only thought you were jealous. You just wanted marriage and a family—the American dream. But if that's the case, I've always been jealous of you too, Sis."

"Sure," Lisa said sarcastically, pushing the glass salt and pepper shakers to the back of the cabinet next to the napkin holder.

"Really . . . I've always been jealous of your spirit, Lisa. You have such a strong positive spirit."

Danielle's comment surprised her. My spirit . . . Lisa thought. That's something I haven't been in touch with in quite a while.

The first Wednesday in December started out as one of the best Wednesdays in Lisa's life. First she picked up her car that morning after a week in the shop. Walter had charged new brakes, shocks, tires, and a tune-up on his Visa card. It rode like a Cadillac. Next she had completed the final revisions and delivered her sixty-page dissertation proposal to each of her committee members.

Lisa had finalized her study of the communication differences between African-American and African couples. Sundi and Chris had convinced twenty couples they knew to participate. Each couple would complete a six-page questionnaire together and another three-page one separately. The questions explored how communication patterns are different based on social norms, traditions, and morals for both cultures and analyze how these differences impact such relationships. They would participate in two in-depth audiotaped interviews: one alone and one with the spouse. Lisa also planned to spend at least one day in the home of each couple. She would collect observational data on how each couple interacted in their natural environment. For the first time in a long time she was excited about school again.

When she drove up to the house, she didn't recognize the black Lexus in the driveway. Cautiously she opened her front door and stopped at the sight of the stranger sitting in the living room. He was dressed in a very expensive suit, but something about him looked sleazy. Lisa didn't know how to explain it, but she knew right away that his presence involved drugs. She stared at him and quickly noted that his face was different from what she expected. Not very womanlike and definitely no Ru-paul. She noticed traces of eyeliner and lipstick lightly applied. Then Walter appeared from the bedroom with money in his hand and confirmed her fear. Walter handed the money to him, and he got up to leave.

"Oh, baby . . . meet Alva, a friend of mine. Alva, my wife, Lisa."

Lisa nodded her head but didn't say anything.

"You call me if you need anything else. It was nice meeting you," Alva told her, and slithered out the door.

Lisa looked long and hard at her husband, who tried to act innocent. "What?" he asked.

"How could you?" she finally asked.

"What's wrong with you now?" he responded, ignoring her question. He stomped into the bedroom and shut the door.

Lisa ran her fingers across the top of her head. She had to think. She needed to deal with this calmly. What should she do? She collected herself and entered the bedroom. Walter was changing from his jeans to a pair of pleated twill slacks.

"How could you bring him into our home, Walter?" she cried. "I can't believe you're doing that shit again."

"I haven't done anything wrong, Lisa. He was a friend of mine long before I met you," Walter said coldly, putting on his jacket.

"But you promised, Walter! You've been going to those meetings!"

He rolled his eyes at her and slipped on his plain toe oxfords. "I don't know why you're tripping. This is my life, and I'm going to live it. Why is it that wives always feel they have to change you? This is who you fell in love with. This is me!" he told her. Then he did that thing that men do: He turned and walked away.

Lisa screamed and pushed him from behind. "I want the truth, Walter!"

Walter fell forward, then swung back around to face her. "I told you, he's a friend. Am I not allowed to have friends or what?"

"Don't lie, Walter!" she yelled, blocking his path.

"I'm not in the mood for this bullshit tonight, Lisa."

"*You promised!* You said you wanted our marriage to work!"

Walter pushed her to the side and hurried toward the door.

Lisa grabbed a glass ashtray and threw it at him. It crashed against the wall.

"You done lost your goddamn mind, girl!" he shouted as he opened the front door.

"How could you bring him into our home?" she yelled. "How could you?"

"You enjoyed his house, and I didn't hear any complaints," Walter told her in a voice that was distant and cold.

Lisa suddenly felt a strange chill. "He is the transvestite," she thought out loud.

Walter hesitated. "He's a lot of things. He's living his life his way."

Lisa found herself searching for something, anything to restore her hope. She cried as she realized that the house where they had fallen in love belonged to that man. It was as if all her memories were suddenly tarnished and dirty.

"I don't care!" she finally yelled at the top of her lungs. "This is my home too, and I don't want that son of a bitch in here!"

"You're acting stupid. I'll be back when you get your shit together," Walter said, slamming the door behind him.

Lisa wearily sat on the living room couch and listened to seconds, then minutes of silence. Instead of thinking about Walter, she focused on how much she hated his ugly blue and gold couch and love seat. She went into a kitchen drawer and pulled out a razor blade. She cut a long gash in the couch and love seat with it. She cut more gashes, digging deeper and deeper until her arm grew tired. But somehow she felt better. She had destroyed something of his the same way he was destroying their love.

Lisa picked up from the coffee table a small glass elephant that Walter had given her on their second date and threw it against the fireplace. It shattered. Then she knocked over the sand-glazed ceramic lamp on the end table next to her. She snatched most of the colored bulbs off the artificial Christmas tree and threw them into the fireplace one by one. Then she systematically started a search for the purchase he'd just made. She pulled books off the bookshelves and threw junk out of closets and cabinets in the den. Next she moved into the bedroom, where she trashed everything in sight until she found it.

This was it! This was her competition! she thought as she held the bag of white powder in her hand. This was the *bitch* who was coming between her and her man. Lisa frantically ripped open the plastic bag and headed for the bathroom. She pulled the toilet seat up and poured the illegal substance into the water. She pushed the handle down and watched the cocaine swirl out of her life.

When Lisa stepped back and thought about what she'd done, she knew Walter would be pissed, but she didn't care. She had to believe in his love or their marriage was over anyway. She had to find out what was more important to him. There was no other way to explain it.

Lisa lay on the bed, thinking about what to do next. As usual the tears came. She couldn't stop them. She lit a small white candle to summon peace and prayed: "Please, God. Help us, Lord. We need your guidance to work this out. I know he loves me, but I don't know what to do, Lord. I can't live like this. In the name of Jesus, I pray, please help me. Amen." That was the last thing she remembered before closing her eyes and rocking herself back and forth to sleep.

Lisa woke up hours later, when she heard the door slam and Walter entered the house. She didn't move from her spot on the bed. Instead she closed her eyes and pretended to be asleep, listening carefully to every sound.

Walter looked around the house at the mess. He picked up his tennis racket, which had a large hole in the center of it, then noticed that his feet were covered with stuffing from the couch and love seat. He walked slowly toward the bedroom. His head felt as if it were about to explode. He stopped at the bathroom door when he saw the empty plastic bag lying next to the stool. He rushed into the bedroom and shook Lisa until her eyes opened.

"What the hell happened?" he asked frantically.

"You lied to me, Walter. You said it was over," Lisa answered, lifting herself up and throwing her legs over the side of the bed.

"You didn't flush it?" he asked nervously.

Lisa didn't say anything. She watched as he stumbled back into the bathroom and picked up the empty plastic bag.

She walked up behind him and held his shoulders tightly. "We need help, baby. I called the counseling center."

"What the fuck is wrong with you, Lisa?" he shouted. He turned around with a look so frightening that Lisa was overwhelmed. She stood stuck in place until he lunged for her and she jumped out of his way. She began screaming and running at the same time. She sprinted back inside the bedroom, slammed the door, and locked it.

Walter beat on the door like a madman.

Lisa had never seen him like this. He was out of control. She watched the door shake from his constant pounding. Then she noticed the phone and picked it up, but there was no time. He hit the door again, it cracked, and he was inside. She spotted her umbrella and reached for it just as Walter approached. He grabbed at her, and she swung the umbrella, hitting his shoulder. But it didn't slow him down. She ran out the door and into the hallway where he caught her, and slammed her hard into the wall. She struggled to get free, but couldn't.

"You fucked up fifteen hundred dollars. What the hell were you thinking?" he screamed.

"We need help. Walter, please, I love you," she pleaded.

"You don't love me. You think you're too goddamn good for me. You and your fuckin' Ph.D.!"

He raised his hand and smacked her across the face. She screamed and fought harder. But the more she struggled, the more vicious he got. He held her against the wall with one hand and hit her several times with the other. After a while all Lisa could feel was numb. She closed her eyes, but she could still see that beautiful black hand raised above her. That hand that she had kissed, caressed, and loved.

Walter finally came to his senses and let her go. Lisa tried to run, but her legs wouldn't move correctly. She stumbled through the living room and fell into the Christmas tree.

Walter walked over, picked up the phone, and dialed 911. "You need to send someone to 9775 Martin Drive before I kill this crazy woman."

Lisa didn't move. She lay on the floor, crying quietly and praying for the police to hurry. She felt so stupid. She had always bragged, "Ain't no man ever gonna beat on me!" And here she was swollen and discolored from somebody's fists. She promised the Lord that she would never judge another woman in this situation negatively again. Then she heard her mother's voice saying, "If he hits you once, it only gets easier next time." She lay there watching Walter pace across the floor and wondered if she could ever forgive him.

Minutes later there was a knock at the door: "Police . . ." they called from outside.

Walter looked at the door, then at Lisa, but he didn't move.

Lisa crawled to the door. And when she opened it, the police-man helped her to her feet. He stared at her busted lip, swollen and bruised face, black eye, and bloody nose. The policeman stepped in and looked cautiously around the house.

"What's going on?" he asked with his hand close to his gun.

Lisa kept watching behind her. So he got more nervous and unbuckled the strap on his holster. His female partner came in behind him.

"I—I need to get out of here. Could you wait while I get my things?" Lisa asked.

The policeman followed her inside the bedroom, cautiously eyeing the mess. Lisa glanced at Walter, who was sitting on the couch with his head resting in his hands.

She went directly to two suitcases that were already packed on the other side of the bed. The policeman helped her with the heavy bags, while his partner cuffed Walter and led him outside.

"It's safe for you to stay here if you want to," the officer said. "He'll be in jail until the hearing."

"No, thank you. I don't want to," she said, looked over at her breakfast nook, and headed out the door.

As they drove away from the house, Lisa realized nothing was broken. She was mainly just bruised. What hurt most were her feelings, her self-respect, her pride. It was the kind of hurt Lisa remembered from her grandfather's stories of how things were in the past. When he talked about slavery, segregation, and civil rights. He talked about how black people had fought and died for opportunities that many today still didn't have or appreciate. It was a hurt that burrowed its way into her soul. For the first time in her life Lisa wanted to spit. She wanted to spit the way her grandfather always had when his tobacco was no good any-more, when its flavor, vigor, and strength were all used up, when he'd given up all hope.

Danielle was in the middle of her exercise routine when she noticed the flashing lights from a police car through her bed-room window. She came outside to see what was going on. The policeman opened the back door, and Lisa stepped out. Gasping, Danielle ran across the drive. She looked at Lisa's face with horror.

"She asked me to bring her to this address," the policeman said.

"Thank you, I'll take care of her," Danielle responded.

"She doesn't want to press charges, but she should. If she doesn't, we can only hold him until he sees the judge—about twenty-four hours."

"I'll talk to her. Thank you, Officer."

Danielle helped Lisa up the stairs and into the living room. Lisa took one look at Roger and fell over onto the couch. She curled up into a ball and began to cry again. She cried not because of the pain from the beating but because her love was gone and her marriage was lost.

Roger went into the bathroom and emerged with a cold wet washcloth. "Lisa, what the hell happened?" he asked, gently wiping the hair from her face.

"I had to know," she mumbled, and wiped her tears with her sleeve.

"Know what?" Danielle asked, handing her a handful of tissues. "What the hell would make him do this?"

Lisa rested her head on the back of the couch. "He's doing drugs again. So I found his stash and flushed it down the stool."

"You flushed his dope and stayed in the house," Roger asked in disbelief.

"It was the only way I could know. I had to force him to make a choice."

Danielle took the wet cloth from Roger and leaned over Lisa, wiping blood off her neck. She wiped more blood away from her face, trying to assess the damage.

Lisa waited for her older sister to start the lecture, but she didn't say a word. When Lisa finally got the nerve to look up, Danielle was crying too.

Danielle and Roger both checked on her several times through the night. Danielle put an extra blanket over her, and Roger brought her a glass of water and aspirin. That night was one of the coldest nights in D.C. history. The temperature dropped to barely ten degrees. Lisa couldn't sleep. She lay wide awake, thinking about how messed up her life really was. She relived Walter's violent anger, over and over, hating herself for not hating him.

Roger took Kim to his parents' house that morning. Danielle suggested it because she knew he needed time to cool off. They left just before Sundi arrived. Sundi and Danielle sat at the dining room table, talking in low whispers that still reached Lisa's ears.

"She won't press charges. She says she loves him," Danielle explained to Sundi, handing her two large peanut butter cookies.

"Well, we can't force her," Sundi replied.

"We can't let her go back to him either."

Sundi dunked her cookie into the cup of coffee in front of her. "How you gonna stop her if that's what she wants, Dannie?"

Danielle slammed her fist down on the table. "You should have seen her, Sundi. He had no right!"

"I've been so wrapped up in my own problems I really haven't been around for Lisa," Sundi apologized.

"We've both been guilty of that. I've been sitting around here feeling sorry for myself when she needed me."

Danielle noticed the tip of Lisa's horoscope book sticking out of her purse, which lay on the table. She pulled it out and thumbed through it.

"If these things were any good, they would have warned her or something. Listen to what it said for yesterday." Danielle read out loud: " 'You can make lasting impressions and may receive a promotion. Be careful in love. It can boomerang this evening. Think things through thoroughly before taking action.' "

Sundi and Danielle looked at each other.

"Look up the day she married him," Sundi suggested.

"Shit, when was it?" Danielle asked, trying hard to remember.

Sundi looked at her pocket calendar. "Late August. The twenty-first."

Danielle fingered through the pages until she found the right one: "Here it is. 'Be conservative in health, travel, and personal matters. Make plans slowly. Be prepared for changes that mean adjustments to new environments. Caution is important today.' "

"She lied. She said her horoscope said go for it," Sundi told Danielle and took the book. "Why would she ignore this book? She *loves* this thing."

The phone rang, but neither of them bothered to answer it. After the fourth ring Danielle's answering machine clicked on. They both looked at the machine and waited. "You've reached the Mead residence. Please leave your name and number after the beep."

It was Walter. "Dannie, pick up the phone. I need to talk to Lisa. Dammit, Dannie, pick up! I want to talk to my wife!"

It was quiet for a moment. Then he hung up.

"He's so sorry. He didn't mean it," Danielle said sarcastically. "We should tell him to come over tonight to talk to her, hide behind the bushes outside, and beat the shit out of him with baseball bats," she said with a chuckle, even though she was very serious.

"Maybe he is sorry, Dannie," Sundi told her. She always tried to find the good in everybody.

But Danielle didn't want to hear anything positive about Walter right now. "Sundi, you are such a diphead sometimes. I knew he was an asshole from the beginning," she explained. "Dammit, I knew I should have done something!"

Both women sat despondently at the dining room table for a while. Sundi skimmed through the horoscope book, reading various days that Lisa had highlighted, while Danielle sprinkled sugar, salt, and pepper into a pile and mechanically mixed them together with her index finger.

Sundi sat in the recliner and Danielle lay on the family room floor watching television when Lisa walked in slowly. The sun was going down. She had slept all day. Her face hurt. Everything hurt. She could barely lift her right arm or open her left eye.

Sundi saw Lisa and reacted for the first time. She stood up and hugged her. Then she cried.

"Don't do that, or I'll start again," Lisa told her.

"How are you doing?" Danielle asked, not really expecting an answer. She came over and hugged her too.

Danielle and Sundi moved several pillows around on the couch. It didn't help. The pain was worse when Lisa sat up, but she was tired of lying down, and she especially didn't want to look at the wallpaper in Danielle's guest bedroom any longer. The ugly green speckled print had started to move around.

"I *hate* for you guys to see me like this!" Lisa said, thinking out loud.

"You don't have any reason to be embarrassed," Sundi told her, holding her hand. Lisa pulled away. She didn't want or need pity.

"I knew something was wrong. I'm gonna beat your ass myself when you finish healing," Danielle joked. Lisa tried to smile but felt a sharp, piercing pain shoot through her right temple and eye.

The phone rang, and when the answering machine came on, the person hung up. Lisa knew it was Walter. She wanted to talk to him.

"I'm gonna get a soda. You want anything, Lisa?" Danielle asked.

"Water, please, and could I have the aspirin from the bedroom?"

While Danielle got the water, Sundi brought the aspirin. It was quiet except for the sound of water running.

Lisa knew they would purposely try to steer the conversation away from her condition, but she wanted to talk about it, so she finally spoke up. "You know the worst thing about this mess? I keep wondering if somehow *I* caused it."

"Why would you say that?" Sundi asked.

"I just feel that I might have encouraged Walter by doing the drugs with him sometimes."

"Yeah . . . that was pretty stupid, but it doesn't mean you caused this shit to happen," Sundi reassured her.

"Why do we do that?" Danielle asked, carrying the water into the room from the kitchen. "When a man is involved, it's somehow always *our* fault!" She shoved the water at Lisa. "We're like those dogs that are conditioned to eat when the bell rings. Or like in those music videos, when the women are always half dressed, showing their tits and asses, and the men are fully dressed in double-breasted suits. Ooooohhh! That shit pisses me off!"

Lisa took two aspirin from the bottle, popped them in her mouth, and swallowed water behind them. "I need to talk to Walter, Dannie."

"You need to press charges," she warned.

"You don't understand. He didn't mean to hurt me," Lisa said, needing to believe that.

"He didn't *mean* to hurt you! What do you think he meant to do?"

"Don't do this, Dannie, I need your support right now."

"But, Lisa, what if he does it again?" Sundi said, genuinely concerned.

"You're not going back to him," Danielle pleaded.

"I honestly don't know what I'm going to do," Lisa said, saddened to some extent by her own response.

Danielle stopped talking when she heard her sister's reply. She didn't know what to say or how to help. She somehow felt responsible but knew Lisa would have to decide for herself. Danielle turned on the television and flipped through the channels. She stopped on an old Doris Day movie. At least that would have a happy ending.

As Lisa watched her sister laugh at Doris making a mess in

the ultramodern, technologically advanced kitchen, she envied her sister. Despite all the bullshit she had put Roger through, he had never hit her.

In the middle of a laugh Danielle turned to Lisa. "Look," she said, "take some time to build up your strength, and if you still want to see the asshole, I'll set it up."

Lisa smiled slightly. She knew Danielle was just trying to buy some time to talk her out of it, and she loved her for that.

During a commercial break Danielle hopped up and pulled several small boxes from under the large white flocked Christmas tree near her window. She always put her tree up right after Thanksgiving. It was loaded with old and new ornaments of every color. The black angel at the top had been with Danielle and Roger since their first Christmas together.

"I think this is the perfect time to open these," Danielle said, handing one to each of them.

Sundi tore into hers, and they all burst out laughing as she held up a bright red miniature dildo. Danielle opened Lisa's box for her to reveal a yellow dildo, and she pulled out a blue one from another box. She immediately put it in her mouth and sucked on it, moaning in ecstasy.

"You're so gross!" Sundi said, frowning.

"You wouldn't feel like that if you tasted the right one," she teased, leaning in closer.

"Like they have different flavors or something," Sundi said, rolling her eyes and motioning for Danielle to get back.

Danielle attached her dildo to her key chain. "Of course there are different flavors. There's chocolate chip, butter pecan, and double dutch chocolate! You haven't lived until you've tasted double dutch chocolate!"

"I know you're not going to keep that thing on your key chain in public," Sundi told her.

"Why not?" she teased, swinging the key chain in a circle.

Sundi shook her head, and they went back to the movie, which ended with Doris Day getting the man of her dreams and living happily ever after.

Danielle started flipping through the channels again. She

stopped on a show called *Video Soul*. She screamed when she saw one of the videos she had described. "That's what I'm talking about," she hollered, pointing at the screen. "Look at that shit; it's disgusting."

"This coming from the woman who sucks on miniature dildos and describes dicks that taste like ice cream," Sundi noted.

"That was a joke among friends. This shit is nationwide," Danielle explained caustically.

They watched as the girls in the video shook and gyrated in tight minidresses. Lisa noted that their breasts were much too big for the bikini tops they wore. She thought it was truly sad when they humped away at various band members, and they all broke into laughter when the girls dropped to the floor and started to hump it.

Lisa caught Sundi staring at her face, and they both quickly dropped their eyes.

Lisa paused. "Don't look too good, huh?"

"I'm sorry," Sundi apologized.

"I haven't even looked in the mirror yet. If it's as bad as I feel, I don't want to see it!"

"You remind me of that time I tried to stop that door with my face," Danielle teased.

"You were trying to be cute in front of that football player Vermin," Sundi reminded her.

"His name was Shermin," Danielle protested. "And never in my life did I have to *try* to be cute. Men flocked around me like birds hover over your car."

"Danielle, how can you sit there and lie with a straight face like that?"

"He was in the room, that's all," she admitted playfully, and stuck her dildo back in her mouth.

"And you always knew what to do when a man was in the room," Sundi continued. "She sure charmed that guy in Indiana. Huh, Lisa? I was nuts to go to Purdue with you guys not knowing anybody."

"The only one who had fun was Lisa. She got a free high," Danielle joked. Then she reached over to touch Lisa, but when she shrank back, anticipating the pain, Danielle caught herself.

Lisa remembered that weekend at Purdue. It was a crazy one. First, Danielle was speeding most of the way, so they decided that if they got stopped by the police, Lisa would act sick to get out of the ticket. Forty miles outside West Lafayette, the flashing lights pulled up behind them, and she went into her act. When the policeman walked up to the car, he glared at Danielle. "Young lady, do you realize you were traveling at ninety miles an hour?"

Danielle replied frantically, "Something's wrong with my sister, Officer, and we don't know anybody in Indiana except some friends at Purdue, so we were trying to get her there."

He stepped over to Lisa's window on the passenger's side and aimed the flashlight toward her face. Tears flowed down her cheeks, and her body shook like a junkie's in need of a fix. She just knew they were all going to end up in jail.

After assessing her condition, the officer told them to wait and he went back to his car. He returned, explaining that he had called an ambulance. So Lisa was really sick, but Danielle didn't sweat it. She quickly told the officer that they couldn't afford an ambulance, so he went back to his car and canceled it, but he wanted them to follow him to the hospital in a nearby town. They did.

"What the hell am I going to do at a hospital, Dannie?" Lisa had asked. She knew they were all going to end up in jail.

"You're doing fine. Just say it's in your head and they won't know the difference," Danielle explained confidently.

After her examination the doctor had left the room and told the policeman it was a legitimate crisis, so he let them go. But the story didn't end there. They reached Purdue about three in the morning and couldn't find the sorority sisters they had planned to stay with. They barely had enough money for gas or food, so a hotel room was out. Danielle decided to find the fraternity house of a guy she had met several weeks earlier.

They found the house easily. It was huge and located on a major street. Danielle parked the car in front and boldly marched up to the door and knocked until a half-asleep guy finally answered. When she asked to see Gage, the guy she knew, he told her that Gage was out, so she proceeded to tell this guy their tale of woe.

After hearing the story, he led them upstairs into a corner room with a terrible musty smell. Three piles of dirty clothes lay in the middle of the floor. At least four or five pairs of filthy tennis shoes were scattered around. Danielle picked up the bedspread and turned up her nose at the stains, then fussed with the guy about clean sheets. Lisa sat down at the top of the steps, trying to avert the headache she felt coming, and Sundi opened up all the windows in the room.

Lisa closed her eyes, leaned her head against the banister, and listened to Danielle harass the poor guy, despite the fact that he was trying to help. She noticed that he had asked Danielle to be quiet several times because she might wake up somebody named Bulldog.

Of course that didn't stop her big sis. Danielle talked even louder, until they heard a slow, pounding sound coming up the stairs. Boom . . . boom . . . boom . . .

Lisa looked down at the landing on the stairwell but saw nothing. Boom . . . boom . . . boom. The eerie sound continued moving upward and rounded the corner.

When Bulldog finally turned the corner, they didn't see the four-headed monster they'd imagined, but a fairly nice-looking guy with a seriously pissed expression on his face. He wore a pair of shorts with no shirt, which enabled them to also see that he was very well built. His shoulders and chest bounced on every step with defined movement. He carried a large baseball bat that hit each stair as he climbed higher: Boom . . . boom . . . boom.

When Danielle saw Bulldog, she quickly analyzed the situation and spoke without missing a beat. "Ooooooooooooooohhhh, Lisa," she yelled. "Ain't he fine!"

That was all it took. Bulldog was like lotion on an ashy leg, and Danielle soaked him up. When she got through with that man, he put down the baseball bat and got the clean sheets himself.

Lisa had to smile at her sister. She was truly one of a kind.

"That gets on my nerves too!" Danielle was still complaining as the video of a young rap group named Kris Kross came on.

"Oh, Lord," Sundi moaned. "She's kicked into her societal problems mode."

"I'm serious. Why don't they let kids be kids? Why can't they let these kids enjoy their childhood?" Danielle continued. "I mean, I like the song, but why do they have these little boys calling themselves Mack Daddys and Daddy Macks? Look at that baby—now what does he know about a Mack Daddy? He needs to be singing about playing video games or eating cotton candy at a state fair."

Lisa and Sundi both laughed. When Danielle got in one of these moods, it was hard to shut her up. Other videos were presented, and Danielle dissected each one. Lisa had to admit it did bother her that rap music seemed to get the most publicity when focused on violence. A series of videos came and went. Many seemed to say the same thing: This is a violent world we live in. It's the truth, Lisa thought. But the truth doesn't always set you free. She pulled a small mirror out of her purse and opened it, determined this time to look at her disfigured face. Then she stopped. She didn't really want to see it. She didn't really need to see it.

She closed her eyes and waited for the aspirin to work. What would she do without Walter? She thought first she might spend some time feeling sorry for herself. She would wallow in her sadness and even throw herself a few pity parties. She knew Walter loved her, but she also knew she needed more than he was willing to give. This time she had to pay attention; she couldn't ignore the warning signs.

Lisa stayed with Danielle and Roger for several weeks. Although the physical bruises disappeared quickly, she realized she was not completely well. Her mental and spiritual senses were lost in a fog of self-pity and disbelief. Being black, over thirty, educated, ambitious, single, and female was a confusing state of mind. She was tired of apologizing for her success, especially to black men. She was tired of being treated as if she were a liability rather than an asset.

Luckily Mrs. Belmont had just put out the tenant in her apartment when she called, so Lisa moved back in as the new year unfolded. Walter agreed to stay away from the house that day so she could get her things. Just for the fun of it, she set her place up almost exactly the way it had been before. The only things missing were the sand-glazed lamp and two mirrors she had broken at Walter's house. Once the smaller boxes were inside, Roger and Chris brought in the bigger pieces: the queen-sized bed, the couch and love seat, and her two steel blue butterfly chairs. As Lisa, Danielle, and Sundi sat on the front stoop to catch their breath, Lisa's vision focused on the house across the street. It hadn't changed. The shutter was still hanging off. The walk hadn't been shoveled.

"I'll be right back," Lisa told Danielle and Sundi as she

started across the street and walked up to the chipped and peeling door.

She knocked several times before someone answered. When the door opened, she was surprised to see an elderly black lady, maybe eighty years old, on the other side, and in a wheelchair behind her sat an even older black man, probably ninety. The woman's face showed hundreds of wrinkles and wisdom lines. And although a hot, musty smell seeped from inside the house, from what Lisa could see it was fairly clean.

"Uh . . . excuse me . . . I—I live across the street, and I was wondering, uh, if you would mind if I fixed your shutter and shoveled your sidewalk tomorrow," Lisa asked.

"What?" The lady frowned and stepped closer to the door.

"I live across the street, and I'd like to fix your shutter tomorrow if it's okay?" Lisa said, speaking louder.

"Well, our son usually does those kinds of things for us because we can't afford to pay for it. He's so busy he doesn't get around as often as he should."

"It won't cost anything, and I'd love to do it for you."

"Just a minute. Matt, this young lady wants to fix our shutter and shovel the snow. She says it won't cost. Do you think Billy would mind?"

Matt rolled to the door in his wheelchair to get a better look at Lisa. "Probably not," her husband replied. "Billy has such a hard time getting away from his business and all."

"Thank you . . . that would be nice," the lady said, opening the screen door and extending her hand. "I'm Gladys, and this is Matt," she said, taking Lisa's hand.

"Hi, Gladys and Matt. I'm Lisa."

"Thank you again, Lisa," Gladys added.

"No problem," Lisa said, and hurried back across the street.

This was Lisa's first step in the healing process. It was a small step but an important one. She was determined to create a new and better life for herself. She would no longer allow people or situations to undermine her control.

Three days later she took a second crucial step. She stood in her black sweat suit in a small, dirty garage among nine other women. She was starting an eight-week automotive repair class. There was a cracked, portable chalkboard and about fifteen old wooden school desks on one side of the room and five auto bays for repairs on the other side.

Lisa had come to truly hate mechanics. She saw her mechanic as another man in control of her life, and since she couldn't afford a new car right now, she decided she should know something about her old one.

"In this class you will learn the basics of auto mechanics," the instructor said, "how your engine works, how to check and change your own oil and transmission fluid, and how to talk more confidently with your mechanic."

The instructor's name was Darin Jackson. Lisa immediately noticed he was a chocolate Tootsie Roll in his late thirties. She had to admit he sparked her interest, especially when she found out he owned the repair shop. But she wasn't ready for another romance. It was too soon, and she didn't have the time or energy to focus.

She watched Darin explain the function of spark plugs in a car and noticed that his grubby overalls were layered with dirt and grease from weeks gone by. She couldn't stand a man with dirty fingernails, and his were awful, but she laughed at herself because he was a mechanic and his hands were supposed to look like that.

"I need a volunteer for this first segment," he said, looking at his all-female student body.

No one raised a hand, so he pointed at Lisa, and she reluctantly walked forward and stood in front of the car.

"Can you open the hood of the car for me and show me how to check the oil?"

Lisa walked to the driver's door and reached inside to unlatch the hood. Then she came back up front and pulled the hood up, but it stopped and caught on something. She tried again. She had seen Roger open it a number of times, and even Walter. She looked at Darin and became irritated when he smiled.

"It won't open," she told him, annoyed. "I've never had to open one before. Somebody always checks the oil for me."

Darin felt under the hood for the latch, and when he found it, he took her hand and gently guided it until she felt it too. Lisa pulled the latch to the side and lifted the hood up. She noticed that his cold touch made her shiver. She knew cold hands meant a warm, loving spirit.

"Now, show me the stick you would use to check the oil," Darin continued.

Lisa stared at the grimy mess for a minute. She saw several metal casings of different sizes and shapes. There were wires everywhere. The only thing she recognized was the battery. She finally said, "I don't know."

"Take a guess," Darin teased.

Lisa hated his smug attitude. She turned and looked under the hood again. "There," she said, pointing at a long metal bar that was sticking out of one of the casings.

"No, but it was a good guess. That's for the brake fluid, and this is the oil," he said, correcting her and pulling out the oil stick.

Lisa felt embarrassed. "If you don't mind, I'm going back over here so *you* can teach the class!" she said and pushed her way to the back of the group.

The third major step in her recovery was to bring God back into her life. Lisa felt she had lost her faith somewhere along the way. She felt empty inside and needed to be filled with His spirit again. It had been several years since she had gone to church on a regular basis, and she soon remembered why. As she attended different churches, she couldn't believe how blatantly superficial many of them were.

Her first encounter was a church she had never been to before. She had passed the First Church of God and Christ every day on her way to work, and it always looked so inviting. Maybe she picked a bad Sunday, but the service lasted four hours, and she was ready to scream. Various people in the congregation testified for an hour and a half. The reverend's sermon was an hour long. It was hot, so the kids got restless, and that made parents obviously tired, but the service continued with reports, songs, and even a good news segment. Lisa quickly decided this church was not the one.

Her major complaint about the second church occurred when the reverend finished a good sermon about the charity of God and they took up the collection. As he stood in front of the money baskets, Lisa was amazed to hear him say: "God bless those who gave." Period. That was it! How about those who wanted to give and couldn't? The reverend also turned her off with snide remarks like: "Religion is more than selling bean pies on the corner."

Next she visited Sundi's church, Brightroad AME. She had heard that Reverend Fields was an egomaniac, but she loved the building so much she figured she could spend the time admiring the architecture if his sermon was boring. Unfortunately Reverend Fields lived up to the rumors. He was so busy speaking to the television camera he didn't have time for his congregation.

Finally she settled on Danielle and Roger's church, Mount Olive Baptist. She had attended a number of times as a guest, but it was different now that she was looking for a church home. Lisa wanted a place she could feel comfortable. She wanted to belong to a church that she knew was sincere about the love of God and not the love of money. She also wanted to listen to a good choir. Although she realized that was not the reason people were supposed to go to church, she needed a good choir. She even thought she would join the choir once she got her life under control again.

She attended several services at Mount Olive, but her contentment didn't last long. On her third Sunday she found herself right back where she had started. She had taken her time getting dressed that morning and ultimately stepped into church late. But she knew she looked good in her new paisley two-piece. The hem fell just below the knees, so she wouldn't be the topic of this Sunday's gossip circle. Lisa sat down in one of the back pews as Deacon Johns finished his financial report.

She found herself in deep reflection that Sunday. While the announcements were being made, she looked around at the many husbands, wives, and kids and wondered why her marriage had to fail. One mother stood up and announced that her son was marrying a wonderful girl and they were so thankful. A man rejoiced about his fourth grandchild. A pregnant woman stood up and with her hand resting on her large stomach praised God for His goodness. In the midst of their joy, Lisa closed her eyes and asked God to help her understand what she had done wrong. She needed Him to show her the right direction for this happiness that everyone else seemed to have. And it was as if God Himself answered Lisa that Sunday morning because the preacher's sermon spoke directly to her.

"The black, educated, ambitious woman is literally killing the black family. She's having fewer babies, raising them less attentively, and not taking proper care of her black man." Reverend Mills's deep voice echoed in Lisa's mind. As her eyes met with others around her, she felt as if everyone in the church knew he was talking about her. There, in the house of the Lord, Reverend Mills stood in his almighty pulpit and chastised her for striving to achieve her dreams, hopes, and aspirations.

At first Lisa felt confused. Then the confusion changed to devastation. She felt sick to her stomach, and her body grew numb. She tiptoed through the back pew, past Danielle, Roger, and Kim, across the aisle, and down the stairs to the basement.

When she thought about her life, she realized it had been a series of choices. And although she had tried to make the right ones, maybe they weren't right after all. When her high school sweetheart had talked about getting married and having a family, that was not her choice. Her choice was an education. Her college boyfriend had asked her to marry him, but instead she chose a career. Then, when she was ready, she had selfishly expected everything to fall into place.

Lisa sat on a bench in a corner of the room, listening to the feet above her stomp in a rhythmic pattern. On the wall behind her was a colorful mural. The design had evolved over the years, created by the many kids who attended the church's day care. There were handprints, chalk drawings, and signatures everywhere. The congregation often talked about covering it with a fresh coat of paint but didn't dare.

She saw Danielle walking toward her and silently groaned. She didn't feel like hearing a "pull yourself together" speech today.

A young boy darted past Danielle, racing from the rest room and wrestling with his pants at the same time.

She stopped and reached for his zipper. "Here, let me help," she said.

He jerked away. "I can do it. I'm not a baby!" he told her, pulled the zipper up, and dashed to the stairs.

Danielle shrugged her shoulders and turned to address Lisa. "You okay?"

She didn't respond at first. She sat there, shoulders and head slumped down. No, she wasn't okay. Danielle should see that. She'd never be okay again. She was tired—tired of searching, hoping, and waiting for something special to happen in her life.

"You going to talk to me or what?" Danielle asked, sitting next to Lisa and putting her arm around her shoulders for support.

"It was like the preacher was talking directly to me, Dannie. I mean, it's my fault I don't have a family. I was too busy, too selfish. I focused on my wants—my education and my career! And when *I* was ready, I jumped into a marriage that was doomed to fail."

"It's not your fault, Lisa, and as much as I want to blame it on Walter, it's probably not his fault either."

"But it didn't work with Kirby and Thomas before him. Why can't I make a man happy?"

"Because you need to concentrate on making your own self happy, Lisa. Fuck a man!" Danielle told her, then looked up at the church ceiling apologetically. "Sorry," she said. "Kirby was a walking zombie, following his dick," she continued. "He's bound to get hit by a bus someday, and you should be thankful you got away from his sorry ass before it happened. You've got everything going for you, Sis, but it doesn't mean nothing until *you* believe it."

"How did I get stuck in this cycle: find a man, lose a man, find a man, lose a man? I'm sick of it," Lisa said, resting her head inside her cupped hands.

"Have I ever told you about my shit-tolerance theory?"

Lisa shook her head and smiled because she knew her sister actually came up with some good theories sometimes.

"I've been thinking a lot about the question you asked me on Thanksgiving. How do we know when it's the right love?" Danielle stood up and used her hands to illustrate. "My theory is based on shit-tolerance levels. That is how much shit a person is willing to take. I believe we all have shit-tolerance levels, and we have to figure out what our individual levels are or how much shit you're willing and able to take off somebody else. Once you know what your level is, all you have to do is find a man with a bowel movement about the right size or smaller."

"That's so stupid," Lisa told her, but she had to laugh anyway.

"It's true!" Danielle replied, barely cracking a smile. "Roger has a very high shit-tolerance level. That's why he can deal with me and the mounds of shit I dish out. But I have a low shit-tolerance level, and he has a small bowel movement, so he's perfect in my life. I couldn't deal with the bullshit that Chris puts Sundi through or even the crap Derrick wanted to give me. That's my theory on why some relationships work and others don't. The shit-tolerance levels have to match!"

Lisa actually left the church feeling better than when she entered. She already knew she had to accept the fact that it wasn't about Kirby or Walter; it was about her. She was holding on to men who weren't ready. She made herself need these men no matter what.

On her way home the car started to sputter and jerk. As if I haven't suffered enough today, she thought. She waited at a red light, praying that it wouldn't die out, when a pawnshop on the other side of the street caught her eye. She looked at the rings on her left hand and realized if she continued to wear them, she was only building up false hope because she and Walter could never get back together, and she had to let him go.

When the light changed, she made an illegal U-turn and pulled into the lot. Lisa jumped out of the car and marched into the mall corridor. She walked past Nine West shoes and JC

Penney into the pawnshop. She pulled off her engagement and wedding rings and handed them to the clerk. "How much?" she asked.

Lisa watched as he examined the rings carefully. Finally, peering over the top of his glasses, he made her an offer: "Five hundred dollars."

Lisa frowned, looking at the man as if he were a fool. "These are fifteen-hundred-dollar rings!" she told him.

He looked more closely at the rings, pulled out a small book from the middle drawer in his desk, and studied them for a few more minutes.

"Seven hundred dollars is my best offer," he finally told her.

Lisa put the rings back on her finger and turned to leave. Then, as if possessed, she swung back around, pulled them off, and handed them to him. "Take them," she said.

She watched as he pulled out a stack of hundred-dollar bills and gingerly counted out seven of them, then pushed them across the counter toward her. While she re-counted the money, he wrote up a claim ticket and set it on the counter. She put the money in her purse and half-turned to leave. The clerk picked up the ticket and waved it in the air. "Here, you forgot this," he said, handing it to her.

Lisa took the ticket, tore it into tiny little pieces, and tossed them in a trash can on her way out the door.

Her final stage of recovery was the completion of her dissertation. It had always made Lisa feel good to accomplish things, and this was something she had control over. She quickly finished the methodology and literature review sections. She was busy conducting interviews when Walter tried to come back into her life.

She rushed into her office late one Monday morning and stopped when she saw the large bouquet of yellow roses on her desk.

"He waited for a while but said he had to leave," her office mate, Vanessa, said as she handed Lisa the card.

She opened it, but she didn't really have to. It was Walter's trademark. Lisa couldn't understand why men thought flowers could solve everything. Women loved to get flowers, but they wanted them to represent love and romance, not a ploy to get over again. As far as she was concerned, a man could send flowers as an apology only once. After that it was a waste of time and money.

She read the card out loud: "I miss you! I need you! I love you!" Then she moved the bouquet off her desk and onto the bookshelf near the window. She sat and stared at them until the phone rang.

A week later she came home to find another token of Walter's affection. She had purposefully forgotten it was Valentine's Day. But Mrs. Belmont stuck her head out the door as she walked up the steps.

"Lisa, come here a minute, please."

"Maybe later, Mrs. Belmont, I'm beat," she replied, taking each step slowly.

"It'll only take a minute," Mrs. Belmont added, and hurried inside her apartment, leaving the door ajar.

Lisa took a deep breath and ambled into the apartment. As she entered, she looked unbelievingly at what seemed like hundreds of helium balloons covering the ceiling of the living room.

"For you," Mrs. Belmont said, handing her the card. This time she read it silently.

"Damn him!" she mumbled.

"You're not happy?" Mrs. Belmont asked, confused.

"Yeah, thanks, Mrs. Belmont," she said, and gathered the balloon strings up in both hands. She took them to her apartment and released them in the living room. They floated up to the ceiling as a reminder of her painful loss.

Lisa canceled all of her social life in order to finish the dissertation. She ate, slept, and screwed those pages until her adviser okayed them and they scheduled the defense. She knew this was a crucial part of her recovery. She had finally begun to feel good about herself again. She was doing what she wanted to do, and things were going in the direction they should.

Lisa was very nervous during her defense. She waited outside the conference room in a lounge for almost thirty minutes while Dr. Javier organized everything inside. Eventually she came out and led Lisa into the room, where her committee members sat, looking formal and serious. Lisa smiled slightly and studied their faces as she sat in that large leather chair at the front of the dean's smooth walnut table.

Dr. Javier spoke first. She laid the ground rules and set the tone. The committee members took turns asking questions about her dissertation. How did she feel her friendship with Sundi had influenced Sundi's and other participants' answers to the interview questions? How might the tape recorder she used to tape each couple's interview have influenced their honesty? What did she see as a future research area for herself in relation to her findings? Lisa answered each question thoroughly, glancing over at her adviser every now and then for a reassuring nod. The defense lasted about an hour. Then Dr. Javier asked her to leave the room again.

Lisa waited in the lounge for another very long twenty minutes. The feeling reminded her of the pressure a woman often felt after her first date with someone she really liked. Sometimes she was not sure if he liked her, and it was pure hell waiting to see if he would call. Lisa was extremely anxious. She was anxious to complete this stage of her life, anxious to move forward into an unlimited future, and anxious to find her spirit again. Finally Dr. Javier walked into the lounge. "Congratulations, Dr. Allen," she said, and they hugged.

There were rows and rows of black graduation gowns glistening in the lucent afternoon sun. Most were plain, but a few were decorated with colorful stripes and hoods. Hundreds of students were graduating, but only twenty-nine were Ph.D.'s.

Lisa stood up when it was time for her row to walk to the front of the temporary stage. She didn't have to wait long because they were going in alphabetical order: Aaron, Abbot, Achey, Adair, Lisa Elaine Allen.

She stepped forward and stopped in front of the first table onstage. She accepted the folder the registrar handed her. She smiled because she could hear Danielle's and Sundi's big mouths yelling her name. She tried to find them in the crowd, but some guy with a huge camera kept flashing it in front of her.

As she walked across the stage to the second table, the dean picked up her hood and carefully placed it over her head. She stood in front of the crowd in a daze, then mechanically followed the feet of the graduate in front of her. Near the end of the stage she shook the hand of the college president. Then she followed her line back to her chair, and they all sat down. That was it! She was Dr. Lisa Allen. She didn't really hear any of the other names they called. She sat staring at the huge piece of paper that represented five years of her life. It said: "The University of Maryland College Park has conferred on LISA ELAINE AL-LEN the degree of Doctor of Philosophy and all the rights and privileges thereto appertaining. In Witness thereof, this diploma duly signed has been issued and the seal of the University affixed. Issued by the Board of Regents upon Recommendation of the faculty awarded on this the twentieth day of May, 1996."

When the ceremony finally ended, the graduates marched off the stage and around the corner, accompanied by "Pomp and Circumstance." Then everyone dispersed into the crowd. Lisa looked for Danielle and Sundi because she desperately needed some hugs. She moved slowly through hundreds of happy parents, friends, and families. She thought she heard Danielle's voice, turned to look behind her, and bumped right into Walter.

"Hi," he said, handing her a single red rose.

"Hi," she replied, taking the rose gingerly.

He reached out to hug her, and to her surprise she hugged him back. Lisa suddenly found herself thinking how good it still felt to be in his arms.

"I'm proud of you, Lisa. I knew you could do it!" he said, awkwardly leaving his arm around her shoulder.

"Thanks. How are you, Walter?"

"Fine, just fine . . . Look, I didn't come to mess up your day or anything, but I needed to see you. I need you to forgive me, Lisa."

She spoke softly, almost in a whisper. "I'm trying, Walter."

She held her mouth tightly shut because she wanted to tell him how much she still loved him and always would.

"That wasn't me. I was upset. I was crazy. I'm really sorry. I couldn't do that to you in my right mind."

She didn't respond. She was confused: Part of her wanted to hold him tightly, and part of her wanted to run.

"You know I didn't mean to hurt you," he repeated.

"I know." That was all she could think of to say.

She looked at him hard, trying to see what was inside his head or maybe inside his heart.

"So, what can I do to win you back?" he asked, flashing his most lovable grin.

"I don't know, Walter. I've gotta be sure that that part of your life is over. I can't do that again. I won't do that again."

"Lisa," Danielle called from behind. She'd seen Walter and kept her distance.

Walter glanced over at Danielle and started to talk faster. "I'm going to finish the treatment program this time. Then I'm going to work on getting you back. I'd really like to try again, Lisa."

Lisa held back the tears that wanted to come when she looked into his tortured eyes. "I can't come back, Walter, not if that's why you're going to finish it. You can't do it for *me*."

She touched his face lightly, then turned and walked away.

"Lisa, wait," he called, but she didn't turn around.

Suddenly Walter grabbed her arm and pulled her back toward him. It was as if her heart were no longer beating. She shivered, turning to face him, and he let go. As she looked into his face, she flashed back to that day in New Orleans when she had given this man everything, and she knew at that moment she could never get it back.

Danielle was the first to arrive at The Bottom, a soul food restaurant and bar on Georgia Avenue. It had been six months
since Lisa's face resembled a plane crash. Danielle waved at her
baby sister when she headed for the table. Lisa motioned to the
maître d' that she planned to join her. When she reached the
table, she leaned over, and they hugged.

"So, did you decide?" Danielle asked before she could sit
down.

"Give me a minute to catch my breath, will you?" Lisa told
her, and took several gulps from her water glass.

"I can't wait, tell me."

"Okay. I'm going to accept Howard's offer. I want to try a
black university for a while. Maybe I can help a few kids like
Arthur get through the maze."

Danielle's smile grew broader. "Sounds good to me. Especially since I don't want you too far away," she said.

Lisa raised her eyebrows and looked at her big sis sarcastically. "Guess who called yesterday?" she asked, changing the
subject.

"Dad. He called me too," Danielle said.

"No. Walter called," Lisa told her. "He's in New Orleans."

"How's he doing?" Danielle asked, faking concern.

Lisa knew Danielle hadn't forgiven him, but she had. "He finished his treatment program, and he's working in accounting at a clothing store. You know, the hardest part was talking to his parents."

"You're still going through with the divorce, aren't you?" Danielle asked, playing mamma, but Lisa didn't mind.

"Yeah. I've got to live my life my way. As Mom always said, 'A weak mind is like a microscope: It magnifies trifling things.' "

Danielle and Lisa heard their names and turned to spot Sundi as she walked toward the table. The bottom half of her body was covered by the decorative railing until she rounded the corner and revealed that she was *very* pregnant. "Hey, you two. What's up?" she yelled.

"Your temperature and your weight. You gonna drop that baby any day now," Danielle teased.

"I hope so. Movies lie, they make it look so damn easy," Sundi joked. She was having such a miserable pregnancy it had made Lisa rethink her plans for a little one anytime soon.

"You and Chris still fussing over names?" Lisa asked.

"If it's a boy, he still wants a junior," Sundi explained.

"I hate juniors. They usually grow up to be assholes," Danielle said as she squeezed the lemon from the edge of her glass into her water.

"I have to agree," Lisa added. "A kid should have its own identity."

"I told him if he names my baby boy a junior, I'm going to name the girl Sundiata the Second."

"Please!" Danielle said, smiling and cutting her eyes at the same time.

"I'm glad you guys worked it out, Sundi. Be happy," Lisa told her best friend.

Sundi looked surprised. She thought for a moment about Lisa's comment. Then she grinned and shook her head self-assuredly. "I am happy. I think *we're* finally happy."

The waiter walked up and refilled the water glasses. "Would you like to order now?" he asked.

"Not yet. Give us a few more minutes," Danielle said.

"I'd like a banana margarita," Lisa said. "You want one, Dannie?"

"Yeah, that would taste good about now," she replied.

"I'd like iced tea, please," Sundi told him.

As the waiter walked away, they noticed a car entering the parking lot outside their window with white smoke blowing out of its tailpipe.

Danielle pointed. "What's wrong with his car, Lisa?"

"Transmission or engine. One is blue smoke, and one is white. I don't remember which is which," she answered in a cocky tone of voice.

"So the class must have helped, huh, Lisa?" Sundi asked.

"Never again will a mechanic be able to treat me like boo-boo the fool," she answered with pride.

"She's gonna change my oil this weekend, aren't you, Sis?" Danielle asked, and winked. She lit a cigarette and waved the smoke away from the table as best she could.

Lisa picked up the menu. "In your dreams," she replied. "Where's Kim?"

"Roger took her to visit his mother for the weekend."

"The barbecue is next weekend, right?" Sundi asked. She knew it was next weekend, but she was really asking Danielle if everything was okay at home.

"Yep, since we missed it last year, Roger is truly looking forward to his annual Fourth of July bash."

"Oh, yeah, did James tell you he and Dorthea will be here for the festivities?" Danielle asked Lisa with a raised eyebrow.

"Yep, and he said he popped the question."

"Did she say yes?" Sundi asked.

"It's scheduled for September," Lisa responded.

Sundi shifted to get comfortable in her seat. "That's nice." Sundi looked at her two best friends as the baby kicked. "Touch right here, Lisa."

Lisa laid her hand on Sundi's stomach and felt several knocks. She chuckled. "It's hard to believe that somebody is in there," she said.

Sundi groaned. "It's a miracle, but it's a painful miracle."

"It's good pain," Lisa added.

"Danielle, I've got to tell you that you and Roger are my heroes," Sundi said. "I'm really glad you guys are back together."

"Yeah, they give me hope for the future," Lisa teased.

"Keep hope alive," Danielle responded, imitating Jesse Jackson's popular line. "I have learned one thing: You *can* teach an old dog some new tricks."

"Just be careful that dog don't turn around and bite you," Lisa warned.

Danielle leaned back and shivered. "Uhmmmmm, I might like that if he bit me in the right places."

"You're sick, Dannie," Sundi said, shaking her head as the waiter brought their drinks.

"And, Lisa, what about you? Any new men in your life?" Sundi continued. She had been dying to ask.

Lisa ignored her. She acted as if she hadn't heard the question.

"Miss Allen, I'm talking to you," Sundi said in an exaggerated tone.

"I'm doing fine, thank you, Sundi," she finally replied. "As Millie Jackson once sang, I don't have to wash nobody's dirty drawers but my own, and I like it like that."

"Girl, please. Everybody's looking for that wonderful feeling of love and happiness with the perfect mate," Danielle said, egging her on. "You can't fool us."

"Excuse me?" Lisa responded, pretending she didn't understand her sister's comment.

"I have to admit," Sundi told them, "I like having a man in my life."

"Well, I'm through running behind men. I'm finding love and happiness right here," Lisa explained, pointing to her chest.

The waiter stood there enjoying their exchange until Danielle told him to get a life.

"You didn't call that guy, did you, Lisa?" Sundi finally asked the real question she had been leading up to.

"Call who?" Danielle echoed, being her usual nosy self. Lisa could tell when Danielle was meddling because her ears perked up just like a dog when it hears a fire truck pass.

"Sundi gave me some guy's number last week. I left it in the women's bathroom at the Marriott. I bet he got plenty of calls," Lisa said, and busted into an uncontrolled laugh.

"Ohhhhh, Lisa, that was ugly," Danielle said, laughing too.

"I don't think it's funny," Sundi told them. "He's really a good guy. You can go with me to his store next week and see for yourself."

"I don't want to meet him or anybody else! I'm happy! Can't you guys understand that?" Lisa asked, sucking in a deep breath. "I'm tired of explaining this every time we get together. I don't want to be bothered. My career is going great. My health is good, and most important, I have peace of mind!"

"That peace won't last long without the other piece," Danielle teased. Then she and Sundi slapped their hands together with a high five.

"You're both hopeless!" Lisa said.

"Hopeful . . ." Sundi corrected her. "You just haven't found Mr. Right yet. He's out there."

Sundi is not going to let it die, Lisa thought. Having this baby has definitely made her more aggressive.

But Lisa was more aggressive too, and she continued to stand her ground. "Well, I ain't looking for him either. I know there are some good men out there, but right now I just don't have the time or patience."

"You're always looking for perfection, Lisa," Danielle said. "You think Roger is so wonderful, but it took him five years to catch on to the date of my birthday. Same date, every year, five years." She held up five fingers to help make her point.

"You think Camille knew what she was getting when she married Bill Cosby?" Sundi asked. "She probably knew he had potential, but a billion dollars' worth?"

"And I know sistergirl helped push him up that ladder," Danielle added, snapping her fingers, twice.

"Read my lips! I'm . . . not . . . interested!" Lisa said, raising her voice this time just enough to get their attention. "If he walked through the door right now, I'd take off running like a jackrabbit. So, could we change the subject, please!"

Just as Lisa finished her sentence, a man who sent her heart into overtime walked through the restaurant door. He was about six feet tall, medium build, and wore a dark gray, double-breasted suit jacket with matching baggy pants that hung just right. With both hands in his pockets, he stood as if he were posing for a layout in GQ magazine.

Lisa stared harder, because he looked so familiar, but she couldn't remember where she had seen him before. He walked over to the bar and joined a couple of other guys. One of them must have said something funny, because he smiled—a warm and inviting smile that caused a volcanic eruption inside Lisa's thighs, and that's when she recognized him. It was Darin, her auto mechanics instructor.

Darin turned and saw Lisa. She flashed him one of her famous smiles, and he sent one of his right back. At that same moment something else very strange happened. Her favorite song, "So Good," started to play on the jukebox. Lisa realized it had to be an omen. As she listened to that soothing, emotional mix, she knew exactly what Al Jarreau was singing about.

Lisa often laughs about her attitude then. Abstinence was an impossibility. She loved black men! She loved the way they walked when they knew a woman was watching. She loved the way they smelled after making love. She loved the way they looked when their muscles contracted on the basketball court, in the weight room, or at a construction site. She loved how they spoke with a powerful, comforting rhythm. She loved the soft feel of their smooth brown skin. She loved the rich texture of their coarse black hair. She loved everything about them.

Danielle looked at Lisa, then over to Darin. "Nothing makes you forget one man quicker than a better one," she said.

Sundi also watched the scenario and shook her head. "You go, girl!" she told her.

Lisa smiled at them both and stood up. "I have to admit when it's right, love is *sooooo gooooood*," she said, then carefully straightened her short black skirt, so that the split came up the left side. She took aim and walked across the room with a slow, deliberate motion, grabbed Darin's hand, and pulled him onto the dance floor.

BERRY   Berry, Venise T.

So good.

Wallingford Public Library
Wallingford, CT 06492

A2170 367358 0

WALLINGFORD PUBLIC LIBRARY
200 NO MAIN ST
WALLINGFORD CT 06492

R & TAYLOR